W9-AWL-571

THE BALANCE OF JUSTICE
THE UTICA STREETCAR MURDER OF 1872

A NOVEL BY EILEEN SULLIVAN HOPSICKER

NORTH COUNTRY BOOKS, INC.
UTICA, NEW YORK

Text copyright © 2017 by Eileen Sullivan Hopsicker

Cover and page vi photos courtesy of the Oneida County History Center, Utica, New York

ISBN 978-1-59531-056-9

Design by Zach Steffen & Rob Igoe, Jr.

Library of Congress Cataloging-in-Publication Data in progress

North Country Books, Inc.
220 Lafayette Street
Utica, New York 13502
www.northcountrybooks.com

Dedicated to my husband
William S. Hopsicker

ACKNOWLEDGEMENTS

A posthumous thank you to Virginia B. Bowers, long-time historian for the city of Albany, New York. She was a wealth of knowledge, exceedingly helpful, and quite excited at our discoveries.

A posthumous thank you to Mildred Miner, founding member of the Limestone Ridge Historical Society in Oriskany Falls, New York. Millie's archival copy of *The Weekly News* put me on track for writing this book.

A grateful thank you to George Newman, former editorial page editor of the Utica *Observer Dispatch*, AP reporter, and United States Foreign Service representative. George provided appreciated research from a distant location. His interest and encouragement kept me motivated.

A hearty thanks to Lisa Rogers, reference librarian at Utica College. She was invaluable in her assistance as I fumbled my way through miles of microfiche to pull out the facts of Josephine's life.

Staff at the Oneida County Clerk's Office, Archives, are deserving of well-earned thanks for locating and putting at my disposal documents pertinent to *The Balance of Justice*.

My thanks to staff of the New York Public Library for locating a pertinent letter from the Daniel Sickles Papers, Manuscript and Archives Division, New York Public Library. Astor, Lenox, and Tilden Foundation.

Janice Reilly and staff at the Oneida County History Center are deserving of well-earned thanks for locating photos used in this book.

Many thanks to Shirley Malarne and the Essex Historical Society of Essex, Connecticut. They filled in the gaps on Captain Isaiah Pratt. The sea captain was an integral character in Josephine's story, and their enthusiasm pushed me onward.

PREFACE

The Balance of Justice is a biographical novel set in the mid-nineteenth century. Central characters, events, and places in this story did exist. My protagonist, Josephine McCarty, was as thrilling a woman as ever graced the pages of fiction. In portraying her life, I made an effort to follow the sequence of her actions. But the book is not a biography; it is a novel set in the context of actual events.

In 1872, an Extraordinary Term of the Oneida County Court of Oyer and Terminer convened in the state of New York for the purpose of trying Mrs. Josephine McCarty for murder in a shooting committed on a horse-drawn streetcar in Utica, New York. It was the most sensational case in the history of the county. Testimony given in the course of the trial was covered in great detail by The *Utica Morning Herald and Daily Gazette* and the *Utica Daily Observer*. These newspaper accountings provide the bulk of the information used in writing *The Balance of Justice*. Background information came from many sources, a full list of which may be obtained by contacting North Country Books. The main characters' thoughts, conversations, and descriptions come from a combination of research and imagination. Secondary characters, in many cases, are fictitious in nature and identity. Mrs. McCarty's connection to persons of historical fame is documented. Selected testimony and written evidence used in her trial can be found within the context of the manuscript. Again, please keep in mind, *The Balance of Justice* is a novel.

Mohawk Street Jail, Utica, New York

THE SHOOTING

The intensity of the explosion failed to penetrate her senses. It was the blood. In reaction to the splatter, her palm flexed open, allowing a gun to fall silently onto the cushioned seat. Acrid smoke became one with the heavy veil drawn over her face. She reached through the haze to retrieve the revolver and moved to the steps at the front of the car. Her foot stretched into space, sending a layer of petticoat fluttering skyward. Releasing her hold on the handrail, she sailed toward the pavement, only to have the action reversed.

"It will be your death to jump while the car is in motion." The comment came from a gentleman who had taken a commanding grip on her arm.

The lady averted her face. Although the horses had bolted at the firing of a shot, a dexterous driver had them under control and was slowing to a halt. Skirting her rescuer, she dropped to the curb without hesitation. A second man stepped forward holding a large fur muff. She accepted the hand warmer and turned from the streetcar, leaving a cacophony of panic resonating behind her. Tiny heels tapped against sandstone as she walked briskly downhill in the direction of Utica's business district.

Another pair of feet hit the pavement. They belonged to a long-legged man who rushed to keep pace with her. The sidewalk beneath them quivered as the streetcar resumed its speed and thundered past.

The two pedestrians halted. They'd reached the intersection of Hopper and Genesee streets which offered a clear view of city hall. Designed by Richard Upjohn, the building included a clock tower that served as a focal point for this burgeoning city of New York State. The municipal structure also housed a police station. The pair watched as two policemen sprinted from the building to run off in the opposite direction. The woman sighed heavily.

"Do you intend to surrender yourself to the police?" the man beside her asked.

"It is immaterial," she answered faintly. "I care not what is done. Are you a policeman?"

The gentleman stated he was not.

"My children are waiting at Butterfield's hotel downtown." She raised a small hand to point northward before moving to complete her journey.

"You should surrender yourself at the police station." The comment carried an insistent edge.

"Let them come for me."

Her walking companion called out to a gentleman on the opposite side of the street exclaiming the need of a policeman. He pointed to the woman with exaggerated gesture when a man in uniform emerged from a doorway beneath the yellow brick tower. The uniformed attendant hastened toward them, introducing himself as Janitor Supple, a special officer of city hall.

The woman appeared confused as he grasped her arm to draw her across the street. The self-proclaimed "officer" was posing a question when her escort interceded, admonishing Supple that he had no right to question the lady.

The woman grew excited, crying in anguish, "Oh, sir! He is a villain. He has robbed me and my family of everything we had."

The men could only guess that her comments were in reference to the shooting victim.

The trio entered the station house where Mr. Supple surrendered his charge to the chief of police. The time read 10:10 AM. The date, January 17, 1872, signified the onset of the most sensational criminal trial in the history of Oneida County. The scope of the case was beyond imagining when the woman first stepped into the building.

Chief Luce had a square jaw and a neatly trimmed mustache. He appeared to be a solid man, muscular in build and staid in character. He conducted the lady to his office with courtesy and requested she remove her veil.

The woman pulled two large hat pins from a brown, plumed jockey cap. A cascade of silk netting slipped to her shoulder.

The three men stared. Her chin rose slightly. The dark eyes glittered in wariness as she returned their gaze from a face chiseled to delicate perfection. They were facing an exotic being of great beauty. Once seen, this woman would never be forgotten.

Chief Luce rubbed a hand over his balding scalp. "You have a gun?"

The lady acknowledged she did. Putting her hand to the pocket of a sealskin jacket, she withdrew a pistol and handed it to the chief. Her gun was a Smith & Wesson, manufactured in Springfield, Massachusetts; one barrel had been discharged. When the chief asked if she had anything else, she offered her wallet, but he pushed it away.

"You do not want my money?" she asked.

"Oh, no," he responded quickly, fanning his arm with an invitation to sit. She took the seat with dignity and responded to his interrogation.

"My name is Josephine McCarty. I reside at 62 Howard Street in Albany."

Though the question and answer seemed simple, her statement would later be refuted. John Maloy, chief of police for the city of Albany, identified the suspect as Emma Burleigh, a notorious character in the capital district.

Maloy was wrong. While the woman regularly used the alias of Emma Burleigh, she bore the legal name of Josephine McCarty. In years past, she'd been known by her maiden name, Josephine Fagan. On occasion, she went by the name of Virginia Seymour. And she no longer lived on Howard Street. The many discrepancies would complicate Chief Luce's report.

Josephine's shadow on the trip down Genesee Street continued to linger at the station house. His interruptions to the interrogation were wearing thin with the chief.

"Your face is familiar," the shadow said. "Have you not lived here?"

"I have lived near to Utica."

"Your children?" he continued. "Would you like me to inform them as to your circumstances?"

"No, sir. Go to the Jones & Babcock office and tell them." She followed

3

the request with an immediate expression of gratitude, a natural reaction in a person of good breeding.

"Isaac Tapping." Chief Luce gave an exasperated sideways nod as he identified the figure departing with her message. He led Josephine to Supple's apartment in the basement where the janitor's wife conducted a thorough search for additional weapons.

When Luce completed what he thought to be an accurate report, he escorted Josephine to a cell in the basement. An officer was assigned to keep suicide watch. The woman's actions had given the chief cause to worry.

The report was preliminary, of course; amazingly, neither the chief nor the prisoner was aware of the facts or the extent of the tragedy that had taken place.

The drama unfolded at Butterfield House. A shout pierced the hushed opulence of the hotel's lobby, informing patrons that a man had been shot. Waiters and guests rushed onto the sidewalk, gaping as passengers stumbled from a streetcar. Milton Thomson, a well known figure in the Utica community, emerged from the vehicle covered in blood. A second victim to the shooting was unable to move. For want of a better conveyance, bystanders placed him on a window shutter.

Three young children were playing in the hotel parlor. They watched with curiosity as two men jostled the shutter through to the billiard room. The man lying on the shutter appeared to be dead. The first procession was followed by a second as attendants guided the injured man to a great velvet chair at the center of the lobby. The surrounding crowd parted when the doctor arrived.

The oldest of the children stepped backward in shock.

"What is it Louis? What has happened?" the smaller boy questioned.

"Juddie, it's Uncle Tom!"

"Where?"

"The man with the bleeding head! He was a visitor at our house. Do you not remember?"

In the midst of the ensuing confusion, the boys held tight to their little sister. All three were pressed to the wall as they observed events with fear and dread. Eventually, the undertaker took the dead man away, and Thomson was escorted to his home. "Uncle Tom" never once glanced in their direction or gave any indication of having known them.

Another child waited in Ogdensburg. Her father, Henry Hall, was dead, his body lying on a window shutter. His wife's familial connection to the Thomsons had put him in the line of fire. Having concluded a visit with the Thomson family, he'd boarded the streetcar along with Milton, seating himself next to the window. When the shot rang out, fate controlled the trajectory. A steel ball entered Thomson's cheek, passed through his nose, and into the chest of Mr. Hall where it severed the aorta causing instant death.

Josephine knew nothing of the man from Ogdensburg until a crowd gathered at the front of city hall. Eager to glimpse the gun-toting beauty, their chatter challenged her weeping lament. Then a voice pealed loudly above the din identifying the murder victim as Henry Hall.

On hearing these words, Josephine halted all action. She knew Milton Thomson. But who, in heaven's name, was Henry Hall? What hand did she have in his death? Grasping her hair with trembling fingers, she released a frenzied scream, "My God! If I have killed an innocent man, take me and hang me at once."

Her fingers twisted into knots as her feet resumed their pacing. The walls drew closer with every rotation. The guard cleared his throat to gain her attention, and then announced the arrival of two Franciscan nuns affiliated with St. Elizabeth's Hospital, a facility situated but three blocks from Josephine's cell.

The nuns entered in a bustle; strings of wooden beads swayed with their motion. The taller nun did the talking; the other smiled, nodding assent to whatever was said.

"Mrs. McCarty, we are here to pray with you and to offer our assistance with the children. We had a nice conversation with them just minutes ago. They are quite charming, truly delightful children. Captain Johnson, the Butterfield landlord, is currently in charge of them. A number of ladies from the community have volunteered to help."

5

"Thank you, sisters." Josephine fluctuated between skepticism and gratitude as she observed the black-clad nuns with their fresh, scrubbed faces. "Louis, the oldest, is twelve. He is self-reliant and very mature. Juddie and Josie are children. I have been beside myself with fear for them."

"Do not fear. God is merciful; he will provide." The sisters kept company with the accused for nearly an hour.

When the nuns left, a reporter from the *Utica Daily Observer* swiftly moved to take their place. Though Josephine acknowledged his introduction with grace, she expressed her unwillingness to grant an interview. "It is my experience that newsmen are too often guilty of printing misstatements."

The pacing continued relentlessly in spite of the influx of visitors. The city was in an uproar. Events were moving forward with great haste.

Lewis H. Babcock, Esq., arrived. Though he and his client had never met, his partner, Robert Jones, had been representing the accused in a suit she'd initiated against Milton Thomson. Babcock pulled up a chair and studied the woman.

"You've come to some serious trouble, Mrs. McCarty. We need to get our facts together."

"Milton wouldn't see me! I had no place to live, no means to care for the children. Mr. Jones is aware of the circumstances. Milton dammed us to hell and put his own children out on the street!"

"It will all come out before we are through. The issue is to focus on your defense."

The glitter in Josephine's eyes turned wild. "Had I been clear in my head, I should have taken better aim."

"Hush! Make no statements in that regard."

The counselor looked over his shoulder. After explaining the route the bullet had taken in claiming the life of Henry Hall, he filled her in on the judicial proceedings.

"Coroner Lawton of Rome empanelled a jury of seven men for an inquest. They will meet at 1:00 tomorrow afternoon. A man has been killed. They will most certainly send the case to a grand jury."

The lawyer looked sharply at his client. "You need to understand the law, Mrs. McCarty. It states that when a felonious act is committed with premeditated design to maim or kill an individual and another is killed in the process, the perpetrator is guilty of murder in the first degree."

Josephine stared back at him. "There is plenty of law in this country, but precious little justice."

"You shot two men on a streetcar filled with witnesses. Oneida County has a penchant for hangings."

Conversation between the lawyer and client continued through the evening. The law firm's other partner, Robert O. Jones, was then on a train bound for Albany. The legal team thought it imperative to retrieve their client's personal papers before anyone else could get hold of them. Jones would also consult with lawyers in Albany who had served the accused in the past. Jones and Babcock were capable attorneys, but Hall's death made Josephine McCarty a candidate for the hangman. Every avenue had to be covered.

Counselor Babcock returned to the city hall cell early the following morning. He handed Josephine a stack of newspapers. "News of the shooting has hit the papers."

It certainly had. The story appeared in papers throughout the country, including the *Washington Sun*, *New York Times*, and *Chicago Tribune*. Coverage could even be found in the *Daily Democrat* in Sedalia, Missouri. The articles were not kind and in many cases totally inaccurate.

Josephine's mouth twisted to a grim smile as she read a *New York Herald* article describing her as "a tall, portly lady," when she had a diminutive figure with height just a smidgeon over five feet. The *Utica Daily Observer* identified her son, Juddie, as being a girl bearing the name Jennie. That same *Observer* story had her married to a wealthy Scotsman. She wanted to laugh. Robert McCarty originated from Lewis County in northern New York, and if there was one thing he'd lacked it was money.

Residents of the Augusta area were disputing another erroneous statement. The *Utica Daily Observer* reported that Milton Thomson's first encounter with Josephine McCarty was a happenstance meeting on a steamboat where she allegedly seduced him. The locals knew better.

The *Utica Daily Observer* also published a statement written by Milton Thomson in response to the rumors being bandied about. It read as follows:

> To the Public–I do not expect to silence the clamor of those who devour character and fatten thereon; but I have a right to demand, and do demand, that all sensible people, and especially those who have professed to be my friends, withhold their judgment till they get the facts.

But on the eighteenth of January, Jailer Cole was still shuffling visitors to Josephine's cell. When he opened the door to her son, Louis, she dropped the newspapers, allowing her child to fall into a sweeping embrace. He'd maintained a strong and resolute demeanor since the advent of their troubles, but he loved his mother and the gravity of the situation did not escape him.

"I've been tending to Juddie and Josie," he said bravely. "A lady from town stayed with us last night. Another woman is with the children now."

"I'm sorry, Louis. Do you know what happened?"

Louis nodded. The two kept their communion for the remainder of the day, awaiting an announcement that would dictate their future—or the lack thereof.

The inquest commenced at one twenty-five with a large crowd of spectators present. One by one, the streetcar passengers gave testimony. Isaac Tapping offered the most lengthy accounting. His statements were accurate and unbiased.

Dr. D.P. Bissell reported on his examination of wounds to Milton Thomson and Henry Hall as they appeared on his arrival at the Butterfield House.

Due to his infirmity, Milton Thomson was sworn at home and gave his testimony at that location.

At eight that evening, just thirty-four hours from the time of shooting, the jury had a decision. Josephine McCarty, in the process of committing a felonious assault, did, without intent, cause the death of Henry Hall.

Each of the jurymen as well as the coroner took a turn in signing the verdict. In deference to a request made on behalf of the accused by her attorney, the jury removed themselves to the jail, where Mr. Babcock read the decision in their presence and explained its ramifications to his client.

The authorities transferred Josephine to the Mohawk Street jail where her sons, Louis and nine-year-old Juddie, joined her. The boys huddled against their mother enclosed by the bars of a damp, stone prison. The cell would be their home for several months as legal combatants struggled with strategy. Their sister fared better. Good to their promise, the Franciscans were housing her at the hospital convent.

Henry Hall's body was taken by rail to his home in Ogdensburg where fifteen hundred people paid their respects and attended the internment.

While reports on the crime circulated with various discrepancies, descriptions of Josephine were uniformly scathing, accusing her of blackmail, abortion, and spying for the Confederacy.

Albany's *Argus* informed readers that for a period of time, she enjoyed a life of high style in one of the principal hotels of New York's capital as the kept mistress of a noted political leader. Reportedly, any bill she put her hand to was assured of passage during the 1862–63 session. The *Argus* labeled her a social vampire.

Albany's *Daily Evening Times* of Saturday, January 20, 1872, claimed that if the facts of her affiliations were divulged, a social earthquake would erupt in their fair city. It was hoped that justice would not require the publishing of names. This same newspaper described her as having been a bad woman always.

Events were playing well with forces who wished to see the woman hang. The jury would be under siege as political machinations took control of the trial.

CHAPTER ONE

In response to the certainty that his client would be indicted for murder, counselor Babcock spent hours reviewing the facts. An insanity defense would require a full accounting of Josephine McCarty's life. His prodding for information yielded a chain of surprises.

He was sitting at a table with pen and paper before him when he asked his client: "Can you recall Thomson's first advances toward you?"

Answering firmly, Josephine replied, "That would have been 1842."

Caught off guard, Babcock's head bobbed upward.

With a finger pressed to her brow, Josephine's thoughts stretched back in time. "For thirty years he stalked me, just another lion hunting meat. I paid little heed, initially. I was very young. He did propose in '43, the year I finished my studies at the Oneida Conference Seminary. I remember events of that year well.

SHE'D ALWAYS FOUND JOY in returning home after months away at private schools. The long periods of absence were bridged by letters, and homecoming had been an instantaneous assimilation into an ever-widening circle of friends.

The year 1843 introduced a period of change. Her graduation from the seminary presented opportunities that would take her far from the Central New York community she called home.

Though the plan she'd formulated had drawbacks, she was operating on the premise that challenges of the past had been far greater than anything likely to come up in the future.

The death of her father, Terrence, had seemed insurmountable, yet she'd eventually managed to master the grief. Her step-father, Camp Williams, died in a horrific accident three years later. Josephine's mother was now a widow twice over. High-strung to begin with, shock caused the woman's agitation to increase. The resultant outbursts had been a trying experience for a girl still in her teens.

Robert Norris, appointed guardian by her father's will, proved the only constant in her young life. He had been true to the assignment. Yet, hard as it would be, the time had come to exert her independence.

Just two days after arriving home, she tied a bonnet under her chin and left the house. She followed a path that took her along a cornfield to the entrance of Parker Cemetery. On reaching the burial site, she climbed a knoll and dropped to the ground beside a marker for Terrence Fagan.

Her slim fingers traced the chiseled characters as she whispered to the rustling grass.

"I'm leaving, Father. So much has happened. I'm sure there is more to come, but I need to move into the larger world, away from the gossip of our little community. I've been a good girl, Father, I really have, and your little Josie loves you still."

On rising, she stood to stare at the next stone in line. The granite recorded the beginning and end of Camp Williams' life. He was killed at the age of forty-three, on June 11, 1841. Without any discernible change in expression, she turned back to the path to resume her journey. It was imperative that she see her guardian, Robert Norris.

The Norris General Store and Post Office enjoyed a steady trade, as did most of the businesses at the five-point juncture in Augusta Center. The moment Josephine entered the store she was halted by a familiar shriek.

"Josie!"

Mary Norris skipped forward, dodging the barrels that crowded the floor. Her corn silk hair and blue eyes contrasted sharply against Josephine's dark features as the two enjoyed a sisterly hug. Friends since childhood, their bond grew stronger the year of Terrence's death. It had been a year of sorrow and tough decisions. Though aware of her daughter's craving for knowledge, Phoebe Fagan had balked at the thought of sending her away to boarding school. Robert Norris, the newly appointed guardian, made an offer of room and board if Josie would attend Augusta Academy. The institution sat adjacent to the store and the living arrangement spawned a sisterhood destined to last a lifetime.

"Josie, I can't wait to hear of your latest adventure. And do tell, what are the Dodge boys up to?" Mary voiced her question with a giggle.

She knew Josephine boarded with the Reverend Dodge and his family while attending the seminary in Cazenovia. She found it an enviable fact that William and Ireneus Dodge had also been classmates.

"Now Mary, the Dodge boys are gentlemen of the highest caliber. They are never up to anything that isn't in every way honorable."

"Josie, you endow every boy with undeserved virtue. I wouldn't care if the devil's blood ran through their veins; the Reverend's sons are smart-looking fellows. I'd accept either as a beau."

A knowing smile crossed Josephine's face. It flickered with humor before sobering to the task at hand. "Mary, I really need to speak with your father. Is he here?"

The postmaster's voice boomed from the back of the building. "Josie, my girl, you're home and a welcome sight indeed."

"Uncle Norris, I'd like to speak with you privately."

Norris took a startled glance at his charge; a bushy right eyebrow shot to an awkward curve as he directed her toward the desk he used for postal business.

"Uncle Norris, I've completed my studies at the seminary and am qualified to teach. I would like to arrange a visit with my father's relatives in the city of New York. There should be an abundant number of positions available downstate, and the metropolitan community would enable me to expand my own education."

Robert looked at her reflectively. Twelve at the time of Terrence's death, she had not been a difficult child. She was sweet and affectionate, and he loved her almost as much as he did his own daughter. But his worry for

Josie went well beyond any he had for Mary.

"What about your mother, Josephine?"

"Uncle Norris, I've been away from home for years. Mother is an independent lady. I don't believe she would be much affected by my moving, whatever the location."

The guardian took a deep breath. He'd felt a moment of apprehension at her request for a private interview. Seventeen-year-old Josie was a vision of beauty and grace. But those eyes, the glint emanating from that depth of darkness, tended to throw one off balance. In the age of Victorian fluff, she often appeared a rebel. Her brilliance and daring could garner chastisement and often seasoned the pot of gossip. Half the young jacks in town were chasing after her skirts. He couldn't protect her forever.

"Write the letter. If it's agreeable to your relatives, I will arrange the trip. Keep in mind; you'll be under my charge until we reach New York."

She offered Robert an appreciative hug. As she backed away, each step accompanied a new expression of gratitude, exuberance overwhelming her senses. The aproned clerk approached unnoticed. Their collision drove him sideways. His foot caught the leg of a table, and he stumbled to the floor, showered by a toppling of bonnets and ribbons. Waving a feather away from his face, he looked up at his lovely assailant.

"Milton, I'm so sorry." Josephine put a hand to her mouth, more to stifle laughter than to mask embarrassment.

Milton Thomson looked delighted. "Any time, Miss Josephine!"

Milton was a recent graduate of the Clinton Liberal Institute. His family owned a hotel and general store in nearby Paris Hill. The position at Norris' offered a convenient transition from classroom to trade.

As the proprietor astutely noted, Milton was infatuated with their Augusta beauty.

After repeating a litany of apologies, Josephine escaped to the furthest corner of the store, where Mary hastened to join her. Their giggling bounced from the walls as they discussed this latest incident in Milton's awkward performance as a prospective suitor.

The girls hadn't seen each other in months, and their conversation quickly expanded to envelop the community at large. After all other topics had been exhausted, Mary moved to personal inquiries. Did Josie communicate with Michael Meyers from Herkimer, and had the Warren boy proposed?

Josephine offered some evasive answers before casting her eye to the sun. It was time to head for home.

She skipped the shortcut, avoiding the marked stones of Parker's Cemetery. Passing the feed store, she caught the attention of Sidney Putnam who'd been loading grain sacks onto a wagon.

"Good afternoon, Miss Fagan. Isn't this a lovely day?"

"Oh yes," she answered with a smile. "It is most certainly a lovely day."

The farmer kept watch as she passed, his own smile widening broadly. Reports on the girl's beauty weren't half good enough.

She'd reached the Josiah Rand farm when a cheerful voice drifted down from above.

"Good afternoon, Miss Fagan."

Josephine looked up to see Nathan Brown peering down from a wagon stacked with hay. "And top of the day to you, Mr. Brown."

"Aren't we formal now?"

Josephine laughed. "Are you working for Mr. Rand?"

Nathan nodded with an annoyed expression.

"You know, when I was a little girl my father would toss me up onto the hay wagon and give me a ride. I do miss those happy days."

"Why should you miss what could be yours right now?" Nathan stretched out a hand to pull her upward.

"Oh, no! That wouldn't do at all!"

"Josephine Fagan, are you afraid of heights?"

An irresistible taunt! Bracing her foot against the iron wagon wheel, she took the extended hand. On reaching the top, she sank to her knees in the freshly harvested forage. Tipping her face toward a smattering of clouds, she met the sun full strength.

A stabbing sensation drove Nathan to speak. "Josie, will you marry me?"

His question drew a quick response. "No, Nathan. I will not!"

"Why?"

"First of all, I'm not ready for marriage. Second, you don't own a white horse and have no coat of armor."

"What are you talking about?"

Josephine fell back onto the soft green hay. "Did you never hear of King Arthur or the ancient knights of chivalry?"

"I don't under…"

Another voice cracked the air, leaving Nathan's mouth hanging open. "What's going on up there?" It was Josiah Rand!

"Is that you, Josephine Fagan? Get down off that wagon both of you. Scandalous behavior! That's what it is! I won't have it on my place. Your mother will hear about this, Miss Fagan."

Josephine jumped from the wagon with skirts flying and raced up the road towards home. Temperatures hovered close to eighty, and the exertion caused her face to redden. The streaking tears were born of humiliation.

On reaching a wooden culvert that marked the northeast corner of the farm, she dashed to the stream in search of relief. With hands cupping water, she splashed her face and gulped. Then closing her eyes, she savored the moment before standing to shake hay from the folds of her dress.

A fallen willow bridged the tributary. She dusted the trunk with her handkerchief before sidling down to meditate.

The brook-side plot with its stand of willows provided an almost omnipotent perspective of the diminishing hillside as it stretched to the valley below. In the days of her childhood, the scene had affected her with an innate sense of power. Over time, she'd come to revere the spot for other reasons.

When Amos Hodges galloped to the house to report her father's accident, she'd run to the brook as a place of refuge. Uncannily, she'd been sitting there when Camp Williams fell and the wagon rolled over his neck. The sacred corner stimulated recall of happenings both pleasurable and tragic.

But she had no time to ruminate on past events. Her thoughts ran to the future. Handling her mother required forethought. If gossipmonger Rand turned this incident with Nathan into an issue, her mother might deny support.

Her mother's unpredictable behavior had always been worrisome. How would she sit with the idea of turning to the Fagan family? Phoebe Burley Fagan Williams could be a volatile woman. When she captivated Terrence Fagan, she was a stunning beauty with a grown daughter. But the porcelain complexion and pale eyes were companion to a rather delicate psyche. Nervous and flighty, she'd been prone to periods of ill health. Their move to Augusta had been a response to the asthma that assailed her in the tidewater basin of Virginia. Yet, Phoebe Williams valued status and appearances above all else.

Josephine's mind wrapped around that last thought. The opportunity to be introduced in good society would most certainly appeal to her mother. She rose from the splintered willow bench with a confident chin aimed toward the sky.

Phoebe seemed a bit perplexed as her daughter recited the advantages of this new proposal. "You've yet to meet your New York relatives. What makes you think you'll be welcome?"

Josephine checked her impatience. "That is the purpose of my writing a letter. Father had great affection for Cousin O'Dwyer. I find it hard to believe he would have felt so were the man not of honorable character."

Phoebe mulled the situation. She'd had no say in the upbringing of her older daughter. Though the girl had married well, she died in childbirth at twenty-five, leaving four babies, the youngest of which would follow her to the grave. Things might be different with Josephine.

Terrence's daughter had a willful streak that ignored proprieties and custom. Yet, the girl was clever. Phoebe could barely comprehend young Josephine's thoughts. It occurred to her that it might be advantageous to have this daughter settled in a big city.

With Phoebe's approval guaranteed, Josephine rode out the following morning with a letter addressed to Thomas O'Dwyer. Johnson, her little black Morgan, tore through the fields in response to his mistress' urging. Saliva foamed at the corners of his mouth as she reined him in at Norris' store.

"You're riding hard for a lady of leisure." Milton stood at the hitching post with a grin on his face and the reins of a saddled gelding held loosely in one hand.

"I have a letter to post," Josie answered with a smile. "I want it to go out today."

"The mail always goes out on time. What are your plans for the rest of the day?" Before she had a chance to answer, the eager clerk extended an invitation. "I have a packet to deliver to Esquire Dean. Would you like to ride along with me?"

The offer connected with the daring tone her mood had taken.

"It would be a pleasure to join you, Mr. Thomson, as soon as I post my letter."

She dropped from her horse and tossed the reins to Milton.

After safely depositing her letter, she remounted, and the two drew off at a trot. It was a leisurely ride with the stinging sound of grasshoppers filling the August air. When the errand had been completed, the horses were turned toward home. Puffs of dust followed their tread as a sober silence fell between riders. Josephine stared straight ahead, conscious that Milton's eyes were riveted upon her.

Pulling abreast of his riding companion, Milton broke the silence. "Josephine, you know I care for you. Why do you put me off?"

The smile, the twinkle…they toyed with her suitor as she issued another flirtatious rejection.

"Milton, I have no serious beau, and I have no intention of acquiring one at this particular moment in life."

"What of Warren Curtis? The mail between you flew back and forth from early spring until you returned this very month."

"Milton! Your handling of the mail should be discreet. You shock me with your comments."

"Well, you haven't answered."

"I feel no need to explain myself, but Warren and I share political ideology that opens the way for intense conversation. Were you of the Whig

Party, we might have more in common."

"It is a divisive party with loose ends that can't be tied."

"Milton, you're not listening to me. I told you: at present, I am satisfied to have a strong contingent of friends."

Josephine tapped Johnson with a crop that sent the horse off at a gallop. Milton followed as she veered to a field, distancing him even further. The little black horse went back on its haunches as it slid down a steep embankment. He jumped a creek and scrambled to the top of another ridge. Rock and clods of dirt rained down upon Milton as he continued his pursuit. The edge of Josephine's dress had been soaked at the creek, but on she went, over rail fences and cobblestone walls, leaving scattered livestock in her wake. The three-mile chase did not slow until they reached the village of Oriskany Falls.

When Milton pulled up beside her, he was facing Diana, the fearless goddess of the hunt. Wonderment flooded his face; it would for anyone having just enjoyed the adventure of his life.

"Josie, I had no idea!" He could hardly get his breath. "You're an incredible horsewoman."

She gave him a coquettish smile. "My accomplishments are many."

And her thoughts were miles away. A cousin whom she'd never met suddenly held the key to her future.

Thomas O'Dwyer and Terrence Fagan had been boisterous friends as well as cousins. Finding Ireland a pie divided too often and the family farms too small, they shook the *auld sod* clear of their boots to take passage on a ship setting sail for America. They arrived in New York in 1821, robust and ready to start life anew.

As luck would have it, the economy of the United States was in the second year of financial depression. Thousands of workers had lost their jobs as factories shuttered their doors. Terrence returned to working the land; Thomas remained in New York to fight his way up a crooked ladder.

As a saloon keeper in the Irish district, he held powerful sway over his New York patrons. It was a position that bought him influence with factions at Tammany Hall. He'd risen from the slums of Five Points to a three-storied mansion above Washington Square. The ascent had been long and slow and often violent. Pride in what he had achieved would further be fed by a visit from his late cousin's daughter. Satisfaction overwhelmed him as he sat at his desk to pen a reply.

His letter put Josephine in a flurry. She ripped the envelope and scanned the text while standing before the postal window. In a rush of excitement, she turned to the postman.

"Oh, Milton! Isn't it wonderful? I am moving to New York!"

Milton stood mum; time had run out, and the love of his life would soon be far away. Desperation prompted a panicked plea. "Why, Jo? The valley is growing. Opportunities abound. We have local politicians whose influence is expanding within the state and within the country."

Josephine shook her head. "I must leave. For me, there is no other choice."

"When will you go? Will you write? Will you give me an address where I may reach you?"

"Of course, I have no intention of forgetting my friends or my roots. I will always be in touch."

CHAPTER TWO

The grand jury of Oneida County delivered an indictment of murder against Josephine A. McCarty on January 25, 1872. The charge of murder in the first degree recorded the aliases of Josephine A. Fagan, Emma Burleigh, and Virginia Seymour as clarification of the defendant's identity.

At the February term of the Court of Oyer and Terminer, Josephine stood before the court of the Hon. Charles H. Doolittle. Doolittle was tall and imposing. A full, dark beard exaggerated an angular face. His eyes were black and probing, his manner one of impatience.

"How does the prisoner plea?" The words were thrown at the defendant as a challenge.

Josephine's composure failed to waver. "Not guilty, Your Honor."

She'd barely brushed the seat of her chair when the district attorney, D.C. Stoddard, took the floor. He moved for the trial to go forward immediately.

Babcock responded, addressing the court with a motion for postponement. He cited the need of additional time to prepare an adequate defense. Judge Doolittle agreed to move the case to March 25.

The *Daily Bee*, a Utica newspaper published by Seth Wilbur Payne, was the only paper to stand with Mrs. McCarty in the charge of murder. The January 26 issue carried a statement accusing Judge Doolittle of accepting—or agreeing to accept—money, pending the result of the McCarty trial. Allegedly, the judge's benefactor, Milton Thomson, wanted McCarty out of the way. Payne reiterated the statement the following day, going further in calling Doolittle "self-seeking, tricky, conniving, and in every way a dishonorable man."

The judge commenced a libel suit. Court assigned a succession of lawyers as counsel to Mr. Payne; each in turn begged for excusal. The reasons for withdrawing varied, but when the fifth lawyer asked to be excused, Payne allowed the trial to go forward offering no defense. On March 9, the jury took but ten minutes to find Payne guilty. He received a sentence of four months at hard labor in the Albany Penitentiary.

Josephine was, in the meantime, dealing with family life in a single cell. A small table separated her cot from one shared by the boys. That tiny space accommodated meals and lesson time. Her request for extra blankets had been granted, and one was used to provide a modicum of privacy while using the chamber pot. Juddie suffered the most from their jailed existence. Due to his maturity, Louis enjoyed a great deal of freedom. Jailor Cole allowed him to pass freely from their cell to the world outside. He had taken a job hawking newspapers, and unbeknownst to his mother, made a deal with a photographer to sell pictures of her as well.

On March 21, Louis returned from the street to enter the cell. Behaving in a covert manner, he moved toward the cot carrying his coat in a neatly folded bundle.

With growing suspicion, Josephine spoke to him sharply. "Louis, what is it that you have hidden in your coat?"

The boy nearly dropped his coat. A quick recovery left him shaking.

It occurred to her that he might have picked up a kitten. When he failed to answer, she asked again.

He opened his coat and his mother's jaw dropped. Her voice trembled as she asked the next question. "Where did you get that gun?"

A small, cartridge-loading pistol rested in the folds of Louis' coat. Tears welled in the boy's grey eyes. "I bought it to shoot Uncle Tom."

Josephine gasped as her heart thumped soundly in her chest. She lifted the gun from its woolen shroud and wrapped her arms around the child. *What have we done! Both mother and father charged with murder, what does that mean for our son? This can't be placed on the boy. He will go to a fine school and grow up a gentleman. He mustn't be bloodied by our mistakes.*

"Louis, my dear, dear, Louis, you must not think such things. You have always been a good boy and must continue to be so. I am relying on you to show good judgment."

"He made trouble for you. It's his fault that we are here." Louis was blubbering and his fist could not keep up with the snot running from his nose.

Josephine raised her head and tried to smile. "We will get through this somehow. Has there ever been a situation from which we did not recover?"

Louis shook his head.

"Well then, tell me how you managed to buy a gun."

Keeping silent on the photographs, Louis told of the newspapers he'd sold and the change he had accumulated in order to make the purchase.

"As proud as I am of your acumen, the gun shall stay with me. And we'll think no more on this subject. Is that understood?"

The youngster smiled and swiped at his tears.

Juddie was asleep on his cot. Josephine moved to reach the little boy's thumb. His lips quivered as she pulled the stubby finger from his mouth. They were deserving children, but should a jury find her guilty, the hangman would make them orphans.

Her eyes rolled toward the window. Soot from neighboring smokestacks coated the thick glass panes. Iron bars reinforced the dreariness of the wet spring weather. A long time ago she'd stood on a precipice in Catskill, her future as sparkling as the sun in autumn. The promise had been thwarted, but the details were mercilessly committed to memory.

THE MAGNITUDE OF HER YOUTHFUL PLANS became clear when the housekeeper broke into tears. The trip to New York would not be another semester at school. She was embarking on a journey without end. How did one plan for a lifetime? With a shake of the head she cleared her thoughts.

"Don't cry, Bridget. It is not my death that causes the packing. I am simply moving to a new chapter of this wonderful vision I have for life."

Bridget produced a tentative smile as she placed another dress in the trunk.

Rail service from Utica to Albany kept a fairly reliable schedule, yet

Robert Norris rejected the cars in favor of traveling by stagecoach. He had an aversion to replacing horse flesh with a chugging, smoking, iron machine. The Cherry Valley Turnpike would take them straight through to Albany.

So, with her trunk strapped to the top of the coach, Josephine took her place inside. Though consumed with excitement, she'd felt tears on her cheeks as her mother embraced her one last time. Whether the tears were hers or those of her mother, she really couldn't be sure. The warmth of their parting stirred emotions that had been dormant for some time.

She was hardly a seasoned traveler. Beyond the move from Virginia, past trips had been confined to the fifteen-mile radius of the schools she attended. The journey she sought to undertake would extend to the farthest reach of her dreams. It would all come about in increments, starting with the trip to New York's capital and a coach rolling forward at seven miles an hour. The dust and discomfort plaguing other passengers seemed not to be noticed at all. Her first complaint came late in the evening when they halted in Albany at Stanwix Hall.

"What is that smell?" she inquired as she stepped to the road with a handkerchief held to her nose.

The barrel-chested driver laughed. "That's Albany, miss, the foulest smelling city in the nation."

Darkness draped their surroundings, limiting the view. Robert Norris guided her up the steps to the Stanwix, hoping for clean beds and a bite to eat. The hotel proved to be a provider of luxury, and the noxious odors were soon forgotten.

Dawn brought the shock of Albany to daylight. Garbage littered the streets. Pigs roamed about, routing and wallowing in mud wherever it could be found. Josephine stepped back from the hotel window, blasted by the stench and filth before her.

The capital of New York State is nothing more than a pigsty, she thought as she tied her bonnet and stepped through the door.

Robert's itinerary included a steamship ride down the Hudson. She couldn't wait to get to the wharf. As their carriage approached the river they witnessed an unruly scene—hundreds of people were milling about in confusion. Agents for vessels docked in the harbor were fighting to ensnare bewildered travelers. When a booking agent reached for Josephine's arm, her guardian cocked his fist. If the man hadn't turned on the run, Robert would likely have knocked him down.

Wrenching free of the mob, they boarded a steamship that guaranteed passage to New York in a single day. Once on deck, Robert turned to his charge and grinned.

"Well, Josie, what do you think of your big world thus far?"

Josephine's face lighted with laughter. "It doesn't look or smell anything like Augusta. I guess we lost all aspects of our old home somewhere along the way."

Travel by boat proved a pleasant contrast to the jolting experience of the stagecoach. The open deck allowed them to glide downstream in awesome appreciation of the Livingston Estates on the east bank and Catskill Mountains to the west.

A telegraphed message to Thomas O'Dwyer had him standing on the wharf when they reached New York. He looked closely at every woman who traipsed down the plank. Then suddenly she was there; he knew her in an instant.

"Josephine!"

She looked up at his exclamation, flashing the dark eyes that tied her to the Fagan name.

"Cousin Thomas?"

"Yes, indeed," he responded, encircling her with great hulking arms.

She introduced him to her guardian. They were cordially shaking hands when a dapper young man with sandy hair appeared at Thomas' elbow.

"Thomas," he said with familiarity, "whom may I ask is this lovely lady?"

Thomas turned to the intruding stranger with a look not altogether pleasant, though his voice and manners held.

"My cousin, Miss Josephine Fagan, and her guardian, Mr. Robert Norris.

Rosie and me are bein' honored with a visit." He introduced Daniel Sickles with a courteous nod.

The gentleman bowed reverently.

As he raised his head, the grey eyes made an appreciative sweep; the intelligence, humor, and daring of the glance became an indelible image in Josephine's mind.

Thomas' voice snapped them to attention as he made a declaration. "We'd best get this baggage into the carriage afore it ends up on some other bloke's rig."

His anxiety had nothing to do with the trunks stacked before them. He wanted his cousin off the street and away from the man he found so unnerving.

Daniel Sickles tipped his hat, smiling from an elegant pose as the three made their way to a brougham. West Street ran along the wharf with a traffic pattern both fast and chaotic. Carriages were driven so recklessly pedestrians had to scramble to keep from being run down. Josephine picked her way, carefully sidestepping excrement on the dung-covered pavement. Once safely positioned in her cousin's carriage, she turned to him with a question about the gentleman who had, so recently, aroused her curiosity.

"Mr. Sickles—what is he about?"

"Sickles is about everythin', a lawyer and scoundrel with unlimited ambition. Though he might look the part, he's no gentleman, but rather an individual to be avoided by any lady who cherishes her reputation."

Josephine's laughter tinkled above sounds of the city. "Uncle Norris, I take back some of what I said earlier. Cousin's description of Mr. Sickles sounds like something issued from a mouth in Augusta."

"Heed me, Missy! Sickles is a dangerous man. Don't let his fine good looks deceive you."

Not wanting to annoy their host, Josephine directed her conversation toward the luxury of the brougham. Removed from the waste and dust of the streets, she took pleasure in the trip up Broadway. Her cousin had certainly done well for himself.

"Will we pass your business establishment, Cousin?"

"Oh, no! The Hoot and Holler's in the Four Ward, a poor community, certainly no place for such as yourself."

"Well," drawled Robert Norris, "it must be profitable to put you in a rig like this one."

"Ha! The Hoot and Holler serves me well, but the real money comes from the land. It's been that way since the beginnin' of time. This city grows like an infant, every day. If you have anythin' to invest, it ought to be in the land or what might be built upon it."

They pulled up to the O'Dwyer mansion where a servant appeared to assist them. Thomas' wife, Rosie, was right behind him, chirping a greeting as she grabbed at bags and guided her guests inside.

Supper was served in a room lit by chandeliers. The food was dished onto fine china and consumed with silver forks. But the fare was plain Irish cooking. Thomas' repertoire of funny stories resulted in peals of laughter. The merry evening might have been termed raucous if not for the omission of cursing.

Robert Norris planned from the beginning to limit his stay to a single night. He'd accomplished the deed he'd set out to do. His charge was in the hands of relatives, and he'd be heading back on the morrow. Previous inclinations were summarily dismissed as he purchased a ticket to travel by rail.

Eighteen hours from the time of his arrival, Robert was on the platform awaiting his first trip in the cars. He held Josephine close for a moment, and then released her and turned away. The distance that would grow between them caused apprehension on both sides. Guardian Norris had been the one person Josephine could count on in any situation, a fact recognized by each of them.

Rosie O'Dwyer possessed the same pleasant manner as that of her husband, welcoming Josie heartily into a home that had been sadly deprived of children. Though Thomas' little cousin had come to them purposely to gain a position in teaching, the hostess felt the initial intent should not exclude a day of shopping on the city's most elegant thoroughfare.

Josephine's beribboned bonnet, delicate profile, and cultivated speech drew smiles and cordial treatment from clerks and patrons all along Broadway. By contrast, her plump companion with the heavy brogue drew looks of distain as another tiresome Irish. Rosie ignored the affront, fully aware that Thomas had the wherewithal to buy any shop on the street. Should such a ridiculous whim overtake him, he could purchase the inventory as well.

The ladies were passing Tiffany, Young, and Ellis Jewelers when Daniel Sickles stepped from the shadows of the doorway. He bowed in deference, grasping Josephine's hand with a gentleman's aplomb.

"What a delightful coincidence! I couldn't have timed it better had I tried." The words flowed eloquently from lips half hidden by a well-shaped mustache.

Josephine responded with a dazzling smile that quickly ignited sparks. The virile energy coursing the young lawyer's body all but singed the tips of her fingers. She jerked her hand away, conscious that she'd never encountered a man of such magnetism.

"Very pleasant to have run into ya, Mister Sickles." Rosie hurried her pleasantries, directing Josie past the lawyer in haste.

The gentleman stood where they left him, his eyes trailing their path while his hand struck a match to light a fresh cheroot. The women melded with the promenade of shoppers, but their disappearance failed to erase the image in Sickles mind. The little lady with the ebony hair definitely piqued his interest.

When Thomas O'Dwyer arrived for dinner, he inquired as to how the ladies had spent their morning.

"We were shopping on Broadway, Cousin Thomas, when quite by accident we ran into Mr. Sickles again."

"Ha, that Sickles! I have little use for the man, but I have to say he does have brass. They threw him over the stair rail at Tammany Hall last night. Didn't faze the bugger a bit; he picked himself up, marched up the stairs, and entered the fray all over again."

Josephine looked aghast. "Why did they throw him over the railing?"

"Emotions run high at Tammany. If they can't shut a man up, they get rid of him, and they don't care how they do it."

Later in the evening, with their guest tucked in bed, Thomas expressed his concern to Rosie.

"I'm thinkin' we don't need that Sickles sniffin' around our gal. She's a bright little lass but certain no match for a dandy the likes of that one. I understand they've been lookin' for teachers up in Catskill. It might be a better place for little Josie. I'll post an inquiry tomorrow."

Thomas received a timely response from Emily Crocker, principal of the Catskill Female Academy. Josephine Fagan's credentials substantiated her fitness for the position they sought to fill. Josephine acquiesced to the offer, concealing her disappointment. Thomas and Rosie had her best interests at heart, but she'd left home with the prospect of establishing residence in the city of New York. Catskill was not what she had in mind.

The O'Dwyers were insistent on accompanying her back up the Hudson. Their plan included a brief stay at the Mountain House before dropping her off at the academy.

An excursion to one of the most famous hotels in America and the excitement of her new role as a teacher erased Josephine's frustration, and the well-dressed man with the keen grey eyes was pushed to the back of her mind.

The steamship provided a relaxing interlude between New York and the city of Catskill. The stagecoach ride up the mountain was another experience entirely. Josephine and her party were joined by a gentleman who had also taken the steamer. He was well acquainted with the district and thought it necessary to give them a running account.

"They're busy around here. Charlie Beach runs the Mountain House; he's the son of the owner of this here coach. Most everything around here is geared to the hotel or the meat-packing business. The cattle yards of Catskill are as essential to New York as the Boston yards are to New England. They slaughter about three hundred head here every day. Ship it all downstream."

Josephine flinched. Being a country girl, she was well acquainted with the butchering process, yet the numbers conjured a picture not altogether pleasant. As business proprietors in New York City, Rosie and Thomas were well versed in the traffic and commerce of the Hudson and had little use for their companion's narration.

But the traveler had yet to finish. "They've got several tanners in the area; there's a good market for hides. Lots of hotels, including the Brossenhan, cater to drovers. It's all big business. Of course, there are the artists—Thomas Cole lives in Catskill, you know." Then he smiled at Josephine. "There's also a goodly number of churches and schools. The girls at that academy should be right proud to have a pretty young teacher like you."

The trip took five tiring hours, the strain of which silenced their chatty narrator about a third of the way from the top. Josephine and Thomas left the coach to walk for a while. Shades of red and gold flashed brilliantly between shadows as the sun lit a path through the towering pines.

The Mountain House sat on a precipice, a huge, white edifice, columned front and back. The O'Dwyers followed their baggage to the hotel desk. Josephine lingered behind. After walking the length of the portico, she stopped to place a hand against one of the massive columns. The breathtaking scene before her reduced the mighty Hudson to a wisp of silvery ribbon. Thoughts of the lookout willow brought a smile to her face. Her little valley was nothing more than a pinprick in the topography of a vast and intriguing world.

The Mountain House offered incomparable luxury. But three days away from New York proved to be more than the O'Dwyers could abide. Relief was evident as they entered the stagecoach for a return to Catskill. Their smiles widened with the speed of the coach's descent.

A boy with a dray moved Josephine's trunks along the street to her new home, which was housed in what had once been a private residence. A young girl stood waiting on the porch.

"Miss Fagan, I'm Gertrude Morley." She spoke with timidity as she made the introduction.

Josephine regarded the girl in wonder. They were separated in age by no more than three years, yet she was the teacher and Gertrude the student. "I'm pleased to meet you, Gertrude. Have you been a student at Catskill for long?"

"No, ma'am. This is my first year at the academy."

An older woman with a bustling manner stepped through the door behind Gertrude. She offered an institutional welcome and introduced herself as Emily Crocker. Having long ago conquered the anguish of being a childless widow, the principal had progressed to the hustle of being a competent administrator.

"We are pleased to have you join us. Isn't that so, Gertrude? Let me show you around." She gave a through recitation as Josephine and the O'Dwyers toured the building. "The seminary is based on religious and scientific principle. We've had extraordinary teachers. Our first preceptor, Professor Rufus Nutting, authored a text on English grammar that has become a handbook in teaching."

The last stop on the tour took them to the third floor where Josephine would have a room to herself. The rectangular bit of space held a bed, a desk, a chair, and a bureau. Most importantly, it had a window with a view of the village below. Overall, it provided her with a private space to think on those rare occasions when she might be free of teaching commitments.

The O'Dwyers moved to leave. The new arrangement would serve Josie well, and they were eager for the sight of New York. They offered their good wishes with the request that she should write often.

Then Thomas turned back. "You know, Josie, you'll always be welcome in the O'Dwyer home. You just let me know if you're not happy here." He uttered the words with great sincerity. His little cousin was family.

There were four new students in addition to Gertrude attending the Catskill Female Academy. Insecure and lonely, they attached themselves to the beautiful teacher who was as new to the school as they themselves. The chair beside Josephine's third floor window provided a quiet confessional as the girls discussed their concerns about suitors, books, and each other. It never occurred to them that their teacher's life experience didn't extend much beyond their own. But she understood their inhibitions, and her popularity grew.

In accordance with custom, she wrote zealously to friends and eagerly anticipated their replies. However, a letter received from Milton Thomson came as a bittersweet surprise. He again expressed his ardor, and this time he offered a proposal of marriage. She gave great thought in penning her reply; not that there was any possibility of accepting his offer, but the refusal would be tendered with kindness.

She had embarked on a new life. Her success with students provided a threshold to new opportunities as the trustees of the academy considered establishing a sister school in the District of Columbia. Miss Fagan had been selected to accompany Mrs. Crocker on an exploratory mission in Washington, D.C.

By steamboat, ferry, and train, the principal and her protégé chugged their way to the nation's capital. The city had much in common with Albany and New York. Filth and neglect supplanted all plans for the rational development envisioned by the country's first president. A menagerie of animals roamed the dusty, rutted streets. Josephine and her companion were fortunate to secure rooms at a boarding house on Pennsylvania Avenue, the one road to be paved and bordered with wide brick sidewalks.

CHAPTER THREE

In March, Governor Hoffman issued a proclamation providing for the holding of an Extraordinary Term of the Oneida County Court of Oyer and Terminer to be held in the city of Utica on the twenty-fifth day of the month, at two in the afternoon. The announcement had been anticipated, and it was generally understood that this new term had been set for the express purpose of trying Mrs. Josephine McCarty.

The *Utica Daily Observer* published the announcement with a six-bar headline: "The Hall Murder / Trial of Mrs. Josephine A. McCarty / The Killing of Henry A. Hall of Ogdensburg / Statement of Facts / A Brilliant Array of Counsel / The Opening of the Trial."

The type grew smaller with each line of the title, but the most enlightening phrase referred to counsel. It was said the best legal minds in Central New York had been called into service for the McCarty trial. The article went on to reveal the uncommon connections between these legal minds.

The presiding judge, Charles H. Doolittle, was to be assisted by associate justices Pratt and Williams.

Attorney Robert O. Jones had been on the case since the day of the shooting. His partner, Lewis H. Babcock, a highly regarded defense lawyer, was designated to lead the defense. Babcock and Doolittle had been legal partners prior to the latter's ascension to judge.

Babcock and Jones enlisted the aid of D.C. Pomeroy of Rome, New York, a lawyer known for success in a host of local criminal cases. The Hon. D.J. Mitchell of Syracuse also joined the team. His dexterous handling of criminal cases flashed brilliantly in courtrooms across the state.

District Attorney Stoddard once served as a clerk in the office of Mr.

Mitchell. The previous fall, he'd defeated Babcock in a run for the office of district attorney.

Stoddard was working with Charles Sedgwick, a former congressman from Syracuse who was serving as a representative of the state attorney general. Sedgwick had been part of the counsel for the people in a high-profile case defended by Mr. Mitchell.

The composition of the trial intimated political maneuvering, from the Governor's issuance of an extraordinary term, to the attorney general's appointment of a representative to assist Mr. Stoddard. But the wheels of justice rolled forward.

At the appointed date and time, Judge Doolittle entered the courtroom. The associate judges followed at a respectable distance. Representatives for the people and counsel for the defense rose as the trio took to the bench. Doolittle introduced the court clerk, James B. Paddon, along with Deputy Sheriff Cole and other officers of the court. Instructions were given in regards to seating. Jurymen and witnesses were to be seated first; the remaining chairs could be filled by spectators, but once filled, the doors would be closed to all others. When court convened, the room was two-thirds full.

The new grand jury was sworn. After being informed of their duties, the jury retired to their room. At 2:15 PM, Josephine entered the court room and the buzz of conversation stopped. The petit jury returned, and those desiring to be excused were heard. There was one excusal based on the grounds that the man was deaf.

District Attorney Stoddard then moved the trial to go forward.

Lewis H. Babcock rose to his feet immediately, moving to postpone until the November term. He read affidavits prepared by Mrs. McCarty and each of her counsel declaring the need for postponement. Counsel, convinced their client was not legally accountable, made a case for the need for additional time. They were searching for several important witnesses, and an individual key to their case was confined to a sick bed. He would not be well enough to travel until the November term of court.

The district attorney stated that he was waiting for paperwork from some of his witnesses and needed time to review affidavits provided by the defense. He asked for an adjournment until the following morning. The adjournment was granted.

One of the issues referred to in the affidavits was the chronic ill health of the accused. Spectators observed Mrs. McCarty as she departed from the courtroom. They found her appearance much the same as it had been in January.

The court reconvened on Tuesday morning. Argument continued with the motion for postponement eventually granted, but not for November. The trial date was set for April 29, 1872.

Counsel had, thus far, been successful in the execution of their strategy. The newspaper frenzy surrounding the crime had spawned misinformation and speculation, and their client faced a biased public. With the passage of time, calm would return and interest in the trial would wane. From this point forward, the facts would be their defense. Individuals who would not be taking the stand included Robert McCarty, Phoebe Williams, Emily Crocker, and Rosie and Thomas O'Dwyer; all were dead.

JOSEPHINE'S FIRST ENCOUNTER with Robert McCarty occurred while having tea with Mrs. Crocker at the boarding house in Washington. He was sitting at a table in the dining room surrounded by a pile of papers. He turned in his seat to lock eyes with her. For the duration of their repast, she remained the object of intense inspection.

Though he was attractive in appearance, his stare made Josephine uncomfortable. She looked to Mrs. Crocker to free her of his attention.

"Would you care to join me for a walk?"

The older woman looked doubtful.

"It's a lovely day, and the sidewalk is so inviting."

They toured the limited vicinity of the avenue, rubbing elbows with elegant ladies, hunched-back maids, and natty politicians, while carriages and coaches drawn by sleek teams of horses trotted the highway beside them.

The following afternoon, Captain Dewey, Emily Crocker's cousin, stopped at the boarding house to share tea with the ladies. Slightly rotund and middle-aged, the captain had a jovial nature.

Josephine acknowledged their introduction and was about to be seated when the captain's voice ripped through the room.

"Hail," he called. "Is that Robert McCarty?"

Josephine stiffened. The gentleman signaled was none other than the annoying individual of the previous afternoon.

"Ladies," said Captain Dewey. "There is a friend. I must introduce you."

Engaged in a hearty handshake, neither man noticed the look on Josephine's face.

"Robert McCarty, I would like you to meet my cousin, Mrs. Emily Crocker, and her traveling companion, Miss Josephine Fagan."

Mr. McCarty bowed ever so slightly. "Pleased to make the acquaintance."

Josephine gave him a purposeful look. "I believe you were in attendance yesterday."

"Indeed I was," the man admitted. "I hope you will forgive the bad manners, but I couldn't draw my eyes away from your face. While wanting to introduce myself, I couldn't come up with a valid excuse. Now thanks to Captain Dewey, the occasion has arisen quite handily."

The directness of the man's manner and remarks was disconcerting. In an instant he'd taken the liberty of sitting beside her.

With eyes still focused on her face, he leaned forward to inquire: "Is this your first excursion south?"

Josephine cocked an eyebrow at his assumption. "As a matter of fact, I am southern born. My family moved north when I was eight. I have relatives residing in Maryland. One cousin has a home here in Georgetown. "

McCarty sat back in surprise, and then recovered himself with flattery. "I should have known: where else would one find such beauty and grace?" Then he began to laugh. "The Yankee is a southern belle, while the gentleman of the south was born in New York State."

"Whatever do you mean?"

"Just what I said. I was born in northern New York."

Josephine giggled. "Isn't life exciting!"

Her initial annoyance faded as Robert explained his situation. Though employed as a law clerk at a Washington firm, he regarded the position as temporary. His plan for the future required a switch to the field of engineering. He had designs and prototypes for a number of inventions but needed money to embark on manufacturing.

Josephine was enthralled at the intensity of his comments. The gray fringe at his temples gave him an air of dignity, while dark curls and a smooth complexion enhanced the impression of virility. He was twenty years her senior, and his attentions were a significant contrast to those of younger suitors. An appreciation for his maturity grew along with an interest in his novel inventions.

"I must take you to see my steam gun," he insisted. "The revolutionary design guarantees its manufacture."

At their next meeting, Robert led her to a barn behind the boarding house while Emily Crocker watched from the porch. He unlocked the barn door and, raising a canvas, proudly displayed his steam gun.

"The rapidity of fire would annihilate an enemy."

Josephine shivered slightly. "What enemy do you target?"

"Any enemy at war!"

"Supposing the gun was to be used against those defending our nation?"

Robert scoffed. Yet Josephine's concern would linger. Innovation and design could be admired, but annihilation of an army without discretion implied a questionable conscience.

They took to walking out together, and their conversations were often animated. The inventor's arms would flail expansively in emphasis of some new technology. At the dinner table, they sat in amused resignation with the unflappable Crocker sitting between them.

In addition to spending time with Robert, Josephine made visits to relatives in Georgetown. But her main responsibility was attending to seminary business with Mrs. Crocker. They were in the third week of their stay when fever struck the principal.

Josephine had no experience at tending the ill. The only remembrances she could conjure were the cold cloths placed on her head as a child. The technique failed hopelessly when applied to Mrs. Crocker. The fever continued to rage. Josephine's plea to the landlord to fetch a doctor was forgotten the moment she turned her back. In desperation, she sought a physician on her own. He diagnosed the malady as typhoid fever. She was instructed to wash the woman with strong soap and to bleach the bedclothes and linens. In nursing the ailing educator, she ignored her own raw and reddened hands. Discomfort was relative, and there were more serious issues to be resolved.

Mrs. Crocker's infirmity forced Josephine to cover their expenses from the small cache of bills she'd managed to save. It was an unsustainable situation. The putrid smell of illness wafted from every corner of the room as she sat in the dark, calculating options. She and her mentor were no longer desirable boarders. Typhoid threatened the establishment and an eviction notice had been served. The proprietor's efforts seemed wasted, however, since guests were already in the process of packing.

Robert's concern for Josephine receded when imaginary symptoms caused him to flee the site well ahead of other patrons.

When they met for breakfast early one morning, she informed him as to her plan of action.

"I am leaving Washington."

The law clerk reacted with sudden alarm. "Where will you go? What are you to do?"

"My cousin has been in contact with Judge Richard Barnes of Port Tobacco. He has expressed the need of a tutor. By accepting the position, I will have income and a home with the judge's family."

"But, my dear Miss Fagan, if only you'd moved from that retched house, I would have assisted with your expenses."

Josephine smiled sweetly as she placed her hand over his. "I appreciate the thought despite the unkindly inference that I abandon Mrs. Crocker."

Robert began to sputter, but she continued in a somewhat condescending tone. "In any event, you know the impropriety of accepting such an offer. Port Tobacco sits much closer than my home in New York. Surely, we will meet again."

"When will you leave?"

"Day after tomorrow. I've been in touch with Captain Dewey, and he's made arrangements for his cousin's care."

"My heart will suffer."

She smiled at the exaggeration. "I will miss you, too."

Dewey directed the transport of Mrs. Crocker's trunks, while Josephine held the woman's limply extended hand. High fevers had resulted in seizures, leaving the lady unable to speak.

"Dear Emily." She'd never addressed the principal by her given name before, but at such an intimate moment endearments seemed more appropriate than the formality of a classroom.

"I'm sorry to leave you in your illness, but I have to earn my keep. Captain Dewey will see that you are well cared for. I hope to hear of a complete recovery soon."

Emily Crocker's breathing grew labored. Her mouth contorted as she stared into the eyes of her young companion. It was a failed effort at communication. Tears were the partner to their silent good-bye.

When Josephine stepped to the stagecoach, Robert took her hand, holding it to his lips well beyond the period etiquette would allow. He did not release her until the driver called for all to board.

The stage ride to Port Tobacco was a scheduled trip of five hours. Mrs. O'Hearn, a woman well known to Josephine's Georgetown cousin, was also an occupant of the stagecoach. She had been enlisted as an accidental chaperone. They'd covered more than four miles when a rider came galloping up behind the coach screaming at the driver to halt. The wary reins man suspected robbery. Jawing at the horses, he cracked his whip, asking for greater speed. The team bolted forward and the coach rocked sideways. Panicked passengers grabbed loops on the side walls as they braced their feet against the floor.

When the rider drew abreast of the passengers, Josephine let out a squeal. "It's Mr. McCarty," she laughed. "It's Mr. McCarty!"

Holding tight to her bonnet, she angled her head through the window. "Stop driver, stop!" Her head hit the casing as she tried once more to gain the driver's attention. "It is my friend. You must stop."

Acknowledging the message, the driver pulled back. They traveled nearly a quarter of a mile before the four, heavily lathered horses came entirely to a halt.

"What in the deuce are you up to?" cried the driver, his face contorted with exertion and anger.

"Sorry, sir," answered Robert. He was covered with dust and coughing. "You see, I could not part with Miss Fagan without getting her answer to a most serious question."

Everyone turned toward the dark-eyed lady. Her bonnet was crushed, and a broken plume dangled off to one side. She moved a hand to cover her mouth, suppressing a willful giggle.

"Miss Fagan," pleaded Robert, "will you marry me?"

Mrs. O'Hearn gasped while an elderly gentleman sputtered in disgust. The other jostled passengers settled back into their seats, murmuring gratitude that they were still alive.

Josephine half sat, half stood, with her head still poked through the window. Looking directly at Robert, she gave her answer.

"Yes, my darling, I will."

With a heaving chest, Mrs. O'Hearn leaned toward the man beside her. "I would like to have killed her had she said no."

The man gave a nod as his lips twitched to a grin.

Robert reined his horse in close to the coach to kiss the hand of his betrothed.

"I will write your guardian today!"

With that, the gallant gentleman turned his horse, giving the stagecoach leave to continue its journey.

Josephine leaned against the cushioned seat, an exultant smile lighting her face. She hadn't thought Robert capable of such a chivalrous gesture. Oblivious to the expressions of fellow travelers or her own bedraggled appearance, she savored the moment, recalling the proposal's every nuance as the stagecoach rumbled onward.

An increase in traffic pulled her from reverie. The coach was approaching the entrance to Hill Top Plantation. A wide-eyed little boy ran ahead, announcing the coach's arrival. A coachman hopped from his position up top to guide her steps to the road. A door opened at the front of the manor house, allowing several children to tumble forward. They were followed by a slim and pretty woman with a wide and welcoming smile.

As Josephine thanked Mrs. O'Hearn for her kindness, the woman looked past her at the gaggle of children. "Good luck to you, Miss Fagan; I expect you will earn your keep."

Mary Barnes introduced herself as wife to the Honorable Richard Barnes, who served in the Orphans' Court. Their family consisted of three biological children and five others who had been entrusted to their care. All were there to greet the tutor.

"Miss Fagan," cried the good mother in alarm, "what has happened?"

Taken by a moment of confusion, Josephine gave her new employer a questioning look. Then, conscious of the plume dangling next to her face, she began to laugh.

Josephine's explanation about her exciting trip drew a joyous response from Mrs. Barnes.

"Oh, it will be such fun to plan a wedding. I should love to assist in the making of your dress."

The warmth of the Barnes family formed a dramatic contrast to the cool relationship she shared with her mother. At the time of her arrival, Judge and Mrs. Barnes were in a custody battle over the guardianship of an orphaned nephew. Fourteen-year-old Barnes Compton had petitioned the Orphans' Court of Charles County for guardianship to be granted to the judge. He'd grown close to his mother's brother and enjoyed his place within the family, with their rollicking household frequented by the elite of southern Maryland.

In spite of the judge's position, the family received notice shortly before Christmas that custody of Barnes Compton had been granted to a paternal uncle, a man barely known to the youngster in question.

It was a bitter interruption to Christmas festivities when the boy left in resignation to enter Charlotte Hall Military Academy. He'd been named heir to a vast estate. In time, he would mature into a fine Southern gentleman with a fondness for his extended family and a remembrance of Miss Fagan. Though his position as the largest slave holder in Maryland would eventually put him in opposition to positions held by the tutor, in 1844 he had yet to ascend the seat of authority.

The southward sojourn had taken Josephine from an abolitionist hotbed in Central New York to the very heart of Southern slavery. Childhood memories were jarred to the forefront. As a six-year-old, she'd been witness to a slave block where children were sold at auction. Impressions of that experience were the backbone of the debates against slavery she participated in while attending the Oneida Conference Seminary. With difficulty, she withheld her abolitionist remarks at Hill Top.

Shortly after the first of the year, Robert McCarty paid a visit to Hill Top. Robert Norris had given his approval to their union. Technically, Josephine was no longer subject to his jurisdiction, but the approval brought joy to his former charge. The future groom sat in silence, furtively glancing at his betrothed.

"What is it, Robert? Have you a change of heart?"

"Oh no! Oh, never! I simply want to apologize. I'm sorry about my behavior on the road to Port Tobacco. Chasing the coach was a fool's mission. I should have done better. Had I to do it over, I would never address you in such tasteless fashion."

Josephine's face fell. "Robert, it was the manner of the proposal that convinced me to say yes!"

Her fiancé drew back in shock. "How could you sanction such a ridiculous display?"

"Your sincerity and the joyous, impetuous nature of your devotion quickened the beat of my heart. Please, don't blight the happiness by withdrawing what I found to be so endearing."

Though somewhat confused, Robert dropped the subject and said no more. The wedding was scheduled for July with the ceremony to take place in Georgetown. Josephine wrote her mother detailing their decisions.

In January of 1845, her commitment was to the position of tutor. She concentrated on honing her skills to work simultaneously with giggling children of varying ages and stages in education. The information dribbled down from one age group to another on a continuing basis. A love of learning made the process more interesting, and the judge approved her order for several new books.

Dedication to duty had no bearing on the passage of letters from Port Tobacco to Georgetown. They passed through the postal system several times a week with each bringing prompt reply. In one correspondence, Robert broached the subject of returning north. Personal contact with New York manufacturers would hasten production of his inventions. She agreed without reservation and sent her mother a detailed letter explaining their plans.

Phoebe made quick work of spreading the news. Josephine received a congratulatory note from Mary Norris with the added message that her pining suitors were much chagrined. Milton Thomson appeared most despondent.

Mary Barnes was ecstatic. The tutor had been accepted as part of the family, and as suggested on the day of her arrival, Mary and her seamstress were assisting with the creation of a wedding gown. At her final fitting, the bride stood before a full-length mirror admiring the finished product.

"It is by far the most beautiful dress I have ever seen," she exclaimed in awed sincerity.

Violet silk rustled with every movement. The dress had been fashioned with appliqués of matching cord and a dropped waistline. The yards of fabric comprising a bell-shaped skirt were meticulously gathered to fit her tiny waist.

"I shall have a pink nosegay to pin at my side. And don't you think the bonnet would look best if my curls fell to the front of the brim?"

Her onlookers nodded agreement.

As the day grew closer, excitement gave way to serious thought. Her life was about to change again. Had she been hasty in her decision? Was Robert truly her lifelong love? How could she know? Then, putting a hand to her pocket, she felt the letter, opened it, and read once more: "My Dearest Love…"

Robert did love her. She held the note to her breast, convinced of the rightness in her decision.

Richard and Mary Barnes accompanied her to Georgetown. On July 28, 1845, Josephine Fagan and Robert McCarty were wed. While the gathering of guests was small, all were in agreement that a more handsome couple could hardly be found, the bride a vision of loveliness next to a groom who stood tall in a cutaway coat and satin weskit.

Robert and Josephine spent the first night of their marriage at the Tayloe Hotel. They arrived late in the evening, and upon reaching their room, Robert whisked his bride into his arms to carry her over the threshold. But the fairytale wedding took a nightmarish turn when the heavy door swung shut.

Initial attempts at intimacy began with tender endearments, but quickly turned brutal. The bride cried out in pain as her husband's fingers dug into her shoulders and his bruising mouth closed over hers. When it was finally over, he rolled to his side and fell asleep.

Josephine floundered in the dark until she found the washstand. As she bathed her body with tepid water, she wondered at the popularity of current novels. Where was the romance she'd read about? Her wedding night represented nothing more than barnyard copulation. Tender romance had no part in the taking of her virginity.

She awoke the following morning comfortable in a firm resolve: if her husband wanted his wife for a lover, he would have to change his ways. There would be no repeat of the previous night's roughness. She felt the rub of his legs against her as he stretched and rolled from their bed.

"Best get up, my Josephine. I am expected to work today."

Life for the couple evolved to a pattern with relatives and acquaintances welcoming them to their homes. A buzz would reverberate through every soiree as women gossiped and men smiled. The vivacious bride was a charmer. If the McCartys had remained in Georgetown their lives might have been very different. But the marriage was still in its infancy when the couple packed for a move to New York.

They boarded the cars in Washington with a stopover scheduled in Philadelphia. Robert's inordinate jealousy had been apparent from the start. He took offense at every glance directed toward his wife. It was a dangerous attitude, especially in the City of Brotherly Love. William Penn's blueprint for city development had been distanced by spilling growth and an influx of feuding immigrants. Bloody riots of the previous year were a result of the city's tinderbox status. When walking the streets of Philadelphia, the wise kept their eyes on the road.

Josephine directed her husband's attention towards architecture, the impressive city water system, and the ongoing construction of highways. It was a skill of manipulation that she would perfect to keep from fostering Robert's jealousy. She enjoyed their tour of the city. Years hence Philadelphia would beckon her return. But the first trip constituted a honeymoon; her only concern was pleasing her husband.

In selecting New York to be their home, Josephine recruited the assistance of Thomas O'Dwyer. He located a room in an old Federal mansion on Greenwich Street. Situated on Battery Park where the sea and grass came together, it seemed an ideal location. As a gift to the newlyweds, Thomas paid the first month's rent. His generous act was nearly erased when fire raged through the neighborhood. The blaze destroyed every house on Broadway. Though Greenwich Street escaped the flames, it was fenced by blackened timbers, and an odor of spent fire penetrated the whole of the community.

Josephine wrinkled her nose as she tiptoed up the steps. Fortunately, the odious scene on the outside had no effect on the interior of the building. Greenwich Street was part of an aging section of the city, but it offered a tarnished state of elegance. Their room had tall windows and a marble fireplace that would hold a mantle clock they'd received from the Barnes on their wedding day. While the bride busied herself at establishing a home, the groom lobbied manufacturers for production of his steam gun.

New York was awash with misery, especially in the Irish district. Thomas had kept his cousin away from the fourth ward when first she'd visited the city. With this second coming, he wanted to see the couple assimilate into a decent environment. He had Rosie arrange a supper party for an assemblage that included the austere but revered Bishop John Joseph Hughes. The bishop's effort to unify New York's Irish appeared to be gaining momentum. Josephine was intensely interested and conversed with His Excellence at length, unaware of the resentment her husband held.

Robert was not a papist. As a Scottish descendent whose grandfather served in the Revolutionary War, he had little regard for immigrants—especially the Irish rabble. He chafed at the society surrounding him, but his disgruntled looks had little effect on the bishop. The prelate found nativists an annoying reminder of England's aristocracy. He would willingly tell them that having a father born in America was not a prerequisite for entrance to heaven.

The success of a party is categorized by the nature of the guests, and Josephine had been pleased. As the cab rolled away from the O'Dwyer mansion, she moved close to her husband and took hold of his arm. The ambiance seemed perfect for confiding a bit of good news.

"It was a wonderful evening, Robert, and I have something to tell you that will make it even more so." She smiled coyly, and then whispered breathlessly, "I am with child!"

Robert reacted with choking surprise.

Josephine laughed. "It is the logical outcome of carnal relations."

Robert pulled out a smile. "I never gave much thought to it."

How typical of an inventor, she thought. His next remark was unexpected.

"This might be a good time to visit your mother. You can introduce your husband and announce the coming of our child as well."

"Oh, Robert, I am anxious to have you meet my mother and to show you the beauty of my childhood home."

Robert shook his head. "I doubt there is much difference to be found between the hills of Augusta and those I knew in Essex County, but it will be a pleasant excursion. I think we shall take the cars."

Their arrival in Augusta was highly anticipated. Phoebe could not contain her pride. The rumors surrounding her daughter would be put to ground forever. Josephine had married a businessman and was living in New York City. Smug with this tidbit of information, she reported the upcoming visit to all of her acquaintances in Oriskany Falls.

The train deposited the couple at the depot in Utica where they hired a rig to drive out to the farm. As they crested the last of the hills, Robert sat forward, his eyes scanning the fields.

"My father took great pride in this farm," Josephine remarked.

Her appraisal was ignored. Her husband was absorbed in an assessment of his own.

Whatever his deduction, it had to be shelved. Phoebe and the housekeeper were on the porch, madly waving their handkerchiefs.

Josephine jumped from the wagon before her husband could offer to assist.

"Oh, Maman, I have missed you!"

There could be no disputing the affection in their reunion. Josephine had been absent for a year and a half, but considering the unfolding of past events, it seemed a much greater expanse of time. She introduced Robert as they entered the house, and then quickly came to a stop.

"Maman! The scent from your oven is heavenly. It's so long since I've tasted the good food of home."

As an introduction to the agricultural aspects of the property, Josephine walked her husband around the perimeter of the farm, stopping last at the point she'd cherished most, the look-out corner by the stream.

Robert pulled on his whiskers. With narrowed eyes, he counted the buildings surrounding the mansion. He gave his head an involuntary shake, realizing that his wife was still rambling.

"Josephine, you really must grow up."

The comment stunned her. "Robert, I have no intention of climbing a tree or playing make-believe, but this little corner is a part of what I am. Have you no interest in me beyond the outward appearance?"

With a disdainful look, he answered, "Should I have saved my baby shoe that you might know the size of my foot when I was two?"

The sarcasm stoked her temper, but before she had a chance to react, the dinner bell rang. The first argument of a newly wedded couple was postponed for another day.

Following a visit with the Norris family, the couple drove Phoebe's old horse to the village. The new Mrs. McCarty found it interesting to see how the appearance of a wedding band could change the attitude of old neighbors. Their final evening on the hill passed pleasantly as they sat on the porch tasting homemade ice cream.

While the return to New York left Josephine somewhat nostalgic, the bustle of the city was invigorating. The relationship with her father's family had grown increasingly close, and she quickly accepted an invitation to join them for Christmas dinner.

Beyond the joy of pleasant companionship, Rosie provided valuable information on midwives and babies and various household functions. Josephine took to accompanying her cousin to mass on Sunday, longing to know more of her father's religion.

Robert felt no affection for the O'Dwyers and disapproved of their taking his wife to the Catholic mass. He kept these thoughts to himself, however, as Josephine's preoccupations left him free to pursue interests of his own.

His bride was unlikely to grow restive. She spent hours at the Mercantile Library absorbing facts and events through a collection of newspapers. Texas had been annexed to the United States; the philosophy of Manifest Destiny was driving President Polk toward war with Mexico; and that handsome dandy, Sickles, was still in a scramble with Tammany Hall.

In the spring of '46 the news became personal. It didn't appear in a newspaper, but came as gossip from Norris' store. The McCartys were visiting Augusta for the second time, when Josephine learned that her mother had encumbered some debt. Though reluctant to discuss the matter, Phoebe nervously admitted that she'd had trouble retaining help. Some of the fields remained fallow and income from those she'd leased had not been sufficient to make up her losses.

Robert's familiarity with farm values prompted a mortgage offer of seven hundred dollars. An agreement was reached, signed, and recorded at the office of the county clerk. His grateful wife envisioned him a knight in armor once again.

A few weeks later in a stroll along Broadway, Robert left her to browse a ladies store while he crossed the street to a tobacco shop. As she stepped from the store to the sidewalk, her eyes connected with those of Daniel Sickles.

"Why, Mr. Sickles, how nice to see you!"

The gentleman took her gloved hand as he had before, but with a question evident in his eyes. "It seems I've lost track of time since our last encounter. I haven't the least idea as to how I should address you."

The insinuation made her laugh. "It has been some time. I am now the wife of Robert McCarty."

"Well, congratulations, Mrs. McCarty. I only regret that the honor of your hand escaped me."

Caught in a rare state of embarrassment, Josephine welcomed the sight of her husband purposefully striding in her direction. With an air of pride, she turned to offer an introduction.

"Robert, I would like you to meet Mr. Daniel Sickles; Mr. Sickles, this is Robert McCarty, my husband."

The two shook hands politely, Daniel with unruffled decorum, Robert in obvious agitation. The former bowed goodbye and crossed the street, leaving the McCartys to stare at his back.

Robert's anger rose. "I return from a few minutes absence and you're flirting with a dandy!"

Josephine's hand went to her hip as she responded in exasperation.

"Robert, look at me. My pregnancy is already apparent to anyone with a discerning eye. No gentleman would flirt with me! I am not dumb. If I see an acquaintance I will acknowledge such, be they male or female."

Her husband didn't look any less agitated after hearing this reply, but he let the matter drop.

Summer arrived, and on a muggy July afternoon, labor pains caused Josephine to send for Rosie, who in turn sent a message fetching the midwife.

When they arrived, they found Josephine pacing the floor.

"Josie, rest. You'll need your strength as time wears on. Where is Robert?"

"I don't know. He left early this morning. I expect he will be back for tea."

They received a note a short time later, stating Robert's apology for being detained. He would try to be home by the supper hour.

Rosie and the midwife worked at relaxing their patient with all the methods at their disposal. They were both of the opinion that she could be in for a lengthy labor. It had been the pattern for women of her diminutive stature.

When Robert returned, he found his beloved drenched in sweat and writhing in pain. In a compassionate move, he took hold of her hand and ordered Rosie to send for a doctor.

"Robert," whispered Rosie in a calming tone. "Babies are not the business of doctors; it's the midwife what does the birthin'. You take yourself downstairs. We'll fetch you when the wee one arrives."

Her comments sent Robert reeling. But he couldn't deny what Rosie had said. It was his duty to preserve decorum. Placing a kiss on his wife's brow, he offered encouragement and retreated to the floor below. In a matter of minutes, sweat had soaked through his ridged white collar.

The child was delivered on July 6, 1846. With cheeks glowing in a pinkish radiance, Josephine pursed her lips in a mischievous smile as she introduced her husband to their son.

"Oh, Robert, it is a boy, a wee little boy; here is our baby, Eugene."

There is no doubt Robert loved them both, and mother and child thrived with the knowledge.

Eugene was only a few months old when Josephine realized she was pregnant again. They bundled their belongings and moved the family to a two-room apartment on Cherry Street, an area swarming with large families. The rooms lacked the elegance of the mansion they'd left and were a greater distance from the park. But the need for additional space was a fact neither parent could dispute.

In the spring of 1847, the family returned to the farm in Augusta. The visit brought relief from the crowds of Cherry Street and a breath of fresh air to the baby.

Phoebe's behavior upon their arrival had an unsettling effect on Josephine. Her concern increased when she found her mother staring blindly through a window with a piece of paper clutched to her breast. The woman started at the sound of her coming and suddenly began to tremble.

"What is it, Mam?"

Phoebe looked down at the paper she held. "The mortgage I owe Robert. I haven't been able pay it back, and the interest is accumulating."

Her daughter smiled. "I'm sure you have nothing to worry about. We're not about to put you out of your home."

While her comments were uttered with complete sincerity, reflection left doubt. Robert was a businessman. But surely he wouldn't foreclose on her mother.

Once back in New York, foreclosure issues receded in importance. The accouchement attendants had an added duty for the delivery of her second child. Someone had to keep track of Eugene. When newborn Ella let out her first cry, the boy looked on in wonder. Climbing onto the bed, he took Josephine's breast to his mouth. Her uterus pulsed in comfort as the siblings nursed in unison.

Josephine resumed her routine and was lugging the children up Broadway when someone called her name. Searching the faces of passing pedestrians, she caught her breath in surprise.

"William Dodge," she called as the gentleman approached. "How good it is to see you. How are the reverend and your mother? And what of Ireneus and the little one?"

William gazed at her with warm affection.

"Please," he said. "There is a place close by where you can sit with the children. I do want to catch up on the events of your life."

Scooping Eugene up into his arms, William led his friend and her children to an ice cream parlor. The toddler swirled his spoon in the creamy confection while his mother and her friend conversed.

"Ireneus is doing well, but we lost little Richard two years ago."

"Oh, no! How could this be? That sweet little boy! I am so ashamed of neglecting good friends. If it isn't too painful, tell me what happened?"

"Scarlet fever," the young man replied. "I doubt Mother will ever recover."

"How could she?" Josephine murmured as Ella fussed and tugged at her bodice.

Sadness shadowed William's face, but he shook it off with a smile.

"What of you?" he asked. "I see you have quite a family of your own."

"I do indeed. They take up all my time and most of my affection." A smile accompanied her last statement.

She went on to relate events of the years since she'd last seen William and his family. "So, I am no longer Josephine Fagan but Josephine McCarty."

"Congratulations on all accounts. As you might expect, I am an attorney. I have been practicing in Oneida County, but recently received an offer from a law firm here in New York. My wife and I will be moving to the city within the next few weeks."

"Can you believe it?" Josephine asked. "We were a happy threesome as we scurried between your home and the seminary, all such serious students, debating and discussing throughout the journey. My life is now a thousand miles from our classes in modern languages and ancient classics. But I like to think those early morning walks cemented our friendship."

"I feel that way also. Josephine, should you ever be in need of a lawyer, please don't hesitate to call on me."

"I hope that won't be necessary, but I shall keep the offer in mind."

The meeting with William left Josephine yearning for another visit to her old home, but the McCarty's did not return to the Augusta farm until the spring of 1848. By then, Josephine was expecting their third child.

She inhaled the air, expanding her lungs. The hills of Augusta were the source of her strength. She put Ella to her shoulder and led Eugene to that wonderful place, the lookout corner. The little fellow held her hand as he climbed on a log and edged his way across the brook. When he reached the other side, he stamped his feet in triumph.

There were advantages to living on a farm, but moving there was an unlikely scenario for her family. She knew Robert would never abide working so far from the city. Even if they could, the complexion of Augusta was changing. When Mary Norris moved to Indiana, her father had sold the store. He and Mrs. Norris were working at the asylum in Utica. She'd heard Milton Thomson was in that city also. Many of her friends were married, and she'd lost contact with most of them.

When they'd left New York, her pregnancy was still a secret. She wanted to share the news with her mother before others made assumptions. The announcement brought the barest acknowledgment. Phoebe's reactions were always a mystery. She seemed to enjoy the grandchildren most when they were miles away. Then she could brag without being bothered.

On their return to the city, Josephine took her news to Rosie, who greeted the revelation with warm Irish cheer. She herself had delivered three children, all of whom had died within days of their birth. Yet she never displayed the least bit of jealousy towards those in more fortunate circumstances. Plump and puffing, she joined Josephine on the floor where they occupied Ella and Eugene with pull toys until Thomas arrived for dinner.

"How's my favorite cousin today?" he asked, giving her a hug.

"I am fine, Thomas. How could I not be with little ones such as these?"

Thomas nodded as he sat himself down in an oversized chair and leaned back in contemplation.

"Josie, what do you know of Robert's business?"

The question came as a surprise.

"Well, he has his inventions and is working to get them into production."

"Has a single item been manufactured?"

"I don't believe so. But there must be great faith in his ability as investors have been purchasing shares of stock. Do you see a problem, Cousin?"

Thomas smiled at the beautiful woman playing her role as scratching post to the two little children who clawed at her skirt.

"No, nothin' to trouble you, Josie. Just inquirin' as a bit o' gossip."

Josephine delivered her son, Terrence, in November of 1848. They were now a family of five. But with noise and commotion bouncing from the walls, Robert found reasons to stay away. Conversations between the husband and wife were limited to whispers made in the dark.

At the end of January, with Terrence an infant only three months old, Robert announced his plan to leave for Europe. Josephine was taken aback.

"I need a new market for the steam gun. Industry has flourished in England. Once I get settled, I'll send for you and the children. It will be a wonderful experience for all of us."

"What, pray tell, do I do in the meantime?"

"I'll leave you with money and see that you're settled. This is a great opportunity; I don't want to lose out."

Josephine looked doubtful, as well she might. Jacob Perkins' perfected steam gun preceded Robert's by over twenty years, and in spite of its accuracy and amazing performance, the Perkins gun never reached production, not in Europe nor in the United States. Yet Robert could not be dissuaded.

He scheduled his passage to England in May. Josephine took the children to the wharf to see him off. Just before boarding, he kissed her and pressed a bankbook into her hand.

"The rent is paid till the end of the month; after that you will have to move." He gave her a slip of paper with the address of another boarding house. "Nora will have a room for you. I have an agent, a Mr. Blackfield. He'll handle our communications."

With a peck on the cheek for each of the children, Robert turned to walk up the gangplank.

It wasn't until she returned to her rooms that Josephine opened the book.

"Fourteen dollars!" she exclaimed to the walls. Her husband had given no timeline as to when they might join him, and when they did, the passage would be costly. "How am I to care for three children on fourteen dollars?"

CHAPTER FOUR

For the second time, Judge Doolittle convened his court for the McCarty trial, appearing at the bench on the morning of April 29, 1872, at 11:00. His assistants were Justice R.U. Sherman, a last-minute replacement for his ailing predecessor, and the returning Justice William Pratt.

Josephine likewise arrived at the appointed hour. She was attired in the same brown alpaca dress and sealskin jacket she had been wearing in January when she arrived in Utica. She looked to be well.

Babcock and Pomeroy were tardy. After hastily taking his seat, Babcock leaned toward Josephine to speak in a whisper.

Daniel Magone had joined District Attorney Stoddard and the Hon. Charles Sedgwick as counsel for the prosecution.

Roll call revealed that only fourteen jurors out of a panel of thirty-six had answered the call. Judge Doolittle announced that without the requisite number of jurors, he would have to adjourn until the following morning.

Babcock and Pomeroy consulted their client once more, and then Pomeroy stood to address the court. He was prepared to make another motion for postponement but would wait until after dinner. Mrs. McCarty's son, Louis, had been placed on the list of witnesses, but the boy was seriously ailing. A doctor had been called to attend him. Counsel wanted to ascertain the child's condition before making his petition.

Judge Doolittle displayed his annoyance, stating that under no circumstances would he allow further efforts to postpone the trial. But there was also an issue with the jury. The case had gained such notoriety that the circumstances were known to almost every man in the county. An Extraordinary

Term of Oyer and Terminer provided the court certain discretionary powers. Among these powers was the right to draw a second panel of jurors, excusing the first, or, if the court chose, to keep both panels. Judge Doolittle exercised his option, requesting the sheriff to summon one hundred talesmen for the selection of a new jury.

Court was adjourned.

When proceedings resumed on Wednesday morning, Clerk Paddon issued his roll call and all absentee talesmen and jurors missing from the original panel were fined a sum of twenty-five dollars.

Mr. Pomeroy immediately asked for a recess that the defense might inspect the sheriff's list. Judge Doolittle replied that if the delays continued, the trial would never take place. Mr. Mitchell argued that defense had a right to examine the names of jurors and had been denied the opportunity when the list was drawn. A half-hour recess was granted.

When defense counsel returned from reviewing the returns, Mr. Mitchell issued a challenge, calling the selection process flawed and illegal. He insisted the law did not give the court the right to draw extra jurors in an Extraordinary Term of Oyer and Terminer. While acknowledging the integrity of the men before him, it was his conviction that allowing the sheriff to call in talesman without concealing their identities could result in a biased jury.

Judge Doolittle stated that he had acted in accordance with law and had chosen the most expedient method of filling the jury box.

The defense's challenge was noted, but the process moved forward.

Although Josephine maintained a demure demeanor, no detail of the court escaped her observation.

Adam K. Adams of Rome was one of the first talesman called. He had no scruples when it came to finding a verdict of guilty in a capital case. He had read the evidence of the McCarty case at the coroner's inquest and had developed an opinion. He admitted to having expressed that opinion, affirming it would take evidence to change his mind. Mr. Adams was accepted.

After lengthy questioning, the court excluded Edwin A. Harvey of Camden on the challenge of favor.

Walter B. Buell stepped forward when called. He said he had read newspaper reports, believed them accurate, had formed an opinion about them, and had expressed that opinion. He maintained, however, that he would have no problem finding a charge of guilty and thought himself capable of being unbiased. Mr. Buell was accepted.

So went the selection process, a gloomy omen for the prisoner. But then, what was abandonment if not an omen of gloom?

EUGENE CLUNG TO HIS MOTHER'S SKIRT as she trudged the streets of New York juggling a baby in each of her arms. A tight little foursome, they bumped their way through the crowded streets looking for the address Robert had provided. When they arrived at the boarding house Josephine looked up in disgust. She turned with a pivot, but then she stopped. It was beyond dispute—fourteen dollars wouldn't buy them a stay at the Astor House. Stepping over the threshold, she walked toward the desk to confront a woman whose hardened features might have been cut from stone.

"Excuse me. I'm looking for Nora."

"That would be me."

"My husband, Robert McCarty, has advised me that you have rooms that might accommodate myself and my children."

"No vacancies," came the cold, flat reply.

"Please. A single room will do."

For a moment, it looked as if Nora might relent. Terrence's sudden squalling killed her compassion.

"I told ya darlin', I got nothin'. You'll have to go elsewhere."

Elsewhere where! If a substandard boarding house won't take us, what are we to do? A cholera epidemic was sweeping the city. Statistics indicated that half the children born in New York would die before reaching the age of seven. On the walk back to Cherry Street, Josephine stopped at the rail station to check schedules and prices. When they reached their rooms, she set the children on the floor and sat down to scribble a note to her mother. She would need cartons to pack their belongings, but she would be out of

New York before the month ended.

The O'Dwyers took Josephine and her family to the station, where trunks and cartons were transferred from the carriage to a baggage car.

"Wish you'd let us help," Thomas sighed.

"You are helping, and I thank you very much, especially for the sandwich box and the sweetmeats for the children. You are so dear to me. I will never be able to repay you."

"There's to be no talk of payment. Family is family. I want to hear no more."

With hugs and tears, the McCartys and O'Dwyers parted.

The train chugged into the Utica station with Robert Norris watching attentively from the platform. When the doors opened he was there to help.

"I appreciate the ride, Uncle Norris."

"Don't mind a bit. I enjoy an occasional trip through the hills. Besides, seeing the babes gives me great pleasure. With Mary so far away we've no chance to see her young'uns."

The sight of the farm was more welcome than at any time in Josephine's memory. While Phoebe and Bridget were again on the porch, their greeting would be different.

"Grandma," called Eugene. "We're going to stay a whole long while."

His statement contained a wealth of truth. But Josephine hadn't time to think on it. She was exceedingly tired and her mother had questions.

"What has happened between you and Robert? Are you separated? You have three children. What are you thinking?"

When the weary, young woman finally crept into bed, she was too tired to notice the hooting owls. It took a direct splash of sunlight against her lids to get them open in the morning.

Unaware of his mother's trials, Terrence tugged greedily at her breast. Bridget busied herself with breakfast, while Eugene and Ella poked noses and fingers into every corner of the house.

Their grandmother appeared out of sorts. "Do you expect Robert to send for you soon?" she asked.

Josephine looked at her mother, confusion clouding her eyes. "I have no idea as to his schedule. I'm not sure what it is he expects of me. Will it be a problem to have us here?"

Phoebe switched topics, ignoring the question.

The children never envisioned the farm as a refuge. They were enjoying a carefree holiday, and their father's absence offered unasked-for freedoms. They picked strawberries, rode with their mother in the two-seated carriage, and sometimes sat on Johnson's back.

The young mother's beauty blossomed anew, and she wrote her husband with energy, relating Eugene's cute little expressions or elaborating on Ella's blond curls. Terrence was simply adorable.

Return mail appeared sporadically, usually with reports on the contacts Robert had made in Europe, the amazing expansion of the industrial world, or the exposition planned by Queen Victoria and her consort, Prince Albert. He'd already been offered a position at the event as a jurist for the United States. There was no mention of his gun being brought to production or any timeline for a reunion. He never mentioned money, and there were no gifts at Christmas.

In February, eight months into her husband's absence, Josephine kissed the three toddlers good-bye. As she boarded the cars for New York, she prayed her mother and Bridget would be up to the challenge of caring for three small children. Mr. Blackfield was the target of her visit, and she wasted no time in reaching his office.

Up until then, she'd known nothing of the agent beyond his name. On their first meeting, she found him to be a lascivious scoundrel. His smile made her squirm as he squinted through a pair of greasy spectacles.

"It must be difficult having your husband gone so long."

"It is a difficult thing to raise three small children while forced to rely on the largess of my mother. I would like an accounting of the money Mr. McCarty has placed in your hands."

The agent stooped to his ledger, opened it, and angled it for Josephine's perusal. Her jaw dropped at the lack of entries. The effrontery of her husband's behavior overwhelmed her. *How could he be so callous? What had he expected when he boarded that ship? What did he care for any of us?* The more she thought, the more frantic she became. But her next stop would be the O'Dwyer home, where she would need to control her emotions.

When she lifted her hand to the knocker of Rosie's front door, she was assured of a welcome. Her note announcing a trip to New York had immediately been followed with an invitation. She could stay as long as she liked. When the initial pleasantries ended, an uneasy silence took hold. The O'Dwyers sensed a problem. Though solid in her resolve to keep the situation private, Josephine's quickness of movement and sharpness of tongue were signs of agitation.

"Does Robert communicate often?" Thomas tried to mask his concern as Josephine continued to hide the truth.

"Yes, indeed. It seems there is a great deal of innovation underway, and he is centered at the heart of it. I'm sure we will be joining him soon."

Her words were unconvincing.

Bishop Hughes stopped at the O'Dwyers the following day and expressed great pleasure at Mrs. McCarty's return to New York. The prelate was, first and foremost, a shepherd to the flocks. He quickly took up on the fact that all was not right with Josephine. He looked to Thomas, whose barely discernible shrug gave credence to his concerns.

"How are those three beautiful children," the Bishop asked, pulling an image from the depths of his memory.

"They are doing well, growing so fast I can hardly believe it." The words reflected a dull sense of pride.

"It is a cold but beautiful day. I have finished my calls and thought I might take a drive through the city. Could you join me, Mrs. McCarty?"

Josephine looked startled. The invitation took her quite by surprise. Yes, a drive in the brisk, seaside air might clear the muddle clouding her brain.

"I appreciate the offer, Your Excellency. If you can wait till I get my shawl I would be happy to accompany you."

The Bishop's driver helped her into the carriage, and then he covered both passengers with a robe of beaver skins. The prelate was a well-known figure in the city of New York. Pedestrians waved from every corner as the rig bumped along frozen roadways. But the priest had a deeper mission in mind when he initiated the outing. A skillful conversationalist, he manipulated the course of their pleasantries to indicate that if the young mother wanted to confide in him, the confidence would be sacred.

"Father, is a woman nothing more than a channel to man's immortality? Does a man not bear responsibility for the children he sires?" The anguish in her voice was evident even to herself. "Excuse me, Father, I don't mean it to sound as if I resent my children. I do not. They are everything to me. But I'm befuddled at the circumstances that currently face me."

"We are all accountable for our actions, men and women alike. Unfortunately, some will fail in their duty. It is always so, in every aspect of life. So," he paused for a moment, "it falls to those of stronger mettle to carry the burdens others cast off. Faith in God is the nourishment that feeds the struggling soul." He smiled kindly. "There is always help to be found in the church, be it to feed the hungry palate or the starving spirit."

Josephine closed her eyes and dropped her head.

"It is enough, Father, to have been given the chance to bare the disturbances of my mind. I thank you for caring, and I thank you for the ride."

The Bishop's driver guided his handsome hackney in close to the curb, depositing his passenger at the O'Dwyer's front door. She alighted from the carriage without assistance, and, waving good-bye, wondered how others could think the bishop fearsome.

The children's welcome when she returned to the farm drew tears she could not repress. Robert's absence had cost him some of the most precious moments life could offer. Their youngest son, a nursing baby when his father left, was now a toddler playing tag with his brother and sister. She scooped the three of them into her arms and looked to her mother in appreciation.

"I'm sorry to have become such baggage, Mam, but perhaps one day I will be in a position to pay you back."

Whatever the grandmother's thoughts might be, the family thrived with country living.

An elderly neighbor had been hired to work at the farm. Slattery had lost his own place to foreclosure and took great pleasure in having the children about him as he worked. They had his permission to play alongside the domed haystacks while he forked the dried grass onto wagons. But when the hops crop ripened, the children were sent back to the house. A flurry of activity would soon encompass the farm, leaving no time for toddlers.

Picking hops provided a sociable opportunity for an agrarian community. Pickers arrived at the farm by foot and by carriage. Girls in bonnets and summer frocks flirted with engaging young men as they filled crate after crate with creamy pods. In a couple of days the yard was cleared, and the troop moved on to a new location. Their chatter echoed through the hills of Augusta from late August until mid-September.

When the hops were dried and baled, Josephine took her children to the dock in Oriskany Falls to watch as the cloth-covered bales were loaded onto barges. Eugene was in awe of the fact that hops from their grandmother's yard would float from the Chenango Canal to the Erie and ultimately end up in the city of his birth.

There were so many things to savor and remember, from spring's awakening to the depths of a snowy winter. Yet under it all, there was the strain of uncertain separation.

In the second January of their stay at the farm, Robert wrote that he had arranged for the family to join him in England. He wanted Josephine to meet with his agent in New York. Blackfield would have funds to cover their expenses. He instructed his wife to brush up on her French as he had business that would take them to Paris, and he suggested that she take up residence at a French boarding house where the language would be spoken more casually.

At the end of February, Josephine was on the cars heading to New York for a second and much-dreaded sojourn to the office of Mr. Blackfield. In accordance with her husband's request, he identified a boarding house in Albany run by an aged émigré from France. He then reviewed a schedule of steamships departing from New York.

"Your family will be united again. It should be a time of rejoicing for all of you." His smile lacked sincerity, and the failure to elicit a response forced him to fill the silence. "Nothing should worry you, Mrs. McCarty. I will arrange everything. You may be assured of my company throughout the voyage."

Josephine's breath caught and stopped. She couldn't abide the thought of this strange little man in her company for as much as three long weeks.

"I'd like to review the schedules again," she said.

The agent nodded slyly. "The packets are cheaper but they take longer." He circled the name of a steamer indicating the sailing date.

Josephine looked down at the schedules. Indeed, passage on a packet could be purchased for a great deal less than tickets sold for a steamer.

"I will be booking passage for myself and the children. I'd appreciate it if you would give me the funds to do so."

"Of course," replied Blackfield as he doled out notes. "But take care you don't end up on the coast of Africa."

She found herself much too upset to work through a decision. Holding the schedule in her hand, she walked the wharf to examine the ships. An onslaught of rain caused the schedule to crumple. She pulled her mantle in tightly, turned toward Broadway, and headed north.

A trip to New York always ended with a visit to the O'Dwyers. She took a cab to the Sixth Street address and was taken aback at the maid's hesitant greeting. Her surprise turned to shock when she heard a wail emanating from the rear of the mansion.

As her cousin-in-law stepped to the entry, Josephine rushed forward with arms outstretched. "Rosie, what terrible thing has happened?"

Rosie guided her into the parlor. "It is our housemaid. Kitty's got relatives that have their way with her. She come in this mornin' all bruised up. Thomas threatened to take vengeance on the perpetrators. That frightened the poor lass even more."

Thomas entered the room with a frown on his face. "If they don't quit, they'll kill her. We need to get that girl away from here." He paused for a moment as he thought. "Josie, can't you take her to the farm? She's a good lass. She'll work."

"I'm sorry, Cousin, but I came to tell you. I'll be leaving for England soon."

"That's fine," Thomas said absently. "That's fine." Her cousin's mind was focused on the problem at hand.

The three of them stood in consternation until Josephine jolted the others to attention. "I have the perfect solution. I will be sailing with the children. It would be wonderful to have a nurse for them. Kitty's relatives will have no idea where she has gone. They'd have no reason to check manifests, and if they did, what could they do once the ship sets sail?"

"Kitty,' called Thomas. A slim, auburn-haired girl shuffled through the doorway. A blackened eye and bruised jaw offered proof of the beating she'd received. "Mrs. McCarty has a proposal for you."

Josephine smiled kindly, noting the maid was likely no more than nineteen years in age. "Kitty, my children and I will be sailing for England. Would you like to accompany us? I can pay your passage and other expenses."

The girl began to whine. "I come on the ship and never sought to make that trip again."

"But this time you will be sailing with me and we will have better quarters. No one can reach you once you board."

Kitty looked doubtful, but a glance and nod from Thomas convinced her. "Faith, if I done it once, I could maybe do it once again."

Josephine deliberately avoided the correction. Kitty wouldn't be making the trip once again. She would be crossing the Atlantic twice. Once over, once back. "It will be another month before we sail. I will post the time and date. Please, Kitty, don't leave the O'Dwyers until I come for you. Everything will be fine."

Josephine's confidence had grown in a matter of hours. By taking the packet, she would have more than enough to cover Kitty's passage.

Once this was settled, Josephine traveled to the French boarding house in Albany. Upon locating the residence, she found the original proprietor no longer in charge. Sebastian Mollet's aging daughter, Virgene, looked ready to give up also. Some of the residents were definitely suspect if judged by their attire and numerous escorts. Nevertheless, the boarding house provided ample opportunity for polishing her skills. She'd been studying French since fourth grade. Conversing in French on French soil would fulfill a childhood dream.

After two weeks immersed in a dubious form of French culture, Josephine left for Augusta to gather her children and pack their belongings. She rode toward the farm with some misgiving. She'd put her trust in Bridget, but it suddenly surfaced in her mind that her mother could dismiss the woman without provocation.

Her fears were assuaged before they could make the turn to the driveway. At the sound of wagon wheels, her children tumbled through the doorway with grandmother and the housekeeper following closely.

Josephine paid the driver and ran to the children, sweeping them up in her arms.

"We are going sailing," she told them. "Remember the rhyme, 'Rub-a-Dub-Dub?'"

They nodded, regardless of whether they remembered or not.

Their mother laughed. "We are all going out to sea." Then looking up at Phoebe, she announced the good news. "It's ended, Mam. We sail the first week of April."

Phoebe sighed in relief. Her response, whether due to the emptying of her house or the respectability of having her daughter and son-in-law back together, stood as a mystery not to be questioned.

Josephine took the children to the Howard Hotel in Albany. From there they would travel on to New York. She'd booked passage on the *Margaret Evans*, a packet ship captained by Isaiah Pratt. Like all of her kind, the fully rigged *Evans* would sail on schedule, ignoring weather or a shortage of cargo. They would be three days out of the harbor before Mr. Blackfield knew they were gone. Prior to the advent of such packets lines, sailing had been a case of catch as catch can.

A cab carried the family directly from the rail station to the South Street wharf to meet the O'Dwyers and Kitty Murtaugh. The children had been absent from New York for two years. While Eugene may have held some recollection of the city, the smaller children had none. The number of people and vehicles and the size of the buildings left all three in awe. But nothing equaled the tall ships with sailors scrambling to the top of their masts.

When the O'Dwyers' carriage arrived, Kitty approached the children with an encouraging smile that instantly bridged to friendship. Rosie and Thomas hugged their good-byes before stepping back to allow the little family to board. Eugene looked up at his mother in merriment. "Rub-a-Dub-Dub!"

CHAPTER FIVE

By Thursday afternoon, May 2, a full jury had been selected and sworn. A large contingent of spectators held seats in the courtroom. Counsel for the people took the floor with Mr. Stoddard issuing the opening remarks.

As prosecuting officer, he promised to review the facts of this case without embellishment. He addressed the jury, remarking on the good fortune of having agreed on the panel in such a timely manner. He pressed them to seek truth from the evidence presented on each side of the case, that when defense and prosecution finally rest they might be prepared to execute their duty fairly. He reviewed the facts of the shooting on January 17 from the point of Mrs. McCarty flagging down the streetcar at Oneida Square until she was as apprehended at city hall. It was their intention as prosecutors, he said, to examine statements made by the defendant in the presence of the jury. Turning to the judge, he asked permission of the court to read the statutes on the subject of murder.

Reading aloud, Stoddard informed the jury that the definition of murder references a premeditated action to willfully cause the death of another person. By statute, the definition included cases where an attempt is made to kill one individual and another falls victim. The district attorney also read from Wharton's criminal law. He concluded his opening remarks by stating that his sole intention was to present the facts in their true form, and that he would then ask the jury nothing but careful consideration of the evidence presented.

He then read the names of seven witnesses he had subpoenaed. Only five of them answered when the names were called. Orders were issued to an officer to locate the absentees.

The five witnesses in attendance included Mr. Reed, the streetcar conductor at the time of the shooting; passengers Adolphus C. Stutt and Isaac Tapping; William J. Supple, janitor at city hall; and A. Charles Luce, chief of police. Each testified as to their memory of events before, during, and after the shooting. A few discrepancies emerged.

Mr. Stutt recalled seeing Mrs. McCarty with her hands raised toward Milton Thomson and that Thomson had put his hands out to push her away. But the conductor remembered her having a muff. Mr. Stutt had no knowledge of a muff, but stated that she had spoken and her words began with "I'll kill," or "I'll murder." Mr. Reed claimed that it was impossible to hear any conversation on the streetcar unless it was spoken directly into one's ear. Mr. Tapping reported being directly beside the accused on the car and hearing her muttering something; the words had been indistinguishable. Stutt stated that he did not think the defendant looked haggard in appearance, although other witnesses swore she was wearing a veil.

Chief Luce produced the gun he had taken from the defendant on the day of the shooting. He identified it as a Smith & Wesson No. 47404. He stated that the gun was exactly as it had been when he received it: one barrel discharged, the other four loaded.

The district attorney took up the gun.

Mr. Mitchell cried out in alarm, noting that in the past, Stoddard had been known to be careless in his use of firearms.

As the district attorney handed the pistol back to Luce, Judge Doolittle ducked in fear, fully conscious that the barrel was pointing in his direction.

The court grew increasingly uneasy as the gun passed from one hand to another. When the firearm reached the clerk, Mr. Paddon, he relieved himself of responsibility by gingerly placing the gun onto his desk.

Members of the court sighed in relief, and then shot to attention at the sound of a rumble to the rear of the room. A drunk had slumped in a chair and was snoring.

Doolittle adjourned the court.

THE SHIP HAD BEEN OVERBOOKED with all of the staterooms occupied. Arrangements were made to place the McCarty family in Cabin 2. Normally used for storage, the space had been cleared for the attachment of beds. Compensation for the lack of finer accoutrements came with an increase of privacy and the luxury of having meals delivered to their room.

Kitty's previous experience had been in steerage. Occupying a stateroom of such generous dimensions overrode the absence of grandeur. Josephine found isolation a desirable feature. Illness could be deadly in a crowded ship. For Josephine, who was always conscious of health risks, protecting her family was paramount.

A questionable feature of Cabin 2 was that it adjoined the quarters of the captain. The ramifications of this juxtaposition would not be realized until after they docked.

Knowing their trunks and baggage had been safely stowed, Josephine took her children and their nurse to the upper deck. Calls of cast off and up and loose echoed toward the sky. Sailors in pea coats and flat hats responded to the favorable winds, their actions precise as they hauled on ropes as big around as a grown man's fist. The heavy sails unfurled and the ship slipped from its mooring.

"What are they doing, Mother?"

"They raised the sails to catch the wind that will blow us all the way to England."

"Could the wind blow me off the ship?"

"Only if you climb to places you shouldn't. You wouldn't want to do that, would you?"

Eugene shook his head, frowning concern.

The *Margaret Evans* was maneuvered out to the harbor in a backward motion. Passengers waved at acquaintances who continued to monitor their departure from the dock. As the distance between ship and shore grew longer, Rosie and Thomas disappeared. A call of set sail sent the rig toward open water. The wharf faded to obscurity, and the coastline narrowed to a diminishing thread stretching between water and sky.

Josephine had escaped the overtures of Mr. Blackfield and successfully rescued Kitty. She should have been in a state of euphoria. But she was clutching her stomach as the roll of the ship sent her spinning. Her face blanched as she staggered down the steps to their dingy cabin.

Kitty was the one to flourish in the briny air. Finally free of abuse, she smiled broadly as she unpacked a small cache of tempting confections. The children's eyes grew wide. In response to their nurse's instructions, they sat on a crate chewing licorice sticks, unconscious of the churning seas.

Their mother's condition worsened. Every movement caused her to retch, and the *Margaret Evans* never ceased rolling. Failure to eat or retain solid food weakened her even further. On the fourth day at sea, Captain Pratt appeared at the cabin requesting permission to enter. At first glimpse of his passenger, he issued orders to have her carried topside. The benefits of sunlight could not be ignored. Kitty smothered her mistress in blankets, essentially blocking the light from all but her face. Terrence, unable to reach his mother while in her berth, climbed onto the bench with impressive dexterity, snuggling as close to her as he could get. The other children whispered to Kitty, asking if their mother was going to die.

"Nay!" squawked the nurse. "It's takin' her longer than most, but she'll get her sea legs in time."

From that point forward, Josephine spent at least two hours of every day lounging on the open deck. The captain insisted she take broth and eventually added biscuits. They were into the second week of the voyage before she could stand and climb the stairs.

"You're looking brighter today, Mrs. McCarty."

The captain stood above her, hands clasped behind his back, feet planted solidly against the deck. The arch of the sails framed the portrait, emphasizing the fact that Captain Pratt was an exceedingly attractive man. A clean-shaven face exposed classic features and clear blue eyes that squinted against the sun. Although obviously accustomed to authority, humor tickled his mouth and crinkled his skin with crow's feet.

Josephine did her best to look pleasant. "My health is much improved.

I believe I owe the gain to you."

The captain's straight, white teeth flashed from behind a mischievous smile.

"The shepherd cares for his flock; I tend to my passengers. If you can work up an appetite, you'll find meals on the *Margaret Evans* to be very fine fare."

"I know it to be true. The children's nurse has been taking them to the dining room to spare me the odor of food; yet, they often come back exclaiming at the tarts and cakes and meats they eat."

The captain laughed heartily. "Perhaps tomorrow you will join them." Then tipping his cap, he moved on.

The following day brought entertainment that enlivened passengers and crew alike. The call of a whale-sighting starboard caused all on deck to rush the rail. The McCartys watched with other onlookers as a mammoth finback cleared the ocean's surface. Terrence was lifted to his mother's shoulder while Kitty held up little Ella. The whale slapped his tail against the water, creating a spray half the length of the ship. The children screamed in delight. Then a huge jet of water soared skyward; the leviathan had taken the form of a fountain spouting a saltwater geyser.

Josephine smiled and began to relax. The playful antics of the whale and the effect it had on the children so absorbed her that she started at the sound of her name.

"Mrs. McCarty, it is a relief to see you smile."

As she turned to the captain the smile widened.

"I have rejoined the living."

"The children tell me they are going to England to reunite with their father. The anticipation must be great."

The smile transitioned to one of reflection. "Yes. It is a good thing."

Captain Pratt looked at the passenger whose health he had so closely tracked. It seemed there might be more to her story.

The packet moved forward without opposition; the currents were steady, carrying no threat of storm. There'd been just a few cases of illness and one broken arm when a passenger tripped on a rope. No contagions erupted to instigate fear, and passengers were safe to loll in boredom. Some read or found partners for table games; others enjoyed uninterrupted sessions of gossip.

With her refurbished stateroom set apart from the rest, Josephine chose to keep to herself. Country air of the recent past had served her as well as a tonic. Clear, cold, ocean breezes did the same, bringing the rose back into her cheeks. Watching the children, whether in argument or laughter, brought her a great sense of peace. Kitty kept their cabin tidy and their clothes clean.

Captain Pratt was a source of intelligent conversation. His interest in the children prompted her to ask if he was married. He told her no.

"The ship is my bride, the sea my home. How could I serve a second family?"

A moment of silence underscored the weight of Josephine's reply.

"There are those who wouldn't worry themselves with such trivial concerns."

"It sounds as if the issue rests somewhere close to home."

The young mother tipped her face upward to look at the captain. His stance made him as much a part of the ship as the masts that towered behind him.

"I have no desire to burden others with the intricacies of my life."

Once again, the white teeth flashed. "I am skipper, physician, and psychologist. I may make reference to the shepherd, but I am not a priest. If it would help to speak, I have an attentive ear."

Josephine sighed. "There isn't much to tell. My husband left two years ago to pursue business ventures in England. We have not seen him since. By the age of the children, you can reason how much memory they might hold of him. It will be an interesting reunion. So much can change in the span of a couple years."

"Ah, to see you all again, such a bright and beautiful family, your husband will, no doubt, be a very happy man. The mood will be infectious. All should go well with this reunion." He ended with a convincing grin and left to attend his duties.

The Atlantic between New York and England is a width of approximately three thousand nautical miles. The *Margaret Evans* had been sailing smoothly from one monotonous day to the next. Night brought a peaceful display of constellations twinkling in the distance. But several days out from the English Channel, Josephine awakened to voices emanating from the captain's cabin. The ship was rolling violently. The children beside her were asleep. Kitty's breathing continued in an even rhythm. It seemed she had no more awareness of the choppy waters than the children under her care. Josephine pulled on a wrapper, and placing her palms against the wall, inched toward the door separating their stateroom and that of the captain. With a determined tug the bolt slid free. Before she could catch it, the door flew open.

"Josephine! What are you doing up?"

"I heard voices and felt the tumbling of the ship."

"We are encountering heavy seas. It is nothing you should worry about. Stay in your room and try to rest. By morning, this turbulence will be well behind us."

While the first mate stood back saying nothing, his surprise at the captain's use of her given name showed plainly on his face. It seemed they were experiencing a chaotic night of firsts.

The storm ended just before sunup, proving Pratt's prediction. For Josephine, the night had been fitful, and she was eager to welcome the new day. She stood at the railing gazing at the nothingness of a morning filled with water and sky. A long shawl trailed behind her carried by a lingering breeze. Wispy black curls escaped from their pins to swirl about her face.

Captain Pratt thought he'd never seen a more beautiful woman, and no array of finery could make her more so than when she opened his door in the midst of a storm. She'd clutched her wrapper tightly, yet light from his lantern defined the breasts that heaved beneath. All through the night he'd fought the winds to keep to his ship on course, but the vision of the woman who stood in the shadows never left his mind.

"You're up early for a woman short of sleep."

Josephine turned with a smile. "I was just thinking of my father and his voyage from Ireland. He sailed in '21."

"A farsighted man," the captain said, keeping his voice on an even keel. "The famine drove millions of Irish onto emigrant ships in the last five years."

"My father knew, from the time of his youth, there would never be food enough in Ireland."

"You were close to your father?"

Her mood turned pensive. "I loved him very much. He was killed when a recalcitrant horse caused his wagon to capsize on one of Augusta's steepest hills. I thought my heart would stop when a neighbor arrived to give us the news."

"Were we docking at Liverpool, our route would have taken us through St. George's Channel along the Irish Coast. Will you visit the Emerald Isle?"

With a shake of the head, she mumbled, "I don't believe so."

A profound expression transformed the captain's face. "The Irish have suffered miserably, but the blight seems to be wasting."

"Yes," came the lady's murmured response. "And the weak are already dead."

Captain Pratt remained silent. What more could be said of the Irish tragedy?

"Mother," Eugene called as he emerged from the lower deck.

The children were finished with breakfast and Kitty had brought them topside. Josephine wrapped an arm around her young son's shoulder.

It suddenly occurred to the captain to ask: "Have you had breakfast, Mrs. McCarty?"

"No," she answered with an embarrassed laugh. "I was anxious to get the air. Now I expect I will miss the meal completely."

"I have yet to eat. Can I entice you to join me?"

"Why, yes. That's very kind of you."

When the two went below, numerous pairs of blinking eyes followed their descent. The passengers couldn't wait to repeat what they had seen.

As the *Margaret Evans* drew nearer the English Channel, ships from various countries and continents bobbed on every side. The children pointed at every new flag and tried to connect it to the port of origin.

"Are we almost there, Mother? Are we?"

"We are getting closer," Josephine answered with patience.

The captain approached. He wanted to offer her some assurance.

"Mrs. McCarty, will your husband be at the dock to greet you when you disembark?"

"I expect he will be."

"I wish all of you well. It will be unfamiliar soil. Should you need assistance, I'll be available until my ship sets sail again. The *Margaret Evans* has a set departure schedule. While I'm at sea, you can always contact the company's agent. He's a good man and you can trust him."

When the coastline finally came into view, the children were ecstatic.

"We are there! Are we there?"

"Where will Father be? How will we find him?"

Josephine smiled. "Your father will be waiting, and he will find us. We have a way to go before we reach port."

Their ship passed the Isle of Wight, the Southampton Waters, and the island city of Portsmouth. Ship traffic intensified in all directions. They rounded the county of Kent and entered the Thames. With remarkable dexterity the crew took the ship into port, sailing it smoothly right to the dock.

Along with a host of fellow passengers, the McCartys and Kitty were making the adjustment to walking on solid ground.

"Mrs. McCarty?"

Josephine gave a questioning nod to the shipping agent who faced her.

"Captain Pratt sent me a message that you might need assistance."

"Why, thank you. As an entourage of two women and three children, there is little doubt we are at a loss to move our baggage."

The agent had their trunks placed in a cart with instructions for the carter to await direction.

After listening to the conversation, Eugene tugged at his mother's skirt and motioned her down to his level.

"Mother," he said in a whisper, "the people talk funny."

Josephine laughed. "This is England, Eugene. They have an accent that is indigenous to their country. If you were to ask, they would say you are the one who talks funny."

The family looked up at the ship to find the captain staring down at them. They waved to each other and turned to go their separate ways.

The Gravesend community teemed with business. People and cargo from incoming ships moved rapidly from one location to another. Coaches from the east, west, and south pulled into the depot every few minutes to change horses or transfer passengers.

Josephine searched the crowded wharf and finally caught sight of her husband. He was striding their way in a top hat and cutaway coat. She experienced a brief palpitation, followed by the feeling she was outside her body, looking upon the scene that was unfolding.

"Josephine, my darling, you're more beautiful than all my musings could conjure." Robert's compliment came with an enthusiastic embrace.

"It's good to see you again, Robert." Their lips met as her mind wandered. Would reconnecting be that easy?

Before she had time to dwell on the question, Robert's attention swerved to the children. "How you've grown! We no longer have babies in this family!"

Eugene's curiosity overrode every other emotion as he stood boldly before the man called Father. His siblings clung to their nurse.

When Robert reached for a valise and withdrew three parcels, Ella and Terrence took notice. "We shall do this by age," he said, handing a package to his oldest son.

Eugene was beside himself, his eyes dancing as he unwrapped a set of small tin soldiers.

"Wow!" he cried.

His mother stepped back in surprise, but bystanders smiled at his use of the old Scottish term. His father laughed out loud.

"Where did you hear that word?" Josephine asked.

Eugene looked from father to mother. "A boy on the *Margaret Evans* would say it whenever he was pleased. Is it a bad word?"

"It is not," answered Robert. "The word means just what you thought it did, and I'm glad you are so pleased."

Eugene was noticeably relieved as he fingered the brightly painted replicas of the Household Regiment of the British Guard. "Thank you, Father. Never before did I have anything so grand."

His excitement proved contagious. The younger children looked to their father expectantly as their brother put his arm around Robert's waist.

The two packets were delivered in one quick movement, allowing the discovery to take place simultaneously.

Ella held a small doll with a china head and Terrence a horse-drawn carriage with a wheel that enabled it to roll along the floor.

Josephine relaxed a bit, pleased that her husband and children were bonding so well.

Robert turned his attention to Kitty. "Kitty Murtaugh, I'm pleased to make your acquaintance."

"Such a gentleman," she murmured, turning away shyly.

The baggage man had been waiting, but his impatience grew at each passing moment. Robert handed the man a couple of coins, instructing him to haul their things to the depot. He looked to his family, encouraging them to move onward. "Our coach to London will pass through in an hour."

Bursting with pride and the opportunity to impress, he led his family along a walkway to the New Prince of Orange, a popular dining establishment located just yards from the depot.

Conversation was a slow integration of past into present.

"Josephine, dear, how is it that you sailed on the packet when I expressly instructed Mr. Blackfield to send you by steamer?"

"The difference in the price of tickets was enough to cover Kitty's passage. I was sure you wouldn't mind if we could provide a nurse."

The explanation seemed satisfactory. Husband and wife smiled at each other as they sent their family scurrying back to the depot. The coach rumbled to a stop right on schedule. With trunks and parcels strapped into place, the four-in-hand lurched forward. It was the onset of an unimaginable journey. Little Eugene was right: the sights and sounds were as strange as the accents.

When they reached the center of London their coach crossed London Bridge. Josephine hummed the centuries-old rhyme, and their voices rang out across the Thames, "London Bridge is falling down, falling down..."

London had nothing in common with Albany, New York City, or Washington. Cities in the United States were struggling to emerge from virgin earth, their identities undefined. Streets in the English metropolis were paved to accommodate fashionable carriages and well-dressed personages. Dignified buildings and beautiful parks complimented a city of thriving commerce and urbane politics.

Josephine felt transported into a long-lost dream. *It is an illusion; it can't be real.*

Their coach passed the Palace of Westminster, home to Britain's Parliament. Big Ben struck the hour as the reinsman turned his team away from the Thames and guided them toward the McCarty lodging in the very heart of London. They stopped at a building near Regent's Park. The coachman unloaded their baggage as Robert ushered his family up the steps. The apartment offered a sitting room, two bedrooms, an alcove for Kitty, and a pantry with the convenience of a small stove.

It had been a long voyage and an exciting day. The children were tired. Kitty fixed a small supper, and then she tucked them into bed. Josephine and her husband were alone again for the first time in more than two years.

Robert gazed at her with admiration. "It's wonderful having the family joined again. You've done marvelously raising the children these last two years. What do you say, would you like to go for a walk? It was our custom when living in Washington, and the roads at the Capital weren't even paved."

Josephine put on a bonnet and grabbed her shawl. Taking hold of her husband's arm, she called to Kitty, informing her that they were out for a walk.

The domestic nodded amiably. Her fears had been foolish. Their passage had been smooth and now the missus and mister were together again.

The McCartys walked the square, passing other pedestrians out for a stroll in the evening air. But unrest existed in the shadows of stately homes. Josephine recognized that London had problems; parks and paved roads gave no indication of conditions for the city's indigent.

When the couple were about to retire, Robert's arousal brought him to his wife's side. He kissed her beautiful neck and pulled her close. Josephine did not respond. Her mind flew back to lonely months of impoverished status.

"What is it?" Robert asked as he continued to nuzzle her hair.

"It's been over two years. You need to give me time."

"Time for what?" her husband asked in exasperation.

"During your absence, I dedicated myself to the care of our three children. If I am to have another, I want to be sure you'll be with me."

Robert turned his back and moved to the sitting room, his disgust at her reticence unmasked. Yet morning brought a return of good humor.

The children were peeking through the curtains when they saw their father pull up with a hired hack. He waved them out, and they called for their mother.

Josephine adjusted her thoughts, finding it prudent to be positive in light of the previous night's unpleasantries.

She reached for a bonnet and parasol. "Come children, your father has planned a grand day for us."

They tumbled from the doorway anxious for a ride. Robert grinned widely as he handed them into the carriage. The hack circled Buckingham Palace and drove them through fashionable Belgravia and out onto Knightsbridge, ending at Hyde Park, home of the exposition. An enormous crowd milled about the pavilion.

"Oh, Robert! This is the Crystal Palace?" Josephine's tone carried amazement.

The structure, made entirely of glass, rose to a glittering height and covered a span of nineteen acres. A beautiful, showy marvel, the palace stood as a symbol of the innovation and technology showcased at the Great Exposition of 1851.

Robert could not contain his pride. As a jurist for the event, he considered himself an integral part of the ingenious technology that was sweeping industry.

Unexpected joy illuminated his wife's face. "I can't wait to see the exhibits. Is your steam gun on display?"

"No. Though the concept of the gun is simple, I run into difficulty when I try to explain its benefits. But I am very involved in the organization of this magnificent event."

Well, thought Josephine; at least he has a job.

Robert helped each of them down from the carriage, keeping Terrence in the crook of his arm. With Ella holding tight to her mother and Eugene walking forward unafraid, they entered an atrium tall enough to hold a full-grown tree. The fountain appeared as a waterfall, cascading from a great height and spraying the air as it fell to pools on a lower tier.

Arts and crafts and engineering projects from around the world were being showcased. Nothing escaped Josephine's notice. She shared her interest with the children, explaining and commenting on various displays to enhance their appreciation.

Robert's pride was bolstered. The girl he'd married remained unchanged —brilliant, interested, and grasping for knowledge.

He committed an error with that assumption. Josephine was greatly changed—older, wiser, and wary.

Their tour continued until the children tired and asked to be taken home. When they reached Regent Street, Kitty greeted them with strong tea and hot buttered scones.

"Lord, 'tis wonderful seein' this family togither," she cried.

Robert drained his tea cup and dabbed his mouth with a napkin. "I'm enjoying this reunion immensely, but I must leave for a while. My position with the commission requires that I be available."

His wife looked dejected. "Mightn't I go with you?"

"Not this time, my dear, but I will return this evening."

"Well, I should think so," Josephine answered, somewhat indignantly.

The memory of past practices continued to gnaw at her.

In the second week of their stay in London, she made a decision to follow her husband when he left in the morning. Passing St. James Park, he continued north. His destination appeared to be a tiny row house in Charing Cross. Josephine watched as he walked to the door and knocked. The light-haired woman who responded looked to be some years older than herself. For one brief moment, it seemed her husband deserved the benefit of doubt. The assumption evaporated as she witnessed their embrace. Disgusted, she returned to her children and waited.

Robert tiptoed through a darkened suite toward the glow of an oil lamp. His wife stood with her back to him. He entered the bedroom admiring the naked body and the silhouette outlined by lamplight. He dropped his trousers in a silent approach, but the smell of whisky gave him away. Josephine turned in a flash, pushing him against the chest of drawers as she grabbed a nightdress and moved away.

Robert howled in pain. How could he be hurt by such trifling contact? Josephine saw that a stain oozed through his shirt. Flipping the fabric upward, she exposed a penis covered with blisters. Dropping the shirttail, she backed away.

"You are diseased!" she hissed. "You come to me to share your plague?"

"Josephine, I'm sorry. It isn't always so. It is a temporary outbreak. It will clear."

"Did it come from that harlot in Charing Cross?"

It was Robert's turn to be shocked. "How could you know about Nancy?"

"How I know is not the issue. You have been keeping house with a woman who brought you disease. It is a befitting penalty."

"Josephine, what did you expect? We've been separated for two years."

"It was a separation of miles, done at your choosing. It was not a separation of our marriage. Would you treat the sin so lightly had I been the one to default?"

Suddenly conscious of her still-naked body, she dragged the nightdress over her head, sending swathes of muslin in a drop to her ankles.

"Don't pretend to be so innocent," Robert chided. "You shared a cabin with Captain Pratt."

"I don't know where you got that information, but the door between us was never opened." She bit her lip at the comment, remembering the night of the storm. "The captain is a gentleman. And I was sharing a room with three children and their nurse. This conversation is not about me. It is you that stands there oozing."

Robert reached for his trousers and pulled them up before collapsing onto a chair.

"What would you have me do?"

Josephine dropped to the bed opposite, trying desperately to compose her thoughts and control the timber of her voice.

"We have three children to consider. They are just beginning to know you. Perhaps we can reconcile enough to live in domestic harmony."

"Are you speaking of a marriage without intimacy? Is that the life for a husband and wife?"

"It will have to do for now. The future will take care of itself."

Robert grabbed his clothes and faded into the dark. The outer door closed and she knew he was gone.

Questions descended on her as she sat the bed staring into the night. What happens now? Would her husband come back? Would she want him if he did? She was in a foreign country with three small children and nothing but a handful of coins. Easing herself down onto the bed, she stared at the ceiling until her tired lids folded.

Eugene, Ella, and Terrence rose in the morning full of anticipation.

"Where is Father? He promised to take us to the park."

Their mother attempted a smile. "I will take you to the park today."

Kitty turned with a questioning look. She'd awakened to a noise during the night and heard the closing of the outer door. *Had the mister been coming or going?* Either way, she sensed there was trouble in her household.

Josephine walked her children to the playground where she sat on a bench in contemplation. She hadn't the money to pay the rent. Even with prudence, food would be a problem. Captain Pratt was the only person she knew in all of England.

Days passed without any sign of Robert. The children were hungry and she was nearly out of money. Round-trip cab fare to the packet-line office required the expenditure of a full crown; yet, it would take hours to walk the route. She agonized over the decision. Leaving Kitty and the children for the entire day was equally worrisome. She took the cab.

As things turned out, she'd wasted her money. According to the shipping agent, Captain Pratt had gone to sea. The *Margaret Evans* would return to port six weeks hence. Josephine turned to leave. It would be a long walk, but she couldn't afford another two shillings six pence.

Her forlorn expression gave the agent pause to wonder what relationship connected this woman to the captain. If he was right, he'd seen her before. "Would you care to give me your name? We have ships departing weekly. I can send the captain a message if you like."

"My name is Josephine McCarty, but I don't mean to bother the captain."

"Mrs. McCarty! Captain left word that should you appear, I was to offer assistance and he would make good on any expense."

Josephine assessed the agent. His features were so unlike the pinched composite of Mr. Blackfield. This man's broad, florid face imparted good cheer and most likely compassion. Still, she had no intention of baring her soul to a stranger.

From the agent's point of view, the Captain had left his orders. He signaled a cab before the lady could move. She looked startled as he opened the door to hand her up.

"The captain would want me to see you home safely, ma'am." He paid the driver, tipped his hat, and stepped backward.

"Thank you," she called as the cabby's little brown horse pulled away.

Kitty met her at the door with an envelope. Robert had sent a message asking that she meet him beside the waterfall at the Crystal Palace.

She spotted her husband from a distance, stopping before he took note of her. Did she really want this meeting? His coming and going would eventually drive her crazy. He shifted in his seat and their eyes met. She sensed his impatience at the halting approach, but he rose quickly as she drew near.

"You look beautiful as always," he complimented, pulling a chair from the table as an invitation for her to sit.

Josephine nodded acknowledgment as she took the offered seat

"Do you remember," he asked, "how we used to sit on either side of Mrs. Crocker at the dinner table in our old boarding house?"

Josephine failed to smile. There was a time when she and Robert had been very much in love; the existence of Charing Cross Nancy, the abandonment of previous weeks, and the years in Augusta without him obliterated memories she once cherished.

Her husband ignored the cool reception.

"You were right," he said, "from the very beginning. It has been a long separation. We need to move slowly if we want to weave our lives back together. I've been busy this last week and have been hired to do some engineering on the Isle of Wight. It is a beautiful place, agricultural in nature; you'd find yourself right at home. The climate is mild. It's almost a resort. I know the children would like it, and I believe I can get a cottage in Niton.

Robert sounded desperate as he oversold his proposition.

"Tell me, Josephine. Can you forgive me? We need to start from scratch and this would be the place to do it."

"I don't know that I can forgive you. The abandonment, the other woman, and the circumstances of these past two weeks have been a great source of agitation. The landlord is harassing me for payment of the rent."

"I will take care of the landlord. For the sake of the children, will you try?"

What was it about this man? He leaves his family with no regard for their well being and suddenly wants them back again. It made no sense.

"You say, for the sake of the children?"

"It is best, my love. They need a father and a mother. Let us go back; we can announce the move together."

Josephine wanted to slap him. If not for the children, she might have done so. Instead, she took a deep breath, grabbed his arm, and walked forward.

CHAPTER SIX

Friday afternoon, May 3, defense lawyer Lewis H. Babcock stepped forward to give his opening remarks. He stated that the case had been assigned to him on behalf of the prisoner and that he accepted the responsibility as an important duty. Being a humble man, he shuddered that someone with his limited experience should lead the defense in a case where the life of a human being was at stake. He admitted to being a stranger to the prisoner at the time he was called in as counsel. Nevertheless, he had labored incessantly on behalf of his client. His learned and distinguished associates had assisted him in the effort to uncover the truths of the case. Investigation of the prisoner's story convinced him of the rightness of an eventual acquittal. If he could aid the jury in reaching that verdict, it would be held with pleasure long into the future.

He pointed to the fact that the talent arrayed against his client seemed unnatural to the process. Never in the history of Central New York had such a powerful team been assigned to a single case.

"Why?" he asked. "The district attorney was capable of prosecuting for the People. Yet, he was being assisted by an eminent lawyer from St. Lawrence County, and the attorney general had assigned another great legal practitioner to represent his office at trial. With this startling array set against my client, I found it prudent to seek assistance on behalf of the defense."

"The fact that the accused had not the means to cover her defense was not the fault of the Prosecution. It was up to her counsel to step forward, and they were personally bearing the expenses of the trial believing it to be their duty. The destitute had a right to expect that the course of justice would proceed with fairness."

Babcock looked pointedly at the jury and continued with an astonishing statement:

We have been met by the wealth of Milton H. Thomson, who is the real prosecutor in this case. Secret pamphlets and libelous falsehoods had been distributed in the courtroom while the jury was being drawn. While operating in the background, Milton H. Thomson was the man above all others who could have thrown light on this matter. When he took from his photographer the negative of his photograph, so that the picture could not be sent for identification to a distant city, I claim that he was making an effort to defeat the ends of justice. This woman has been confined to a sick bed in jail all of the time since her arrest. Her child is sick, and if he comes to Court to assist his mother he must come on a sick bed. Here this woman is in Court, sick, haggard, crushed in heart and body, with her case in your hands. We all lament the death of the unfortunate man Hall. Why should he die instead of Milton H. Thomson is a question we cannot answer. Milton H. Thomson may not be answerable to the law for this man's death, but the moral sentiment of the community will hold him guilty. I think, gentleman, you are satisfied from the facts as sworn to, that the killing of Mr. Hall was entirely accidental. The prisoner had never seen him. She bore him no malice. I submit, with the utmost respect for the authorities cited by the District Attorney, I think he will look in vain to find where the accidental killing of a person will be called murder by an American jury. Those laws were instituted in England, when the property of a criminal reverted to the Crown. Whether that pistol was fired intentionally or whether the pistol accidentally went off when Mr. Thomson rose, has not yet been proven. You must not be satisfied that the accused discharged the pistol intending to take Thomson's life.

Babcock continued his oration, emphasizing that the real question confronting the court was intent—what had been in the mind of the accused when the act was committed, and did she possess the soundness of mind

85

that would make her legally accountable for the crime?

He outlined the tragedies that followed her from the time of her marriage to Robert McCarty. He addressed her relationship with Milton Thomson and how he had tracked her.

In closing, he remarked, "Thomson's words fired the mine which caused the explosion." His client had been pushed beyond the border of sanity.

Babcock finished his opening statement at 5:45 that evening. The *Utica Daily Observer* classified the speech as a supremely able effort.

Reporters for some of the other papers appeared to be less impressed. During his oration, they expressed their boredom with hand gestures and flippant remarks that could be heard by jurors. Mr. Pomeroy had risen in the midst of Babcock's presentation to object to the behavior of these newsmen. Judge Doolittle ruled against the objection. When the trial adjourned for the day, Pomeroy approached the reporters with an apology.

It was noted by the *Observer* that a similar incident could be found in *The Pickwick Papers* by Charles Dickens.

THE ISLE OF WIGHT FULFILLED ITS DESCRIPTION. Niton, a fishing hamlet at the southernmost tip of the Isle, truly looked to become a resort. Mansions and cottages were springing up along its shores. The McCarty children explored every nook and cranny, dragging their nurse from the water's edge to the hills that rolled above the village. It was the first time in their memory that they were living in the presence of both parents. Their happiness and the balmy weather gave Kitty to believe that all was well.

Yet, the betrayal of trust and harsh words were invisible barriers between husband and wife. The bliss of earlier years seemed irretrievably lost. Robert often left for days at a time, using his surveying as an excuse to remain in more rural areas of the isle. Josephine suffered from a sense of isolation greater than anything she'd known on the ship. She was slow to make friends and missed the culture and intellectual stimulation of the cities. Newspapers kept her abreast of world news; they also informed her of the departure and arrival of ships from New York.

It just happened that the *Margaret Evans* had docked at the Port of London when her husband announced his need to visit that city on business. After days of pleading, he agreed to take the family with him. The trip involved a six-mile ferry ride from the Isle of Wight to the main coast of England. The total distance between Niton and London ran close to one hundred miles. But the family embarked in a happy state.

Josephine justified her purpose thus: she and her husband would enjoy a vacation together, but when business took him elsewhere, she would take the children on side trips, to attractions that only London could offer. Of course, at the first opportunity she took the children to the harbor to visit Captain Pratt.

She went first to the shipping agent who pointed upward toward the deck of the *Margaret Evans*. And there he stood just as he had when they departed the ship, a solid figure, a man of integrity.

"Look," she pointed.

"It is the captain," shouted Eugene. "It is our ship! Can we go aboard? Oh Mother, I do want to see the captain."

Josephine walked toward the ship with her children in hand. The captain watched for a moment before moving to meet them.

There was no embrace. But a catch in the young mother's breathing drew a look of concern as the captain hoisted Terrence onto his shoulders.

"My agent reports that you were looking for me."

"Yes." Josephine dropped her eyes.

"Please, tell me what happened."

"It was nothing. At any rate, all has been settled."

"Josephine, please be truthful with me."

She looked up at him, fearful that the beating of her heart might be seen through her bodice. "I will never lie to you, but there are things that should not be discussed. You will have to trust me in that."

Isaiah nodded before turning his attention to Ella and Eugene.

The children were still in a state of excitement when their father joined them for supper.

"Father, we saw Captain Pratt this afternoon."

Eugene's report came to a halt as anger distorted his father's face.

Robert struggled to keep from raising his voice.

"That was it all along. You accompanied me on this trip to rendezvous with your lover."

"Yes, I hoped we would see the captain. He is a kind man, has been good to the children, and directed my care when I was ill. The skipper is not my lover and this was not a rendezvous. I would gladly have told you of our meeting if it weren't for your unreasonable jealousy."

"Jealous! It was you who went sneaking around and followed me."

"You had given me reason. Let us not quarrel before the children."

The excursion created a widening gap in spousal communications. Robert's surveying trips suddenly lengthened in duration. Josephine didn't bother to follow, though it might have been better if she had.

In years to come, journalists more concerned with supposition than fact would record a lack of religious training as a precursor to Josephine's downfall. While she never committed to a single religious sect, she'd been a practicing Christian all her life. As a child she was influenced by a revivalist preacher lecturing at the Methodist Church in Oriskany Falls. When an effort to convert her playmates failed, she gave them up for lost. At fourteen she was baptized by a redheaded revivalist at the Baptist Church in Augusta Centre. Her association with the O'Dwyers drew her into the fold of the Roman Catholic faith.

In Niton, her church of choice was St. John the Baptist. Once a medieval monastery, it had been occupied by more than one denomination throughout its long existence, ultimately serving the Church of England. If the services within a church could change in structure, then what difference would it make as to where she chose to pray? She attended services weekly.

She and Ella were returning from church on a balmy Sunday morning when she began to reflect on her circumstances. Robert came and went as a guest in their home. The arrangement allowed for a separation that kept them together. It wasn't the best of solutions, but the arguing had come to an end, and the children seemed to be happy. Who knew, reconciliation might be possible after all. She looked at Ella as they turned the corner.

"We're almost home. Tell me, did you enjoy the service today?"

A woman's hysterical wailing silenced Ella's response. Realizing the scream had come from the vicinity of their cottage, Josephine grabbed her daughter and ran. They entered the house to find their nurse half out of her mind.

"What is it Kitty? What has happened?"

"The mister," she blubbered. "The boys, he went and took the boys!"

"What do you mean? Where are the boys? Tell me what has happened."

"The mister came and took the boys."

As if on cue, Robert crashed through the door, scooped Ella into his arms, and fled to a waiting carriage.

Stunned initially, Josephine suddenly came to life. "Robert, Robert come back! Where are you taking the children?"

She raced down the road oblivious to anyone who might be watching. But the driver continued to whip his horses as the carriage rolled out of sight. She hugged a light post in search of support. Her chest was heaving and her legs were weak.

"Oh, missus…"

She turned to see Kitty trotting toward her, arms outstretched and a shawl clutched in her hands. Kit's face was mottled and streaked with tears.

"Oh! I am so sorry. I couldn't stop him." Her sobbing began anew as she sought exoneration. "You see, I couldn't."

Josephine's words came softly to the surface. "Yes, Kitty, I understand."

The nurse took her mistress home, helped her to a chair, and took to brewing tea. There is a time and place for everything, so as Kitty poured the tea, she added a dose of whiskey.

The alcohol was an effective narcotic. Josephine ceased to shake and began to think. She'd made it a habit to put coins aside. The nerve-wracking weeks in London had taught her a lesson. The cache was small, but it would get them to London.

"I'm sure Robert is headed for London. We're going back, Kitty, and I'm going to find my children."

"But ma'am, how do you propose to do so?"

"I'm not sure, but I won't give up until I do."

When they arrived in London, she took a room for herself and Kitty on Bloomberg Square. Her first order of business was to write Captain Pratt. She needed a friend who knew the geography of the city.

The following morning she began her search, going first to their former lodging on Regents Square. The landlord's haranguing began the moment he opened the door. She stepped back at his accusations of running off without paying the rent. Foolishly, she'd taken Robert at his word, believing the rent to be paid. Humiliation sent her skulking. There was obviously no need for questions. Robert couldn't go back to a landlord he'd cheated.

Her next stop was Charing Cross, home of the harlot. The woman looked startled as she answered the knock. Josephine put a hand against the door to prevent it from slamming shut.

"Please, Robert McCarty has kidnapped my children. I need your help in finding them. The man doesn't matter. You can have him. Just spare me the children. I tell you, you wouldn't want them. They are a handful. Please, oh please, don't turn me away."

"I ain't seen him in months."

"Please," Josephine begged again. Her pain was real and the accused woman felt it.

"I could maybe ask around. Don't promise nothin'. You're wrong about one thing—I'd love to take them babies." She shook her head sadly. "My brother's will keeps me in this here house, but I ain't got the wherewithal to care for young'uns."

Josephine took her hand from the door, said thank you, and handed Nancy a scrap of paper.

"What's this?" asked the woman.

"My address."

"Don't read none, but I know some what does." Nancy slipped the paper into her pocket while appraising Josephine from top to bottom. "Remember, I don't make no promises."

The woman had no idea that the fancy clothes she'd been appraising were the result of a deft needle and a talent for transforming the style of old garments. Josephine's predicaments were never exposed by careless dress. In truth, her ability to care for the children wasn't much better than that of Nancy. She scoured the city without success.

Two weeks after the meeting with Nancy, a boy appeared at her door.

"Nancy said to give this back to you."

She glanced down to see the address she'd scribbled for the woman in Charing Cross. Turning it over, she found a second address had been written on the back.

"Thank you," she said as she looked into space. The boy had disappeared.

The address provided by Nancy took her to a tidy cottage in Chelsea. She approached the building cautiously, having been an unwelcome visitor at each of her previous encounters. To her surprise, a buxom woman with a domestic appearance came to the door with a smile.

"What can I do for you, dearie?"

Doubt clouded the woman's face as Josephine described the kidnapping. She hesitated in her reply, but their voices had carried throughout the house, prompting a response from someone inside. The women listened as quick little steps were heard running in their direction.

"Mother," cried Terrence as he flew to her arms.

The woman put a hand to her mouth and moved aside. Inviting Josephine to sit, she began an explanation as to how the children's situation evolved. Robert's concocted story of being a widower in need of help had been very convincing. The woman and her husband agreed that for a price they would take the children and treat them as their own. She was apologetic, acknowledging that the children needed their real mother. Eugene and Ella were taking some lessons from a woman who could read. They were expected to return within the hour.

When all three children were within her reach, Josephine hustled them to the door. Before they could lay a hand to the knob, Robert burst in upon them. The children clung to their mother, fearful of their father's rage. But the perspiration on his brow was a sign of illness, not anger.

"I am taking the children to my lodging. You are obviously ill and in need of care. Should you come to me, I will attend your needs. In either case I am taking my children."

The carriage had been waiting for some time and she thought nervously about the cost. When she reached the house on Bloomberg Square, a message awaited stating that Captain Pratt had docked. Fearful of leaving the children at night, she sent a message that they would meet on the morrow. With three little bodies asleep in her bed, she informed their nurse that an errand would take her from the house at sunrise.

"Lock the door behind me and under no circumstances are you to open it. You understand how dangerous that might be?"

Kitty nodded with tears in her eyes. "I know not how you managed to get those children, ma'am. But the mister, he's a bad one."

Josephine shook her head. "You mustn't speak of it, Kitty. Not when the children are near. Now get your sleep. I will be up at dawn."

She dressed hurriedly the next morning and stepped to a cab, instructing the driver to take her to the pier. Thoughts of the fare disturbed her, but she was exceedingly tired for having spent the night in an armchair. The morning sun flared between buildings, burning her eyes until she turned away. The impending reunion made her nervous. So many issues swarmed through her head she could hardly think at all.

The captain was waiting and stepped to the cab the moment it came to a halt.

"Josephine." He said the name softly, ignoring her objections as he paid the driver. Guiding her to the agent's office, he took her to the back of the room and signaled the agent to leave.

"What is this about the children? Robert has taken them away?"

Josephine nodded. "I have them back. It happened yesterday. He tried to stop me and will again. I've instructed Kitty to keep the door locked."

"But how have you been getting on? Has Robert been paying your bills?"

She shook her head in the negative. "What little I'd saved is gone."

"What do you want to do?"

"I want to take my children home."

"To New York?"

"Yes."

"That can be arranged. I'll put you on the passenger list and…"

She put up a hand to halt him. "Not at this time, Isaiah. The children and I will go back on your next voyage. I need to plan. If Robert suspects, he will pull his tricks to stop us. But Kitty is another matter. Since our arrival, she's been witness to a great deal of grief, which is what she sought to escape in fleeing New York. While a true and trusted ally, she needn't be exposed to my dilemmas."

"I will take care of Kitty. She can sail with us three weeks from today. In the meantime, you have no money?"

"No." Her shame was apparent as the answer came in a hushed tone

"Twenty pounds should keep you in decent housing for the next few months."

"Isaiah, that's too much. I don't have the resources to repay you. I can't let you do this. What would it say of me?"

"It says you've been badly abused and that you and your children are in dire straits. It says I am a friend who wants to help. Should you turn me down, I will take it an insult."

Josephine blushingly gave him her schoolgirl smile. "Nothing can crush our Captain Pratt."

The captain laughed and took her hand. It was a strong hand, one that chased fear to the bottom of the ocean. But they weren't floating on water; they were standing on English soil.

Her circumstances were changing daily. Robert appeared at her door that afternoon, barely able to stand. She eased him onto Kitty's bed, stripped his clothes, and washed his body. Leaving the nurse with orders to brew some broth, she went in search of the landlord.

"I need an additional room," she said.

The landlord squinted his eyes in disbelief. "You can't pay the bill for the room you have, and now you want another? You're a fine-looking woman, but I don't give out favors."

Her temper flared. "I didn't ask for a favor." She plunked down payment for the existing bill. "Now, I want more than just another room. I want two rooms joining, and I need them right away. My husband is with us, and he is ill."

"All the more reason to expect a caper."

"I will pay you in advance, but I want the rooms today." As she took the money from her bag, the landlord stood and gaped. "Well," she asked, "do I get my rooms or do I find another landlord?"

The man had to close his mouth before he could speak. "I don't know where you got those notes, but I'll double your rooms before nightfall."

With Kitty and the children in a separate room, Josephine was free to move about as she nursed her husband day and night.

"You are a treasure, Josephine. Really you are. I have been very foolish." Robert stretched a limp hand in his wife's direction. "I am sorry. Things will be different from now on. I promise."

She left the room without comment. Taking Kitty aside, she told her passage had been arranged for her return to New York. She would be sailing with Captain Pratt.

"We'll sail togither? Like before?"

"No, Kitty, that won't work for us this time. You will be going alone." She gave Kitty the date of departure with assurances that the captain would look to her well-being.

Kitty's initial happiness collapsed. "Oh ma'am, I don't know as I can leave you."

"Nonsense, Kitty. We will be fine. You made the trip to America to begin a new life and I brought you back to the old country. I'm sure things will be different when you return, and all will be for the best."

"Yes, ma'am. But what'll happen to you?" The nurse's distress returned.

"I will be fine. I have a plan, but I must keep silent lest it goes wrong."

The plot to escape remained secret. She couldn't divulge her plans to anyone, not to Kitty nor to the children. She didn't dare. She didn't trust Robert.

Eugene was the one to notice the captain. Fascinated with action on the street, he'd been watching from the window when Captain Pratt dismounted in front of the house. The last time he mentioned the captain's name, his father had been very angry. He let the curtain fall and approached his mother to whisper: "Captain Pratt is out on the sidewalk."

Josephine kissed her son with a warning not to tell anyone that he'd seen the captain.

She walked to the front of the house, nodding pleasantly from the door and speaking clearly, "Captain Pratt, how nice to see you."

"It is quite a surprise to see you, madam. A very good friend of mine lives in the house next door. I'd thought to pay him a visit, but it seems he isn't at home. I trust all is well with your family?"

"I've been quite busy of late. My husband is ill and I have been caring for him."

A furrow creased the captain's brow as he gleaned her situation. "Has there been any change in your plans for the future?"

"Not at all," she said with a smile.

"Very good." The captain returned her smile and tipped his hat. Then catching sight of the boy in the window, he raised a finger to his lips.

Eugene repeated the gesture with a slight nod.

On the day of her departure, Kitty's wailing reached every ear on the wharf. Josephine did her best to establish calm. "Remember, you are traveling with Captain Pratt. No one on the sea is more capable than he. Take your fears to him, and he will reassure you."

"Yes, ma'am." Kitty wiped her tears with a handkerchief. The captain's actions in recent months left no doubt as to his courage and kindness.

"And one other thing, Kitty. I haven't been diligent in letter writing. The news of Rosie O'Dwyer expecting a child demanded greater attention. It is the biggest event of their lives. Please give the family my regards and keep our troubles silent. It's best they remain ignorant of our situation."

With Robert's recovery, the family took what was meant to be a brief excursion to Paris. The length of their stay grew to months. Josephine's fluency in French brought her husband's negotiating tactics up to a competitive level.

France was under the rule of Louis Bonaparte's Second Republic. The country's crowning city was a center of high style and modernization. When not with her husband, Josephine educated her children in the culture and arts facing them on every front. Terrence giggled delightedly as they viewed a street-side puppet show. Although it was her goal to expose the children to culture, it came as no surprise that they preferred a circus to browsing the work of struggling artists.

On an afternoon of freedom, she visited the Hospital de la Salpêtrière. France's proclaimed progress in health care included declining death rates, surging inoculations, and a quiet move toward birth control. The issues were fascinating. Yet a tour of the hospital left her appalled. It wasn't the hospital but the patients that shocked her. Lovely young girls, their faces contorted in pain, gave birth to the babies of wealthy bourgeois who would never claim the child or acknowledge the mother. Older women suffered from disease, a result of mistakes made when they were young and fair. All were condemned to a sordid life. There seemed little help for the lot of them. She returned to the hospital often, serving as a volunteer. When permissible, she sat in on medical lectures.

Her joy in Paris might have been greater if the dream had not gone sour. A host of issues now scrambled for attention in her beleaguered mind. Getting back to New York had become an obsession. In the months since Captain Pratt's sailing, she had worked on plans of escape. Should one scenario look to fail, she had an alternative to back it up.

The planning proved useless. When the captain arrived in Paris, Robert went into a rage. Spying the seaman as he passed their hotel, he ran to the carriage screaming profanities.

Pratt halted with an indignant look. "My dear man, if it is your wife's honor that spawns this tirade, I assure you nothing untoward has transpired. However, if you wish to pursue the issue, I invite you to ride out with me where we can settle the matter as gentlemen."

Blanching in fear of a duel, Robert ran back to the hotel where he locked his family in their rooms. When the captain's carriage turned the corner, he pushed Josephine aside and dragged the children into the hallway. Before she could catch him, he pulled the door shut and turned the key.

Patrons of the hotel could hear her pounding. But the scene unfolded as in the past. She was freed from her room, but not in time. Robert and the children were gone.

Déjà vu, without the company of Kitty. There was no one left to assist her other than Captain Pratt. She sent him a message and waited, circling the room until his knocking halted her pacing. She struggled to set the key in the lock and fell as the door swung open.

"Josephine!"

The captain lifted her onto a settee. A clean lavender scent filled his nostrils. *She is a remarkable woman, sharp and self-reliant, but she is engaged in war, and combatants in every battle need time to collect and regroup. My lovely Josephine has been pushed to the limit.* He caught himself at the thought. Josephine did not belong to him; she was the wife of Robert McCarty.

"I'm sorry," he said. "The confrontation this afternoon, undoubtedly, compounded your troubles."

She shook her head. "Robert is an out-of-control coward. As soon as you left, he ran off with the children. I believe he does it to spite me. For two years, he ignored them entirely."

The captain poured sherry into a tumbler, suggesting she sample the liquid. He smiled as it caused her to sputter. "Do you have any idea where they have gone?"

"I feel he must be on his way to England."

"We'll leave for London tomorrow."

He cradled Josephine in his arms much as her father had years before.

She closed her eyes, absorbing the strength and warmth of real affection. How was it that one man could be so good and another such a cad?

"You sail this week." She knew the timetable. She'd planned to be with him when he left. "I shall be lost without you."

"I wish I could tell you all will be fine, but I'm afraid it mightn't be so. Your passage is set. Can I convince you to sail?"

"Isaiah, they are my children, my flesh and blood. I gave them life. I have to keep trying."

The following day, Isaiah accompanied Josephine across the channel to London. Before returning to sea, he handed her another twenty pounds. "You need the protection and independence that only money can offer. I pray that on my return you will be waiting to sail with your children in hand."

The *Margaret Evans* departed, leaving Josephine in a gloomy mood. Then word came from Isaiah's agent that at least one of the children had been located at a home in Camden Town. She ascertained the location and approached the house on foot. The two older children were nowhere in sight, but she found Terrence in the care of a rough sort of woman with hardened features and long bony fingers. If this keeper possessed an increment of compassion, she managed to keep it hidden.

But where kindness was absent, fear stepped in. Having a well-bred lady on her doorstep gave the woman pause to think. Begging Josephine not to take the child directly, she explained there were those who might be hard on her if the boy should disappear. A two shilling offer bought information. Terrence would be traveling on a railcar two days hence.

Josephine entered the car at Waterloo Station just as the woman instructed. Terrence spotted his mother immediately and raced to her arms with Robert in pursuit. The boy's terrified screams alerted passengers who quickly stepped forward to intervene.

When the police arrived, they escorted Josephine and her son to the depot. Terrence trembled with apprehension. The actions of his parents were beyond comprehension.

"Mother, I want to go home."

Josephine swallowed hard as she realized they had no home. She couldn't be sure what dwelling the child had in mind.

"The ship? Would you like to go back to the ship?"

Terrence nodded. "Cap'n Pratt."

The toddler related strength and protection to the persona of Captain Pratt. In an uncanny way, the seaman represented stability.

They were still in protective custody, but a little past noon police assigned care to a railroad detective. A short time later, two of McCarty's mechanics jumped them in an attempt to snatch the child. The detective put up a fight, drawing a new contingent of policemen. They were taken to a justice at the London police station where the case came abruptly to an end.

The officers in London wanted nothing to do with the incident.

Josephine procrastinated as long as she could. Then taking a deep breath, she stepped from the station house to face the worst of her fears. Robert lunged from the shadows to snatch the baby. With one quick shove, he sent her sprawling to the bottom of the stairs. Terrence stretched toward her but was swallowed by darkness.

His wailing continued to ring in her ears as she lay crumpled on the sidewalk at the entrance to the London police station.

Law laid custody of children with their father. Nevertheless, Josephine searched for legal counsel. Passing beneath the Doctors Commons Archway, she approached an office in the first court where proctors administered ecclesiastical law. There were several clerks working in the outer chamber. They raised their heads simultaneously as she entered the room.

Her situation did not seem unique. She was asked to produce a marriage certificate.

"I have none. My husband stole the document when last we were together."

She caught the glimmer of a smirk. "I am sorry, madam. We cannot proceed without a marriage certificate."

In fact, Josephine was considered a *femme couverte*, a woman covered by her husband's identity. In the eye of the court, she had no individual rights. Returning to Robert's most recent residence, she explained the situation to his landlady. The woman's sympathies were with the children's mother.

They searched his room together. The marriage certificate could not be found. Josephine wrote to Lyman Warren, a justice in Augusta, asking if he could locate a copy. Warren's response acknowledged her letter, but the certificate never arrived.

She called on Robert's lawyer, but her plea for information generated a chilling response. The children had been taken across the channel and were hidden on the continent.

If she didn't have enough to worry about, the original London landlord had sued Robert for rent. The case was settled in the office of Robert's lawyer with Captain Pratt being charged the bill.

Lost to her children and to herself, she ambled the city aimlessly. Walking along St. James Square, she turned into the London Library where an exhibit on the feminist Flora Tristan captured her attention. The circumstances of Tristan's ugly marriage and her crusade for women's rights illuminated the limitations of life in a world governed by men. Knowledge wouldn't lighten her mood nor could it bring her peace. But understanding the challenge invigorated her strength.

Kitty wrote faithfully, informing her of tragedies on the other side of the ocean. Rosie O'Dwyer's pregnancy had been fraught with complications. The dear little lady passed away with the baby still in her womb. Thomas was crazy with grief and cared not a bit for the mansion. Since he no longer had need of her services, she'd taken a job caring for children at a baby farm in Pennsylvania. It seemed sadness had no boundaries.

When the *Margaret Evans* docked again, she waited on the wharf, anxious for the return of her captain. Spotting the upturned face, Pratt sent a mate to fetch her.

He tilted his head to examine her features. "There is sadness in your eyes, but certainly no loss of beauty." He put his arms around her, and she smiled for the first time in months. "Will you have supper with me here on the ship? The *Margaret* provides privacy, and the fare I can offer will be to your liking."

Their meal was made peaceful by the gentle roll of the ship and the lap of quiet waters. But in gazing at the woman through candlelight, Isaiah was transported to a midnight of violent seas. The memory and her presence were overpowering. "Josephine, you need to go home."

His guest did not respond.

"England's declaration of war against Russia will affect every aspect of shipping. Many of the country's merchant vessels have been pressed to transport troops and supplies to Crimea."

"I don't know." Her voice was filled with doubt.

"You had difficulty finding the children while they were in London. You scoured Paris without success. Europe is a continent of countries and languages foreign to you. Your search is an impossible task, but if by chance you should succeed, you'd be subjected to heartache all over again. You need to go home."

Her pitched response was testy. "I have no home. The man who pledged to love me destroyed all I held dear."

"Get away from here and give yourself time."

"There is no home in my future. I won't have Robert and will never marry again."

The captain's somber expression mirrored hers as he replied. "And I shall never marry at all."

"You mustn't say that, Isaiah; you have so much to offer a family."

"Josephine, in your time of greatest need, I was an ocean away. The hardships you endured in the years of Robert's absence are identical to those of a seaman's wife; only, for her, the absence goes on forever."

Josephine stared at the darkened bay. "When I left home, I thought I'd been through the worst life could bring." A melancholy smile pulled at the corners of her mouth. "I now take stock in the phrase 'things are never so bad that it can't get worse.'"

"And one is never taxed beyond their ability to survive."

Josephine laughed nervously. "That sounds like a sermon from Bishop Hughes."

The captain's laughter rumbled. "The Bishop and I are cut from different cloth."

The unintended pun against the bishop's mantle brought another laugh. The tension binding Josephine was broken.

The captain turned serious once again. "You must go home, but not with me. I'll arrange for your passage on the *Hermann*, out of Southampton. It is a steamer and will have you home quickly."

She sat motionless. "You wouldn't have me with you?"

"I have my faults, dear Josephine, but I won't be the next to bring you grief. I refuse to spoil that which I find to be perfect."

Sagging against his chest, she wept quietly, barely aware of the fingers that toyed with her hair. His kiss came unexpectedly, with an urgency bespeaking great passion. Yet he pulled away to drape his cloak across her shoulders.

Signaling a cab from the top of the plank, he assisted her to the waiting hack and took his place beside her.

Fighting another spill of tears, she made an attempt at normal conversation. "I've been so self-absorbed, I haven't asked about Thomas O'Dwyer. Do you have information on how he has adjusted?"

"I'm sorry to say he has taken to drink. He won't last long at the rate he's going."

"So, one misfortune has led to the next." She put a hand to her mouth, choking on grief.

The cab reached Bloomberg Street where Isaiah handed her down to the road.

"The *Hermann* leaves Southampton day after tomorrow," he informed her as they walked to the door. "I will drive you to the rail myself." He lifted her chin with his finger, offering one last kiss.

She let herself into the cubicle that had been her home for several months. The closed drapery created a morbid, cave-like setting. She tried to catch her breath, but her knees buckled, and the floor came cold against her face

Sobbing racked her body as it had on that occasion so many years before. She'd been a child then, racing across the field. Tall grasses had gripped her ankles until she tripped beside the stream. Trickling water had cooled her face as she lay grieving the loss of her father. No soothing rivulet came to her this day. Her marriage had ended, the children were lost, and she was alone once more. She had no future, no hope, no interest in anything.

CHAPTER SEVEN

Court resumed on Saturday morning, May 4, with defense calling Mrs. McCarty to the stand. Pomeroy would pose questions assisted by Mitchell. Spectators were sparse.

Josephine wore the same outfit as on previous court days. After she took her seat at the witness stand, a constable stepped forward to offer her a handkerchief.

Babcock had been chronicling his client's life. Her response to questioning substantiated his accounting. Yet her answers were issued impulsively, often in advance of the Court's ruling on objection.

While Milton H. Thomson provided testimony for the inquest, he was excused from the trial on the basis of illness. Nonetheless, he used the newspapers to express his stance, denying any personal association with the accused. But when the question was brought to Josephine, she referred to his proposal of marriage. A letter offered as evidence was marked by the court reporter and read to the jury in spite of the prosecutor's objection.

Waterville, April 24, 1845

Miss Josephine: I have concluded to take the benefit of a few short moments by dropping you a few lines, hoping at the same time that you will excuse the impudence of one who dares to be so presuming. I finally received a paper from you a few days since, directed to Paris (after its having lain there some time.) saying that you were in Port Tobacco. You inquired about your friends. Now, I should be very happy to oblige you, but they are so numerous that I can not well inform you respecting the whole of them. But for one of them I can assure you he is enjoying rather pleasant times, notwithstanding James K. Polk is elected, for there is some satisfaction in knowing that the "Traitor John" has at last become politically defunct in the eyes of every honest person. But this "Annexation question" has been about as troublesome as anything amongst all your Whig friends; but I think most of them will eventually recover from their now, hopeless situation if they can only manage to keep sane awhile, at least until you return! However, I think it will be very doubtful, considering the prospect, that your return will be so distant. I suppose you long since heard that one of your democratic friends, William M. Fairchild, Esq., has gone like the rest of party, and united his destiny with a Miss Stuart, of Smithfield. Now Josephine, don't you think he is rather hasty for a young gentleman of his age? I think that you must have had a very pleasant time at Washington during the present winter, but from you not returning once in an age, I have about concluded that you have at least partially forgotten most of your friends, or that there is such a place as Augusta. Perhaps you may say no! to this; but if you do I shall most certainly conclude that some young gentleman has stolen your affections, heart and all: a circumstance I should much regret, for "you know" they constitute the most essential parts of a young ladies attractive qualities.

I heard some time since at Augusta a conversation (and a very interesting one) between a couple of ladies at a certain table: they were gossiping, of course. One of them says "Don't you think" Josephine Fagan is not coming back this winter. I want to know replied Mrs. H–, Well, my opinion is that when the duck comes she will fetch a Husband with her any way. Miss B. replied that she did not think you had any such intentions. I said nothing, but thought Mrs. H. was a woman of uncommon, good judgment, which I suppose you are too much of a lady to deny. There is nothing new of importance in Augusta, everything appears to pass along in about the usual routine with little variation. Samuel L. Rose was here a few days ago since, who said there was nothing new. You know he carries the "Augusta" mind generally. I suppose you must be enjoying yourself very pleasantly on the plantation you spoke of at Port Tobacco, and perhaps as well that it may be a long time before we see you this way again. But have you forgotten Augusta? the ride from Oriskany Falls to Esq. Dean's? I think that on our return you proved yourself quite a "Horseman," I have many times thought of it, as well as many other pleasing incidents, which took place at Augusta, which I shall ever remember with all their pleasing associations. Your friend—Mary F. Norris is at home and has become very adept on the piano. Frank Curtis is at New Hartford teaching and Warren as you "well know" remains in Augusta, and it would be useless for me to say anything concerning one from whom you hear so often.

I am now engaged in the Post Office at Waterville (Oneida Co.), at the American Hotel, where I shall probably remain at least a part of the summer. One of your former acquaintances, G.F. Havens, is boarding here, formerly from Hamilton. He was married a short time since to a Miss Welton, of Paris. Now Josephine I should be much pleased to hear from you; to know that I may remain your friend, and believe me when I say I am sure it would be in vain for me to aspire or hope beyond. In closing allow me to offer you my best wishes for your success & Happiness.

Most Respectfully Yours, &c.,
Milton H. Thomson

This rambling letter offered concrete proof of Thomson's early acquaintance with the defendant as well as his show of affection. His subsequent advances would be brought to the court's attention at a later date.

JOSEPHINE LACKED ENTHUSIASM as she boarded the *Hermann* to exit England. Improvements built into the modern steamship made no impression on her whatsoever. She saw nothing but a cold, lonely ocean, a mirror of her life and expectations. Giving up on attempts to be present at meals, she glided from her compartment to the deck with an ethereal grace that drew the attention of curious passengers.

Day after day, she sat on the deck, a ghostly figure huddled in the folds of a blanket. One afternoon, while sitting thus, a shadow crossed her face. She raised her head thinking a cloud must be passing.

"Good afternoon," said the gentleman standing above her.

She opened her mouth, but failed to respond.

"Would you mind if I took this chair?" he asked, pointing to the seat beside her.

Her tongue gained mobility with three one-syllable words: "Not at all."

"Please, allow me to introduce myself. My name is Alanson Jones. I am a physician in New York and have been enjoying a holiday abroad." He said this with a happy grin as he lowered himself to the chair in question. "I notice you've not been to the dining room lately. It is my hope that you are well."

She made a weak attempt to return the smile, amazed that someone should notice her absence. "It's the constant rolling of the ship," she explained. "In spite of my travel, I've failed to grow sea legs."

The doctor nodded. "Perhaps I can be of help."

"I've taken the powders to no avail."

"Why don't you come to supper tonight? The right choice of foods can make a considerable difference. It would be a delight to have you at the table."

Josephine was tired, tired of everything, including the blank walls of her tiny compartment. "Perhaps I will," she answered slowly. "I can't promise, but I will consider the invitation."

Dr. Jones was intrigued as much as anyone on board. The woman's beauty had caught his attention when she first appeared on the Southampton railcar. A veil of sadness enveloped her. It would be a joy to dispel those clouds.

"Look at that man," he exclaimed, nodding toward a stoop-shouldered fellow exiting the dining room. An oblong shape burgeoned through his wrinkled shirt. "What do you think his story might be?"

With an unexpected smile she answered, "I'd say he's preparing for the day when Captain bans him from the dining room entirely."

The haze lifted proportionately as she became increasingly aware of the lives surrounding her. Speaking with a prestigious surgeon stimulated an interest she had long since abandoned. As the *Hermann* rippled across the Atlantic, Dr. Jones enticed his new friend to join him in table games, and as red and black checkers slid from square to square, Josephine directed their conversation to the subject of medicine. While the afternoons passed pleasantly, joy remained an elusive target. When another passenger chided Dr. Jones with the once popular song, "Go Call the Doctor," she found it impossible to join in the laughter.

Their ship slipped to a berth in New York's harbor in the spring of 1854. Josephine stepped from the plank to the wharf on South Street, steadying herself against the illusionary tilt of ground beneath her feet. There was no one to greet her. Rosie had taken her kindness to the grave. That family's tragedy went beyond reckoning. She would remain in the city overnight and pay her respects to Thomas on the morrow.

Her trunks were delivered to an off-Broadway hotel. Accommodations on the fringes of fashion were less dear. With her baggage in route, she followed on foot. No stimulus hurried her onward; no one awaited her coming. A child chased a hoop along the sidewalk as drays and carriages rolled by. She experienced a moment of confusion when her name floated over the plethora of sound. A stylish carriage with a pair of matched bays came to a halt beside her.

"Mrs. McCarty, may I offer you a ride?"

"Why thank you, Dr. Jones, but I think I will walk. The sights and sounds of New York are a comfort, though I appreciate the offer."

"You are quite welcome. And remember, if ever I might be of service, don't hesitate to call on me." Alanson Jones tipped his hat, and then shook the reins to move his horses onward.

The man was a capable surgeon, but Josephine would have been surprised had she known his skill would one day save her life.

The first order of business on reaching her hotel was to pen a note to Thomas, promising a visit the following day. She set the pen down to reach for her stomach. Ache and torment gripped her. *The children are gone and I don't know how to find them. Oh God, it sounds like a rhyme, but the reality is unbearably painful. What kind of mother could lose her babies?* What should she do? Where would she go?

Morning brought no respite from agony. The walk to O'Dwyer's deepened her depression; the sight of Thomas pierced her heart. The boisterous giant had dwindled to a shadow of his former being, hair and beard unkempt, the whiskers dotted with crumbs.

She threw her arms around him. "Oh Thomas, I am so sorry. If only I might have been here."

He studied her for a moment through bloodshot eyes and shook his head. "There was nothin' to do, Josie. She was so happy. I knew trouble was brewin', but I never thought to lose her. Then Kitty came back tellin' what Robert had done. If I could get my hands around his neck I'd kill him and be glad." The outburst seemed to exhaust him as he wiped a tear from the corner of his eye.

"Cousin Thomas, you must take better care of yourself."

"Josie, you're the closest I've ever had to a daughter. There's nothin' I wouldn't do for you, but I can't live without my Rosie." Dropping his head onto trembling hands, he sobbed unabashedly.

"Please, Thomas. Have you been to the saloon?" He shook his head. "You have to get down there. You have to take control. Who knows what an unsavory bloke might do to your business."

"It doesn't matter anymore."

"It does matter. Promise me you'll try."

"You're a lovely lass, little Josie. I give you my promise to try."

Josephine scoured the kitchen for ingredients that they might have tea. She suspected it would be the first solid food her cousin had eaten in weeks. She was also sure he'd fail in his promise. She could only hope he would try. They parted as the afternoon waned, two sorely injured souls sympathetic to each other's grief.

From the O'Dwyer home, Josephine went straight to the rail station to check the schedule of trains. She would be heading north as soon as she could get a seat. Isaiah had been right. She needed to get back to Augusta if she were to find her way out of the nightmare.

The visit with Thomas was a revelation. As the train chugged alongside the Hudson River, she thought about their trials. Thomas had lost his wife and child, not to a forest of trees, but to eternity. For them, there would be no tomorrows. Her children were alive—bright, handsome, and hopefully healthy. She couldn't see them; that was her grief. But the future stretched forward endlessly, and her babies still had their tomorrows. She needed to sort these thoughts and establish goals if there was ever to be any order in life.

When the train pulled into Utica, Robert Norris waited at the siding. Her telegraph message probably left him wondering if he would ever be rid of that girl. But he held out a hand as she descended from the car.

They were in the buggy before a single word was spoken.

"I'm alone, Uncle."

"I know."

And that was it. The road to Augusta passed beneath the carriage wheels in silence.

The adopted uncle drew back on his reins as he turned down the driveway to the farm. "You'll be okay, Josie. You've made it through more than any could rightfully expect."

Wrestling with emotion, she expressed her doubts. "I don't know, Uncle; I just don't know." Then grabbing a bag she followed Robert as he transported her trunks to the house.

Phoebe greeted them stiffly. Her warmth was crippled, her joints rigid. "What happened?" she asked. "When you left, you were a married woman with three children."

Josephine looked to her former guardian, but he had turned away.

"It's a long story, Mother. We'll have ample time to discuss it. Where is Bridget?"

"I let her go."

It had been unavoidable that Bridget would eventually be dismissed.

Subtle diplomacy had its limits with Phoebe. Josephine climbed the stairs to her old room where familiarity coaxed her onto the bed. Down pillows supported a night of tumultuous sleep, and morning sunshine did nothing to brighten her spirits. The confrontation she had been dreading awaited in the kitchen.

Phoebe turned from the stove at the sound of her step. "Listen to me, miss; I'm telling you right now, you can't dance in here whenever you like and take up residence. You'll have to pay me rent."

Josephine's retort came quickly. "Father put both of our names on the deed to this farm. We share equally in ownership. You have a right to the profits you earn. But you cannot turn me away.

"I'll have papers served on you!'

"Do that, Mother. I can assure you it will be a waste of time."

A letter arrived from Milton Thomson; she dropped it into the fire unopened.

Days and weeks tumbled together in a blank block of time. Decisions were made and discarded as she continued to flounder in depression.

Brian Kerry, a young Irishman, had taken the place of old Slattery. He watched through the summer as his employer's daughter moped about the farm. He'd heard rumors about her troubles and thought it wrong that a woman as young and beautiful as Mrs. McCarty should be giving up and calling it quits.

On a brilliantly sunny afternoon, Phoebe asked him to fetch oats at Newell's Corners. He'd saddled Johnson and was about to ride off when Josephine appeared at the fence. "Mrs. McCarty, ma'am," he said, "I'm off to fetch some oats. Would you like to ride along?"

Josephine looked confused. "You are riding the only horse we have. How could I possibly accompany you?"

"Johnny's a fine, broad horse. I'll give you a hand to climb on behind. When you were a mite, there must have been a time when you rode double."

Her quick laugh was the first to erupt since she'd arrived at the farm. "I rode behind my father many times." She looked up at the merry Irish eyes, and the good times rushed to the forefront of her mind. "Thank you, Mr. Kerry; I accept the offer."

Pulling the back of her skirt up between her legs, she tucked it into the waistband. Brian hoisted her onto Johnson's back and they ambled downhill toward the feed store.

They reined to a stop at the loading dock where numerous eyebrows flew upward. Josephine McCarty riding behind a hired hand? There was a gasp as she slid over Johnson's rump, her petticoats riding up to the knee. Ignoring the stares, she followed Brian inside. He went directly to the oat bin, filled a bag with oats, and cautiously looked around.

"Wait for me outside and be prepared to run for it."

"Brian, what are you talking about?"

"Just do as I say."

Josephine stepped out onto the dock. She was making an appreciative scan of the hillside when Brian exited the store and jumped onto Johnson.

"Mrs. McCarty, hurry. Give me your hand and hurry."

They were across the road when Mr. Smith ran from the store shaking his fist.

"I'll have the sheriff after you."

"What have you done?" asked Josephine in bewilderment.

Brian laughed wickedly as he jabbed Johnson to a trot. "We stole the grain."

"But why?"

The farmhand laughed again. "To provide the neighbors with a shocking new rumor."

Josephine choked at the reply as she burst into peals of laughter that sent tears rolling down her face.

"Smith keeps your mother on the books. She never gives me money. All I had to do was sign for the oats. Your mother is good for twenty-eight cents. Smith knows that, but they'll be buzzing for months on the robbery at the feed store."

Out of breath but in a more sober state, she questioned Brian again. "I still don't understand; why did you do it?"

"Mrs. McCarty, I've observed such sadness in your face, I knew it would take some sort of shock to rouse you from the malaise. It's a harmless deed we've done, and it brought you to hearty laughter. Whatever the penalty, it was worth it."

Brian didn't understand the extent to which the tale would grow. Gossip took the town by storm—and Phoebe subscribed to all accusations.

"Josephine, how many times are you to bring shame to this house?"

The daughter looked purposely at her mother. "Your marriage to that useless truck, Camp Williams, brought more joy to the scandal mongers than any action I've ever taken. The lady on the hill marrying a hard-drinking farmhand! Your union took place while I was at school. When I returned, the shock was accompanied by sly looks and untoward remarks from some of my very best friends. Don't talk to me about shaming the family."

Charges of larceny were dismissed, but Brian Kerry was fired. Josephine left for New York shortly thereafter.

She reached the city to learn Thomas O'Dwyer had sold his mansion. He'd gone back to Five Points, the community from which he had come. She thought it would satisfy Robert perfectly to know the Irish parties on Sixth Avenue would never occur again.

Sorrow sent her to mass on Sunday morning. Her friend, Bishop Hughes, had been elevated, becoming the first Archbishop of New York. Spotting her from the altar, he rushed to make contact at the close of the mass.

"Mrs. McCarty, how good to see you again. I understand you've been abroad. Now where are those children?"

Josephine took a deep breath. "I don't know. While I was in England, my husband took the children from me. I have not seen them since."

"Praise God," the archbishop said solemnly, making the sign of the cross. "First the O'Dwyers and now you! There is no understanding the ways of the Lord in times like these, but you must keep faith."

Josephine failed to smile. "The theory is good. The practice is fraught with disappointment."

The prelate's frown was rescued by the call of another parishioner.

Josephine strolled to the corner and bought a newspaper. Checking advertisements for employment, she skipped anything with a reference to teaching. Dealing with other people's children would be more than she could ask of herself. Her eyes fell to a notice recruiting lady agents with the requirement that they be of good moral character. The position involved selling subscriptions to a medical journal. The prospect stirred her interest.

Her interview with A. Ranney Publishers and Dealers in Maps and Books impressed the company's owner. She was an exceedingly beautiful woman, bright, and interested in the contents of the journal. How could he lose? He offered a commission on every subscription sold.

In her first venture as a saleswoman, she stopped at a bookstore on Broadway. A sign on the door listed Morgan Haversy as proprietor. Noting only one individual occupied the store, she approached the gentleman with smiling confidence.

"Mr. Haversy, could I possibly have a moment of your time?"

"You can have all the time you want, miss, but I'm not Mr. Haversy."

Taking in the man's brown apron, she concluded he must be an employee.

"Could I speak with Mr. Haversy?"

"I don't believe so, but then how am I to know?"

Josephine felt her face redden with annoyance. "Can you tell me if he'll be here soon?"

"No."

Getting increasingly agitated, she begged for clarification. "You can't tell me, or he won't be here."

"Oh, it's for sure he won't be here. He's in the cemetery,"

Her look of shock forced him to explain.

"Died three years ago. I bought the shop but never bothered to take his name off the door."

Balancing between the desire to laugh and the urge to scream, Josephine plunged onward. "I am selling subscriptions to *The People's Medical Lighthouse*. If Mr. Haversy had been aware of the information in this publication, he might be with us today."

"It's doubtful. He was drunk and hit his head falling down stairs."

She was not about to be put off. "Among the many enlightening articles contained in this periodical there is an explanation of the affects of alcohol on the body. Two subscriptions are essential for a merchant such as yourself. A single issue will fly off the shelf before you have a chance to absorb our valuable information. May the ghost of Haversy preserve you."

The store owner's laugh was surprisingly hearty for a man whose pale skin and concave chest suggested a lack of exercise. "I have to say, your spiel tops anything I've heard before."

Josephine topped her pitch with a dazzling smile. "Can I sign you up for two subscriptions?"

"Make it five, and the name is Albert Van Nort."

As she went on to target all points of New York for sales, she never repeated the error of assumption.

The People's Medical Lighthouse appeared in some of the city's most fashionable houses and in a goodly number of book stores. The journal contained essays by Harmon Knox Root on the function of and diseases afflicting human organs. She herself became one of the periodical's most avid readers, making the publication an easy sell.

From New York, she moved on to Philadelphia. The city had been a point of fascination since the days of her honeymoon. Those happy days had passed, but there was a chance she might begin anew in this same city. Known as the City of Medicine as well as the City of Brotherly Love, Philadelphia was home to the first all-female medical college in the world. The school had been established five years earlier, and the Female Medical College of Pennsylvania was her targeted destination.

She smiled as the Arch Street building came into view. The school was smaller than and not nearly as modern as the Augusta Academy she'd attended as a child. Augusta's three-storied brick construction had a domed roof, flat back, and round front, and it had seventeen windows facing the road. The medical school stood tall and narrow with three long windows aligned on each of the top two floors. An addition fell off to the right of the structure, destroying the symmetry of the original design. Comparing architecture seemed a foolish thought, but it was the first thing to cross her mind.

The facade of the school in Augusta reminded her of Humpty Dumpty's brick wall. Education in the healing of injured bones and broken bodies took place in the lopsided college on Arch Street. One thought connected to the other.

Though somewhat in awe, she approached the registration desk and introduced herself as a prospective student. The secretary reached in a drawer and pulled out a copy of the college's *Sixth Annual Announcement*. She explained that the curriculum, fees, and general requirements were outlined in the booklet. Opening the booklet, she pointed to a section describing terms of admission. The five-month term ran seventy dollars with an additional fee of five dollars for the course in practical anatomy.

Applicants suffering financial difficulty were encouraged to apply, as each year six needy individuals were admitted at twenty dollars per session excluding demonstrator and graduation fees. Josephine left the Arch Street building in a lighthearted mood. If she were to continue with her subscriptions, come fall she should have enough in her savings account to cover the enrollment fees. The thought of becoming a doctor filled her with a sense of purpose.

Late in the summer of 1855, she received a summons to appear in Augusta. Robert McCarty sought foreclosure of his mortgage on the farm. She'd been subpoenaed as a witness. Tossing the notice aside, she placed a hand to her forehead and closed her eyes. At the time of its origination, the document seemed a formality elevating her husband to hero status. Images of the honeymoon years retreated in a mist. A few days later, she rode the train northward, gloom again her traveling companion

She went with her mother to the court house, wondering what it would be like to face Robert again. The aged and soured expression he wore took her by surprise. With a rueful smile, she imagined he'd been unsuccessful in the manufacture of his precious steam gun. A downturn in fortune could be a reason for the lawsuit. But then, she knew first hand his tendency to operate from spite. He'd ignored her pleas for information on the children. Now it was her turn to seek satisfaction. She tipped her head upward ever so slightly.

Early questioning established the relationship between the witness and Robert McCarty. It was a meandering route that eventually got to the topic of the loan. Her answers were simple.

"I failed to notice if my husband had the mortgage with him when he left my mother's home.

"I don't remember a green trunk being left in my care when he sailed for England.

"I never removed the mortgage from any trunk."

Robert's failure to produce the document in question caused the case to be adjourned.

When they returned to the farm that afternoon, Josephine turned to her mother with a firm directive.

"You escaped eviction this time. You'd better be careful in the future."

Phoebe walked stiffly to the house. Josephine unhitched the horse before leading him to his stall. Placing one hand on the silky neck, she slipped the other under his chin. With her head resting against his coat, she murmured into the ear of her dear old friend.

"You are a fine fellow, Johnson, kinder and more faithful than those of my own species."

As she left the barn, her feet tracked northward, seeking the place that had been a refuge so often in the past. The willow log once used as a bench had disintegrated to a crumbly pile of detritus. Planting herself amongst the reeds, she dipped her hand into the cool flow of water. Eugene had been two when he crossed the creek, stomping his feet on the log with delight. The child had now passed his ninth birthday and was halfway grown to manhood.

A horse's neighing invaded her thoughts. The sound of carriage wheels rumbled nearby. She looked up to see both the carriage and the horse standing in the road before her.

"Can you tell me where Mr. Hunter lives?" called the reinsman.

"To my knowledge, there is no one of that name in the neighborhood."

"Do you remember me?"

Josephine knew the intruder well, yet pretended to be at a loss.

"My name is Thomson. You must remember. I worked at Norris' store."

"Ah, you must be Milton. I didn't recognize you with the beard."

The gentleman nodded in amusement. "It's nice to see you, Josephine. Is your mother at home?"

She acknowledged her mother was at home. Milton continued on up the hill, turning off when he reached the driveway. He tied his horse and entered the house at Phoebe's invitation. When Josephine finally joined them they were in the midst of a lighthearted conversation. The guest stayed for supper, prolonging the visit until his presence became awkward.

When he finally left, Josephine's mother commented, "I told you years ago Milton would be a good catch. He's a wealthy man now, and Miss Uppity is peddling books." The words sputtered from a raspy voice as Josephine struggled to control her anger.

Milton returned a few days later to invite Josephine to drive out with him. "You know," he said as the carriage rolled forward, "I married just three years ago. I should have waited longer."

"To delay on my account would have been an error. I shall never marry again."

"I'm sorry for all that has befallen you, Jo, but you never know what the future will bring. I've been very prosperous. If you need help in getting settled, I could be useful."

"I've given it a great deal of thought, and my wish is to go to medical school."

Milton drew back at the announcement. "I think that would be a grave mistake. I'm prepared to stake you with $1,000 if you want to go into business."

Josephine's smile belied her thoughts: never again would any man dictate her future.

"Is Johnson still in your mother's barn?"

"Oh, yes, he is aged but doing quite well."

"Would you like to ride with me tomorrow?"

"I would enjoy that very much, but there must be a pact to avoid any discussion of my future."

"I agree, but please, don't disappear on me again."

The next day, Josephine felt the tingle of past excitement as she mounted her beloved horse. She held the Morgan to an easy pace, riding beside Milton as he reported on the circumstances of mutual friends. She informed him that she would be returning to New York within the week.

Two days later, Milton was again at the door. He made his stay brief, but on his departure she found an envelope containing ten dollars. An accompanying note requested her to use the money for stamps.

CHAPTER EIGHT

The May 4 court proceedings were still in session. The day had progressed rather oddly. While the courtroom was nearly full, both Pomeroy and Sedgwick arrived late that morning. Counselor Jones was tardy in returning from the noon recess, while Mitchell and Sedgwick had to be retrieved by the sheriff. Judge Doolittle remarked, with a quizzical smile, that his allowance for the recess might have been overly generous.

When court was gaveled back to order, Josephine walked calmly to the witness box where she continued to accommodate questions.

Pomeroy took up the fact that Thomson had approached his client shortly after her return from Europe, having done so at a time when she was sick and vulnerable and suffering from grief at the tragic loss of her children. He then asked his client about Thomson's approach.

She dabbed at her eyes and answered, testifying that Thomson told her he regretted having married. "He stated his ongoing affection, insisting that in spite of the situation he would willingly stake me in business. He wanted to be informed of my every move."

Her recitation continued. Events were reported as they had transpired over the course of many years. Letters written by Milton Thomson became a source of controversy between defense and counsel for the people.

Mr. Mitchell interrupted the questioning, stating that his client showed signs of fatigue. He had two or three more important matters to investigate, and Mrs. McCarty seemed hardly able to answer. He requested that court be adjourned.

Judge Doolittle looked at his watch and noted it was not yet 4:00.

Mitchell responded that perhaps the watch was slow.

The Judge shook his head, remarking that in the morning and at noon his watch was found to be fast. Before adjourning for the day, he alerted all present that anonymous letters had been passed to jurors. The constable had been remiss in his duties, and the Court would see him punished.

NEW YORK BRIMMED WITH POSSIBILITIES IN 1855, and Adolphus Ranney had a plum to offer Josephine. Dr. Frank Grant Johnson had designed a series of philosophical charts. He and a group of supporters, including Ranney, wanted the New York State Legislature to include the charts in the curriculum of the common school, and they needed someone to lobby the legislature. As presented, the venture had the potential to be quite lucrative. Ranney offered the position to Josephine.

"You will be compensated for your efforts regardless of the outcome. But should the bill be approved, you stand to earn substantially more. And of course, we will pay your expenses. It is imperative our agent be well positioned to entertain key officials."

She was mulling the logistics of the proposition when she emerged from the publisher's Broadway office.

"Good afternoon, Mrs. McCarty." The smooth voice drifted from beneath a graceful mustache.

"Why, Mr. Sickles, how nice to see you." Her melodious response erased the span of a long ten years.

"And where is your entourage today?"

"It is a tangled story, but I now travel singly."

Sickles digested the information with a degree of satisfaction. The lady was free? "Did you know a search is underway to discover your whereabouts?"

She looked at Daniel with some confusion.

"There is an advertisement in the *New York Herald*."

"Whatever do you mean?"

"Someone is looking for you. Information is to be sent to the office of the Thomson Insurance Agency in Utica."

Josephine's jaw dropped. "That is certainly news to me."

"It seems we have some catching up to do. Would you like to ride out with me tomorrow?"

"Indeed I would." The thrill running through her body came as a surprise. She handed him a card displaying her address.

She awaited his call in a cloud of violet silk, a wedding dress restyled. The selection was an act of defiance. In spite of having born three children, her measurements remained unchanged.

The gentleman called at 2:00, looking especially fine in a top hat and pale grey, cutaway coat. Josephine swished her tailbone to hear the silk rustle, and then she stepped through the door to raise a lace parasol. Her beauty had survived the test of time in spite of the many tragedies that followed her.

Sickles made a sweeping bow before handing her into a covered carriage. "So what were the circumstances, Mrs. McCarty, which altered your life so drastically?"

"First of all, I am once again known by my maiden name, Josephine Fagan." She summarized five years of her life with eloquent simplicity.

Sickles frowned. "My daughter, Laura, is the pride of my life. There is no limit to what I should do if anyone threatened to take her away."

She studied Daniel Edgar Sickles. He was an infamous philanderer; yet, she believed him sincere as he spoke of his child. "And what of your wife?"

The expression changed immediately. "My wife remains beyond the borders of this conversation."

"She is certainly beyond earshot, but her unseen presence sits boldly between us."

"Do you find that troubling?"

Josephine seemed fixated on the distant horizon. "I am not sure. At one time, I would have. I don't know where I stand right now."

She knew the uproar he'd caused as secretary of the United States legation in London. His young wife had been pregnant and unable to travel when he made the trip overseas. He filled the void by taking his concubine, Fanny White. The indiscretion might have been overlooked if he hadn't presented the prostitute to the Royal Court of England. Giving Fanny an alias, he'd had the gall to introduce her to Queen Victoria, a reproachful action on every front.

"So Mr. Sickles, what is your prediction for the senate race?"

A wide smile lifted the smooth canvas of her escort's face. "You're taunting me now. I am a minority, middle-of-the road Democrat. The Soft-Shell and Hard-Shell Democrats will battle the Whigs and Know-Nothings to the end. Strategy triumphs, and I've plotted my steps with care." His grin was devilish. "You do keep abreast of things, don't you?"

"Of course. Observing the machinations of politics reinforces my opinion of the citizenry in general."

He appraised the woman beside him. Her comment was caustic, her intelligence keen, yet the sweetness of temperament and ladylike demeanor created a magnificent composite of opposing characteristics. What a fool her husband must have been. The observation came to him without any thought to his own situation.

"Do you have news on my cousin Thomas?"

"He lives in a room behind the saloon, hasn't been sober in weeks. Thomas was a fine man, fearless in the defense of what he felt right. But the future looks bleak for him now."

Their drive had taken them through a large section of the city. "I see we've skirted the perimeter of the Central Park project."

The gentleman lifted his hat and laughed. "There's no fooling you. You must then be aware I convinced the city council to expand the park to seven hundred and fifty acres."

Josephine nodded. "I was, just yesterday, offered a position to lobby the state on behalf of my employer. Whether or not to accept is something I have yet to decide."

"Do it!" he crowed. "I'll be a part of the legislature soon and able to lend my support."

"Your confidence is infectious."

Sickles grinned again. "I'd like to think so."

When the carriage returned to Josephine's lodging, it was evident the excursion had fanned flames of mutual attraction. The parting left each with more questions than answers. But both were too mired in other projects to pursue the relationship further.

Adolphus Ranney looked up with pleasure as Mrs. Fagan stepped through the door. "Have you made a decision?" he asked.

"I will do it, as long as I'm free to pursue my plans for medical school."

Ranney's pleasure turned to admiration. He'd known she was bright. He had the impression she read his publication front to back. Being a medical student would make her an excellent witness to the advantages of the charts.

She took the cars up the Hudson carrying rolled copies of *Johnson's Philosophical Charts* and a well-crafted bill prepared by Ranney's lawyers. She settled herself at Congress Hall, one of Albany's most fashionable hotels.

She'd been to Albany many times, but the process of lobbying required inside information. She made an appointment with Hugh Hastings, owner and editor of Albany's *Knickerbocker News*. Hastings had an intuitive feel for the temper of the legislature. As a green-hearted Irishman and devoted Whig, the keen-eyed newsman had as much interest in Josephine as he did for the charts she was trying to sell.

His fleshy, pink cheeks widened to a grin. "Tell me, how did you become involved in the business of lobbying?"

"I am a former teacher and currently work as book agent for A. Ranney Publishing. Knowing that I will be attending medical school next month, Mr. Ranney thought me a match for the project."

She unrolled her charts, stretching them across the editor's desk. He scanned the material and nodded carefully as she answered each of his questions with patience. "Senator Wadsworth sits on the Committee on Literature. It might be beneficial to speak with him," he advised.

Josephine wrote the senator requesting an appointment and was surprised at the quickness of his reply. Determined to strike while her name remained fresh in his mind, she draped a cape over her shoulders and walked toward his office with a determined step.

Senator Wadsworth was a tall, well-built man with handsome features and a commanding presence. Hastings alleged that Wadsworth garnered great respect for his independence and strong public spirit.

"How can I help you, Mrs. Fagan?"

"I am here on behalf of Mr. Adolphus Ranney and his associates. They support the introduction of Johnson's Philosophical Charts into the common school system. Mr. Frank Johnson has developed a series of charts exhibiting diagrams, equations, and other properties of mathematics and science in a manner easily understood."

She placed the roll of charts on the senator's desk and continued her explanation. "It is an opportunity to give our school children a decided advantage in the classroom at nominal expense."

Wadsworth unrolled the drawings, inspecting them with interest before returning his gaze to Josephine. "And how do I fit into this project?"

"You are my first call, well, second, really; as mentioned in my letter, Mr. Hugh Hastings advised me to contact you. Obviously, I'm hoping to get enough interest in the bill to get it introduced in the Senate."

"Can you give me actual figures on the cost of this venture?" The senator's eyes were rimmed with kindness, but the brilliant flicker was hinged to a keen intelligence.

"The price for a set of ten charts will be twelve dollars. Each chart is guaranteed to be well mounted in a sturdy and attractive frame."

"I can get your bill through committee and report it on the floor. But first, you need someone to introduce it."

Josephine was brimming with enthusiasm.

Senator Wadsworth caught the look and hastened to set her straight. "Don't get too far ahead of yourself, young lady. Obtaining support for anything in the Senate is an uphill battle."

He might have saved his words. Josephine was ebullient. She gushed her thanks and left his office with the promise to keep him informed.

In the course of a week, she managed to meet with numerous members of the legislature, all of whom seemed amenable.

Her next stop was Harrisburg where she engaged Pennsylvania legislators in discussions about the properties and benefits of Johnson's Philosophical Charts. Her schedule was tight.

On the last Saturday of September, she appeared at the Female Medical College of Pennsylvania to begin her first term as a medical student. With her dark hair coiled beneath a starched white cap, she presented an image of eagerness and intensity.

The program required a stout constitution. Her lectures in surgery, obstetrics, physiology, anatomy, and chemistry ran Monday through Saturday from 10:00 in the morning until six at night. Patients who visited the clinic came from destitute circumstances. She witnessed and assisted in the treatment of coughs and fevers and quickly learned the process of cleansing and bandaging gangrenous sores. Thinking back to Emily Crocker, she wished she'd been familiar with these practices while treating the unfortunate principal.

Professor Ann Preston was an early graduate of the female college and carried the distinction of being the only woman on the teaching staff. She taught physiology, a subject that had sparked Josephine's interest while attending lectures in France. She thought to pattern herself after Dr. Preston, attacking each segment of study with great diligence.

She was immune to the queasiness assailing others in the operating theater. Younger women blanched to the white of their uniforms while she stood resolute. The aspects of surgery appealed to her probing mind. She followed each lecture with an examination of papier-mâché reproductions of organs.

Milton Thomson's letters appeared no less than once a week. She did her best to respond, but his avid need for details exceeded the time she had to reply. It was all she could do to keep the pot simmering in regards to Senator Wadsworth. It would work against her if the bill should come to the floor before the new session was seated. Freshman senators were freshman votes. She needed to get to Albany where she could reestablish contacts.

When the five-month program at the college closed at the end of February,

Josephine boarded the train once more. This time the cars would take her to New York. She made the transfer from train to cab and was soon on the sidewalk heading toward a pale, granite building with Doric columns. A baggage man followed with her luggage. She had once been too poor for the lowest of boarding facilities. Now, through her own hard labor, she was registering at the Astor House.

The state of her accommodations represented an overall change in her financial status. Her next order of business was to establish an account with a banking firm. She paid a visit to the offices of Livingston, Meyers & Fundley where she asked to see one of the partners, Michael Meyers, formerly of Herkimer.

A glint appeared in Michael's eye when he learned Mrs. Josephine Fagan had asked to see him. He'd been little more than a boy when he joined the crowd of Josephine suitors. It stirred him to find her as much a beauty as she'd been at their last encounter. "It's been a long time, Mrs. Fagan, but I'm pleased to know you will be banking with us."

"I didn't choose the firm. I chose you. I want all deposits and withdrawals channeled through you." She wanted a banker who would be familiar with her dealings. Michael was someone she knew and trusted. He appeared flattered at having been selected.

"You needn't come to the office to conduct your business. Send me a note when you wish to make a transaction, and I'll arrange our meeting for a location convenient to you."

In the future, banking would be conducted at the Astor House. But on this occasion she kept their meeting brief. The Johnson bill had been introduced to the Senate and was currently in the hands of the Committee on Literature. Thirty thousand dollars in potential earnings rested in the hands of Senator Wadsworth. She had to be in Albany before the bill reached a vote.

The Delavan House sat directly to the front of the rail depot. The proximity made for an easy commute, and being the most elegant hotel in the city, the Delevan was host to legislators from both the Assembly and the Senate. Josephine's reservations had been in place for weeks. Before descending the stairs to join the fray, she stood for a moment to assess the activity in the lobby. A familiar voice floated upward, and she caught a glimpse of Daniel Sickles.

He had been victorious in his campaign for senator, but his opponent's allegations of fraudulent voting left him fighting to retain the office. His prediction of a tumultuous campaign had been correct. She had no doubt the strategy he used to take the office would continue to work in his favor.

Grasping her coffee-colored skirt in one hand, she placed the other on the railing and floated to the mezzanine in grand style.

The rustle of silk turned a good many heads. Senator Sickles walked toward the staircase to meet her, encouraging his colleague to follow suit.

"Mrs. Fagan, what a nice surprise. I have someone I would like you to meet. Samuel Cuyler is a Senate freshman from the twenty-fourth district. Sam, might I introduce my friend, Mrs. Josephine Fagan."

Senator Cuyler bowed pleasantly. "Pleased to meet you, ma'am. I expect Senator Sickles knows just about everyone. He is far more experienced than I, having served the state assembly in '47 and '48. All in all, I expect we will work well together." Cuyler bowed his head and moved on.

Daniel gave her a snide grin. "It's unlikely Senator Cuyler and I will work together at all. He is a Republican, a temperance advocate, and an abolitionist. I am a hard-drinking Democrat who believes in states' rights. Then again, I am one of only four Democrats on the floor." He looked thoughtfully at the lady before him. "I note your bill on the philosophical charts is up for a third reading."

"Yes! I hope I can garner the support we need."

"Dine with me tomorrow evening. I will introduce you to some of the state's most powerful leaders."

In state legislatures throughout the country, debate focused on one important question—whether Kansas would be a free state or a protectorate of slavery. Albany followed the same pattern, except the debate came with a preamble: Have you seen the female lobbyist? She's courting votes for a bill on charts of some kind.

There was a gentleman on the fringe of the chamber who knew the lobbyist well. Alanson Jones quietly observed her deft handling of a group of polished legislators. The woman had come a long way since that sober voyage on the *Hermann*. In shedding the sadness of the past, she'd gained an electric energy that was taking Albany by storm. Dressed in a blue poplin Zouave jacket and wide, swaying skirt, she sparkled with the intensity of a gem in a room full of drab politicians.

The moment their eyes met, she turned to the desk beside her, jotted a note on her card, and had it delivered by messenger. Upon reading that she was using her maiden name, the doctor signaled approval and smiled.

They connected again at the Delavan House where she explained her interest in Johnson's charts and brought him up to date on her medical studies. The conversation was warm and pleasant—and disappointing. The doctor had hoped the door might be open for establishing a new relationship. Yet, her manner implied a staid friendship, and the door remained as tightly closed as it had in the days of the *Hermann*.

The lovely lobbyist held a series of conferences from her parlor at the hotel. The last of her guests had left the room when a knock called her back to the passageway.

"You've certainly been busy," observed a grinning Senator Sickles.

"Yes indeed, Mr. Senator."

"Tell me, did your forlorn suitor ever discover your whereabouts?"

Josephine laughed. "Yes, he did. We correspond on a regular basis."

Sickles' smile was somewhat tight. "Very good. I thought his technique quite ingenious—not very subtle, but quite ingenious."

Her face reddened as she changed the subject. "Have you any news on Cousin Thomas?"

Sickles looked stunned. "Have you not heard? Thomas passed away sometime before Christmas."

Tears flooded her eyes as she choked on the shock.

The senator extended his condolences as he guided her back to her room. Once inside, he kicked the door closed with the heel of his boot.

She felt the urgency as his breathing grew heavy: "Josephine, we are so alike. We are a match that should have been consummated years ago."

Josephine's heart thumped strangely. It had done so at every encounter she'd had with this man from the time of their very first meeting.

"I believe dear Thomas had my best interests in mind when he arranged the move to Catskill."

"Do you think he advised you wisely?"

"Probably. Had we married, which is unlikely, it would have been me waving from the dock as you sailed away with Miss Fanny. On the other hand, a brief affair would have left me shamed and forgotten." Tears came again at the thought of Thomas and the misfortune he had suffered.

"Josephine!" His kiss sent a jolt through her body as he lifted her until her feet danced in the air. And still, her composure remained intact.

He released his hold as her toes touched the floor. Her aloofness irked him. He had a knack for reading women and was not accustomed to such a cool reception.

"Is it this fellow who advertises in the newspaper? Does he satisfy you more than I?"

"I should slap you for that remark. Milton Thomson has been chasing me since I was a child of fifteen. He writes constantly and seems disturbed if he doesn't know where I am."

Were Sickles a man of different mettle, he might have cringed at her remark. After all, his Teresa was fifteen and pregnant when he'd married her. But the man lived on a plane above shame or blame or backward reflection.

He kissed her again, his lips hard against hers, and this time she was lost. Her brain ranted: *This is a mistake. Get out while you can.* But she could not quell the urge.

Conjugal relations had ended with Robert's departure in 1849. Starved for affection and sexual gratification, she responded to every nuance. Daniel treated her with tenderness and greater respect than the man who had chosen her for a wife. Latent passion had been aroused, and she gave herself with complete abandon.

When their bodies lay quiet, entwined in the darkness, she accepted the harsh reality of her station. This lover collected women as if they were charms. Over the long haul she would mean nothing. Yet, in the battle between knowledge and emotion, desire had triumphed.

Turning, she looked to him for some small response.

"Would you mind terribly if I called you Edgar? I know it's your middle name, and I find it quite charming."

He wrapped her tightly in his arms and kissed her again before answering. "You may call me anything you like. I will always answer."

For Josephine, a name change would better the situation; it would give their relationship a different twist, set her apart from his long list of women. Insane? Yes, insane. How could she abide such debasement? What would Thomas have thought? Biting her fist, she made a resolve: when the chart business was finished, she would leave Albany for good.

On March 24, 1856, Senator Wadsworth submitted Bill 279 to the Senate, authorizing the Superintendent of the Public Instruction to purchase *Johnson's Philosophical Charts* for use in the common schools of the state of New York.

The bill passed the Senate on March 31, 1856. For a time, Josephine thought Johnson's Charts would actually make it to the classroom. Then resistance from a recalcitrant Assembly spilled to the Senate. Senators who initially voted for the bill suddenly withdrew support. Josephine pushed to table the bill for further discussion, but her efforts failed and the proposal went down in defeat.

Her time at the state capital was about to end. She hoped her absence would be enough to stifle wagging tongues.

While she and Edgar met openly at political gatherings, their private trysts had been discreet. She cringed at the thought of public exposure, fully aware their relationship was both illegal and immoral. Yet, she had come to love this wily politician, and she would savor their fleeting moments together. His affairs had been numerous. If his marriage was in trouble, the blame could not be laid on her.

The dawn of their final morning peeked past the edge of a pulled shade. The wonder of their last night together warmed her body as she stretched and rolled in preparation to rising.

"Will you go directly to Philadelphia?" he asked.

"I'll make a brief stop in Augusta before moving on to Philadelphia. I will be lecturing in Pennsylvania until the new term commences. The lecture circuit is lucrative, and I won't be dependent on anyone for wages or for votes."

He stroked her chin as he digested the answer. Josephine's perfectly chiseled face and overall elegance rivaled the beauty of any women he'd ever met. She had brains and an ore at her center that could harden to steel. A bewitching lady—and he wanted more of her.

"Keep me informed as to where you will be staying." As her expression turned doubtful, he smiled. "Advertising shows a complete lack of manners, but it's obviously very effective."

The chart episode, the affair, and Sickles' tenure in office were just the beginnings of an interesting year.

Daniel Edgar Sickles drew on every resource he had to push James Buchanan up the steps to the White House. In his maneuverings for a Buchanan nomination, he set himself up to run for Congress. Though he'd spent less than a year serving the state senate, his name appeared on numerous bills and resolutions. His stock was running high.

Josephine spent the summer lecturing ladies on the connection between hygiene and health. She also covered the important subject of ways to limit one's offspring. The women were eager for knowledge and she delivered it with eloquence and wit. The proceeds of this lucrative venture were deposited with Michael Meyers in the vaulted rotunda of the Astor House.

When she returned to college that fall, Josephine was one of a handful of students given tickets to attend a lecture at Blockley Hospital. Dr. David Hayes Agnew was the disgruntled presenter, upset at the fact that females had been allowed in the hall. He refused to acknowledge the women as students, referring to them as "misguided creatures." From that point on, women at the Female Medical College were jokingly labeled Agnew's creatures.

At the culmination of the national election, Sickles celebrated Buchanan's inauguration. It was a double dose of euphoria, as Sickles would be serving as a newly minted congressman.

Milton Thomson remained in Utica writing and answering letters. Correspondence from his friend, Leyland Stanford, described the exhilaration of striking gold in California. He'd invested his proceeds in railroad stock and was well on his way to making history. Meanwhile, Milton's business continued to thrive. He had a nice wife. She held a position of prominence in local society. But somehow, the thrill of living was passing him by. He yearned for a bit of excitement.

Josephine exuded frenetic energy. The sight of her when she stepped from the train in Utica caused Milton's heart to race. She had completed her second year of college. On the walk to Bagg's Hotel, she informed him of thoughts she held on obtaining a divorce.

"I think it an excellent idea," he said, struggling to mask his pleasure. "I'll be out to the farm in a couple of days, and we'll discuss the matter further."

Josephine spent the night at Bagg's, and then took the stage coach on to Augusta. She missed the usual sighting of Robert Norris waiting as the train pulled in, but he and Eliza had moved to Indiana to be near their daughter. Change was everywhere, some of it personal, like the Norris' move, but most came in the context of political, social, or industrial developments.

While divorcing Robert would have no influence on her actions, it would legalize her independence. For once and for all, she wanted to be released from the throes of *femme couverte*.

Two days after her arrival in Augusta, Milton appeared at the door. He paid his respects to Mrs. Williams, and then he took Josephine's arm to urge her outside.

"I did some checking, Jo. You can obtain a divorce in Indiana with a six-month residence. If you left immediately, you could be back before the next term commences."

"I'm not sure about Indiana."

"I know you're worried about expenses, but one hundred dollars should help to tide you over." He took the money from his billfold.

"Oh Milton, I couldn't!"

"You can and you will."

She could and she did. Phoebe expressed surprise that her daughter would be leaving so soon. But then, she'd always been unpredictable. The astonishing issue was Mrs. Williams' acceptance of Milton Thomson, a married man, habitually visiting her daughter.

He was there again, in Utica, accompanying her to the train station where she boarded the New York Central Express. It was 5:30 in the afternoon, and she wouldn't arrive in Cincinnati until 3:30 the next afternoon.

The land flattened out before she reached Buffalo, and from there onward not a single hill came into view. As the train turned south, temperatures rose. The heat proved stifling in spite of the open windows.

Josephine had a sack of oranges and biscuits, and Maria S. Cumings' novel, *The Lamplighter*. As long as they kept the oil burning, she could read and have something to eat.

The connection in Cincinnati put her on the Ohio and Mississippi cars with a clear run into Seymour. It was a long journey. When the train finally chugged into town, she was rumpled and tired and out of sorts. Grabbing her valise, she stepped onto the siding, scanning the street for signs of a boarding house.

A good night's sleep put her in better spirits. After breakfast she walked to the post office. In a matter of minutes, she'd established a post-office box issued in the name of Josephine Fagan. Milton Thomson would be sending her letters for proof of residency. At the end of six months, she would go to the Jackson County seat to sign the proper documents.

Summer's heat had come early and the indoor temperature at the boarding house was stifling. She prayed to God it would not last.

The city was double the size of Oriskany Falls. While inhabitants were optimistic about the future of their community, Josephine's opinion of it could be summed up in three simple words: small, dull, and isolated. Her destination had been selected by Milton. He could keep tabs on her more easily if the parameters were tight.

When word spread that the visitor in town was almost a doctor, she became a popular personage in women's circles. The ladies could question her without embarrassment on subjects considered taboo with a male physician. She was back in the business of lecturing.

But the days passed slowly, and the nights even more so. Images of Edgar and the lightness of his touch were poignant memories that had her tossing and turning on hot summer nights.

She received her divorce the first week in September. The following day, her bags were hoisted aboard a train and she began the long trek back to New York State.

If she were to reach Philadelphia in time for the fall semester, her time in Augusta would of necessity be short. On arriving in Utica, she went immediately to Bagg's Hotel. Milton appeared in a matter of minutes. He must have had someone watching.

"Did you get it? Do you have the papers?" The man couldn't contain his excitement.

"Yes, Milton, would you like to see them?"

They were standing in the lobby where their interaction garnered stares.

"I'll be out to see you in a few days," he answered softly.

"No, Milton," her response came quickly. "I have to get back to Philadelphia. I made the stop in Utica in order to go to see my mother. I can't stay more than a day or two."

Milton took her remark as a rebuke. After all, he'd given her the money to go to Indiana. "I don't understand this doctor business. It was a mistake for you to leave Augusta in the first place."

Josephine's eyebrows rose. "I can tell you this, I will never go back."

It was a stiff and bristly parting.

Phoebe took the news of divorce in stride. What more could she expect from her intractable daughter?

Josephine reached Philadelphia on Friday, the twenty-ninth of September.

Lectures began the following day.

Within a week she received the following note: "I have word you are again in Philadelphia. Where have you been hiding? Would like to see you on Sunday next. ES"

The wait had been long, but the words could not have been more welcome. She scribbled a response indicating she would take the cars to Baltimore late on Saturday and register at Barnum's Hotel.

She was pacing the hotel room when a knock on the door sent a thrill coursing through her body. Telling herself the knock might not have been Edgar's, she regained her composure and gave the doorknob a twist. The grey eyes that met hers ignited an uncontrollable blaze of feeling, and the passionate lovemaking that followed was heightened by their prolonged separation.

"You know," she said in a breathless whisper, "Robert and I were husband and wife; yet, our reunion, after two long years of being apart, stirred none of the emotions I experienced tonight."

"Ours was a mating destined by gods. But as a congressman, I must be exceedingly cautious. And by the way, where have you been these past months? I'd hoped to see you at Saratoga."

"Indiana."

Edgar looked puzzled.

"I spent six months in Seymour, Indiana, just long enough to get a divorce. I'm no longer bound to any man."

Sickles laughed. "Somehow, I don't believe you ever were." Then his mood grew more serious. "The fall session has just begun and the Capitol is buzzing. I'm not sure how much time we will have together, but I promise you I'll find a way."

Twenty-four hours with Sickles could keep a woman satisfied for weeks. Josephine went back to Arch Street content with herself and the knowledge she would finish her studies by spring.

Milton wrote with regularity, and twice on trips to Philadelphia made it a point to stop by the college for a visit.

Graduation was scheduled for February 28, 1858. A week before the event, another note arrived. "I will be in Baltimore for a week beginning March 1. ES"

When lectures concluded, Josephine packed her valise and took the cars to Baltimore, registering again at Barnum's Hotel. The lovers had an entire week at their disposal; the closest they'd ever come to such an extended rendezvous had been their time at the Delavan House. Baltimore offered greater freedom; their trysts in Albany had been covered by the blanket of night.

Edger grinned above his breakfast plate: "Can you enlighten me as to what your next project will be?"

"I've completed my studies, but I need to perfect my skills. I'd hoped to enter Blockley Hospital. Unfortunately, political wrangling has upended everything at the hospital.

"A committee called the Guardians of the Poor controls the entire quadrangle of buildings: hospital, almshouse, orphanage, and insane asylum. They recently suspended all medical instruction. I was one of many who signed a petition asking the committee to reverse their decision.

"I don't know what will happen, but in the meantime, I am dependent on the ladies who attend my lectures. Starving artists are martyrs to their trade; a starving physician is a starving physician."

It was late summer when Josephine made her next visit to Augusta. Milton appeared at the door three days later with another invitation to join him on a carriage ride.

"I'm sorry, Milton, but I haven't much time. I'm leaving tomorrow to visit a friend in Oswego."

"What a coincidence. I have business in Oswego. I've put it off longer than I should. Perhaps we could ride the cars together."

Josephine fought annoyance with courtesy and acquiesced. "That will be fine. It's most pleasant that you should think of it."

The following morning, she stood with Milton waiting for the train to Syracuse. The trip involved a connecting rail to take them on to Oswego. Throughout the trip, Milton's solicitous attitude grated on her nerves. When they disembarked, Josephine's friend ran forward to meet them.

"Milton, this is my friend, Miss Sarah Stanley. Sarah was a classmate of mine at the seminary."

Milton beamed. "Do you ladies need transportation? I'm hiring a carriage and would be pleased to drop you off at your destination. Against better judgment, Josephine accepted.

When they passed through the door to Sarah's home, she let out a sigh of relief.

"Who is this Milton?" Sarah questioned.

"Don't you remember? He was the gawky boy who would visit Leland Stanford at the seminary and spend half his time hanging over my shoulder?"

Sarah's mouth fell open. "You mean he's still courting you after all these years?"

"Oh, yes. I received a letter from him shortly after I returned from Europe. And he's a married man! I'm afraid it doesn't say much for marriage vows. But quite some time ago, I came to the conclusion that marriage is only for women. Men go on as if the contract had never been made; unless, of course, the woman should transgress. Then it's another story. But please, tell me what's happening in your life."

The women spent hours catching up on each other and discussing the status of friends from the past. Sarah had been teaching, and she was highly impressed that her friend had graduated from medical school. The visit lasted five days. When they arrived at the station for Josephine's journey home, they were surprised to see Milton on the platform.

Sarah was stunned. "Jo, this doesn't seem natural," she whispered.

Josephine smiled. "Don't worry. I've known Milton most of my life. He's harmless."

The train arrived at Syracuse in late afternoon. Milton went to the ticket office to inquire on the connecting train. When he returned, a peculiar expression had taken residence on his face. "There is a problem. Our connection to Utica has been delayed. They don't expect it to arrive until eight tomorrow morning."

Josephine's agitation was undisguised. "I don't understand!"

"Don't worry. They have to do some track repairs, but this is Syracuse. I'm well acquainted with the area and familiar with hotels here. We'll spend the night and leave in the morning."

A cab dropped them off at the Globe Hotel where each registered for a room of their own. Josephine's was the larger with a parlor bedroom. She had just settled in when Milton tapped on her door. He carried a tray of refreshments and a bottle of wine.

"I don't know that this is appropriate, Milton."

"We've known each other for years. And it would be a crime to waste this tray. We are in an emergency situation. Emergencies require extraordinary measures."

"The sandwiches do look tempting. But I'm not accustomed to spirits."

"I'll pour you a glass and you can sip it at will. It's a very fine pinot noir. I think you will find it pleasing."

Though she hadn't intended to have more than sip, the delicate sandwiches were salty and she drank to quench her thirst. The refills slipped by unnoticed as Milton spoke of the past.

"What about the skating party on the Chenango Canal? You disappeared with Dewey Potter, and there was great speculation as to what you two were doing."

Josephine blinked at the remembrance. "That was such a long time ago. But I can tell you, I skated out alone. It was such a beautiful evening. I skated to the lock at the edge of town. Dewey came looking for me. He said he was worried." Her giddy laugh was a telltale sign of just how much she'd been drinking. "He couldn't understand my lack of fear. He said other girls would never go off on their own as I had."

Milton studied his companion as he continued to ply her with questions. "Why weren't you frightened?"

She chortled. "Why should I have been frightened? The ice was twelve inches thick; I couldn't pound my way through it, and there were banks on either side. I knew the town like the back of my hand. I was never in any danger." Warm and relaxed, she took a deep breath and sagged.

Milton wrapped his arms around her and began to nuzzle her neck. As he turned her head to face him, he kissed her parted lips and found them responsive.

It was well past dawn when she opened her eyes. *Thank God the drapes are closed. I don't believe I could abide the light.* Groaning, she put a hand to her head, and then suddenly shot to a sitting position. *God, oh dear God!*

Her clothes were lying on the floor. "Milton, you scoundrel! You rotten, cussed scalawag!" Lying back on the bed she cursed him with every bad word she'd ever heard. "It took fourteen years, but you finally got what you wanted."

Milton was spared her disparaging remarks. The room was empty; he'd been gone for hours.

Josephine's eyes were glued to the ceiling. *What have I become? Can I condemn the actions of one married man while sleeping with another? The more I venture toward independence, the more I find myself entrapped.*

It came to her as she considered the situation that Milton hadn't the imagination to orchestrate such a seduction. She wouldn't put it past Mortimer. Devious schemes were his specialty. Milton's brother would have delighted in planning the previous evening's scenario.

There was a light knock on the door. "Mrs. Fagan, you must hurry along or you will miss the train."

My God, she thought; hadn't she heard similar words the morning that followed her wedding night? Robert had ravaged her, and when it was over it was time to move on. The male gender had no conscience.

She dressed hurriedly, but a stoic presence had taken hold by the time she reached the lobby.

"Did you sleep well?" Milton's cheek fattened with the hint of a smile.

"Of course I slept. I was barely conscious."

Her companion smiled more broadly. "It's a little late for breakfast."

"It's a little late for a lot of things. My stomach is in rebellion."

Milton called a hack with instructions to get them to the station as quickly as possible. When they were comfortably seated in the cab, he looked at his companion adoringly. "It was wonderful, wasn't it?"

"How am I to remember? You put me in a stupor, and then you satisfied yourself."

"Please don't be angry. I've loved you for such a long time. I promise you will be as my wife forever."

Not quite, she thought, *as*—not *is*—being the key designation. It didn't escape her that he'd waited until they were enclosed in the cab before stating his devotion.

"By the way," he said as an after-thought, "From now on, I will be signing my letters with the pseudonym A.C. King."

Nausea gripped Josephine's innards. The only thing separating her from the women she once despised was the fact that she was self-sufficient.

CHAPTER NINE

A t the close of the May 4 proceedings, Josephine returned to her cell where the boys pushed and shoved in their effort to reach her. Juddie coughed repeatedly as he sought his mother's hand. She opened a window to increase ventilation before scooping him into her lap. Her eyes closed as she thought of Josie. As bad as prison might be for the boys, it was certainly no place for a little girl.

Then she envisioned the environment that had been home to so many of her patients at Blockley.

JOSEPHINE'S TENURE AT BLOCKLEY HOSPITAL began in August of 1858. The upheaval of the previous year had finally been settled.

The issue that created the problem had been the Guardian's decision to transfer the chief resident position from Dr. Robert K. Smith to Dr. James McClintock. McClintock had allegedly been expelled from the American Medical Association for copying prescriptions and selling the list of ingredients to individuals who would pestle them under McClintock's name.

Incensed that this renegade physician had been awarded the chief position, Blockley's visiting doctors resigned, resident physicians walked out, and medical instruction ceased.

The standoff ended with Dr. Smith's reinstatement, and Josephine entered the hospital to perfect her skills. The hospital held over three hundred and fifty patients, all indigent of Philadelphia's ghetto. Josephine's assistant was also her roommate and one of the few to appreciate her diligent efforts. Men dominated the medical profession. Throughout the hospital, it was her beauty, not her skill, which captured attention.

Dr. Smith was different. As a dedicated administrator, he kept careful watch over resident physicians, mindful that long hours could induce stress with tragic results. Josephine was in the nursery when the chief resident first approached her.

"Good afternoon, Dr. Fagan. It seems obstetrics are of special interest to you."

"That's true," she answered pleasantly. "It's something I'm familiar with on a personal basis."

"Do you have children?" he asked.

"Yes. It's a long story, but I haven't seen them for quite some time. I'm arranging for the adoption of a baby born here at Blockley. The mother has no means of support. The birth was difficult and the child's condition is critical. I don't know that she will survive; nonetheless, I've named her Angeline."

"I wish you the best of luck." A lock of sandy hair fell over the doctor's glasses, covering a deeply furrowed brow. Then a smile brightened his clean-shaven face, belying the weight of responsibility. "Keep me posted. And by the way, I find your work exemplary."

Two weeks later, baby Angeline died. She was buried in an unmarked grave with Josephine the only person to grieve her. *It's not fair* screamed the thoughts wracking her brain. *There are women at Blockley who never should have a child. Yet, destiny, in the form of Robert, has robbed me of a precious brood.* It seemed she would never again hold a child of her own.

In November, Sickles was elected to a second term as congressman and was promptly appointed to the prestigious Committee on Foreign Affairs.

The note came in late December. Edgar wanted to meet her in Baltimore. Josephine agonized over her response. She loved the man, in spite of his reputation, and had been willing to give herself solely to him. The dynamics had changed with the Thomson seduction.

In a foolish mental game, she derided herself for being unfaithful. The Syracuse episode had damaged her self-esteem. Could she meet Edgar without guilt? Should she confess her night with Milton?

She carried the note in her pocket throughout the day. Her thigh burned when she climbed into bed. The spot where the note had rested felt sore. Heat from the site crept upward until her body was afire. Her need for Sickles was greater than his for her, and she would not be denied the pleasure of another encounter.

She dashed her response first thing the next morning. "My darling Edgar, I will be waiting at Barnum's when you arrive." Her lips caressed the paper before she attached the seal.

They would have but one night together; yet, Josephine's guilt continued to nag her. They were dining in their room when she decided to raise the troubling subject.

"Remember the man who placed the ad in the paper in an effort to discover my whereabouts?" She nervously played with the food on her plate. "He pursues me still."

Her tone and anxious attitude gave Edgar reason to wonder. He leveled his eyes to hers. "Josephine, our relationship is a difficult one. I do not give or ask for promises and cannot expect you to wait on my calls. You have a life to live and I want you to live it to the fullest. What we have is ours to enjoy as fate permits. Whatever the outcome, I treasure your love and hope you are satisfied with what I can give in return."

Perhaps that was the draw binding her to Edgar. Other men subjected her to castigation without any apologies for the promises they broke. She wrapped her arms around her congressman, and their intimacy took the path of reconciling lovers, though no dissention had occurred.

A month later, Josephine felt ill and soon discovered she was pregnant. She thought, *My God, it has happened; I will have a child, and the child will be mine and mine alone.* She wrapped her arms about herself, breathing deeply to quell the rolling of her stomach.

She sent a note asking Edgar to meet with her as soon as he could wrench himself free.

Sickles read her request in surprise. She was not a woman to trouble him unnecessarily.

When she opened the door to her room at Barnum's, she was glowing with happiness. Edgar stepped back, aware of the change.

"You are positively radiant. Tell me what has happened to put you in such good spirits."

"I am pregnant with your child." Hurrying her words, she was eager to reassure him that she had no ulterior motive in issuing the statement. "Oh, Edgar, I am happy. You've given me the greatest of gifts." With that remark, tears came to her eyes.

"You are not upset or angry?"

She shook her head. "No. Robert stole the other children. Now I shall have one of my own. I expect nothing of you, except to hope that you are happy too."

"You know it is your reputation that I seek to protect. My infamy goes back to the days at Glens Falls Academy." He approached to put a hand on her stomach. "It will be a handsome child, fortunate to have such an extraordinary mother."

They loved each other and expressed it without restraint.

Unfortunately, Josephine was often ill. She did her best to hide the problem, but the long hours were taking a toll. Dr. Smith summoned her to his office.

"Dr. Fagan, you have not looked well of late. I'm not inquiring into your condition as chief resident, but I am sorely worried. Is there anything I can do for you?"

Under ordinary circumstances, the question would have been dealt with lightly, but her hormones were in flux.

"There is absolutely nothing wrong." Her face reddened before blanching to a faint.

When she awoke, Dr. Smith was standing over her. "Doctor, are you pregnant?"

"Whatever makes you suspect such a thing?"

"You must understand; resident physicians are expected to be examples of good health. You must take care of yourself, and you must see a doctor."

"I can't see anyone here."

"Is the father someone attached to the hospital?"

"I never told you I was pregnant."

"I will see that your hours are shortened. Please get some rest."

With that, the interview was over. Her hours were shortened, and gossip began to circulate that she was receiving favoritism. As soon as the morning sickness abated, she returned to a full schedule of work.

On February 29, 1859, she was arriving at work when the desk receptionist called to her.

"Have you seen the *Philadelphia Inquirer*?"

She shook her head, and the woman's eyes brightened. This was her chance to pass a bit of juicy gossip. "It's the biggest story in the District of Columbia. Congressman Sickles has killed Phil Barton Key. He is now in jail and will be tried for murder!"

Josephine fell to a dead faint.

She awoke in her room with Dr. Smith and the receptionist observing from the side of her bed. Smith asked the woman to leave them alone. As soon as she was out of earshot, he confronted Josephine with a series of questions. "What happened? Have you seen a doctor? Are you getting enough sleep?"

She summoned a weak smile. "I fainted; I've seen you; and I'm sleeping just fine."

"I want you to stay in bed. We'll discuss your duties tomorrow."

With Dr. Smith's departure, Josephine took a deep breath and tried to retrieve the conversation she had been having prior to losing consciousness. *Edgar murdered someone?* She had to get a copy of that newspaper. She climbed from her bed, inched down the stairs, and approached the front desk with dread.

"Helen, do you, by chance, have a copy of the morning paper?"

"I do, Doctor. Would you like to see it?"

She thought no; the last thing she wanted was to read the fearful words; yet her reply came in the affirmative.

It took a great deal of effort to walk to the window with a semblance of calm. She settled herself on a chair and allowed her eyes to drift toward the *Inquirer*. The newspaper rattled in her trembling hands, its bold headlines jolting her backward. She scanned the article quickly. The description was ghastly. In a screeching rage, Edgar had advanced on Key as he stood in the street just yards from the Sickles' home. The congressman fired multiple shots, fatally wounding his wife's pleading lover. When bystanders prevented him from shooting again, he pulled free of their grasp and walked away, leaving the dying man slumped on the sidewalk. The incident had taken place in full view of passersby who were returning from services at St. John's Church.

Tears ran rivulets down Josephine's cheeks, puddling on the printer's catastrophic words. She pressed a hand against her lips to keep from spewing grief. If Edgar were convicted, he would be hanged. A chill struck her body. She ignored the newspaper as it dropped to the floor and crept to her room to slip under the covers. A host of conflicting thoughts ran through her mind as shock wracked her body with violent tremors.

Had Teresa Sickles sought vengeance on Edgar's paramours, she, herself, might have been the victim. But such behavior would be unlikely. In a strange twist of ethics, a husband's infidelity was expected behavior. Had Edgar killed Key in a gentlemanly duel there would have been no call of murder. The death would have been given a legal "pass." She was bothered by the fact that her own actions indicated approval of this corrupt moral code.

Though hollow-eyed and pale, she rose the next morning and donned her uniform for another day at Blockley.

Her fastidious Edgar sat in a D.C. jail. Having declined special treatment of any kind, he accepted the vermin-infested cell assigned to common criminals. After four days of bedbugs and foul air, he changed his mind and gratefully took to new quarters.

Lawyers James T. Brady, John Graham, and Thomas Francis Meagher, all of New York, were at his side and ready to work on his defense. Phil Barton Key had been United States Attorney for the District of Columbia and was the handsome son of Francis Scott Key, author of "The Star

Spangled Banner." No trial could gain more publicity than that of the murder in Lafayette Square.

Brady held a private interview with his friend. "Are there any women who might stir up interest should the press gain knowledge of their whereabouts?"

Sickles' mouth drew a grim line. "At the moment, there is one, a doctor in Philadelphia who is carrying my child. I guarantee she will never come forward on her own."

Brady didn't turn a hair. Men, especially the wealthy ones, had illicit relationships all the time. But this one needed to be hidden.

Samuel Butterworth had been with Sickles at the time of the shooting. It was suspected that he willingly detained Key until Sickles reached the street. In defense of himself, he provided a statement of innocence documenting his actions the morning of the crime. His statement failed to reassure the defense. They were convinced that his disappearance would, at the very least, delay further questioning.

It was decided that Butterworth should go to Philadelphia. No one else could be trusted with the errand. He would contact Josephine Fagan and insist that she leave the hospital. It was also to be suggested that she take an alias at her new location. Once the arrangements were made, Butterworth was to take a lengthy vacation somewhere between the Mississippi and the Pacific Ocean.

Feeling foolish in a stealthy disguise, Butterworth traveled to Blockley where he requested an interview with Dr. Fagan. When she arrived, he insisted on finding a private alcove where conversation could flow without interruption. Josephine suspected the visit might in some way be connected to Edgar, and she quietly complied.

"The defense considers it imperative that you leave the hospital and change your name. It could sway the jury in the wrong direction if your relationship with the congressman were to be revealed."

Josephine was aghast. She'd gone through hell in the days since the shooting. Her health was poor, and in her condition she couldn't possibly go home. The two of them sat in consternation. Uneasy with the whole situation, Butterworth regarded Dr. Fagan with empathy. Would it help if he told her that he was also being banished?

She pondered the issue for several minutes. "It won't be that difficult," she finally concluded. "I have given public lectures, but am not well known amongst the general population. With a change of name and residence, it is doubtful that anyone should find me. I'll write an advertisement for the newspaper stating that I am a single woman looking for a room where a friend may call."

Butterworth looked askance.

"I am carrying a child; I may need a doctor. But we must be discreet in every action."

Butterworth looked relieved, but Josephine wasn't finished. "There's just one thing. Will you post the advertisement for me? I'll have responses sent to a post-office box, but it will be best if I keep my description hidden from the newspaper."

Butterfield agreed. Dr. Fagan was obviously a bright and accomplished woman. How she managed to get involved in such a dreadful mess was something he could not understand. Had he given it further consideration, the dawn of injustice might have ignited his mind.

Josephine took a room on Sansom Street run by a woman named Price. She was transporting her trunk on a cart when the police wagon stopped beside her.

"You're Fagan, aren't you?"

Her heart stopped as she stood dumbfounded before the accusing officers.

"I asked," said the heavy, red-faced policeman, "if your name is Fagan."

As they continued to prod her, she found her tongue. "I don't understand?"

"It's fairly simple, lady. If your name is Fagan, there's a charge of larceny against you. Open your trunk."

She stepped back without speaking as the trunk was searched. The police ruffled through her nightdresses and withdrew a couple of anatomical plates.

"You are under arrest."

They pulled her into the wagon, tied her trunk on behind, and drove immediately to a judge who filed the charge against her. In the course of an hour, she was remanded to Moyamensing Prison until such time as her bail should be paid.

She grabbed the bars on the window of her cell, wondering at the charges. She had stolen nothing. It was all a mystery. She had no idea how the plates had gotten into her trunk. The clothes were rightfully hers. There seemed no connection to Edgar, unless it was a trumped-up charge to get her out of the way.

Mother, father, and baby all in jail. What a fix!

It came as still another surprise when the jailer unlocked her cell, announcing an immediate release. Her reaction grew to amazement when she found Dr. Smith waiting on the steps in front of the jail.

"Josephine, I can't keep up with you. But what happened here was not your fault. Politics run the hospital, and as is always the case in politics, the loser is likely to hold a grudge. Gossip has linked us together. You were charged as a way to get back at me. I read of your arrest in the evening newspaper. The article fits the definition of libel. I came right away knowing something untoward had transpired. But how is it that you have been released?"

"I have no idea. When I saw you waiting, I just assumed you had paid my bond."

"I wish I could take credit. I'm terribly sorry about the whole affair. Please tell me, is there anything I can do to make it up to you?"

"Get me away from here."

Once in his carriage, he asked for a destination.

"I have a room on Sansom Street, between 12th and 13th. I gave my name as Emma Burleigh, my mother's maiden name. The incident was in the newspaper?"

"Yes."

"They mentioned me by name?

"Yes. Josephine Fagan."

Tired and weary, she mumbled her state of confusion. "I don't know if I'm coming or going."

Smith handed her twenty-four dollars.

"What is this?

"You've been on the payroll for the last two months. This is money the hospital owes you."

She was determined to hold her tears. It seemed she'd become quite a crybaby over the past few years. "I don't know what I would have done without you. I don't know what I shall do without you."

"I assume there is a problem with your health."

Smith got a nod for an answer.

"I promise to attend you if it is in any way possible."

Josephine smiled grimly. "I've already tarnished my own reputation by taking a room on the condition that I entertain a friend. You had better change your name if you choose to visit."

"You're doing well to keep your sense of humor."

The statement was not a joke. Retaining a sense of humor can only go so far. Though the charges in the article were beyond ridiculous, she found it impossible to laugh. In addition to accusations of peculation, she had been called a sultana around whom all male hospital personnel revolved.

Dr. Smith brought a suit of libel against the newspaper as the charges involved the hospital. Bail was posted and the editor returned to his office to find a seething Josephine waiting at the door.

"The charges in your paper were false. By publishing that story you have tarnished my good name."

At the editor's snort, Josephine raised her arm and, using a crop, lashed the man twice across the face. Her dexterity with a rawhide did nothing to clear her name. The entire episode was reported in the next day's paper.

Harm was done on all sides, as the editor got eighteen months in Montgomery Prison.

The Sickles' trial commenced April 4, 1859. It was a circus environment in a dingy courtroom heavily laden with reporters. Josephine followed the proceeding in the newspapers. A cartoonist's drawing had Edgar praying in his cell, eyes gazing toward heaven.

Edwin Stanton joined the defense. He and Sickles shared a friendship with President Buchanan. As a powerful orator and a respected member of the Washington bar, Stanton—with a trio of lawyers beside him—far outweighed prosecutor Robert Ould.

Ould had been Key's assistant, and, upon Key's death, he was elevated, on the directive of President Buchanan, to District Attorney of the District of Columbia. His job was to combat the defense that Daniel Edgar Sickles suffered from temporary insanity on the occasion of the shooting. It was the first such defense in the history of the country.

Newspapers increased their circulation. America's readers sought knowledge of every salacious tidbit.

Josephine's skin went clammy as rumors circulated that Sickles had been involved with a woman from Philadelphia. Word had it that he and this woman enjoyed trysts at Barnum's Hotel in Baltimore. How could they know? What did they know; and would they find her? The newspapers would certainly try. Their slogan against the defense followed an old cliché: what's good for the goose is good for the gander. And there were those who would see her lover hang.

She kept to herself as much as possible. Dr. Smith made periodic visits to monitor her health. Though obviously concerned, he politely refrained from asking questions.

With the prowess of his defense, Edgar was acquitted on April 26, 1859. After twenty-two days of testimony, the verdict was met with cheers in a courtroom packed to the rafters with spectators and newsmen. Josephine sighed in relieve. It was finally over.

Of course it wasn't; Sickles' political career had been shattered, and public support would dissipate, leaving him open to ridicule and disgust. Surprisingly, the issue that riled people most was not his shooting of Phil Barton Key but his refusal to divorce a cheating wife. He went so far as to insist that she remain in his home.

What annoyed others pleased Josephine. Where Edgar had failed in his vow of fidelity, he had honored the pledge to care for his wife.

The month of May put Josephine well along in her pregnancy. She was naturally slim, and the constant stress had kept her from gaining any noticeable weight. To be on the safe side, she selected clothing to hide a slightly bulging belly.

Residents of the Price house were an unsavory group. Without a doubt, they scrutinized her every move. She was taking a dinner plate back to her room when a heavily bearded man with wild hair and bloodshot eyes stepped to block the way.

"What's the matter? You too good to sit with the rest of us?"

"Excuse me," she answered. "But the quiet of my room allows me to read while dining. Please let me pass."

"Not this time, girlie. You're no better than the rest of us. You got a muffin in that oven of yours and you're tryin' ta hide it." He laughed gruffly. "I bet the bastard's daddy is some big mucky-muck." He reached for her chin. "I'm right, little girlie, ain't I?"

Josephine flew backward and in a flash had a dirk gripped in her hand. The bully backed off. His jaw had dropped and his face was paper white.

The daggers in Josephine's eyes matched the weapon in her hand. "Don't you touch me! If ever you do, I will slit your gullet side-to-side."

Chairs overturned as guests at the table scattered. Mrs. Price ran into the room. Two of her children raced forward to see what had happened.

"What is the meaning of this," she screamed. "I won't have weapons in my house."

"If you can't protect me from the likes of this, I shall have to do it myself." Josephine pointed the dirk at the man opposite her. "Remember, if you ever come near me, if ever I hear you spreading stories, your life won't be worth a rotting handkerchief."

She went to her room, sat on the bed, and shook. She had less than four months to go. If she could deliver her baby at Price's, she would leave the following day and take up residence elsewhere. At that point, she could explain the child as being adopted. Tears welled in her eyes as she placed her arms protectively across her stomach.

When Dr. Smith came by the next morning, she told of her experience the night before.

"You must get out of here before you come to harm."

She smiled dubiously. "I doubt I have much to worry about now. They all think I am mad. I'm watching the advertisements for rooms to rent. I will leave when the child rests in my arms. It won't be much longer."

"You need to deliver in a hospital," he said flatly.

"You know that isn't possible. Everyone in the place knows who I am. They will immediately conclude the child is yours."

"I want to assist you, but how will I know when to come? There has to be a better way."

"I bore the other children in my own bed without a doctor present. If need be, I can do so again."

"This is the first time you've ever admitted to being pregnant."

She lifted an eyebrow and responded slyly. "I never mentioned the word pregnant."

Dr. Smith looked dismal. "When it gets close to your time, I will make a habit of stopping more frequently. It's probably the best I can do."

Josephine perspired through the hot months of June and July. The third week in September, she noted an advertisement for a room to be let on Filbert Street. When Dr. Smith came to visit, she asked if he would lease the room in her name, telling the landlord that she was his sister and would arrive in the city within the week.

The doctor looked overwhelmed. "Do you really think you are but a week away from birthing?"

She gave him a look of contentment. "It has been a long journey. All will be well, and it will be very soon."

She was alone when she went into labor. Her bed was spread with the clean white clothes she had set aside. There were two pails of cold water beside the bed and the water in her basin was warm. She remained on her feet as long as she could, then shedding all but her camisole, eased herself down onto the bed. Reaching backward, she took hold of the headboard and clamped her teeth on a dampened towel.

Dr. Smith arrived early that evening. Knocking softly, he announced his identity. When she called for him to enter, he opened the door to halt in shock. The new mother put a finger to her lips to hush his exclamation. The baby in her arms slept peacefully. Smith closed the door silently and continued to stare.

"Isn't he beautiful?" she asked. The softness in her voice came in part from fatigue. The birth had gone well; the clean-up had been exhausting.

"How did you do this?"

She laughed ruefully. "Women have been giving birth since the origins of the race. I've done nothing spectacular. Besides, I am a doctor."

"I find you beyond belief."

"Well, it would be better if you could tell me you had found the room on Filbert Street."

"I did." The doctor looked down to check a note. "The place is run by Germans. Their English is very poor. I told them my sister would be coming and gave your name as Emma Burleigh."

"Well done, Doctor. Do you think you can help me move tomorrow? A single trunk is all I have left."

The doctor assented, and she gave him a cloth folded over into many layers. "I'd appreciate it if you could dispose of this for me."

Smith gazed at the package. "What is it?"

"The placenta. I want no evidence of birth at this boarding house."

The next day, baby Louis was wrapped in a blanket and placed in a valise. His mother settled his needs before he had a chance to cry, and they left the Price house without anyone the wiser.

The doctor helped them down from his carriage when they reached Filbert Street. The door to the rooming house opened and a short, round-bellied woman appeared.

"Come in, come in!" Looking down on Louis, she began to coo. "Eez so tiny. Eez newborn?"

For the first time in a long time, Josephine was relaxed and at ease. "Yes, indeed. His mother died in childbirth, and I rushed to Philadelphia to adopt him. I would have been here sooner but was, unfortunately, delayed."

"Ohh," said the little German. "Dat ez so sad, but ez good you could come."

The fact that residents of the house spoke German made it easy for Josephine to avoid conversation. She renewed her habit of long walks, and for the next three months mother and child bonded in peace. The only break to their routine came with rare but welcome visits from Dr. Smith.

She mulled her options carefully before deciding that it would be best to leave the area, at least for a while. With her education and lecturing experience, she felt well equipped to support herself. One question remained: where to go? She made a decision and packed her bags. Dr. Smith was the only friend on hand as she climbed the steps of a railcar heading west.

Louis rested in the fold of her arms as city turned to country and then to a forest wilderness. A sense of anticipation had risen within her. This trip would acquaint her with some of the greatest engineering marvels of the day. The Baltimore and Ohio Railroad had cut its way across the state of Pennsylvania through a series of bridges and tunnels until it reached Wheeling, Virginia, where a suspension bridge provided travelers a means to cross over the Ohio River.

When the train made its final stop, she exited the car and was stopped by the shadow that fell over her. The suspension bridge towered above the city. Its massive stone anchorage stretched skyward, leaving one to think the whole assemblage a monument to the gods. It was the longest suspension bridge in the world, but the drawings she'd seen had not done it justice.

She'd sailed the ocean, walked London Bridge, and stood at the pinnacle of the Mountain House. Now the urge to walk across the bridge and trap its vibrations in the soles of her shoes was almost irresistible. But her breath spewed a cloud of icy mist. She was well aware of the dangers in that cold winter wind.

She adjusted the blanket swaddling Louis and signaled a cab. They rolled over the bridge and stopped at the depot on the Ohio side. From the onset, her destination had been Cincinnati. The city was a thriving metropolis on the edge of the undeveloped west, an ideal location for a woman seeking anonymity.

For several months, she lectured under the name of Emma Burleigh. The sessions centered on diseases of women and children and were often attended by those involved in the feminist movement. The desperate and destitute called between lectures. Then a backlash against her feminist followers prompted demonstrations that interrupted her lectures. With a sigh, she packed and moved on to Missouri.

The bustling activity of St. Louis rivaled the action she'd witnessed in Cincinnati. An advertisement in the daily newspaper announced the opening of her medical practice. Her bank account grew in proportion to her practice. She could care for Louis without help from anyone.

"Just think, my darling baby, you are now in a city that carries your name. Don't you find the coincidence appealing?"

Louis chirped an unintelligible response.

Milton's letters had followed her. She decided to update him on the success of her venture and relate the news of having adopted a child. She pursed her lips at the last thought. No one would ever know the truth about Louis. Sitting at her desk, she wondered at being so tired. It had been a busy but not overtaxing morning. She'd treated one woman suffering from hemorrhages and another with an extended uterus. The sun poured through the window, blinding her attempt to pick up a pen. The pain came swiftly, paralyzing her hand. Ink splattered the paper as her pen fell to the floor.

Josephine had been plagued with headaches since England, but this one left her sprawled on the desk unable to lift her head. She put her hands to her ears to stop the ringing, but the vibration only intensified. The syndrome expanded into acute sensitivity, magnifying sound to the point that she could hear through walls.

She took to her bed trying desperately to smother the sound. Yet her actions failed to still the ringing. When she recovered enough to walk, she sought the opinions of other doctors. While several physicians conferred on the nature of her problem, there was no consensus on a diagnosis. Hyperacusis had yet to be fully understood. She was given powders to treat the headache, encouraged to remain quiet, and advised to curb all daily activity.

Rest was impossible. The states' rights argument had exploded. Violence erupted with regularity in what had once been peaceful neighborhoods, and the noise of angry demonstrations penetrated windows and doors.

Abraham Lincoln's election to the presidency did nothing to quell the tide. Before his inauguration could take place, South Carolina seceded from the Union, Fort Moultrie was seized, and Fort Sumter threatened. Just days after the president took his oath of office, South Carolina fired on Sumter, initiating the War Between the States.

As a border state, Missouri provided men and supplies to both sides of the rebellion. Fighting raged without letup in cities and towns throughout the state, with brother against brother and friend against friend. The arguments reverberated in Josephine's tortured brain. By summer, it became clear that she needed to remove herself to the quiet environment of Augusta.

The tiring train rides heightened her longing for the farm's cooling breezes. The clean white buildings were a welcome sight as a hired rig climbed the hill and passed over her little stream. Seth Mayo was the latest farmer to work the land; the fields appeared well tended.

But all was not peaceful in Josephine's hometown. The penchant for gossip flourished. Her appearance with a small child and no husband added spice to the web of rumors. Neighbors refused to accept her explanation of adoption, in spite of the fact that no one could disprove the story.

Far too young to understand the surrounding atmosphere, little Louis splashed and laughed and soaked his mother as he played in the stream at the lookout point. Old Johnson was gone. A mule had become the beast of burden, and his coat tickled the toddler as his mother led them around the yard. It might have been a pleasant summer if not for the animosity of Grandmother Williams.

Phoebe had always been cool toward her grandchildren. Louis was subjected to open disdain. The very notion that Josephine could have delivered a bastard filled her with shame and anger. The boy's blond curls and bright little eyes failed to penetrate the wall she'd erected.

Her disagreeable personality deepened into bitterness. A forced annulment had ended her teenage marriage to Hastings, and their baby had been put out for adoption. It seemed propriety was only relevant when applied to her. Now the firm lip, the imbedded frown, and the dreary calico dress were visible signs of mental turmoil. The old woman was devoid of joy.

When Milton Thomson made his customary visits, Phoebe turned from his company in shame. Perhaps realization had come to her that Milton might father a child out of wedlock. Her rejection was ignored.

If anything, Milton's advances increased. He would send a horse from Butterfield's Livery, enabling Josephine to join him in a secret assignation. They rode side-by-side through the hills and gorges, their conversations inevitably falling to politics. Milton craved intimacy with this dark-haired firecracker from the days of clerking at Norris' store; yet, his efforts to gain favor habitually failed, thwarted by his own ineptitude.

He was immensely proud of his friend, Leland Stanford, who'd been elected governor of California, the first Republican ever to attain the seat. And Milton supported Lincoln's defense of the Union, though he wanted no part of the fighting. Owning no stake in the rebellion, he thought one a fool to run off with a gun. The true cost of battle had been evident at Bull Run where casualties ran into the thousands. He wouldn't play the fool, but he'd gladly sell insurance to those who did.

Boasting about his profits and status with the world's mighty brokers made no impression on Josephine. She grated at his overall attitude. With friends on both sides of the conflict, she took the suffering and loss of the war personally. Daniel Sickles was hustling to muster a regiment out of New York City. Archbishop Hughes was touring Europe as a personal envoy of President Lincoln, an extremely difficult task considering the history of commerce between the Confederate States and Europe. If an aged priest could contend with such a grueling assignment, others should do the same.

Her headaches had subsided. The remarkable sharpness in hearing was under control. As a doctor, she had training that might be of service on the battlefield. She dashed off a letter to Dorothea Dix and announced her plans to move to Washington.

Milton's frustration increased. He wanted to follow up on the romantic ties he'd sought to establish in Syracuse. His first line of thought was to see her off at the Utica depot, but he quickly realized it would be a better choice to ride with her to Albany. He took a seat opposite his desired paramour, assessing her attributes as a connoisseur might examine a work of art.

The arrangement in seating worked from both directions. Josephine cuddled her son as she did an appraisal of her own. Milton had gained a good deal of weight since their first meeting at Norris' store. The weight sat well on him; most would find him handsome. Yet, the aura of self-importance hid an underlying weakness. She noted the affected gesture as he crossed his legs and flicked ash from the end of a fat cigar.

When they reached the capitol, Milton took a commanding hold of Josephine's arm, escorting her to Stanwix Hall where he used the situation to extend his sexual overtures. Circumstances of the past few years had dispelled Josephine's youthful inhibitions. She acquiesced to his advances in mechanical motion. He wasn't Edgar. He didn't have Edgar's gentle touch or innate sensitivity; however, there was little chance she would ever thrill to those touches again.

The following morning, professing a matter of unfinished business, Milton boarded the train and trailed her through to New York. In New York it was the Brandreth House. He registered for separate rooms, and then he promptly moved in with Josephine. As Louis slumbered, Milton's hands were roaming his mother's body. The room registry fooled no one. The staff had seen it all before. But Milton intended to go one step further, accompanying his amoret on to Philadelphia

They were at the Perth Amboy ferry dock waiting to cross to New Jersey. A large group of people crowded the dock and an elderly gentleman bumped elbows with Milton.

"This is a busy place, but I never expected to run into you, Mr. Thomson. How is it you've come so far from home and with such a lovely lady?"

"Mrs. Burleigh, may I introduce you to Mr. Churchill."

"Pleased to make your acquaintance, madam."

Josephine made an effort to be charming but her tone was cold. "Will you be traveling to Perth Amboy as well?"

"I will indeed."

Mr. Churchill had removed his hat and was bowing as Milton's hand waved frantically from behind the stooping back. At first opportunity he leaned into her and whispered, "I won't accompany you any further. The man is from Utica and a consummate gossip. He is the last person I would want to have seen us."

Milton had been at ease as he drove to the Williams place, but that was in the country where he couldn't be seen. His reaction at meeting Churchill painted a picture of hypocrisy.

Remaining aloof, he offered nothing more than a casual wave as the ferry took Josephine and her child downriver. As a sharp wind rocked the ferry, she used the occasion to shelter Louis further. The action was taken not to defend the child from the wind but rather from the cold and penetrating eyes of Churchill.

Washington and Philadelphia would be tricky places with a small child. She had no credentials, and with habeas corpus suspended in Washington, she could be arrested and jailed without trial. Warned by her experience in Philadelphia, she sought a safer haven for Louis.

Kitty Murtaugh was now Kitty Muldoon, married and living on a farm just beyond Perth Amboy. Her response to Josephine's letter had been yes. She would care for Louis as long as need be. Remembering her mistress' sorrow at the loss of the McCarty children, she took the responsibility to be a solemn trust.

Kitty's hulking Irish husband, Sean, answered Josephine's knock with a convivial sweep of his arm.

"Lordy, ma'am." Kitty rushed forward at the sound of Josephine's voice. Tears seeped from the corner of her brilliant blue eyes. "I've longed so to see you. An' the wee one! Isn't he somethin'?"

While Josephine enjoyed their reunion, the separation from Louis was hard on her mind. He trusted her. His security and comfort were her responsibility. How could she tell him that he would be left behind?

The issue became moot. Kitty had to pry the boy from Sean's shoulders to get him to say good-bye. "Now give your mum a kiss."

Louis laughed delightedly as Sean swung him towards his mother and quickly swung him back.

Josephine closed her eyes for a second as relief replaced her qualms. The boy would be fine with this loving couple. Whatever should come, she knew he was safe. "I'll be back, little Louis. I promise. Dear, dear baby, I do love you so. But we are on our own, us two, and Mommy must see that we survive."

Kitty swiped at another tear as Josephine slipped past and closed the door.

CHAPTER TEN

When Court convened on May 6, about a third of the courtroom was filled. Prior to their cross-examination, counsel for the people held a brief consultation. They began their questioning with a review of previous statements, and then quickly jumped to a letter written by Josephine. This correspondence was penned in answer to the Thomson letter read earlier by the defense. As a mark of reference, the Thomson letter bore a date of April 24, 1845.

St. Johns, May 8, 1845

Friend Thomson: Your unlooked for letter was read with much pleasure, not only that it reminded me of friends unforgotten, but somewhat dim in memory's eye, was it welcome, but it apprised me of the convalescence of one I feared had already suffered beyond recovery. It is a fearful malady that of political disappointment and mortification and in extreme cases a hopeless one. You, however, are young, and probably repeated attacks have not yet ruined or impaired your constitution. Believe me, you have my warmest wishes for your entire recovery, and accumulation of strength sufficient to meet unharmed a similar disappointment.

Do you think it possible I could forget "ould" Augusta friends? I assure you I have made acquaintances in that town I can never cease to remember with feeling of satisfaction and pleasure. Although my lot may and I sincerely trust will not be cast in that section of country, yet I shall often, during my future life, recall the winter of 1843–4, and live them over as among the happiest portion of my existence. I have been in many communities, have made many friends, and have parted so often that I have become somewhat calloused, but still there are those so intimately associated with my wild days that they seem to form a part of past happiness. I have no desire ever to look upon a single spot of Augusta's soil (save my father's grave) again, and were it not the home of my mother, should probably never visit that place. There are many that I love and who I would gladly meet again, residents there, but I have suffered too much from bitter malicious words to wish ever to encounter the same. Yet I shall probably see all in June or July. I am delightfully situated now, but the extreme unhealthfulness of the season forbids my remaining late, and, too, mother is very anxious to see me.

Josie A. Fagan

The purpose of introducing this letter was to underscore the "bitter malicious words" phrase as an indication that scandal forced Josephine to leave Augusta in 1845.

When court returned from dinner recess, little Josie accompanied her mother to the defense table and sat with counsel. Her mother took to the witness box and continued the recitation of her life experiences: the breakup of her marriage, her relationship with Captain Pratt, lobbying in Albany, the problems with her mother, and the arrest in Philadelphia.

The last incident mentioned seemed to be of particular interest to the prosecution as Sedgwick came at her with the question: "Were you arrested in 1854?"

Mr. Mitchell objected, and the Court ruled that the witness need not answer questions which might incriminate her.

It became a legal tug of war with Sedgwick demanding answers and Pomeroy objecting.

"Were you arrested in 1862?" Mr. Sedgwick pressed.

Mr. Mitchell advised his client not to answer and the Court reiterated that the witness was not bound to answer.

In a self-possessed manner, Josephine bypassed her attorney's objection. "If I could explain, I would answer, and the answer would not incriminate me: I was arrested in 1862, I believe; the charge was made by my mother. I presume Abner Green made the arrest; the magistrate was Mr. Warren. I made my complaint before Mr. Warren afterward; Justice Warren advised my mother, who was partially insane; I testified on that trial."

Counsel for the defense objected, asking for an exception. The tug between counsels continued with Sedgwick questioning Josephine's actions on August 16, 1862. Had she testified as to her mother's temper and accused her of pinching and torturing the child, Louis?

Unruffled by the badgering, she responded by explaining that Justice Warren had drawn up an affidavit which she had signed. The occurrence took place at the time she was expelled from her mother's home. She'd left the area after the complaint was made.

Counsel for the people took up the issue of Juddie's birth and her charge of having been slandered at Milton Thomson's behest.

Then, to season doubt, Sedgwick questioned why she would bequeath her entire estate to Louis while carrying another child, if Louis was not her child by blood.

PHILADELPHIA HAD ALWAYS BEEN A BUSTLING CITY, but war brought intensity to the traffic and solidarity to its citizens. Like Congressman Sickles, the city had abandoned its pro-southern sentiment and was embracing the cause of the Union. Uniforms and military equipment were produced in Philadelphia's factories. Troops from New Jersey, New York, and New England arrived by the thousands as the Delaware River ferry was the connection between the Camden Amboy Railroad and the Philadelphia-Wilmington-Baltimore line. Add these transient soldiers to the thousands of infantry and cavalry commissioned from within the city and there existed a course for collision.

Pedestrians scrambled before the pounding hooves of couriers and watched appreciatively as cavalry units paraded on avenues lined with gracious homes. Shouts and curses pierced the air as cargo moved from ship to train. The city had changed, and Josephine took care in seeking friends from the college and hospital.

Meeting with Dr. Smith, she described her son and the adventures they'd encountered over the past eighteen months. He listened attentively before offering his own unexpected slice of information.

A gentleman named Wikoff had inquired as to the whereabouts of one Josephine Fagan. He'd left an address where he could be reached if she should ever return. She left Dr. Smith with Wikoff's address in hand and two cleverly confiscated bottles of quinine.

A letter posted to Wikoff earned a quick reply and a set of instructions. She window-shopped before entering a haberdashery where she purchased a pair of grey trousers, a broadcloth coat, and a black slouch hat. She cut her hair and packed anything vaguely feminine into a trunk that she would leave behind. Her reflection in the mirror came back as a satisfactory transition. No one would guess her gender. She went so far as to be photographed before boarding the train for Washington.

A Union officer was waiting when she disembarked. He accompanied her through the chaotic city to a third floor room at O'Donnell's Club House on 13th Street. She had taken the name of Johnny McCarty and was registered as the officer's valet. The two spoke in undertones until late into the evening when the lieutenant led her to a room on the second floor.

The officer twisted the doorknob with caution. He encountered no resistance. Stepping aside, he allowed Josephine to enter and silently departed. Through the dim candle light she saw a man move forward. Holding her breath to keep from screaming, she fell into the arms of General Daniel Edgar Sickles.

"Josephine, my darling, where have you been? I've turned Philadelphia upside down. When you were told to disappear, it wasn't meant to be forever." He drew back slightly to appraise her appearance. "You look to be a fine young man. Perhaps I can entice you to join our troop." Then with unaccustomed timidity he asked if she'd been well.

"I am very well indeed and mother to a handsome son named Louis."

"Louis… I heartily approve. The treatment you received at the time of the trial was a regretful situation. Remorse sits poorly on my shoulders."

With her arms around him, she pushed her face into his chest. It was in muffled tones that she replied. "I never expected to see you again, not up close, not in any sort of intimate encounter."

"Oh, my Josephine, I've thought of you often."

At Edgar's urging, she explained the details of her months with Mrs. Price, excluding any reference to the dirk. She painted a warmer picture of life in the German house on Filbert Street.

"You know my intention on coming to Washington was to work with Dorothea Dix."

Sickles burst out laughing. "Dragon Dix! You wouldn't have had a chance. Beautiful women are banned from the hospital corps."

"Please don't tease me. I'm serious."

"I am not teasing you. Two of Dorothea's requirements of a nurse are that she be plain and over the age of desirability."

Her mouth went slack. "I can't believe it."

"It's true. Now tell me about Moyamensing."

"Oh, dear God! It was a nightmare. How did you know?"

"As I said, we tried to track you, but in that case it was easy. The incident made the newspaper."

Josephine sighed. "Yes. It was a setup involving politics at the hospital."

"I know how that works." Sickles hadn't meant to interrupt, but he did understand. He was in danger of losing his rank as brigadier general due to partisan politics.

"Someone put up bail." Her voice grew thoughtful. "I was never able to find out whom."

Edgar smiled as he pulled her close. "I owe my life to you. I shall never forget, nor will those who were near me in those dark hours."

The lovers shared the night with a constellation of stars winking beyond their window. In the wee hours of the morning, the lieutenant reappeared and escorted her back to their room.

A broad ray of sunshine brought wakefulness. A noisy scuffle seemed to be taking place just beyond their door. The lieutenant had informed her on arrival that O'Donnell's was home to Sickles' Excelsior Brigade and therefore an unsavory place for a woman. She'd assured him that she would not be seen in anything other than men's clothes and would take care to avoid the raucous front room where cigars and whiskey were sold.

The young officer had spent what was left of his night sleeping on the floor. He'd been charged with escorting this he-she girl, but it was an annoying charge that left him perplexed. At the crack of dawn, he slipped from their room wondering what made this woman so special. She might be good looking, but the general was going to a whole lot of trouble to accommodate a pretty face.

Josephine's original intention in traveling to the capital had been sidelined by Sickles' unexpected presence. Nonetheless, she spent days exploring the bulging hospitals. All of Washington was mired in turmoil. Much of the area had been churned to mud; soldiers and horses pounded the ground, even trampling the White House lawns. Political compromise had come to an end. With the suspension of habeas corpus, tight restrictions were imposed on movement. Politicians suspected of Southern sympathy were jailed in the Old Capitol Prison without recourse of any kind.

Positioning herself at various locations, she listened to the conversations taking place around her and attempted to sift fact from exaggeration. Wikoff's name surfaced often. He'd come under suspicion of having used his friendship with First Lady Mary Lincoln to gain and pass information to the *New York Herald*. Wikoff was known for his wily ways, and her Edgar had come to Washington to assist in his defense.

A visit to the home of her cousin, Edward Fagan, provided further evidence of the temper and change taking place. Entering from the back of the house, she ran into the barrel of a gun.

"For heaven sakes, Edward, what are you doing?"

Her cousin halted, but kept the gun in hand. Peering at her more closely, his eyebrows shot up in surprise, and the revolver spun toward the floor.

"Josephine, whatever are you doing in that outlandish outfit?"

"I am without credentials, posing as an officer's servant."

"It is not my desire to be insulting, but your appearance is more the thief than the servant." Laughter rolled up from Edward's deep chest. "Only you would pull such a stunt. But mind, if you are caught, it could mean prison."

The stealthy process of the first evening was repeated on subsequent nights. Each morning the sun sent Josephine out onto the street. On visiting a house owned by the Barnes family, she discovered it occupied by Charles Butler and his clan. She made her excuses and left. Once on the street, she was startled by a shout.

"Hey there, stop at once!" A colonel moved toward her from across the street. "I want to know what you are up to."

When she refused to answer, the officer took hold of her arm, insisting they were on their way to the Old Capitol Prison. She knew the dangers in parading about openly; nonetheless, it perturbed her to have been apprehended.

"Take your hands off me," she screamed, trying to wiggle free. "Haven't you sense enough to know North from South?"

"Hold your peace!" ordered the colonel. It was a useless command as she immediately bit him in the hand.

"Zowie!" he cried. Pulling his punctured hand away, he used the other to tighten his grip on her shoulder. "You are a feisty fellow, but you're on your way to prison just the same."

The prison wasn't really a prison at all, though it was a place of confinement. Originally an inn, the building had been converted to use by Congress when the British burned Washington in the War of 1812. Its stint as a prison would be the most legendary use of all.

With Josephine seated in his office, the colonel tried reasoning with a softer tone and found himself dealing with a more obliging prisoner. He'd given her a thorough looking over by then and was satisfied that the apparel belied her gender. A pretty thing, he thought. In that get-up she looked to be a boy of nineteen.

"You cannot run around in men's clothes without drawing attention to yourself. That can get you into trouble."

"A boy is not to dress like a man?"

"Not if he's not a boy."

"If I look like a boy how do you know I am not a boy?"

"Would you like me to check a little further?"

Josephine drew back, ready for another fight.

"Calm yourself. I see no problem here. If you promise to leave the city in twenty-four hours, I will let you go."

She relaxed a fraction. "You give your word?"

"I am Col. William Wood. I give my word and I tell you it is golden."

She made haste to get back to O'Donnel's, reporting the incident the moment the lieutenant arrived.

In the dark of the evening, Sickles inquired, "You've gotten yourself into trouble again?"

The remark warranted a rejoinder. Her first reaction was to resist his advances, but the mood dissipated quickly. Their moments together were fleeting, and it would have been foolish to waste the opportunity.

Early the following morning, the lieutenant rode his horse to the back of the Club House with a handsome gelding trailing behind him. He offered the reins of the second horse to Josephine. They rode off together, two rod-straight bodies sitting squarely in U.S. Cavalry saddles. The Excelsior Brigade no longer occupied the muddy meadow that Sickles had nick-named Camp Stanton. The troops had moved south along the banks of the Potomac and were headquartered at Port Tobacco, an area familiar to Johnny McCarty.

A loosely run operation, the Sickles encampment was known for bawdy, undisciplined behavior. Another anomaly from a military perspective came with the contingent of civilians who regularly visited encampments hoping to observe battles from a viewing area. The weird fascination made it easy for the impostor to assimilate. Everyone understood the need an officer had for a valet.

Three noblemen from France were traveling with the Sickles brigade:

the Comte de Paris, Prince de Joinville, and Duc de Chartres. The gentlemen were charmed at the valet's ability to converse in their native tongue, with wit and knowledge that took them by surprise. If Josephine's gender had been exposed, they never made mention of it.

General Daniel Butterfield was another matter; he hailed from Utica. The socially prominent Butterfields were vastly wealthy. The general's father had established the longest overland stage route in the world. Though no longer involved with the American Express Company, John Butterfield had been the company's founder. Josephine's encounters with the son had been incidental; yet, his stare reflected skepticism.

"Tell me, little Johnny," General Butterfield said, "how is it that you speak such fluent French?"

"Oh," she boasted with improvised bravado, "my dad was a sea captain. I sailed with him often, took to languages quick like." Dropping her head in mock embarrassment, she qualified the statement. "I'm good at talking, but I can't write a lick."

The officers laughed, and Butterfield gave her a slap on the back.

Edgar observed the scene with pleased amusement. Her quickness was charming in spite of the nondescript valet attire. Butterfield was one of his very best friends. He would confide in him later as to the truth about Johnny. His friend enjoyed a good joke and would certainly get a laugh at having been duped.

Josephine expected to stay with the brigade in the capacity of a field nurse. Colonel Sickles, however, had errands in Washington. When the Judiciary Committee subpoenaed Wikoff on February 10, he felt obligated to assist in his friend's defense. He insisted the encampment would be no place for Josephine if he couldn't be there to keep an eye on things. She argued the point, but in the end, the lieutenant was again her escort.

He guided her back to the capital when the sun had yet to break the horizon. At the rear of O'Donnell's Club House, the officer saluted his charge, then turned and trotted away, leading her horse back to the encampment.

Their association lasted no more than a couple of weeks, yet the lieutenant had gained an appreciation for the lady's powerful draw. Her looks were merely the topping on the cake. She was clever, daring, and desirably soft. He licked his lips as he merged with the shadows.

Josephine faced a decision as to what to do next. She had no idea when Edgar would arrive. The army was preparing to cross into Virginia. Despite Edgar's derisive remarks, she thought it best to follow her original idea of joining Miss Dix's Sanitary Commission. As a nurse, she might have the opportunity for an occasional tryst with the general. Still she procrastinated, convinced that something would happen to influence her direction.

Observing traffic on the Potomac, she couldn't help but reflect on how the scene had changed since her trip with Mrs. Crocker. There were no blockades in '44. Tall ships had bobbed in harmony with the geese that commanded the river each winter. The passage of years nagged at her as she meandered toward the Capitol.

George Vanderhoff was giving a reading in the Senate Chamber. She sidled toward the back wall. The actor-poet had her mesmerized until movement to the side of the chamber caught her attention. The detective, Colonel Wood, appeared to be advancing in her direction. Still in male attire, she was in violation of her promise. Slipping from her stool, she ducked through the doorway, hoping to lose her pursuer in the dark.

At 9:00, a pounding fist rattled her door. It was the first evening she'd spent alone in the room, and the skirmish she'd just escaped caused her to pause in answering.

"I'm here to take you to the provost marshal's office," a young voice charged. "General Porter wants to see you."

Her eyes searched the room. There was no escape. A sinking feeling hit her stomach. She had no option but to answer.

General Dix occupied the desk of the provost marshal. He was no stranger to Josephine. His family holdings in Cooperstown, New York, were not far from where she'd grown up, and his involvement in state and national politics made him a familiar figure. Major General Dix's responsibility on this occasion was commanding the Department of Maryland and the Department of Pennsylvania.

Josephine lifted her chin as she entered the room. With her shoulders square and the slouch hat clutched in her hands, she looked the general straight in the eye. The man had a reputation for toughness, having given the command to shoot without question anyone attempting to haul down an American flag. Yet it relieved her to notice the heavy white brows sheltered eyes that seemed free of malice.

"What is your name, young man?"

"Johnny McCarty, sir."

"It's come to my attention that you've been visiting the likes of Mr. Charles Butler."

Darn that Colonel Wood. He is the cause of my trouble.

"He and his friends are all secessionists with sons in the Rebel army. It appears you may be a Southern sympathizer. It is my responsibility to keep the State of Maryland from seceding. Your actions, however innocent, could be the source of further rebellion. You were once warned. This time, we have no choice but to lock you up."

It wasn't the first time she'd gone to prison, and feeling plucky, she convinced herself that it was nothing that couldn't be handled with a bit of resolve. But when the officers took her to a room to be searched, placidity turned to frenzy.

"I must see General Porter. I was told I was being brought here to meet with him, and I must see him at once." She squirmed from the soldier's grip with a look of fright in her eyes.

"What's the matter, little fellow? You afraid some big hand might come up from behind and get you with a goose?" The officers guffawed at the joke.

"I tell you, I have information vital to the general. It will be your heads if you fail to let me see him."

She was led to the general with skepticism. The general, in turn, looked annoyed.

"If you please, General, I need to speak with you privately."

The general sighed as he nodded assent. His country was warring within itself, and this little dandy wanted to sit and visit? The door closed, and in a matter of minutes, laugher rolled through windows and cracks and rumbled down the hallway. Ducking his head to the outer chamber the general did his best to stifle another outbreak. "Get Colonel Allen's wife and bring her to me."

The officers exchanged bewildered stares. What sort of information did the little rascal hold?

Josephine submitted to a search by Mrs. Allen and was allowed to keep her male attire. The trunks she'd left at O'Donnell's had been confiscated, and she was asked to identify the contents. Admitting to the revolver, she claimed ignorance as to the spurs. "I have no idea where they came from. My baggage appears to be a constant source of mystery."

She had been incarcerated the better part of three weeks when the realization hit her. *I'm pregnant again. This child would be Milton's—and won't he be surprised.* Beyond chastising herself, she subscribed to the notion that what was done was done. A sardonic grin crept across her face. The lusty Milton would be mortified. She sat down on the spot to write him the news.

A week later, another individual appeared at the prison dressed in disguise. He looked to be a minister and asked for Colonel Wood. When informed that he was speaking to the colonel, he commenced a line of questioning.

"Can you tell me if a woman dressed in male clothing has been incarcerated in the Old Capitol Prison?"

The colonel frowned. "I believe someone of that nature may have been brought to the prison. What is it to you?"

The man became agitated. "I just wanted to warn you; she is a very dangerous woman."

The colonel assessed the black habit and pious demeanor, finding it puzzling that there should be a connection to the recent McCarty caper. "What is your name? And what is your connection with this woman?"

The would-be minister refused to identify himself or divulge any information of a personal nature.

With his ire rising, the colonel made his demand clear. "Your name and business are of consequence here. If you fail to answer, our conversation will end, but I tell you, all parties in this city are subject to search and those dubbed suspicious will ultimately be jailed."

The nervousness of the man in black increased. "I apologize, Colonel. My name is Milton Thomson. I hail from Utica, New York, where I operate an insurance business."

"So, why the deacon's clothes and what is your relation to our prisoner?"

Milton ran a hand through his hair in desperation. "Mrs. McCarty has been my mistress, but she is driving me to distraction. Day after day I think of nothing but her. She's costing me money and I want to be free of her."

"Is there a child?"

"I believe there may be, but that doesn't matter. I am a rich man and will do well by you if you can get rid of her." Milton pulled a stack of bills from his pocket. "This ten thousand dollars is yours if you will dispose of her."

"You lascivious, white-livered scoundrel! You have misjudged me entirely!" The colonel had taken to shouting. "You would spend your money to have this woman's blood but chafe at providing for her and the child. It is by your sin that she has been ruined." Milton tried to interrupt, but the colonel left no opportunity. "You have four hours to leave this city, and should you dally, my boot will be there to assist you."

News that Johnny McCarty had been incarcerated did not reach Sickles until his return to Washington. The information sent him in search of Edwin Stanton. An audience with the secretary of war was limited to publicly posted hours with but two exceptions: the president of the United States and Daniel Edgar Sickles. The secretary spent evenings in the telegraph room avidly scanning reports from the scattered divisions under his command. Sickles walked confidently in that direction. A tight friendship had developed between himself and Stanton, and as a friend of the first family, he had easy access to the White House and other facilities with restricted admission.

Stanton saw him coming and rose. His lip curled to one side as he made an observation: "I see you've arranged another furlough."

His remark referenced reports that Sickles fought his war from the Willard Hotel in Washington. The general remained unflappable.

"I'm on my way back tomorrow. If McClellen would get his army into action, I wouldn't have time for furloughs. But I am here on another matter."

Stanton waved his arm to indicate a chair.

"You may be aware that a woman dressed in men's clothing was recently arrested and sent to the Old Capitol."

Stanton nodded and reached to his chest. When occupied in thought, he had a habit of stroking his long, gray beard. "Yes, she gave the town quite a stir. Saw her myself at the Vanderhoff reading. My wife and I were enjoying his narration when Colonel Wood caught my attention. He was moving in the direction of a little fellow sitting on a stool at the back of the hall. The boy saw him coming and ran for the door. I didn't learn the gender until later."

It was Sickles turn to smile. "Now, do you remember the woman we sent into hiding during my trial?"

Stanton's eyebrows rose. "No! You're not telling me this is that woman!" The general nodded. "One and the same."

After a moment's pause, the secretary explained his reaction. "Somehow, I expected your woman to be of much larger proportions. You know, the sturdy type. This woman is but a slip of a girl."

"Believe me," replied Sickles, "she is fire and steel. But I would appreciate it if you could order her release. She is not a rebel and means our army no harm, quite the contrary, really."

"Do you think she would work for us?"

"Knowing Josephine, anything is possible."

The following day, Wood was summoned to the secretary's office.

"Colonel," said Stanton gravely, "our enemies have an excellent spy system working against us. We need to improve our own intelligence."

Wood dropped his head and chewed on his lip. "I have a number of individuals under surveillance. But I would need to get someone in closer."

"Do you have anyone in mind?" the secretary prompted.

The colonel could not control the smirk on his face. "I do indeed, sir."

"Can you enlighten me?"

"We have a woman jailed at the Old Capitol. She might do well by us."

"Would that be Mrs. McCarty?"

"That it would!"

"I want you to interview her on the prospect. If you're satisfied, invite her to join our service. Whatever your decision, I want to meet with this woman myself."

"Yes, sir."

Josephine jumped to her feet when Wood entered her cell. Smiling broadly, he allowed his eyes to travel downward along the sealed door separating her cell from that of her neighbor. A narrow shadow between the door and the floor gave credence to the possibility of a slivered crack.

Josephine stiffened.

With his smile still in place, Wood stepped back, signaling her to exit the cell. "If you please, I would like to speak with you where we can conduct our conversation privately?"

"Do I have a choice?"

"Not to my liking," he laughed. Wood was conducting himself most pleasantly as he directed her to his office. "Please sit down. We need to discuss a visit I had with an individual known well by you."

He appraised the woman, taking special notice of her trim figure and alluring face. She was tough. He rubbed his hand, remembering the puncture she'd inflicted. In spite of the information, so literally at hand, he had no inkling as to how she would react to what he was about to say.

"You are familiar with a man named Thomson, Milton Thomson?" Mention of the name seemed to catch her off guard. "He came to my office looking for you. He was dressed as a deacon, said you were his mistress."

Dressed as a deacon in Washington? Milton was worried that someone might see us together; yet, he confronted the colonel to ask my whereabouts? What on earth was he up to?

The colonel decided to plunge to the meat of it. "I'm afraid this will come as a shock to you, but this Thomson fellow plunked ten thousand dollars onto my desk and said it was mine if I would dispose of you."

Josephine's throat constricted. Her hands went cold. *Milton! He chased me for years, and once he'd had me, I wasn't what he wanted at all.* Grim humor came in the fact that she'd tried to tell him that long ago. But she'd underestimated the man. Never would she have thought him capable of such a calculating maneuver.

The colonel paused, giving her time to digest what he'd said before continuing further.

"Now Mrs. McCarty, I want you to know when I sent him packing, I chastised him for his cruel meditation. I assure you, he won't want to face me again. If you don't mind my asking, what are your circumstances financially?"

"You've searched me as well as my baggage and should know I haven't a penny to my name." That wasn't quite true. The money she'd received from Edgar was hidden in the lining of her sleeve. And, of course, she still had money with Michael Meyers.

"I have a proposition to make." The seriousness of the offer erased his smile. "Secret information is being passed to the enemy. We are fairly sure as to the culprit's identity. We need to prove his actions if we are to foil the operation."

"You want me to act as a spy." Her mind had kept pace with the conversation. She knew exactly where it was going.

"You've a sharp wit or we wouldn't be presenting you with such a delicate task. Careful action and a clear head are essential requirements. There are no guarantees. Rogues exist on both sides of the line and the army can't answer for any of them."

"What am I expected to do and how will I be compensated?"

"Your assignment will be the dangerous service of a double agent, acting as a courier for a turncoat captain. You will be left much to your own initiative. When you have information, you will contact me. The transfers will be direct with no middle person between us. Beyond that, you will follow the orders of our treasonous captain.

"You will receive a stipend, an appropriate wardrobe, an initial place of shelter, and a minimal expense account. Keep in mind you will also be paid by the captain. Of course, he will be dealing in confederate notes, which is nothing but worthless paper here in the north. It will be up to you to gain this captain's trust."

Josephine sat in silence. Rose O'Neal Greenhow occupied the cell next to her. They'd been passing messages beneath the door for days. She knew Rose as a native of Port Tobacco. Before his death, her husband, Dr. Robert Greenhow, had served as the highly respected librarian of the Department of State. He'd taken Rose on a whirligig ride to the pinnacle of Washington society. When she agreed to spy for the Confederacy, the doyenne forfeited everything, including her magnificent mansion. She and her eight-year-old daughter were, at that moment, struggling to survive the vermin and diseases that had infiltrated the Old Capitol Prison.

Confederate prisons were even less accommodating. Louis is waiting and I have another child growing within.

Wood watched as she calculated the risks. "You will have the support of the federal government as far as we can take it."

What do I really believe? For what am I willing to fight? Counting both north and south there've been over 4,500 casualties in the recent Battle of Fort Donnelson in Tennessee. Many more would fall. Where would I stand when it finally ended? Father had been a patriot. He loved his adopted country; it was the land of the free—at least that was what I was brought up to believe. Edgar abandoned his defense of states' rights with the Rebels' first attack. Should it be any different for me?

She looked up at Wood. He'd been waiting patiently for her thoughts to reach conclusion. "I will do it."

The colonel rubbed his hands together and smiled. "You're up to the challenge, Mrs. McCarty; I have no doubt of that. The secretary of war has asked to meet with you before you leave. In the meantime, you might want to spend an hour or so exchanging notes with Mrs. Greenhow. Your reputation will fail sooner if Rose can add her input."

Josephine reflected on the colonel's words as he escorted her to Stanton's office. How could her reputation be tarnished further? She'd lost the luster years ago.

The secretary was familiar with her background, and she had the facts in regard to his. He'd been a highly esteemed attorney long before Buchanan appointed him attorney general. His greatest passion seemed to be work. He'd mourned the death of his first wife for ten years, marrying for the second time in 1856. And he'd saved the life of her beloved Edgar. The thoughts scurried past as Stanton stood to greet her.

"Mrs. McCarty, I've long wondered at your tenacity and courage. It is a pleasure to finally meet you."

The secretary's superior intellect was apparent from the moment he opened his mouth. Perhaps that was the gift of an orator. In the span of their brief conversation, she judged the eyes to be hard and unyielding, and the full lower lip with its fluff of whiskers gave an inkling of interior warmth. Regardless of politics, she had no doubt as to his fitness for the difficult position he held.

By the time she said "good day," the tenor of the meeting had grown to one of friendly admiration. The secretary assured her that in the future she would have his unfailing support.

She left his office to confer again with Colonel Wood. She would impart her secessionist sympathies to the imprisoned Mrs. Greenhow. It was almost certain the woman would spread her tale to others in the Confederate community.

From the Old Capitol Prison, Josephine traveled directly to the train station where she took the cars to Philadelphia. Thanks to the United States government, her trunks contained an attractive wardrobe. She entered the train in a two-piece, brown, taffet dress that turned the heads of men and women alike. The white collar was a complement to her creamy complexion; the small-brimmed hat sitting coquettishly to one side set an image of lightness and youth.

On emerging from the cars, she took a hack to a small but respectable boarding house. Her stiff, taffeta skirt billowed above a swaying hoop as she stepped down from the cab and walked to the door. Lodgers looked up from their chairs in the sitting room, eying her openly as she sashayed to a desk in the center hall. In the time it took to register, female boarders had memorized every detail of her dress, shawl, and parasol. One of the admirers was sister to the infamous Captain McGuire.

According to background material, the girl had been educated in Philadelphia and took pride in being a proper lady. Josephine bestowed a friendly smile. She had set her plans for making contact. The first step would take place at the dinner table, where she introduced herself to the other diners.

"Mrs. McCarty, I couldn't help but notice your shawl when you came in. I can understand having a fine dressmaker, but wherever do you find such beautiful accessories?" The young Miss McGuire was enthralled with the latest fashions.

Josephine smiled confidentially. "I have to take care in giving my sources with the war making such a mess of things." She lifted her teacup and sipped, allowing her comments to penetrate the female minds that surrounded her.

"But what does the war have to do with buying a shawl?"

The landlady, Mona Whiting, laughed. "It has everything to do with it. The blockades go both ways. The North may cripple the South, but the South will certainly annoy the North."

Good, thought Josephine. The conversation was traveling in the right direction.

"But," muttered the girl, "what sources allow you to buy a shawl?"

"Confidential sources," was Josephine's whispered reply. "You must excuse me. I have some notes to write, but I did enjoy our visit."

In later conversation, it became obvious that Mona was involved with Captain McGuire. When he stopped at the boarding house the following evening, Josephine brushed him in passing, and then jumped back with a startled expression, laying the fault on him.

Captain McGuire worked his bulging jaw and gulped at his failure to locate a spittoon. Her gracious smile convinced him that his own misstep had caused the collision, and he gurgled a profuse apology. The sparkling black eyes had him mesmerized as she nodded her head in forgiveness.

On his next visit, McGuire made it a point to speak to the stylish Mrs. McCarty. "My sister thinks you're upset with those troublesome Rebel boys."

"There must be some misunderstanding," Josephine blinked sweetly. "I am myself a southern girl. To the fact, I was born in Richmond." She followed her remark by looking furtively over a well-carved shoulder. "I wish I could take an active role in this terrible war. I'd be willing to do most anything to preserve my family home."

"You know you're talking to a faithful Union man!"

"Please don't turn me in, Captain. I mean no harm." She gave the captain another flirtatious glance. "You know how silly we southern girls are."

Ordinarily, such coquettish behavior would appear ridiculous in a woman of Josephine's age. But whether it was the effect of her indomitable personality or the knowledge of cosmetics she'd accrued in Paris, men in her presence melted.

McGuire was grinning. "Nannies and mammies a hangin on ever word while ya stepped to the dance with nary a thought in yer haid."

"To be sure, Captain, to be sure."

"Did you never learn to ride a horse?"

It was Josephine's turn to laugh. "Of course I ride. Every southern girl is taught to ride."

"Did you ever ride astride?"

"Now, a gentleman shouldn't be asking such things. But yes, I'm very good at sitting a horse, sidesaddle or astride."

"Compliments to you." Captain McGuire made an acknowledging nod as he moved on to visit his sister's landlady.

A few days later, the captain approached Josephine again, asking to speak with her privately.

"I've been thinking on our visit the other day."

"Oh, Captain McGuire. You're not going to turn me in for a bit of reminiscing?"

"Oh, Mrs. McCarty, you ave nothing to ear wit me. I was jus thinkin on how courageous you dounded, talkin about doin most anything fer your home. Like a true Irish lass you are."

Josephine grew increasingly serious. "It's just that our menfolk take all the chances and it really doesn't seem fair. There's no reason why women shouldn't take part in defending our rights."

"That's just it. Not many women think like yourself. But there's a place for you if you're looking to do some good. It would help to end the war a lot sooner if we could get word back and forth."

Josephine nodded vigorously. "You are right in your summation. Nothing would be of better help."

"I'm thinking you might get involved, but 'tis daring and dangerous work."

Josephine's eyes lit up, a telltale sign of her penchant for excitement.

"Can you follow a map?"

"Absolutely." The answer came with firm conviction.

"There's someone what needs to get a message across the lines. If you're willing to take some chances, I could set you up with the delivery."

"Oh yes! Just tell me what I have to do."

The risks involved in this little venture weighed heavily on Josephine's mind. The casualties of war were growing at a staggering rate. An April battle at Shiloh in Tennessee left 23,500 dead or injured. Blood was spilling from brothers on both sides of the conflict. This wasn't a game she was playing. The stakes were too high for such designations.

She took the cars to New York to visit William Dodge, her friend from Cazenovia. He'd offered his services long ago, and the time had come to ask for help. Attorney Dodge prepared her will. The farm in Augusta held considerable value; she wanted it in writing that on her demise the property would go to Louis. Attached to the will was an address where her child could be found

From New York, she took the Perth Amboy Ferry, stopping at the Muldoon farm to visit her toddling son. The cars returned her to Philadelphia. Within twenty-four hours she had a map and was given a location outside of Washington where she could pick up a horse. She would be without contacts until the meet in Virginia. Josephine insisted she understood. She expected no help and would protect her source. Should she be caught, the message would be destroyed.

Captain Patrick McGuire slipped her a sealed envelope and offered his wish for her safety. Step one completed.

Her prearranged rendezvous with Colonel Wood took place at the Washington rail station. The envelope passed quickly from one pair of hands to the other. In return, she was given a pass to visit an ailing relative. This arrangement allowed for the purchase of a stagecoach ticket, the destination, Port Tobacco. It was a non-threatening and transparent mode of travel. It took some explaining to convince the driver of her need to bring a horse.

Wood caught up with her at the stage stop. McGuire's message had been copied and the envelope resealed. It slipped to her hand as he stooped to tie his shoe. The colonel felt a pang of guilt. She'd been given a difficult assignment. The safest place in the world for this woman had been her cell at the Old Capitol Prison.

"If you've had a change of heart," he began quietly.

She interrupted him with a quick and hushed reply. "No. I've made a choice and it will be done. Just wish me a bit of Irish luck."

The coachman pulled his horses to a stop on the Anacostia Bridge, where a baggage inspection commenced. Passengers were required to empty their pockets and upend their hats. To Josephine's relief, no body search had been required. She'd hidden the message well. But having been through the humiliating process of searches before, she was loath to the thought of enduring the procedure again.

Their coach resumed its journey, bumping along roads heavily damaged by regiment horses and bulky cannon traffic. Fields bordering the turnpike wilted in neglect. She pulled her shawl in closely, conscious of the garish impact her finery might have in the midst of such desolation.

Miles away, on the other side of the Potomac, General McDowell and his First Corps made preparations to join McClellan as his army fought toward Richmond. The home of her birth had become the capital of the Confederacy. By all reports, it would soon be under siege, and she was to have a hand in it.

Though the reaper followed battles in Virginia and Tennessee fields, penetration of the North had thus far been limited. Fields in New York were planted and harvested as if the war were taking place in a foreign land. Work might be done with fewer hands; nonetheless, the farms in New York produced in abundance. Not so at Hill Top. Josephine walked the path to the house in stillness. The door did not open; there were no hands in the fields. The voices of children hung in the past.

She didn't expect her knock to be answered, but Moses, the Barnes' old butler, opened the door with a dignified bow.

"Is the judge at home?" she asked.

Moses smiled. "Masta Barnes is in de study, Missus Josephine. He be right pleased you come to visit."

Judge Barnes was exceedingly pleased. "Mrs. McCarty, it is a delight to see you. Other than the military, very few travelers visit Port Tobacco these days. General Hooker's encampment at Budd's Ferry was disassembled just recently. Ironically, he conducted war from confiscated space in one of our churches."

"What of Mrs. Barnes and the children?"

"I sent Mary and the two youngest to her cousin's in Atlanta. I doubt the war will get that far south. I think it the safest place for them. The Rebs are doing a pretty good job. As you can see, most of the coloreds are gone. I'd given many their freedom long ago, but some of them stayed by choice until the war broke out. Fear sent most of them packing when the army trooped through. Since we haven't seceded, the Yanks protect our shipping. But you can't bring in crops without labor. I suppose I should be thankful the house is still standing." The judge put a hand to his head and sank to a chair. "It is a dreadful situation."

Josephine knelt beside him. "What can I do for you? Do you have a cook or anyone other than Moses to assist you?'

Judge Barnes laughed. "Mina wouldn't leave. We have a few still with us. But enough of this! You are a guest. I should not be remonstrating."

They dined in the flicker of candlelight. Josephine noticed only four candles were used and the meal, though tasty, was light.

"Tell me," her host inquired, "What brought you to Port Tobacco in the middle of this rebellion?"

"I have some errands to run. Can we speak freely?

Judge Barnes looked troubled. "We can. Besides the two of us, Moses and Mina are the only ones left in the house. We've had a few Yanks stop by, but there hasn't been much action lately. What is this errand you mentioned?"

"I need to cross the Potomac."

Surprise raised the judge's eyebrows and pushed him to a moment of silence.

"I'll not ask why, but how do you propose to cross?"

"That is the problem," she answered warily. "I've thought of crossing just below Chicamuxen. I have a stout horse but doubt he could make the swim."

"No, no. You can't swim across. Even if the horse could make it, you'd likely be carried downstream." Barnes scratched his head. "I'm assuming this must be an important mission. Why else would you be here?" He looked up at her solemnly. "Is this to Maryland's benefit or detriment?"

"It is to the betterment of us all." She felt a shudder run through her body. The easy part of the assignment was behind her. What faced her in the next few days, she could not imagine.

"The river in the Quantico area is guarded by cannon. If you cross it should be to the north of the creek. But you are looking at a dangerous mission." The judge eyed his visitor. He wasn't telling her anything she didn't already know. "Old Yu is still with us and very devoted. Moses has always been a houseman, but his hobby was fishing. He knows the river well. I'll speak with them."

"You're sure about them? My life hangs in the balance."

Barnes let out a weary sigh. "Why? Why would you do this?"

"Because I was asked."

The judge quietly left the room. Josephine watched the stooped body as it disappeared into darkness. He was a good man. The weight of the war left him helpless.

A few minutes later he returned. "I've spoken with our old fellows. Their suggestion is to cross in a canoe. They'll pause to see you onto the shore; from that point onward, you will be on your own. There's nothing I can do to get you back."

"I'll meet Yu and Moses in the kitchen at 10:00."

Josephine went to her room and worked at the row of buttons closing her dress. She pulled the heavy taffeta dress up over her head and tugged at the ribbons of her petticoat to undo the contraption that formed her hoops. Muslin and wire dropped to the floor. When freed of her corset, she reached into the trunk to pull out a thick roll of fabric. Wrapping the stripping about her torso, she flattened her breasts and bulked up her middle. Within the folds of finery were hidden the articles of male clothing she'd worn a short time before in Washington. After donning the pants and jacket, she went to the fireplace to blacken her face with ash.

When she stepped into the kitchen, three startled faces gaped at her transformation.

It was a covert mission to be brought to fruition by the most conspicuous trio imaginable: a white woman in male clothing and two stoop-shouldered, old black men riding through the night with a canoe strung between them.

They were following the only plan available. The men were too old to carry the canoe any distance, and dragging it would create an obvious path and could result in the craft being damaged. Suspending the canoe between saddles was a cumbersome feat, but it eliminated the problem of a telltale trail. The horses were guided over well-trampled ground. Their hoof prints mingled with the tapestry created in the cavalry march.

Josephine held two items of passage in this dangerous territory—a letter addressed to a Confederate general and a letter of recommendation from the

Union's secretary of war. The trick was to produce the right envelope at the right time. The simple thing would have been to put the North in one pocket, the South in another. But both were hidden least either side learn of her dubious allegiance. The bottles of quinine she'd acquired at Blockley were still in her possession, useful commodities in a situation that required dickering.

Moses had explained before leaving that scavengers might still be camped at the former site of Hooker's army. When the military broke camp in enemy territory, they burned or spoiled everything left behind. Though Maryland was rife with Confederate sympathizers, the state had not seceded and was not subjected to enemy treatment.

The clear sky provided a bright moon and a heavenly web of quiet brilliance that increased visibility and magnified the snap of every twig. Nocturnal creatures were heard scampering through the shadows, but silence ruled the triumvirate as they moved closer to their destination. Cool Potomac breezes swept their faces as they reached the edge of a rippling plain of silver. They had, thus far, evaded detection.

The horses were tethered to trees. It had been understood from the beginning that Josephine's horse would be led back to Hill Top. If she didn't return, the horse was theirs. They slipped into the canoe, still without speaking, and paddled toward the opposite shore. Yu and Moses had labored since childhood, and paddled the waters smoothly in spite of their age.

On reaching the western shore, they braced their paddles against the river bottom to push the craft onto more solid ground. With gestures rather than speech, the two men directed their passenger onward. She climbed from the canoe and merged with the night as she scaled the bank beside the river.

Her goal was to locate a Confederate division camped between Manassas and Fredericksburg. Walking and running in turn, she traveled northwest until she picked up the sound of picket guards checking with one another. The sun had another two hours to sleep. Fishing McGuire's letter from the sleeve of her coat, she looked for a place of cover. When she thought herself safe from a preemptory shot, she called out to the pickets to hold their fire.

"Show yourself!" was the sharp and somewhat frightened reply.

"It's Johnny McCarty from Captain McGuire," she called without moving. "I have a message for the general commanding this brigade."

"Show yourself!" the picket commanded.

Creeping from behind the trunk of a large pine, she waved her handkerchief, praying the nervous picket would not be tempted to pull the trigger.

"Come forward." The picket looked at her suspiciously. "Are you armed?"

"Fix my flint! Of course, I'm armed! Do you think I want some Yank to catch me by surprise?"

A semi-grin flickered in the muscles of the young soldier's face. "Hand over your weapons and do it carefully."

She removed a revolver from inside her coat and a knife she'd hidden in her boot.

"A pepperbox and an Arkansas toothpick—you certainly were prepared."

The picket pushed his kelpie toward the back of his head and gave his prisoner a shove, forcing her to march toward their encampment. Her direction was marshaled by the barrel of his rifle. A campfire flickered some distance beyond, barely discernible through the trees. A second flicker appeared and then another until a hundred giant fireflies dotted the landscape before her.

It was a difficult path they were treading, and every so often she looked over her shoulder, but each turn of the head brought a sharp reprimand.

They cut through the slumbering encampment, stopping at the entrance to an officer's tent. The picket spoke to the sentry on duty in whispers Josephine could not decipher. The sentry entered the tent and a few moments later she and her guard were called inside. An officer with a major's insignia turned and blinked the sleep from his eyes. "What do we have here?"

"Caught this fellow on the perimeter. Says he has a message for the general from an informant named McGuire."

The major was smiling. "There must have been an assignation prior to or shortly after these orders were fixed."

Josephine's look of bewilderment matched the picket's dismay.

"The handkerchief," mused the major. "Unless this fellow possesses dual gender, I'd say the lace belonged to a lady."

In her nervousness, Josephine had forgotten the handkerchief dangling from her hand. Stuffing the object of laughter into a pocket, she thanked the good Lord that her anxiety had been judged as embarrassment.

"Your name, young man?" The question snapped from the major, keeping the messenger on edge.

"Johnny McCarty, sir."

"Now, what is this message?"

With the envelope in hand, she gave the major a defiant scowl. "My message is for the general. I'm to hand it to no one else."

"You are in the midst of a military encampment, surrounded by thousands of Confederate soldiers. Do you really propose to hold out?"

"But I was told..."

The major cut her off. "I am General Stuart's chief of staff. After I've read the letter and verified its authenticity, I will transfer your message to the general. Now give me the envelope." The small talk had ended.

The chief of staff checked the seal before slicing it open. Josephine held her breath as his eyes ran down the paper. Dismissing the picket, he called a sentry into the tent. "Watch this Johnny until I return."

Time passed, and a bugle sounded the first of the reveille calls. The scuffling and mumbling that followed were an indication the camp had come to life. When an aide finally drew the canvas door back, General Stuart entered the tent followed by his chief of staff. In the wake of her amazement, Josephine had all she could do to keep from gaping. General James Ewell Brown Stuart, known to everyone as Jeb, could easily challenge the aristocracy of Europe in the raiment of royal splendor. His heavy beard had been carefully tended. His uniform had designer touches. The red-lined cape, the yellow sash, the peacock feather in his hat, and the perfect rose that bloomed in his lapel set him off from any man serving the military north or south. A fourth signal from the bugle had sounded, marking the time at 5:30 in the morning.

He appraised the courier intently before speaking. "You've done well to travel so far. Did you encounter any trouble?"

"No, sir. I came by way of the Maryland peninsula and crossed near Chicamuxen."

The general raised an eyebrow. "And how did you cross?"

"With a canoe, sir."

"And what did you do with the canoe when you reached the Virginia bank?"

"Scuttled her, sir."

Stuart seemed impressed. "And how do you propose to get back to Philadelphia?"

"I'll use my wits, sir, same as on my way down." The spy grinned.

"I'm glad you're working for us."

Still under guard, she was taken to a campfire and handed a biscuit and a mug of coffee. Sunlight had fired the horizon before the chief of staff appeared.

"You are to deliver the general's reply to Captain McGuire. Have you need of any provisions?"

Johnny grinned. "A couple of those biscuits would be nice, sir. And I'd much appreciate it if you would return my revolver." She needed a horse, but knew that to be out of the question. The cavalry was always short of horses.

The major took another look at the little spy. A cheeky fellow, he thought; but then, he guessed he'd have to be.

She was led to the edge of the encampment and given her bearings.

"Here's your gun," the picket guard said. "You'd best git goin'. To double back would be a mistake. But I wish you luck." He needed the luck for himself. Pickets were often the first to fall.

She positioned herself in a stand of evergreens to await the return of darkness. The trees offered protection from a threatening rain and a vantage point where she could view the encampment without being seen. She munched on a biscuit and mulled her next move.

Major General John Pope's encampment lay somewhere to the north.

Unfortunately, locating the camp would lead her further from the Potomac and Port Tobacco where her trunk sat in a room at Hill Top. The cross into Washington would be easier from Maryland than from Virginia. There was no way she could paddle the Potomac alone. And she certainly couldn't swim.

She needed a horse. If he wouldn't swim the Potomac, he could, at least, get her to the shore. She'd noted the location of Stuart's herd. Getting in close would be dangerous. Horses were at a premium and stealing was punishable by hanging. Yet, it was the only plan she had.

Under cover of darkness, she crept closer to the campground, patiently monitoring the pickets and the horses they guarded. Every now and then one of the animals would raise its head and sniff the wind. She wished something would come along to take attention away from her location. She had the picket's schedule clear in her mind and a dark-colored horse in her sights. Taking a deep breath, she wiggled through the grass until she was splayed at the very edge of the rebel encampment.

Luck was on her side as shots fired on the other side of the camp turned all heads in that direction. With the flick of her hand she had a rope around the horse's neck. She ignored the shouting behind her and never stopped to look back. Moving in a crouched position, she led the horse toward a thicket of brush. Should a picket detect their movement, she would release the rope, drop to the ground, and crawl away. Once free of the camp, she thought it doubtful that her theft would be noticed before the full light of day.

A good springing jump landed her on the horse's back. The pressure of her legs against his body determined their speed and direction. She moved off at a walk to keep the hoofbeats light, and then gradually picked up speed riding ahead of a west wind, its powerful force her only compass. With a prayer that her stead would not stumble, she held tightly to both his mane and the rope.

When the lapping of water reached her ear, she slipped from her horse and removed the rope. Slapping the animal on his rump, she sent him off to find a new home. While most women traveled with a "housewife," she gave credit to God and her father that she'd had sense enough to trade the sewing kit for a rope. Memory of her father drew a shudder. The shame in things she'd done over the past few years would lie heavily on his grave. But she had no time to dwell on that thought.

An orange glow brightened the horizon, spreading daylight along the shoreline. She realized that she'd reached the area just north of Dumfries and Quantico Creek. Following a tree line that bordered the road, she kept watch for roaming sentries. Getting caught was not the danger; she could answer any question put to her. Fear came with the thought of itchy fingers. A single shot and she could be dead with no explanation needed. Boats bobbed in the water at intervals all along the river. Most sat opposite tiny cottages. She scanned the assortment for something substantial.

A lone craft docked approximately a half mile north of the harbor looked to fit her needs. It appeared to be a boat used for commercial fishing purposes. Whatever the circumstance, she would wait for the sun to set once more. She'd been gone two nights and hoped to be back on Maryland soil before another day passed.

It began to drizzle late in the afternoon. She had a bit of oilcloth to pull over her head, but it was no help against the chilling wind. She'd expected as much with the cloudy sunset the night before. Thankfully, a repeat of clouds brought the night on early.

She approached the cottage next to the dock with her heart in her mouth and her feet barely skimming the ground. Laughter could be heard from the opposite side of the window, and she counted three voices, perhaps a father, mother, and son. *Please have the door unlocked.* It was a little prayer, but infinitely helpful. Surprise could be an asset if it didn't get her killed.

She opened the door, gun in hand. The inhabitants faced her in shock.

"Put your hands in the air," she commanded.

The hands moved upward slowly.

"What ya be wanting from us?" the older man questioned. "We got no money. We're fishermen. Ya want our catch, take it. Ain't worth a bullet."

This family wasn't nearly as humble as they appeared. She noticed the father's eye roaming the room, seeking a weapon most likely.

"Listen," she said. "I'm here for the Cause. I spoke with Jeb Stuart not twenty-four hours since. But I need to cross to Maryland tonight."

They looked at her doubtfully.

"I tell you, I want nothing from you but to cross in your boat."

"A man could be shot a comin' an' goin' on that river."

"You fish the river, don't you? It is a very dark night and difficult to see through the rain. You have no neighbors to spy on you. It will be an aid to the Confederacy if you were to say yes. If not, I will scuttle your boat."

"Like 'ell you will!"

As the man moved forward, Josephine aimed her gun upward and pulled the trigger.

"What ya doin' now? Ya put a 'ole in mah roof!"

She had indeed, and hoped to God no one had heard the shot.

"All of you, to the boat. Now!"

"But the missus? She's no part of this."

"No. But as soon as she can get behind me, she'll put a club to my head. Let's go."

"Kin we get our oil clothes?"

She saw the raincoats hanging on a hook and moved to take them down, one at a time. "You'll have your coats when you're on the boat. Now go!"

When they were all on the boat, she ordered the woman off. "I tell you, I mean no harm."

"It's harm to put us in the water this night."

"If that is the case we shouldn't run into traffic. When you get out away from shore, I'll give you your coats."

"By then we'll be soaked through," the son grumbled.

The men rowed hard and Josephine gave them their coats.

"How can you be sure we're takin' you across?" the boy asked. "We could be doin' circles."

"We were at right angles to the shore when we left and you haven't pulled right nor left. Should we come up anywhere but Maryland, I will shoot the old man before anyone knows what has happened. It will be much easier for all of us if you get me ashore and go back to your mother."

The talk ended. Tough as she sounded, Josephine was highly anxious, chilled to the bone, and had all she could do to keep from shaking. The pelting rain made visibility close to zero. They came close to going aground before they saw the shoreline.

"I thank you, gentlemen." She reached into her pocket and pulled out a couple of McGuire's confederate notes. She handed the bills to the boy.

He looked up in surprise.

She smiled. "Take care going back. Your mother will be worried." With that, she climbed the rocks and was gone.

Nine miles of rough road separated her from Hill Top. It was more than she could handle. The leavings from Hooker's encampment had been picked fairly clean, but she examined the ground in desperation. In a pile of weeds, she found several torn pieces of canvas. With the canvas tucked between low-slung branches, she curled up on a bed of pine boughs, put fear and fatigue behind her, and drifted off to sleep.

She awoke with a shiver. Though fever had gripped her, she moved quickly to conceal herself in a thick patch of woods. Wheels rolled somewhere nearby and the stodgy rotation signaled a taxing load.

Oxen appeared through the screen of trees. The beasts hauled a cart loaded with stone and were prodded occasionally by the driver's staff. She stepped before them with a decided gait.

"Good morning, sir. We have a fine day following the rain of last night."

"That we do," answered the old man as he inspected her appearance. "Spent the night on the ground, did ya?"

"You know how it is. When a pretty miss turns your head it's easy to lose track of time. I decided to finish my walk in daylight."

"You're welcome to come along with me then, should my direction fit your destination."

"Port Tobacco, that would be, sir."

"Ah. I'll be turning off long before we get that far, but I'd appreciate the company just the same." He passed a bottle to his newfound friend.

The home brew raged in Josephine's throat, lighting fires as it spread through her body. But the old man's comments were a decided relief. Stopping at Hill Top while with him would have spawned new questions. She wanted no lines drawn between her and the Barnes family. The significance of caution was underscored by her companion's innocent confession. He told her he feared the armies on both sides of the rebellion and worried that his team might be confiscated.

"I'm sorry our routes must diverge," he said. "The presence of a young man gives me confidence."

Josephine smiled inwardly. What a loss of assurance he would suffer if he knew the truth of her gender.

Once she and the old man parted ways, it was determination alone that drove her on through the final six miles. At last, she staggered to Hill Top's door, exhibiting the gait and smell of a drunken sod. Mina greeted her with a fluttering hand and a forehead puckered with frown lines.

"Lawdy! Lawdy! Moses! Moses, come hyah!"

Moses hustled his big frame through the door. "Missus Josephine," he exclaimed in shock.

"Missus Josephine?" Mina repeated, looking curiously at the boy who had fallen through the door.

Moses scooped her up into his arms as Judge Barnes came running. They took her upstairs, and Mina helped her into bed.

She was comfortably covered with blankets and a coverlet when the judge knocked at the door.

"Please excuse the intrusion, but I need to know what has happened? Are you being pursued?"

Josephine appreciated the kindness in the old man's eyes. Rolling her head from side to side, she answered. "I am sought by no one. I've had an adventure-filled couple of days and spent last night in the rain. I need to sleep for a while but will be leaving first thing in the morning."

"I think it would be better if you extended your stay a day or two. The rest would do you good, and I'd be pleased to have company."

She managed to produce a faint smile. "I need to be on tomorrow's coach. I have to get back to Washington. My son is awaiting my return."

The judge pulled back at the mention of a son. "The children have been returned!"

Though the weight of fatigue pressed heavily on her, she repeated the story of Louis' adoption. Judge Barnes' experience with the orphans' court and his own adopted children came through in his congratulations. He smiled warmly and then excused himself that she might sleep.

The next morning a coach dropped her off at Willard's Hotel. The note she sent Colonel Wood requested a meeting at the Capitol. When she arrived at the Senate Chamber, she was dressed once again in crinolines and silk.

The colonel took a seat beside her. "You look in fine fiddle, Mrs. McCarty. Did you enjoy your visit to Port Tobacco?"

"It was an interesting trip." She slipped him an envelope.

"Had you planned on listening to the Senate proceedings?"

"Yes, I will remain in the chamber throughout the afternoon."

At that the colonel nodded and strolled off in another direction.

Perspiration beaded her forehead. With trembling hands, she fanned a feverish body. One more day, she thought. One more day and this assignment will be over.

It was midafternoon when she sensed a presence behind her. Colonel Wood dropped the envelope into her lap. His instructions were whispered softly.

"One of my men will be following you. It is for your protection as much as ours. When you hand the envelope to McGuire, an officer will make the arrest. You will be taken into custody along with our traitor, but your release will come within the hour."

She caught a change in his voice as he added one last comment.

"Should permanent employment be appealing, you have a standing offer."

The arrest of Captain McGuire unfolded as planned. Josephine was taken into custody just as expected, but the charges were quickly dismissed. On her release she took a hack to a neatly tended house on the far side of town. The home was owned by a pleasant family who wished to rent a room. It was a suitable place that put her at minimal risk of encountering Nuala McGuire or her secessionist landlady.

She ordered her trunk delivered to the lodging house, where she sank to a chair in total exhaustion. She had two more tasks to complete: pick up her mail and retrieve her son. Both would have to wait. A fitful sleep shortened the night, leaving her as tired in the morning as she had been when she retired.

Hot coffee gave her a lift. She was perusing the morning newspaper when a name leapt out at her from the myriad of type. Daniel Edgar Sickles had been reinstated as brigadier general and would be serving in Hooker's Second Brigade. She'd been unaware that his status as general had been rescinded. Recent preoccupation left a giant gap in her knowledge of current events.

Josephine walked to the post office wondering what unexpected news might await her. She took the packet of letters she'd found stuffed in her pigeonhole back to her room to read at her leisure.

The first letter she opened wrought an unmerciful shock. A.C. King had written again on an untitled sheet of paper. He'd found a Dr. Williams in Syracuse who would be willing to perform an abortion. He wanted her to return to Utica immediately.

The promises, all those wonderful promises were made by A.C. King. Well, King and Thomson were one and the same—and they could go to hell together. She seethed in anger as her fist crushed the hateful letter.

She spent the next three days in bed, finally rousing herself to ride the cars to Perth Amboy. She and Louis had been separated for four months. Her warm greeting was met with shyness.

"Oh, Louis! It is Mother! Won't you come to me?"

The boy walked forward slowly, ready to retreat at the slightest excuse. As she drew him to her he balked. Kitty read her expression and was quick to cover the boy's reticence. "Don't worry, ma'am. He'll come round in a bit. He's a friendly little fellow."

"Would you like to ride on the train with me?" Josephine asked. The boy nodded. "Good. We will have a gay time and I will buy you sweets." But she lacked animation as she made these remarks.

The slowness of her actions roused Kitty's concern. "Pardon me asking, ma'am, but are you well?

"I have been through some trying times, Kitty. It's nothing for you to worry about."

It seemed to Kitty that the madam lived in a confluence of troubled waters.

Josephine knew her health to be ailing. The movement within her uterus seemed slight, causing her to wonder at the condition of her unborn child. Life outside the womb had certainly been harrowing.

Having a room in a private home offered a quiet respite. She made a determined decision to rest and take pleasure in the time she had with her son. She summoned enough energy to take him to the shipyard. The boy seemed enthralled by the ships and the men who climbed the rigging. Noise and activity had the child's head spinning. Then it came to her that she'd done this before with other children. She pushed the thought from her mind and turned back toward their lodging.

A note awaited her, announcing that a gentleman had called. He promised to return. It could have been any one of a number of men. The mystery nagged at her until Milton arrived.

His well-fed face disgusted her, and without remorse, she addressed him abruptly. "Why are you here, and what do you want?"

"Jo, you didn't answer my letter. I came to check on you."

"Oh, I'm sure you did." Her dark eyes flashed in anger. "You want me in your sights until you want me no more." She snickered sarcastically. "What's troubling you, Mr. King? Can't fulfill your promises?"

"Jo, please keep your voice down. I should have handled things differently. I know that now. You have to understand. My business and reputation are on the line."

Jo turned toward the stairs to escape, but Milton caught her arm.

"Please, come out with me for just a few minutes. We need to talk, but we can't do that here."

"I'm rooming with good people. They would find it suspicious if I were to go riding with a man not my husband. Good night, Milton." At that she called for one of the landlady's children to show her visitor the door.

It was a joy to regain her relationship with Louis. His presence seemed to renew her strength. Though still pressed for news on the war, *Harper's Weekly* provided a running account.

The Army of the Potomac's Peninsula Campaign had been moving forward successfully with the Yanks no more than six miles from the Confederate capital of Richmond. Then on May 31, the rebels bombarded the Union with a powerful offense at Fair Oaks Station. Her Edgar had been in the thick of it, and at least one newspaper praised his actions. But the battle had been costly in terms of casualties. General McClellan halted all forward action, bringing the Peninsula Campaign to an end. The slogan: "Ninety days and we'll have them licked" had been abandoned long ago. Within a month, the Seven Days Battle would result in another 36,000 casualties.

Josephine wondered at the significance of the messages she'd carried. Had her work accomplished anything? Whatever the situation, she was done with the war for a while. It was time to leave for Augusta and give her attention to those she loved. Before setting foot to the cars, she contacted her mother's former lawyer, Mr. Morgan, of West Winfield, New York. It was a precautionary move, and her reception in Utica proved the wisdom of her thoughts.

Milton stood waiting on the platform with a stranger at his side. He hurried toward her and commenced a quick introduction. "Josephine, this is Dr. Williams. He's here at my telegraphed request. The doctor assures me he can perform a safe abortion even at this late date. I want you to get back on the train and travel with him to Syracuse."

Josephine stepped back, aghast. The doctor's clothes were crumpled and stained and his shoes were covered in dust. "Send your wife to him if you are abhorrent of having children. This man will never lay a hand on me." With that, she gave a baggage man instructions to remove her trunk to Bagg's Hotel.

She had just taken Louis up to their room when a rap on her door led her to think that Milton had returned. But the visitor was a heavyset man with a shock of gray hair. He introduced himself as J. Thomas Spriggs, solicitor to the Thomsons. He understood that she was in a difficult situation and was authorized to offer $150 dollars toward her expenses.

"My expenses! He was willing to pay $1,000 for an abortion. I have no means of support at this time. He leaves me in a delicate condition with $150 to cover my expenses. I think not."

Negotiations resumed when Mr. Morgan came to town. The resultant award gave Josephine $1,000. She signed an agreement excusing Milton Thomson of all responsibility in regards to the unborn child. She also agreed to turn over all correspondence she'd received from Thomson. The letters spanned a decade, and the predator suddenly wanted all evidence destroyed. She then took Louis to visit his grandmother, thinking the matter with Thomson settled for all time. Not so!

Within a few days rumors began to circulate throughout the town of Augusta. It seemed Mr. Spriggs had been visiting acquaintances in the area. At each stop, he asked if Josephine was known to them. He then made it a point to disclose her condition. When word reached Phoebe, an explosion occurred that tore the family apart.

"You slut, you whore, with your parcel of bastards!" Phoebe swiped a hand toward Louis, knocking the child to the floor.

Josephine gathered the boy into her arms, but his frightened screams could not be stilled. No matter. Phoebe overrode him.

"The shame you bring on this family! You've had every opportunity, and what have you done? You've reduced yourself to a common hussy. Get out! Get out and take your bastard with you. I pray never to set eyes on you again."

Josephine was gone the next morning. With her face buried in Louis' soft, curly mop, she stepped onto the eastbound car heading for New York. She took a window seat, but she stared through the glass unaware of the scenes that streamed before her. The train raced alongside the Mohawk

River in its curvy route to the Hudson. Every few miles, Louis would reach up to wipe his mother's tears. She drew her son closer, hugging him until he fought his way free.

Phoebe had been right, she thought. She couldn't believe what she had become. It was never her intention to do anything wrong. All she'd wanted was to learn a profession and support herself as a man would do. It wasn't she who had wrecked the marriage. Robert lured her to Europe before making the break. It was his way of keeping her helpless and devoid of recourse.

Yet if she were so innocent, why did she push away thoughts of her father? Her shame would have hurt him severely. Why did she avoid Isaiah Pratt? Trips to New York often coincided with his docking schedule. At the thought of Isaiah, her lids tightened, forcing tears to seep from the depth of her unfathomable eyes. His vision of her future had been accurate. She couldn't bear to have his image floating through her mind.

The ache in her chest intensified, and then the baby kicked in her womb. She would care for these children no matter what. And all the men be damned. Then lifting a hand to her head, she realized they couldn't all be damned. She still needed a couple to get her through the next few months.

Lawsuits were commenced by both Josephine and her mother—Phoebe's with accusations of larceny and her daughter's with charges of battery against a child. At the end, the old woman's prayer would be answered. Contact between them had been permanently severed.

Josephine found an apartment in New York located on 28th Street. The rooms were part of a large home owned by a widow with a family. But before she could have the key, she had to satisfy the landlady's awkward glance at Louis and the noticeable bulge in her belly. In a tearful stammer, she explained that her husband was serving the Union's cause in the war.

The address of the apartment was no accident. Dr. Alanson Jones lived on 28th Street. Her apartment sat no more than a block from the doctor's home. She wanted the comfort of knowing that should she run into trouble birthing this child, Dr. Jones could be called to assist. Barring the onslaught of complications, she would count on the midwives to deliver her child.

August had yet to turn, and she wouldn't reach term until October. Several weeks could pass before setting up an accouchement team. The days of confinement were past. With no one to help her, she completed errands and made appointments as if the pregnancy did not exist.

One of her appointments was with William Dodge. The attorney had drawn up her will; now she needed him to initiate a suit against Mr. Morgan. It seemed Thomson had agreed to give her fifteen hundred dollars, but the lawyer had slyly deposited five hundred into an account of his own. She wasn't about to let this dishonesty go unchallenged.

New York, like Philadelphia, changed in complexion with the advent of war. The city had been growing at a maddening pace. The current conflict stimulated greater production. Industry and ship building were operating at full tilt. But lucrative contracts give rise to corruption. Supplies intended for the Union were often rerouted to Confederate strongholds.

Amongst the general population, patriotism bloomed. Volunteer soldiers from New York and New England collected in the city as they made the journey south. Political sentiment, divided at the onset of the war, had gradually diminished, with support shifting toward the Union. New York newspapers hawked contrasting opinions to a nation eager for news.

The fevered pitch of the populace acted as a stimulant for Josephine. Summer turned to fall, and her health seemed much improved as she toted her son through throngs of people. She made arrangements for a midwife to attend to her accouchement. She'd given birth to one child on her own; she had no intention of doing so again.

The careful planning proved crucial. Her fifth child would not come forth without a fight. The midwife insisted she could accomplish the delivery on her own, but Josephine clutched at the blankets and screamed for someone to fetch Dr. Jones. The infant was badly positioned. Her old friend displayed his expertise in saving both mother and child. Her recovery came about slowly. She had no mother, sister, or faithful husband to offer encouraging endearments. But the tug of the infant at her breast and the worried expression on Louis' face established the fact that she did have a family. And God help her, she would strike down anyone who threatened to take them away.

The child was three weeks old when Milton Thomson stopped to inquire on the birth. He gazed at his son without comprehension. "What have you called him?"

"Ernest Judson. I haven't decided on a last name yet."

Milton looked up in alarm. "Just make one up!"

"Such as?" Her eyebrow accented the question.

"I don't know. How about Seymour? That's where you got your divorce. It's also the name of one of our most illustrious Democrats."

She couldn't help but giggle at the idea of the staunch Republican naming his son for a Democrat. The smile softened her face. She was thirty-seven years old, had given birth to five children and suffered numerous episodes of tragedy, and still she looked a beauty.

"Well, little fellow. What do you think? Ernest Judson Seymour?"

"You know," Milton said to Josephine, "you should have the same last name as the child. It will make things easier."

She closed her eyes and shrugged a shoulder. "I'm already known by Fagan, McCarty, and Burleigh. I suppose it wouldn't make much difference if another name joined the mix. But if that is the case, I'm changing my first name to Virginia."

"Why Virginia?"

"After my father died, my mother changed my middle name from Augusta to Virginia. I'm not sure why. Perhaps she never liked Augusta, accepting it as a way to placate my father." It never dawned on her that Milton might be suggesting a change to further distance himself from Josephine Fagan McCarty.

She spent three months nursing her infant in New York, and then she took the children to Kitty at Perth Amboy. From there she made a stop in Philadelphia where Milton Thomson caught up with her again. They met at the Continental Hotel, and a discussion ensued concerning her suit against Mr. Morgan.

"What is your wish in this regard?" she inquired with a disgruntled tone.

"I want all of this to end," he cried, dropping to his knees. "If only you will forgive me. I know I am guilty of ill usage, but should you forgive me I know we can be happy again."

"I've spoken to Colonel Wood. He says you offered him money to put me away."

"Oh no!" exclaimed Milton. "I would never do any such thing. The colonel misunderstood."

"So, why did you go to Washington? What was your business there?"

Milton smiled weakly. "You know how prone you are to trouble. I wanted to watch over you as best I could. This has all become such a mess. Do you have any idea of the mortification I have endured at the exposure of our relationship?"

"Did it occur to you that I have a right to the same charge? You had me exposed to my neighbors in Augusta and drove a wedge between Mother and me that will never be withdrawn."

"I'm sorry, Jo. Can't we somehow put it behind us?"

"Well, I can tell you the suit against Morgan had nothing to do with you. Morgan kept five hundred of the settlement money, and I am looking to have him make good."

"You needn't worry about money. I promise I'll provide for you and the child." Milton gave her one hundred dollars, and they parted on friendly terms.

She was back in Washington in 1863. Slaves had been freed in all but the Border States. Though Maryland was a Border State, officials would free the blacks through an amendment to the constitution. The cost of this freedom was dear. In the span of two years, combined casualties reached a total of 574,900 men. Some wanted the conflict ended regardless of the outcome.

Colonel Wood informed her that in spite of the occupancy by Union troops, Port Tobacco was home to a dangerous group of southern sympathizers. It was felt that with her connections, she might infiltrate the rebel society and gather information on these secessionist activities. She would not be required to don male clothing or cross the Potomac River. She'd proven herself on the last assignment. In fact, Secretary of War Stanton showed preference toward her service.

Josephine knew the secretary's opinion was based, in part, on her cooperation at the time of the Sickles trial. They'd avoided the subject at every meeting. She wouldn't allow it to be broached. The activity in Philadelphia was a secret that would be taken to the grave.

The current task produced a bit of a dilemma as it had the potential to pit her against friends. She felt a sense of relief knowing Barnes Compton had crossed the Potomac into Virginia at the beginning of the war. There was no reason to be concerned for his welfare. But there were others still active on Maryland soil. She couldn't possibly know that the plot to assassinate President Lincoln would be hatched by a group from Port Tobacco.

Mary Barnes was back at Hill Top. Early expectations that the war would be of short duration had dissolved in sorrow. Two of the Barnes boys were fighting with the Union army. Mary's return had been a harrowing effort to keep what was left of the family together. She welcomed Josephine's visit without question.

Her assignment on the peninsula was to last through spring, but she kept her role a secret. From the beginning, dissenters tended to be young and were often deserters or those who avoided the militia entirely. Subversive meetings were held at inns where conversations took place in soft tones. She gleaned her information through visits with neighbors or in what she could learn from Moses or Mina. She kept records of names, dates, and locations, sending reports through the United States mail with all correspondence addressed to a fictitious gentleman. Colonel Wood picked up the envelopes and deciphered her messages. Years later that unfailing loyalty caused Wood to speak on her behalf.

When her work for the colonel culminated in the early summer of 1863, she picked up her children and took them to Philadelphia. It was there that she learned of the battle raging in a small Pennsylvania town. That the Rebels had advanced so far was shocking, and Gettysburg burned on everyone's lips.

General George Gordon Meade then commanded the Army of the Potomac. General Sickles, his subordinate, was in command of the Third Corps, a wing of twelve thousand soldiers hailing from eight different states. Sickles' men were a prideful group, loyal to their often recalcitrant leader.

Josephine walked the floor of her rooms in terror as Philadelphia awaited news. Then word came down the wire that the Confederates were in retreat. Cheering crowds tumbled to the street in celebration. But the victory had a price; forty thousand men lay dead or injured on a bloody field of battle. It was with wringing hands that she awaited the list of casualties.

The newspapers knew of Sickles fate before the list could be compiled. Ignoring the whistles of cannon fire, her Edgar left himself open to enemy fire as he rallied his men to battle. Evening had fallen when the cannon ball caught him. His right leg was torn from his body with nothing to hold it but shreds. Heavy loss of blood put him near death; yet, in his ever-flamboyant style, he asked the stretcher bearer to light his cigar.

Her heart raced, and her mind fought torment as she set the paper aside. "Dear God," she cried, "please don't let him die."

"Who die, Mother?" Louis asked in alarm.

The child's innocent face took her to task. "No one darling." Her voice had taken a reassuring tone. "No one is going to die!"

She scooped the boy up into her arms, but could not withhold a fall of stubborn tears. Sickles was his father.

She tossed and turned throughout the night, her brain tortured by the images of field hospitals and bloody barrels of severed limbs. She knew infection claimed at least a quarter of the amputees. *If Edgar lives, how will he handle his disability? Could such a vital man survive on a stump?*

She needn't have worried. The indomitable Sickles would not only survive, but would keep the severed leg as a memento of glory. The day after his amputation, he'd been carried by stretcher for fourteen miles until reaching the Littlestown rail station. From Littlestown, he rode the train to Washington along with another fifteen hundred injured men. His still critical condition prevented further movement, and a contingent of close friends sheltered him in a house on F Street. The general remained on his stretcher with no one allowed to visit beyond those who were tending his needs. Exception was made when President Lincoln left his summer retreat and rode astride to Washington for the express purpose of seeing his injured friend.

Sickles reputation had reached the level of legends, after rising from the depths of shame. His supporters would forever hail his gallantry.

There were others who saw things differently. The general had moved his corps in defiance of orders, creating an isolated unit that lacked support. Accusations abounded that the loss of over a third of his men had been the result of a poor, unauthorized decision. Further to the point, his detractors stated, the hole he left in the line of defense nearly cost the Union its victory.

Josephine read it all and shook her head. She knew Edgar to be impetuous; it had been apparent in the horrible case of Barton Key. Just the same, she knew that whatever he'd done, he'd believed in it fully. The debate might rage for a century, but in the general's mind, Gettysburg had proven his most glorious moment.

Josephine was sick at heart. She loved Edgar intensely, but she was a person on the fringe of his life with no rights or expectation. Seeking escape from the war and its gory ramifications, she packed her belongings for another move, taking the children to New York.

CHAPTER ELEVEN

T he prosecution's aggressive bent on May 6 seemed tame when compared to the stance Mr. Mitchell had taken. His initial questioning proceeded routinely. Then staring squarely at Josephine, he'd dropped a bomb.

"Did you ever have anything to do with any other man except Thomson after the child Juddie was born, and if, so with whom?"

The defendant twisted in her chair and began to cry. Her frame shook with sobbing as he hammered away, repeating the question over and over.

The jury appeared perplexed. Mitchell was part of the defense. What prompted him to so ruthlessly batter his own client?

Court interrupted by calling a recess.

When proceedings resumed, Mr. Mitchell directed his client to put the handkerchief aside and answer his question directly.

The sobbing spilled onward. The handkerchief never moved.

Mitchell's prodding was insistent. "I will ask you here, did you ever go to Massachusetts?"

With the handkerchief still clutched to her face, his client replied that she had been to Massachusetts and had, there, known a man named Thompson. Unlike the surname of Milton Thomson, this Thompson was spelled with a *p*.

"I afterward had intercourse with this Thompson; Milton H. Thomson knew of this immediately after it occurred." She went on to describe a suit she had filed and how Milton reacted at learning she was again in the family way.

When she had finished, Mitchell asked why she thought Josie was the daughter of Milton Thomson.

She answered that the times she had been intimate with him corresponded to the date of her daughter's birth.

Defense had probed every aspect of their client's life.

Swimming in testimony, the jury asked for another brief recess.

Josephine returned to the witness box when proceedings resumed. She testified on her actions the morning of the shooting.

I saw Thomson come out of the house; when I saw him I stopped the car and took a seat; Mr. Thomson came in with another gentleman and took a seat directly opposite me; I did not speak immediately; I thought it was about a half-hour after I got in when I spoke to him; I said "Tom, I have brought you your children to support that you turned out in the street to starve—I cannot support them any longer;" he answered. "Go to hell with them!" the next that I recollect, I was standing in the middle of the car; I saw on the seat before me my revolver; I recognized it by gum or candy which adhered to the barrel; the barrel was bent; I saw no one in the car but Mr. Thomson and myself; do not think there was any one else there; I saw Mr. Thomson sitting on the seat; I observed the expression of his face; and noticed that everything about him was bloody; I don't know if I went to the front of the car or not; think that some one was holding me onto the platform of the car, think I was helped off the car; I walked down the street; I remember that some one offered me my muff; two or three spoke to me; I don't remember who they were; I remember being asked where my children were; some two or three went with me on the other side of the street and took me to the Station House; I saw or heard nothing of the shooting whatever; have no knowledge of taking out the pistol or cocking it; I don't remember seeing the pistol until I saw it on the seat; I did not hear any report or see any smoke; I did not have any intent of shooting Thomson or anyone else when I entered that car; I had never seen Mr. Hall before; I did not know him; on that car I had no thought whatever of returning to shoot again; I have no knowledge how that gun was fired; I do not know where my pocket handkerchief was; I don't know how I came to leave my muff; I was soon after put in jail and have remained there ever since; in jail Juddie and Louis remained with me; the little girl is with the Franciscan Sisters at St. Elizabeth Hospital; I never intended to do Thomson bodily injury at this time; after that transaction I had no knowledge how it occurred.

At that point, the defense concluded its examination.

WHEN JOSEPHINE ARRIVED IN NEW YORK with her little family, they came face to face with another crisis. Burned-out buildings were gruesome reminders of a murderous week of riots. The Conscription Act passed in April of 1863 contained a commutation fee. Impoverished workers subject to the draft resented the three hundred dollar exemption fee available to the wealthy. Riots erupted and increased in violence until murder and mayhem rocked the city.

The smell of wet ash assailed Josephine's nostrils the instant she stepped from the train. The odor resurrected memories of the city as it stood when she and Robert arrived in 1845. Unlike the fires that swept New York in those early days, the devastation of '63 had been perpetrated by a mob. Regiments returning from Gettysburg were ordered to take control. Weary from battling the enemy, they found themselves fighting their neighbors. The violence eventually ended, but an aura of danger remained; perhaps it was due to the blackened images the rioters had left behind.

"Mother, what is that smell?" The curious expression on her son's face caused her heart to constrict. Louis was less than three years old, yet his aptitude in speech and understanding went well beyond his years.

"There was a big fire in the city. But you needn't worry. The firemen put all the fires out."

Louis looked around. Seeing no cause for alarm, he gave his mother a confident smile. Unfortunately, she had little faith in the words she'd spoken. Pulling the children in close, she sought a hack to transport them to their hotel.

She was not surprised that the carnage had been attributed to the Irish. They were easy scapegoats, but once upset, they were difficult to control. Governor Seymour had called on Archbishop Hughes to intervene. Though weak and ailing, the prelate rose to speak to a crowd of five thousand and directed them to keep the peace. Ultimately, the draft was suspended, order was restored, and pride in the archbishop gave dignity to the Irish populace.

Within the week, Milton Thomson announced himself at the hotel. His mood was genial as he offered small gifts to the children. His expression changed as he turned toward their mother. "I've missed you." he said with intensity. "I want you back."

"It won't mortify you to do so?" She commented, with mock indignation.

"Please. Let's not start another quarrel. You know I love you. I always will." Pulling her towards him, he kissed her hungrily.

"Not now," she stated nodding at the children.

"I'll return this evening with a bottle of wine." Milton kissed her tenderly and backed away. He'd been without hope when he knocked at her door. This hint of promise sent a rush through his body. *Damn but that vixen can boil a man.*

Their intimacy resumed, and the following day he rubbed his hands together in contemplation. "We'll have to find you a suitable boarding house. The hotel is no place for children."

"The children are going back to Kitty," she announced decidedly. "I will be working in Massachusetts."

Milton drew breath as if punched in the stomach. "What are you talking about?"

"I've been engaged as an agent with Grover & Baker's Sewing Machines. My district encompasses Pittsfield, Great Barrington, and several other communities in that area."

A fish peering from a bowl couldn't look more bewildered. Milton opened his mouth several times before he was able to utter the question. "Why?"

"Experience has taught me that work is the only reliable source of income."

"I told you I would take care of you!"

"Yes, I've heard you state so many times. I will be traveling between Pittsfield and New York on a monthly basis. I'll notify you when I have assembled my schedule."

Milton clawed at his beard. "I think it will be best if you channel my mail through Ephraim Chamberlain."

"I suppose Ephraim understands your dilemma." The comment was delivered with unmistakable sarcasm.

"Jo, why don't you just stay put?"

Anger flared in her retort. "I'll stay put when I have a home of my own and a place to rear my children. Do you think that a goal beyond my scope of achievement?"

She took rooms on the second floor of a house on Pittsfield's main thoroughfare. Milton had returned to Utica and the boys were with Kitty. She surveyed the empty flat in contemplation. The largest room would serve as her showroom. She needed at least a few pieces of furniture. A smile crossed her face as she glanced through the window. A furniture store sat directly across the street.

Bells tingled as she stepped over the threshold. An August sun flamed at her back, creating a slim silhouette. In response to the bells, a bright-eyed young man zigzagged across a floor cluttered with furniture, some new, some used. He introduced himself as the store's proprietor, stating his name as Thompson.

Josephine started.

"Thompson," he said again.

She raised a hand to stifle her laughter. Of course, there were hundreds of people, more likely thousands, who carried that name.

"My name is Seymour," she said pleasantly. "Virginia Seymour. If you don't mind, I'm interested in the spelling of your name."

With a confused expression, the man answered, "T-h-o-m-p-s-o-n."

She smiled. "Yes, of course."

While Josephine paid for her selections, she frowned as she looked across the street. Mr. Thompson read her thoughts and offered to deliver the items to her rooms. She had a bed, a chest, a table, two straight chairs, and a small rug. After several trips across the street and up the stairs, the young proprietor took a moment to catch his breath. His thin chest heaved from exertion as he leaned against the door frame. He was a small man with heavy, dark sideburns, a characteristic his neighbor found amusing - a sort of hangdog, puppy look.

Taking pity on the fellow, she made her excuses. "I'd offer you a beverage, but I have nothing in my cabinet."

He nodded at her and continued to stare. Josephine thought: *In another few minutes his little pink tongue will be hanging to the point of his chin.* "I appreciate your assistance, Mr. Thompson. Now if I can get my business settled everything will be just fine."

"I'd be happy to stay and help, Mrs. Seymour."

"That won't be necessary, thank you. I expect you should get back to the store before some sly soul empties your cash drawer."

Thompson jumped with a cry: "Great balls of fire!" He bumped into the walls from side to side in his haste to get to the bottom of the stairs.

He returned the next day to hang her sign on the front of the building. The sewing machines were expensive, and though traffic at the shop remained steady, sales were few and far between. She traveled to other communities within the district hoping women would be convinced that her machine could save them both time and money. The tiring process left little patience for Thompson with a *p*.

He stood in the doorway of his store when she left in the morning and was standing at her door when she returned at night. His main occupation seemed to be wheedling an invitation to her second-floor rooms. What she didn't see was his figure slouching in the shadow of the store late into the evening.

Thompson smoldered as he watched her move between the oil lamp and the curtained window. He'd never encountered a woman of such appeal. She had become an obsession. He grunted and grinned at a new thought. *She's probably no cook. My wife is a great little cook, but somehow that's just not enough.* He left the thought there, ignoring the fact that his supper had been waiting for over an hour.

Josephine did her best to push Thompson to the very back of her mind. Men were driving her loony. If they kept it up, she would likely end up at the asylum in Utica.

Edgar was convalescing at Lake George. Newspapers stated that a large contingent of caretakers tended his needs while well-wishers kept him company. Though anxious to see him, she thought it doubtful that the two would meet again. After all, his wife seldom saw him. Teresa Sickles lived as a vanquished recluse in an elaborate Bloomingdale tomb. She wondered about his daughter, Laura. Once the apple of her father's eye, it seemed she was as much a prisoner as her mother.

Josephine's jaunts to New York to settle accounts with Grover & Baker invariably led to a rendezvous with Milton. He would arrive before her and routinely register at the Brandreth. On occasion, he would escort her to a performance of some sort. A darkened facility lent itself well to covert liaisons. When attending the Fashion Course harness track, he introduced her openly. The status of the clientele determined the manner of his actions.

It happened that she was in New York on January 3 when Archbishop Hughes passed away. He was one of the most cherished people of her acquaintance. She stood amidst the thousands who mourned his death. His accomplishments had been many; his success was an inspiration. An Irish immigrant who worked in the gardens at Mount St. Mary's College in Maryland, he entered that same institution as a student on the recommendation of Mother Elizabeth Seton. Once ordained as a priest, he'd risen through the hierarchy of the Catholic Church, and during the War Between the States had been welcomed in courts throughout Europe. Yet he never forgot the working class from which he had descended.

He labored for his church and his country, founding St. John's College, an institution that would later be known as Fordham University. Under his guidance, ninety-seven churches were constructed and the cornerstone was laid for St. Patrick's Cathedral. Revered by the Irish and respected by many, he was eulogized by President Lincoln.

For Josephine, Father John's death was a personal loss. She ached for the friend who'd been so caring in some of her most trying times. She knew her actions were a betrayal to what he might have expected. But her eyes were dry, for there was no turning back. She hoped he would understand.

The relationship with Milton continued. There seemed to be no escape. Then one evening she put him off with a complaint of not being well. Milton took a flask from his pocket and fed her a couple of spoonfuls. The liquid had a sweet taste that she found agreeable. He explained that it was bitters and fed her some more. Within an hour, her stomach revolted and vomiting accompanied the pain at her temples.

Milton watched from a chair until the early hours of the morning, when he got to his feet, exited the room, and locked the door, tossing her key back through an open window.

She thrashed on her bed for nearly a week, slipping in and out of consciousness. When recovered enough to think things through, she suspected Milton of poisoning her. It fit with the incredible scenario described by Colonel Wood. His attention was an obsession; he couldn't bear to leave her be.

For her sewing machine business, she worked outward from Pittsfield to Great Barrington in the south and North Adams to the north. Her district encompassed a strip that ran the length of the border between Massachusetts and New York. While the machines were in great demand, a dear price put them beyond reach of the average household. Profits were not what she'd envisioned, and her frustration grew every day. Neighbor Thompson's hovering became an increasing annoyance.

By April, she knew she was pregnant again.

Announcement of the news disgusted Milton. His language blistered the walls. "If you don't get an abortion, we are through. I refuse to be drawn into another damaging scandal."

"And I will not destroy the child."

Milton left with his back hunched and would be out of her life for several years. Josephine considered herself safer with him gone. Since the incident with the flask, his presence made her increasingly uncomfortable.

Thompson with a *p* continued to press her, and she felt it time to teach him a lesson. The punishment for lust would be honeyfuggling. She had no conscience when it came to Thompson with a *p*. She led him to her chamber as the spider might draw a fly. He was a clumsy lover, but she satisfied his craving.

When the door closed behind him, she pondered her motive. *What is wrong with me? Father would shun me and I wouldn't blame him.* Then, squaring her shoulders, she lifted her chin in defiance. *Father was one of a kind. Men are users. They take what they want, casting off what is left. It might be a game to them, but I have my own set of rules.*

Carnal relations continued with Thompson for over a month. If she had no conscience, neither did Thompson. His innocent wife would be shocked and humiliated when his infidelity became public. And Josephine made sure the affair reached the newspaper.

She appeared before a magistrate in the village of Lanesboro and had Thompson charged with a paternity suit. Then removing herself to Albany, she left her suit in the hands of a lawyer. A settlement was reached. The action besmirched the man's reputation and forced him to compensate her with five hundred dollars.

The announcement caused Josephine's jaw to tighten as a single eyebrow formed an arch. *Thompson thought himself a master of conquests; well, he deserved to have that victory haunt him.*

She retrieved her sons from Perth Amboy in 1864 and settled them in an East Albany cottage leased from Warren Kelley. Apart from their time on the Isle of Wight, she hadn't had a home since leaving Augusta. Marriage to Robert had been the beginning of a life lived in boarding houses and rented rooms. While the new arrangement offered privacy and comfort, for the first time in her life she would have full responsibility for the care of a house as well as the preparation of meals and the stocking of wood and coal. She shrugged her elegant shoulders. Her life in Augusta had been an education in housewifely duties.

Albany had changed significantly since her trip with Robert Norris. The prospect of life in the capital filled her with anticipation.

These musings drove her as she shoved furniture across the bare wood floor and looked for wall space to hang a picture. "We're home, children, and we'll never be separated again."

Louis whooped and jumped up and down. His exuberance was contagious as laughter pealed from the jolly cheeks of his little brother, Ernest Judson Seymour. Ernest was nearing his second birthday and had been dubbed with the nickname Juddie, a happy name for a happy child. Louis had a tendency to be more serious, but on this occasion his reaction was joyous.

September brought a sobering letter from Lyman Warren saying her mother had passed. It had taken some time for the news to catch up with her. Phoebe had been buried for weeks and questions had arisen. She dropped the letter in the midst of its reading. The infant within her moved, and her heart felt as if it had been passed through a ringer. She'd loved her mother and despised the bitterness that had driven them apart. Tracing backward in time, she tried to remember the happy days, but the dancing images that made her smile were always those of her father, Terrence, and his merry Irish eyes. Phoebe's haughty demeanor discouraged affection. Expressions of love came at arm's length, yet she'd considered her mother a most admirable lady deserving of great respect. Change had been wrought with her marriage to Camp.

Desperate for someone to lean on, her mother betrayed all principle in one fell swoop. As a man of refinement, Terrence reaped the respect of his community, but Camp's penchant for liquor had a negative impact. To the extent that she was able, she'd skirted the perimeter of Camp's bloodshot gaze. But Phoebe had taken the man into their house and into her bed, staining the image she'd carried for years. Memory of past troubles raced through Josephine's mind. The conflict had ended. She could only hope that her mother would rest in peace.

The unborn child moved again, giving her to wonder what her children thought. Louis and Juddie had been farmed out for months. While she'd spent much of her youth at boarding schools, her formative years had been with her parents. She would have to do better in the future.

Retrieving the letter, she read on. The farm had come into question. With a settlement elusive, Robert McCarty had sold the mortgage to Oliver Curtis. Curtis took the paper on speculation, allowing Robert five hundred dollars on a mortgage of seven hundred. Interest had been accruing since 1846 and had grown to a value of one thousand dollars. From Curtis' point of view, it looked to be a lucrative transaction. Josephine hoped the money would scorch Robert's fingers.

She shook her head in an effort to temper her thoughts. Facts were jumbled and order escaped her. The farm would have to wait. At present, she believed Homer Stewart to be working the land. He'd been a good steward in the past; she trusted him as an able farmer.

Though wanting to resume her practice of medicine, she lacked the energy to do so. Her body seemed sluggish in this sixth pregnancy. For the next three months she managed the house and tended the children. Recalling the complications of Juddie's birth, she made a resolve to take better care of herself.

Dr. Straats delivered her sixth baby in an Albany hospital on November 14, 1864. She named the child Josephine Seymour.

Little Josie gazed upward from a cradle as the boys tiptoed toward her for an introductory view. She was fighting the air with clenched fists.

"Sissie's boxing," cried Louis.

"Thissie," mimicked Juddie in a lisp.

Two sons and a daughter; Josephine observed them with tenderness. Her family was complete once again. The McCarty children were ghosts of the past, but no one could touch the Seymour children.

By 1865, the long days of the Confederate rebellion were giving way to hints that the conflict might end, bolstered by a string of Union victories. Lincoln had been re-elected, making him the first incumbent to regain the White House since Andrew Jackson in 1832. General Sickles was stomping through Washington, hoping to regain his command before the war ended. Josephine shared in the surge of hope with an advertisement announcing her services as a female medical practitioner. This fragile euphoria constituted a high point between two hurricanes.

When the army of Virginia surrendered on April 9, there was little opportunity to celebrate. Troops to the west were still in conflict, and before the War Between the States officially ended, fate took another swipe at the country.

A group of radical secessionists had formed a plot to kill the Union's leaders. They acted on Good Friday, April 15, just six days after the surrender. Secretary of State William Seward was stabbed repeatedly as he lay in his bed recuperating from a previous injury. The attack took place at the former Club House on Lafayette Square, site of the Phil Barton Key shooting. Seward survived the knifing, as did his daughter and sons who were cut while trying to protect him. General Grant and Vice-President Andrew Johnson were also targeted, but due to a confluence of circumstance the assault on them never took place. John Wilkes Booth achieved his goal in firing the shot that killed President Lincoln.

Josephine suffered the shock with great remorse. She'd spent months gathering information in Charles County, Maryland. What had she accomplished? The greatest tragedy that could befall the conflicting states had been hatched in that very location. Her heart grew heavier still on the news that Barnes Compton had been jailed on suspicion of conspiracy. While she knew him to be a secessionist, it was beyond belief that the child she'd tutored in Port Tobacco could be involved in an assassination. Later reports confirming his innocence produced a modicum of relief.

Compton's arrest was indicative of the chaos and fear running rampant in the capital. The country's secretary of war was proving to be a cool administrator. Yet calm would not come to Washington; avarice had fired the city.

The original conflict had been fought under the guise of high purpose. Post-war action was an open quest for power. Newly seated President Johnson set a policy of leniency toward the South. His philosophy met with quick opposition from radical Republicans seeking to humble the secessionist states. There were no halfway measures on either side. An unbridgeable chasm split the president and the secretary of war in an ultimatum that left most of the South under martial law. Honor and respect were virtues of the past, and the political storm spewed treachery that would ultimately call for Johnson's impeachment.

Sickles had been serving as Lincoln's envoy to Columbia when the assassination occurred. The 2,500 mile excursion back to Washington came at a slow and tedious pace. By the time he reached his destination, his president had been buried, Booth shot, and the Confederacy reduced to a topic of history. A friend had passed, but it was no time to cower. Reconstruction offered unique possibilities, and the one-legged general parlayed his way to command of the Department of the Carolinas.

Josephine followed the moves in Washington, but all energy was directed toward her medical practice. She had once again taken the name of Emma Burleigh.

The women she saw were often ignorant of the organs and processes within their own bodies. She encouraged them to be aware, offering advice on hygiene, nutrition, and protection against pregnancy. She treated diseases and executed procedures. The patients who worried her most were pregnant and desperate. They begged for their lives, threatened with murder should husband, father, or brother learn of their secret. The pretty little girls were less fearful. False confidence gave these childish women the expectation that the father of the child would continue to care for them. Seduced by gentlemen out of their class, these youngsters would be burdened for the rest of their lives as the gentlemen moved to their next paramour. It was a replication of the misery she'd witnessed at Blockley and the Hospital de la Salpêtrière in Paris.

Josephine deliberated as to what she should do. Abortions done elsewhere would likely take place in a filthy environment. The desperate were doomed whichever way they turned.

She moved her family to a spacious house with a large, treed yard on

Clinton Avenue. The new residence offered better accommodations for her patients. It also required the hiring of a housekeeper.

The children were enchanted by Mrs. Grant, a pleasant black lady who gave orders in a soft voice and chastised them without ever tattling. But Josephine's spine straightened when she heard their voices floating through an open window.

"Tinkle, tinkle, here's a new wrinkle, we've got a maid and you've got a sickle."

She looked out to see her children taunting the boy next door. Experiences in the schoolyard led Louis to the practice of teasing chants. It was behavior she would not tolerate. On her way to the yard, she passed Mrs. Grant, who was standing near the kitchen window. The woman appeared to be stifling a laugh, but Josephine charged on.

"Louis! What is this chant I'm hearing?"

The children looked up in alarm.

"You should be ashamed of yourselves. Louis, get the sickle from the back of the house and help this boy with his chores. Juddie, take your sister into the house and go to your room."

As the children grew, the outside world was bound to penetrate the shell of their home. It didn't take long to realize that Louis had learned more than just chants on the playground. He was bright and observant and his questions were troubling.

"Who is my father and why don't we see him? Joseph's father is a merchant. He drives Joseph to school every day. Where is my father, and what does he do?"

His mother replied without hesitation. "Your father was a hero killed in the war."

The housekeeper lifted her head at mention of the children's father. Josephine noted the movement, calculating the need to deflect further inquiry. While she cared nothing for what people might think of her, protecting the children remained an issue.

"Do you like children, Mrs. Grant?"

"I do indeed," the woman answered.

"Then please be good to my children. They lost their father in a great battle down South and need to be treated gently."

The woman nodded and went on with her dusting.

While the household ran smoothly, the suit against the farm hung like a millstone around Josephine's neck. She owned a deeded half interest to the seventy-five acres. On Phoebe's death, the remaining half had been divided between herself and her sister's heirs, Charles and Griffin Coffin and their sister, Miranda Coolidge. Her lawyer, Hiram Jenkins, encouraged her to fight for the estate, but she hadn't the funds to do so. The farm meant nothing to her relatives. Reflection produced a single option. She contacted Michael Meyers, and he took the assignment without consideration. While nothing more than a temporary fix, Meyers' action would stave foreclosure for a while.

There were other situations for which no fix could be found.

Teresa Bagioli Sickles passed away in February, 1867. Though married to Daniel Sickles at the time of her death, there had been no place for her in his life. Teresa's existence had been one of a living creature haunting a lonely mansion. In the strict moral code of the day, there could be no forgiveness for a woman who betrayed her husband. Murder could be pardoned, but nothing would exonerate Teresa. In a strange twist of values, those who condemned her most became mourners at her funeral. They spilled from the pews of St. Joseph's Church, paying belated respect to this chastened woman of thirty-one.

The parallels that connected Josephine to Teresa made her sympathetic to the wife she had cheated. No such feelings existed when it came to Helen Thomson. Acquainted with Helen Welton before her marriage to Milton, she'd labeled the woman a silly goose and beneath consideration. An image of Helen crept through her mind, stirring annoyance, as she moved to answer a knock at the door.

It was a blustery night of heavy rain. She drew back the bolt and stepped back in surprise. Milton Thomson stood before her.

"You look like someone in need of shelter," she said, grinning at his dripping beard.

"I would appreciate it, Jo." Milton's expression was unusually serious. "We had some problems on the road. Could you possibly put the driver and me up for a night?"

"I guess we can manage. Tell the driver to go to the back of the house. I have a man named Harry who cares for the grounds. Your driver can stay with him."

She directed Milton to a chair by the fire and hung his coat to dry. "Would you like a glass of brandy?"

"Yes, I would. Thank you."

He watched tiredly as the children played on the floor. The game was supposed to be checkers, though Louis appeared to be the only one with knowledge of the rules. They were beautiful children, all three of them.

"You probably didn't know," he said to Josephine. "But I've had someone watching the house. I wanted to be sure you and the children were safe."

"I observed the policeman on several occasions. I believed our location to be a part of his beat."

Milton shook his head. "I do care, you know." He looked strained and his tone was one of pleading. "What do you say, Jo. Can we bury the hatchet? It would be so much nicer if we could be friends."

Her smile was wary. "I expect that might be possible."

When Milton returned a few weeks later, he had some things he wanted to settle. "Jo, in the event that anything should happen to me, I want you to go to Doonsticks."

"I beg your pardon?"

"I mean my brother, Mortimer. There is a paper, in the safe, relating to the children. I've made provisions for all of them. I also want to assure you that if you should die first, they will be taken care of. I make that a promise."

With this understanding set between them, he made it clear that he would be a regular visitor. The next time he appeared at the door, the reins were in his hands and the driver had been dismissed. Once he was confident that the children were safely asleep, he approached Jo with the amorous expression she'd been dreading.

"Jo, I've missed you so." Cupping her face in his hands, he bent to plant a kiss on her lips, but Josephine was twisting away. "I can't get you out of my mind. I've tried. God knows I've tried."

"There's no way our relationship can succeed beyond the bounds of friendship. All past attempts have failed. You have a wife; your place is with her."

"But don't you remember? I said you would be as a wife to me! I've told you the children will be cared for. What more do you want?"

She thought of Edgar, of the precious moments they had shared and the excitement she'd felt at his touch. Directing her attention back to Milton, she saw the awkward clerk who'd tended the post office at Norris' store. Nothing he'd done through the past two decades had impressed her one iota. It didn't matter, his arms were around her, and his lips pressed her skin as he pushed her to the bedroom.

It was a scene that would be replayed every two or three weeks from August through December. The children referred to him casually as "Uncle Tom." His visits extended to the wee hours of the morning, when he would steal from the house leaving a sum for the children's welfare.

Thoughts of these circumstances weighed on Josephine's mind when he returned the week before Christmas. She tried to explain that his visits had become a problem, but her remarks ignited an argument. As he stood to leave, his mood slipped from anger to deliberation. "Well, Jo, shall I say goodbye?"

"I think that would be best." Maintaining the relationship had been increasingly difficult. To continue would be impossible.

They shook hands in the manner of business associates. In both minds this was the end.

On the national front, President Johnson's rapport with Congress was permanently fractured. Congress had control of everything but the military. The president was frantic to keep what leverage he had, and his faith in Stanton had dwindled. He sought to replace him with a man he could trust.

But the secretary of war adamantly refused to leave, remaining at his desk day and night. He served as Congress's connection to total control. In an effort to keep him in place, Congress enacted the Tenure in Office Act to restrict the president from dismissing any Cabinet member without approval of the Senate. A bitter struggle ensued, and whispers of impeachment were out in the open

As Josephine read the reports she envisioned Stanton—a little man with graying brows knit together, the sharp eyes missing nothing, and the self-satisfied smile that would leave the corners of his mouth pointing downward. No one disputed his brilliance in law. Had it not been for that shrewdness of mind, her son's father would be dead.

Edgar was destined to suffer from this political tug of war. His friendship with Stanton put him at odds with President Johnson, and there were no tenure bills to bolster his position. At the end of August, Sickles received notice that he had been relieved of his command over the Department of the Carolinas.

Congress voted to impeach the president on February 24, 1868. The resolution failed in the Senate. Stanton, however, had lost the fight and was preparing to vacate his office.

Within days of the failed impeachment, the one-legged general appeared in Albany. The former Democrat was now firmly supporting Ulysses S. Grant in his bid to capture the White House. Chosen chairman of the New York delegation to the Republican National Convention, Edgar was on his way to Chicago.

A crowd surrounded the general as he walked from the train depot to the platform. Josephine was caught in the press of pedestrians. As she peered through the maze of bobbing heads, her eyes met Edgar's. He tipped his hat with an engaging, roguish grin and boarded the train and was carried away.

She walked on toward an office on Broadway. She'd moved her practice downtown and had a schedule of patients waiting.

CHAPTER TWELVE

The May 7 proceedings opened with less than twenty people in the audience and counsel for both sides tardy. Mrs. McCarty entered punctually with Josie to one side of her and Juddie at the other. The *Observer* noted that they were bright and handsome children—whoever their parents might be. Mary Jane Grant, the housekeeper they once bragged about, was seated at the back of the courtroom. Her expression indicated grave concern.

Sedgwick's questioning stepped back in time, centering on Josephine's behavior in Philadelphia, her confrontation with a news reporter, and her arrest for larceny. The prosecution insinuated that an affair with Dr. Smith had caused a scandal at Blockley Hospital.

Throughout the morning Josephine responded to the ongoing list of repetitive questions. Her answers appeared straightforward, yet her loyalty belonged elsewhere, and not to the oath she took that day. She denied having pulled a dirk on anyone and insisted she never gave birth to a child in Philadelphia. Louis was adopted.

There were questions as to her occupying a room with an officer in O'Donnell's Club House. Did she know the club house was home to the Sickles Brigade? She answered again that her purpose in Washington was to assist at the medical facilities and that traveling in male attire had been expedient throughout the rebellion.

So, why was she visiting the Sickles encampment? Again she referred to her medical mission. There was no examination of any personal involvement with the general.

Though newspapers in the past named Edwin Stanton her patron, the man had, by then, expired. His name did not appear in the transcript of the trial.

It was after a short morning recess, while describing her meetings with Milton Thomson, that she broke from testimony to ask the prosecutor if he expected her to repeat every conversation that had occurred between them.

Her counsel, Mr. Pomeroy, objected immediately, repeating his client's question.

Mr. Sedgwick answered, "I do not expect to be chastised by the counsel. I shall get all these answers so that they shall be understood after a while."

When court reconvened from the noon recess, the audience had burgeoned and all were present except the judge. Doolittle was tardy.

Throughout the afternoon, Josephine's testimony again traced her actions in Washington and her ongoing relationship with Thomson. The mortgage situation was reviewed without any new facts being added. Her answers in regards to life insurance did prove helpful in clarifying the issue of providing for the children.

"I had put a life policy of five thousand dollars for Sissie; I proposed that Thomson should put one of equal amount on his life for Juddie; I don't know what Spriggs said to that. When I got back I presume I wrote him, but I have no recollection how many letters I wrote him. From 1864 to 1867, Milton Thomson supplied no support whatsoever."

Counsel for the people pushed onward. Entered as evidence was the advertisement she'd published in reference to her medical practice. Mr. Sedgwick was looking to establish her as an abortionist. When asked by counsel for the people if she had in her house instruments of abortion, she replied that she had an ax which she presumed could be used for that purpose.

Mr. Sedgwick pressed her further, insisting that she had yet to answer the question. She denied ever having seen such an instrument or any knowledge that such an instrument existed.

Sedgwick then asked if she hadn't confided in Hortense Martin that studies she'd undertaken in Europe were preparation for the business of performing abortions. Over the objection of her defense, Josephine insisted on answering, stating that a blow or kick could easily have the effect of causing an abortion. She did not study abortion in France. Her activities in that country were to assist Robert McCarty in his business ventures. Her advertisement for the removal of obstructions involved the interruption or retention of the menses. She'd known a woman named Martin, but she never told her that she was going into the abortion business and would not have been likely to as the woman was a talking newspaper, distributing news to every home in the neighborhood.

Two letters were entered as exhibits. Both were addressed to Mr. J. Thomas Spriggs, solicitor to the Thomsons. She identified each as bearing her signature.

Sedgwick read a message written across the top of one of the letters: "I parley with you only to give you a chance to do as you propose to do. Because the next step will be forever irretrievable, and I shall spare no pains in the future to torment the Thomsons."

Listening to the words, she admitted to herself that she'd meant them. The Thomsons had caused her insurmountable pain; she wanted retribution. But the intent to kill never had home in those thoughts.

"I supported three children by my own exertions," she stated in a harried voice. Then turning to her counsel, she asked if she might be excused. "I feel unwell and unable to continue."

Counsel prodded her. "If you are able, you should continue."

She was handed a fan and questioning continued until a recess was called some sixty minutes later. At one point, Sedgwick had become so confused that he addressed the accused as Mrs. Thomson. The flustered prosecutor quickly corrected himself.

"Did you throw vitriol upon Mrs. Dennison?" he asked.

"Mrs. Dennison attacked me and I threw what I held in her direction."

"Did it take her hair off?"

Josephine withheld a smile. "I imagine she had none to take off."

"She had none left afterward?" Sedgwick inquired.

"It might have taken off her waterfall."

The day finally ended when Mr. Pomeroy petitioned for an adjournment due to Mr. Mitchell having been called to a family emergency.

This was the end of Josephine's lengthy stretch on the witness stand.

TO JOSEPHINE'S ANNOYANCE, Milton returned in the spring of 1869. Grant's inauguration had taken place, and the lifelong Republican seemed desirous of celebrating. "Are you happy to see me, Jo?"

"I believe your children would be happy to see you. But you must cut your visits short. The late hours of past visits compromised me with my neighbors."

He sidled toward her. "Come on, Jo. You're still my girl."

His comment brought a sigh. It was obvious that he'd been drinking. They'd said their goodbyes months before, and "his girl" would not be cajoled.

"I think it would be best if you discontinued these visits and mailed your support for the children."

"Never shall I do so," he blustered. "If I cannot spend time here, you will have to make do on your own."

She was on her own; it had been so for quite some time. She closed the door without regret, leaving Milton to shuffle off toward his carriage.

The men in her life were as chess pieces, every movement calculated to gain advantage. Upon his election, Grant appointed Sickles Minister to Spain. Edgar would be gone for years. Edwin Stanton had serious health problems, but his ambition would eventually flourish in Wheeling, West Virginia.

Josephine was doing well on her own. The children were attending one of the best private schools in Albany. Through the years she'd maintained her connections with the powers in the state capital. Her bank account had grown, and she had serious thoughts of buying a house.

What she hadn't expected was another round with Milton.

When he knocked at the door, she led him to the parlor where he sat in a chair observing her actions with the children. His fists tightened. He hated the woman, hated her for the hold she had over him. She'd never loved him. He knew that. Yet he'd followed like a puppy lapping at her heels.

Every farewell had been recanted. Her beauty, the scent of her hair, the softness of her flesh as his hands roamed her body...it was a pull he could not resist.

She turned from ministering to a bump on the younger boy's knee. The motion was slow and graceful. Milton's hands fell limply toward the floor.

"Isn't our Juddie a handsome fellow?" She patted the boy on his behind, sending him off to play.

Milton watched, and as he did, thought bitterly: *Why couldn't Helen have given me children? Is my only heir to be a bastard?*

"What is it?" Josephine asked. "Why do you look so strange?"

Milton shook his head. "I've been feeling a little strange. I'm sure it's nothing to worry about, but I must be getting along."

She watched as he exited through the back door and drove his horse down the driveway. His complexion had grayed. His step appeared halting. She didn't think him well. He'd made numerous promises to her over the years. The children were to be provided for, but what of Milton's family? She had no faith in their good will.

The children's welfare had been nagging at her for weeks. It was the occupation of her mind as she walked down State Street one April morning.

Justice McNamara sauntered toward her. With a tip of his hat, he offered a greeting. "Good morning, Mrs. Seymour."

She responded politely and was about to pass when he spoke to her again.

"I have been thinking of you. If I remember correctly, you mentioned, not long ago, that you were interested in purchasing a home."

"I have given it much consideration," she replied. "Unfortunately, I am not in a position to act on a purchase at this time."

"Well, I am overseeing the sale of a house on Howard Street. It will be going up for auction. If you have a moment, I'll give you the particulars."

McNamara guided her to a park that bordered the Capitol building. Daffodils dotted the lawn in great profusion, while fluttering breezes made folly of serious conversation.

Ignoring spring's seductive overtures, the judge proceeded in his description of the Howard Street property. "As you know, the most fashionable real estate now lies north of State Street; nonetheless, Howard is still a good location with close proximity to the Capitol. I won't lie to you, the building needs work. But there are any number of workers capable of making the improvements. Repairs shouldn't run over five hundred dollars."

Josephine looked doubtful.

"It's a lovely home, Mrs. Seymour, and it's going up for auction."

"I'll walk by and take a look."

Howard Street sat one block south of the park and ran east toward the Hudson River. Number sixty-two stood on the first block, one of six houses commonly joined with the last sitting on the corner where Wendel Street ran into Howard.

She stopped at the entrance to gaze at the wide stone steps. A solid double door was graced with heavily leaded windows and a brass knob and lock set that would glisten with the rub of a little polish. Her eyes trailed the bricks to the cornice trimming the roofline. The three-storied house was narrow and deep as were all the houses in the row. A stable was located in the alley off Wendel Street, giving each of the homes on Howard deeded stall and carriage space.

Her brows came together as she sighed. Was she in any position to buy such a place?

On her way home she stopped to telegraph Milton. Never one to wait once a thought took hold, she caught the 5:15 train to Utica the following morning.

Milton stood waiting at the depot. His look of appraisal hinted at scorn. "So you want to buy a house?"

"Do you think it a foolish idea? I've been approached about a house that's going up for auction. It is a fine building, but I will need your assistance if I am to take any action."

"Are you able to contribute anything toward this deal?" he questioned.

"I have a thousand dollars to invest."

Thomson registered a look of surprise before nodding his head in affirmation. "I will contribute an amount equal to your own." A look of satisfaction smoothed his face. "Can you spare the time to have dinner with me?"

She nodded pleasantly. "Of course, don't I always make time for you?"

They had finished with dinner and were returning to the depot when Thomson suggested she have a mortgage made out to him. It was Josephine's turn to react with surprise; she had taken his offer to be a gift.

"It will be a safeguard," Milton assured her. "If you fall ill or have a problem arise, I'll be in a position to settle things. In fact, I think it would be best if you had Meyers assign the mortgage on the farm to me as well. That will allow you to keep the bulk of your paper with a single entity."

While their relationship had been tumultuous, she'd retained her trust of Milton when it came to business decisions. "That will be fine."

As the train clacked back to Albany, her eagerness grew. She couldn't wait to share the news. The children would surely be surprised. It came as a shock that the children had doubts.

"Why do you want to move?" asked Louis.

"Well, this will give us a home of our own."

Juddie looked at her curiously. "Isn't this our home?"

"No, darling, it is not. I pay a man to let us live here. The building belongs to him. If he wishes to put us out, he can do so and we will have no recourse. If I buy a house, it will be our home and no one will have the authority to make us move. Besides, the new house has a stable. We may be able to buy a horse and, perhaps, a cow." The last statement clinched it for the children. Louis' inherited love of horses endowed him with a gift the equine species understood. He would take on the stable chores if the family were to own a horse.

When the house went up for sale, Josephine received a message from the auctioneer asking if she would like him to bid on her behalf. Her response was that the bid should not exceed $4,500. Justice McNamara contacted her some days later stating that her bid on the house at 62 Howard Street had been accepted subject to a $3,000 mortgage and a down payment of $1,500. Josephine expected the repairs to run $500, so she was in need of $2,000.

Milton took a second mortgage in return for lending her the promised

$1,000. That sum, along with the $1,000 she'd saved, fulfilled the requirements of the purchase. She signed the papers thinking the transfer to have been handled in a very efficient manner. The ink had barely dried when Gilbert Oliver, the seller of the house, assigned her $3,000 mortgage to a man named Mark Wilde. Josephine shrugged her shoulders without concern. That was the nature of business.

She dickered in the purchase of a horse and ended up with a ten-year-old gelding. The carriage horse held no resemblance to the little black Morgan she'd loved. Yet, the rangy, old bay had spent years in a harness and would be a reliable beast on the streets of Albany.

Keeping her economic situation in mind, she bought a two-wheeled buggy with a collapsible hood and side curtains. The single bench seat held herself and Louis with Sissie sitting between them. Juddie crouched in the storage box behind them.

The children were bursting with pride. Views from the buggy were far superior to those of a pedestrian sidewalk. As for the horse, they believed him the finest steed in town, christening him with the name Fleet Feet. Bragging about the maid had gotten them into trouble. Repeating the horse's name would give the desired impression without having to do any bragging.

A country boy delivered the cow by driving her with a stick. As they rounded the corner from Wendel Street, he gave the cow a tap that sent her trotting down the alley. When they reached the stable behind number 62, he led the silky, brown Guernsey to her stall and turned to face the accusing Seymour children.

"Why did you hit our cow?" demanded Louis.

"I didn't hurt that cow any. Just guidin' her so she won't run off." Josephine sparkled with approval at the children's concern. The larger house and the arrival of animals greatly increased her workload, but the advantages it brought to the children made the effort worthwhile.

Unfortunately, her finances were in shambles. The indoor plumbing and gas installations were yet to be completed. Initial estimates for the work had multiplied to thousands.

The need for money drove her to compose advertisements for the Albany newspapers:

To Ladies,

Mrs. Burleigh, M.D., offers a safe and effective remedy for all female irregularities and obstructions, of however long standing, without injury to the health of the patient. Ladies are provided with the best medical care and nursing. All chronic diseases of the uterus are permanently cured. Mrs. B. is not only a graduate of medicine, but spent four years in the hospitals of London and Paris, and possesses a knowledge of all French discoveries. Ladies desirous of availing themselves of the appliances of modern science should consult

MRS. BURLEIGH, 62 Howard Street, near Eagle
Letters must contain one dollar and be addressed,
Box 979 P.O. Albany, N.Y.

While Josephine's practice flourished, success brought notoriety, and her advertisement drew the attention of zealots. They were anxious to exercise laws passed in 1845 making abortion a crime, not only for the practitioner but also for the woman submitting to the procedure. An indictment was sought not on Josephine's actions but on the wording of her advertisement. Though the charges were dismissed, another layer of tarnish had garnished her name.

The mechanics running pipe in her new house snickered as they held the newspaper in the air. The entire project had become a nightmare. Though relief wafted through her when the repairs reached fruition, she hadn't the resources to pay the contractor.

His demands for payment came with the threat of a lien. She couldn't afford a lien on the property but hadn't the means to stave it off. Pleas to Milton brought another $1,000 and a third mortgage as she'd had the mortgage held by Meyers assigned to him.

The Meyers mortgage originated with her former husband. Word had come to her that Robert had died. Her mouth drew a grim line at the thought. The man might be dead, but his deceit lived on. She was now indebted to Milton three times over.

She was rocked with yet another surprise when she learned that the mortgages held by Milton had been reassigned to his friend, Ephraim Chamberlain, who was the mayor of the city of Utica. When she asked if the mortgages had been recorded, Milton said no, and she believed they were listed with no consideration.

She was neglecting the particulars of these transactions under the illusion that Milton had been the bearer of a much-needed gift. It was the same grievous error she'd made with Robert.

Christmas Eve she buoyed herself to trim a tree for her family. Gaslights flickered as she surveyed her efforts. The tree, with its popcorn and cranberries, was a symbol of hope. She climbed into bed with a temporary sense of peace.

Sissie rose first on Christmas morning. Sighting the tree, she ran to fetch her brothers. Josephine turned up the gas in the fireplace, prepared hot chocolate, and walked to the corner to purchase a newspaper. She smiled; the children's happiness was contagious.

Stepping to the parlor, she opened the paper and gasped. Edwin Stanton was dead! She shook her head in disbelief. He'd been appointed to the Supreme Court just four days earlier. His passing robbed her of a staunch ally.

Demands for money dragged into the new year. She hadn't the money to pay the contractor in full. April brought the judgment of a mechanic's lien. The house was slated to be sold. Milton failed to respond to her flurry of messages.

LeGrand Bancroft's charity and kindness were legendary in Albany. He was also the most highly regarded real-estate lawyer in the city. Josephine humbled herself to pay him a visit.

"Well young lady, you seem in a bit of a dither. Come sit, and tell me what set of circumstances brings you to this state."

Her explanation of the facts drew a frown to the lawyer's face.

"I'll look into the matter and see if we can't derive a solution."

Bancroft contacted her two weeks later. "I find the entire business quite unorthodox, but if we can work something out, I'll bid on the house myself. Perhaps we'll be able to untangle this mess after the sale has been finalized."

LeGrand Bancroft and his wife purchased the Howard Street house for the amount of the mechanic's lien. On June 30, the Bancroft's deeded the house to Josephine's son, Ernest Judson Seymour. This arrangement freed the house of the mechanic's lien, but responsibility for the original mortgages had been put to the shoulders of a boy.

Regardless of the name attached to the deed, Bancroft's action could be termed nothing but generous, and he'd bought Josephine some desperately needed time. She gave the Bancroft's a mortgage on her personal property and a second mortgage on the farm in Augusta. The value of the farm remained well in excess of the mortgage held by Chamberlain.

Though she tried to work, stress had been building in pyramid fashion, one layer at a time. Days were lost to her medical practice as she fought for control of her destiny. By the spring of 1871, she found herself insolvent, unable to pay even the interest on the mortgage held by Mark Wilde. On May 30, 1871, Wilde commenced a foreclosure suit. She wired Milton and boarded the train for Utica. When she reached the depot, she dispatched a note to his office. An office boy carried a response stating that Milton had gone to dinner. This announcement was followed by a visit from Mortimer Thomson. He insisted that illness had taken Milton from the city and that he was under a doctor's care.

Josephine had penned a second and more thoughtful letter while awaiting an answer to her first enjoinder. "I must get this message to Milton. I've expended all the receipts of my business to cover repairs to the house. I am no longer able to meet interest on my mortgages." The letter wavered in her hand.

"Can't the mortgage be renewed?"

"I've tried and failed. You do understand that Milton and I share an interest in the children."

"I am fully aware of your relationship. You've been bleeding my brother for years."

"How dare you make accusations! It wasn't I who pursued Milton, quite the contrary. Did you think you were orchestrating the *Rape of Europa* when Milton waylaid me in Oswego?" She doubted Doonsticks had any familiarity with Greek mythology or the Phoenician woman for whom the continent of Europe had been named.

But for reasons known only to him, Mortimer's only reply was to cough up a harsh laugh.

"I long suspected you were coaching him. Well, I've given Milton a child which is more than his wife could do. It's his responsibility to provide for the boy. I would appreciate it if you could do the courtesy of delivering my letter."

Mortimer took the envelope roughly and stomped off toward Genesee Street. A few days later, the unopened letter came back. An accompanying note stated that the doctor would not have Milton disturbed. Mortimer's nickname, Sticks, was the signature scratched on the back of the envelope.

Abandoning her efforts to reach Milton, she returned to Albany and paid another visit to LeGrand Bancroft. Bancroft consented to take an assignment of the Wilde mortgage.

She then visited the law office of Warren Kelley. The man was not a stranger. He had been her landlord in East Albany. He was also the lawyer handling the Wilde foreclosure. She wasted no time in presenting her case. "I have a party willing to take assignment of the Howard Street mortgage."

Kelley looked toward the open door of a side office. Josephine followed his gaze to find Mortimer Thomson sitting in a chair with his back to them. Mortimer had been gifted with good looks and a commanding figure, qualities lost to Milton. It was Mortimer's reputation that lacked substance. She directed her attention back to the lawyer, asking if the mortgage had been assigned.

Kelley fiddled with his fingers before replying. "Parties from Utica who hold subsequent mortgages offered to buy the assignment. I had no choice but to make the transfer."

"Can you tell me who the parties are?"

The man's flustered reaction caused Mortimer to turn toward her and nod. She took his nod as an admission. "Are you acting on the advice of your brother?"

"I am. I spoke with him a week ago and concur with his course of action."

Looking back to Kelley, she asked if the money had been tendered.

"It has."

Josephine left the office in disbelief. She reported her findings to LeGrand Bancroft. "I can't fathom Milton ever selling the house. He may think me embarrassed by the situation, and, in keeping with his promise, is trying to straighten things out."

Bancroft shook his head. "I'm afraid I don't see it that way at all. On the day of the sale, Kelley was with Milton's brother, LaMott. They bid the house in the name of Charles S. Green of Long Island."

"I know the man. Mr. Green is from Utica. He drives and trains trotting horses. I believe he and Mortimer are associates in the horse business."

Her knowledge was useless. Charles Green had filed claim with the Albany county clerk's office for surplus mortgages. Milton had taken total control of her property and finances. She returned to Utica with Juddie in tow. When she was again denied access to Milton, she made the decision to broadcast his actions. The first door she knocked on was that of his mother.

The maid regarded her with suspicion. But Irene Thomson heard the ring of the bell and was capable of answering on her own.

"Bring the young lady to me, Mildred."

The maid acquiesced by ushering Josephine to Mrs. Thomson's parlor.

"Why, look at this handsome little fellow. What is your name, boy?"

"Ernest Judson Seymour," Juddie answered.

Josephine quickly interrupted. "I'm sorry to intrude on you, Mrs. Thomson, but there are things I think you should know."

The matriarch appraised her with a wise and knowing smile. "Mildred," she called. "Take young Ernest to the kitchen. I'm sure he'd enjoy a straw-berry tart, and see he gets a glass of milk."

When Juddie and the maid were out of sight, she invited Josephine to take a seat. "Now, tell me what it is that I should know."

"First of all, Juddie is your grandson. Milton and I have been intimate for years. He is now threatening to foreclose on my property and will put his child out on the street. I'm here on behalf of our boy but have been de-nied the right to speak with his father."

A mist clouded the old lady's eyes. "I do remember. Milton was so taken by you. What a shame that sweet and innocent love should be brought to such a deceitful state. Of course, this needs to be settled in the child's favor. I suggest you meet again with my sons. I should hope they will do the right thing."

From the very beginning, Josephine had been willing to see the sons. The stumbling block lay at their doorstep. With Juddie in hand, she walked up the hill to Milton's home at 321 Genesee Street. A maid answered her ring.

"I'm here to see Mrs. Thomson," she said in a pleasant tone. There seemed no point in giving the woman forewarning.

"Mrs. Thomson is not at home."

She went next to the Rev. Doctor Edwin Van Duesen, pastor to Grace Church. She explained her situation, ending with a question, "Do you not think Mr. Thomson owing in regards to his child's welfare?"

The minister raised an eyebrow and a sly smile twitched at his lips. "I believe the five hundred dollars Milt gave toward the steeple has garnered him absolution."

Josephine lifted her chin. "It appears to me that you and I are on the same level when it comes to conducting business."

The clergyman's jaw dropped as she turned on her heel and marched from the rectory.

Juddie hopped from the chair where he sat waiting and followed her onto the sidewalk. Their next stop was to Milton's agent, J. Thomas Spriggs. The man had replaced Chamberlain as mayor of Utica, and while she would never forgive him for broadcasting gossip in Augusta, he had been courteous in all subsequent encounters. She explained her version of recent occurrences and related her visit to the old Mrs. Thomson.

Spriggs listened to her tale with a troubled expression. "I'm sure we can establish an understanding. The house should be deeded back to the child. Give me two weeks. Remain as you are on Howard St. and do not fret. I have no doubt that Mr. Milton will do right by you."

Spriggs' efforts at negotiation failed. When Josephine returned home, she went straight to her desk and in a cold fury penned the following letter:

Albany, July 3d, 1871

My Dear Sir:

I send you the letter relating to the farm. On my return home I found half the carpets up, and things generally out of place. The fact of the house being sold found its way into the newspapers, and people called to hear about it, and when I proposed to move, etc. I have all my life had such an abundance of human interest expressed in my affairs that I am thoroughly surfeited. I was more incensed than ever with the Thomsons. If Mrs. Milton had been within hearing she would have heard a "plain unvarnished tale." I did not give you all my programme. I intend to call upon the offices of all the insurance Co.'s with which the Thomson's are connected, with Juddie and the papers. He shall have some celebrity—Do not misunderstand me, Mr. Spriggs. If you are temporizing all worse for your client, I will punish him the more.

It is no use to talk of half-way measures. This house must be deeded unencumbered to Juddie, under any restrictions they please. That farm must be taken off my hands at $5,000. An insurance of $5,000 put on my life for Juddie, paid up to Milton's death, after that I will take on the policy.

I send you a release of Mr. M's. mortgage on farm. I have not paid the taxes this year. If the time is past and any trouble in prospect, send the amount $20.33 and I will settle with you. I have repeated your answer to

Mr. Bancroft that you will see this child provided for, and he hopes that there will be no more exposure. I don't care a rush if there is. I enjoyed it in Utica, all but the interview with Mrs. Thomson... I expect to see you soon. I wonder you have never called to see me. Send me a day or two in advance, if possible, the day you will be here, as I am just now running about settling up my affairs and out a day at a time.

Yours truly,
J.A. McCarty

Her letter failed to elicit any response from Spriggs. What she did receive was one of Thomson's unsigned, cut and paste messages. A shiver jarred her shoulders as she read.

The thorn is <u>often</u> plucked for the rose, Fools and <u>obstinate</u> people make lawyers rich, Fools have liberty to say what they please, Much is expected where much is given.

Milton's behavior had grown increasingly strange. Nonetheless, she continued her barrage of letters. The intricacies of daily life commanded constant attention. The headaches returned and hemorrhages that been a scourge since Sissie's birth plagued her on a monthly basis. The heat of August was upon them and summer would soon be lost. She needed a break from the ongoing pressure and decided to take a holiday. Her friend Henrietta Cooper had, on several occasions, invited her to visit Charlton.

With the boys in the care of a friend, Josephine and Sissie embarked on this excursion in high spirits. An early rain had settled the dust and dampened the road, allowing Fleet Feet to travel with ease. Mrs. Cooper appeared before them the moment his clip-clop hit the driveway.

"Emma," she called as she ran from the house. "I am so relieved. The drive from Albany is long, and I was very concerned."

Henrietta's first encounter with Josephine happened while accompanying a friend to the medical office of Dr. Emma Burleigh. As their friendship expanded, the doctor revealed another identity. But Henrietta never addressed her by any name other than that of Emma Burleigh.

"So," she said in a pleased manner. "How is our little girl doing?"

Sissie lifted her eyes and spoke clearly. "I am fine, thank you." *Why had this woman been worried? My mother can handle a horse as well as any man.*

The friends ignored Sissie's obvious indignation, greeting each other warmly. Josephine's previous correspondence raised questions, and they were soon immersed in hushed conversation.

The weather held, and the following day, Mrs. Cooper's nephew stopped by with a sweet invitation.

"I have business in Ballston Spa tomorrow. If you ladies care to join me, we might have tea at the San Souci."

Young Mr. Conley owned a sleek phaeton and a team of dapple-gray horses. With his rig and team, they could shop and be seen at the grand hotel, and still make it home by the supper hour. Smiles brightened the ladies' faces as they gave their answers in unison. Of course, they would go! Mrs. Cooper's maid would mind Sissie while they were away.

Henrietta dressed for the outing in a flouncy pink organdy dress and a hat streaming with pink ribbons. Josephine emerged in a green-striped taffeta with a small green hat set to one side of an upsweep of black ringlets. They adjusted their bustles and opened parasols, creating a picturesque presence in the speedy phaeton. The carriage rolled swiftly along graveled roads, arriving at the spa a little past noon. The shops were dappled by rays of the late-summer sun, and the women joined a strolling convoy that entered every store. Neither had money to spend, but no one would guess from their stately demeanor.

Mortgages, debt, and dominating males had all been left in Albany. A teasing smile parted Josephine's lips as she and her friend met Conley for tea. "The elegant San Souci," she observed with an arching eyebrow. "Would you venture a number on how many of these gentlemen are actually here with their wives?"

Confusion clouded Henrietta's plain face, and Conley was lost for words.

"Accept my apology," Josephine said in quick contrition. "The remark was crass, but experience has been a merciless teacher."

Aunt and nephew gazed at the diners without comprehension, and then looked to each other and shrugged. It had been an enjoyable day, unfolding as promised. They returned to the phaeton in a lighthearted mood.

The gray team raced along Charlton Road until a cumbersome dray emerged from a driveway. Conley slowed to avoid a collision and withdrew his watch to consult the time. The hands were pointing toward 4:00. Charlton was still four miles away. The road ahead stretched upward in a monotonous climb. The young man chaffed at the slowness of their journey. On reaching the top of the hill, he shook his reins, encouraging his team to pass. But the road curved inward, narrowing their path. Though he tried to correct his actions, the outside wheel rolled into a ditch. The tilt of the carriage caused the tongue to twist. The phaeton flipped with the horses rearing and screaming in their struggle against the entanglement.

Conley had been thrown clear of the crash. He scrambled to reach his team and worked feverishly to set them free. The panicked grays crested the hill and disappeared. Henrietta seemed dazed as she struggled to stand, her dress streaked with dirt. She stared at the wreckage dumbfounded. As awareness dawned, she was filled with dread.

"Emma," she screamed. "Where are you? Tell me; are you hurt?"

Josephine's muffled response came from beneath the carriage, her voice distorted by pain. "I fear I have broken an arm."

The creeping dray that had been such an annoyance pulled to a stop behind them. After assessing their situation, the elderly driver climbed to the ground to offer help. Tipping his hat, he introduced himself. "Name's Simpson, Joseph Simpson. Might I be of assistance?"

"Yes, sir," said Conley exhaling relief. "Our first priority is to free Mrs. Burleigh."

The men struggled to lift the splintered wreckage as Henrietta eased Josephine free.

Conley appraised the good Samaritan. "Mrs. Burleigh is seriously injured and my aunt is in great distress. I would appreciate it to no end if you could transport them to my grandfather's house. His farm sits to the left of the crossroad beyond, just a mile down on the right."

"That's an easy chore. What of yourself, sir? It looks as if you could use some help."

The younger man shook his head. "This mess can wait until tomorrow. But I must find my team before dark."

The men lifted Josephine into the old man's cart, doing their best to spare her pain.

"I'm afraid she needs medical attention." Conley's sorrow was plain on his face. Had he not been in such a hurry, the accident would never have happened. "Tell me?" he asked looking to his newfound friend. "Are you, by chance, on your way to Charlton?"

"I am."

"Would you do the additional favor of contacting a doctor? Mrs. Burleigh needs to be seen right away."

Though the distance to the farm was short, every bump in the road produced a new shock of pain, and tremors set Josephine's limbs to twitching.

It was well into the evening when Dr. Young arrived. He found his patient delirious and suffering from shock. Her injuries included a fracture to the left arm, a dislocated shoulder, concussion, and bruising about the temple. Her pulse was abnormally high, and her nervousness seemed to intensify the pain. After administering a dose of chloroform, he set the fracture, worked on the dislocation, and wrapped her in bandages. He left Henrietta with a set of instructions and the promise of returning the following morning.

Dr. Young kept his promise. He appeared at the house midmorning and went about the process of applying a splint. His patient's condition required constant monitoring, and he continued to check on her daily. Josephine was bedridden for the next ten days. She suffered from an incessant hammering within her head and was at times delirious.

Sissie had been brought to the farm in the hopes that she might have a calming effect on her mother. She sat beside Josephine and read from her books. She thought it ironic that Mrs. Cooper had been so worried about the trip from Albany when the real devastation had come at the hands of her nephew, and not five miles from the Cooper home. But her meditations were reserved for her brothers.

On the second Sunday of her intended vacation, Josephine countermanded the doctor's objection to travel. Her boys were in Albany and she needed to retrieve them. The splints prevented her driving; so, she elected to take the cars. Mr. Cooper gave assurance that he would deliver her buggy within the week.

As she was about to board the train, she grabbed hold of her friend. "Henrietta, I am afraid, very afraid. Someone is watching me. I fear for the safety of my family."

"What are you talking about? You haven't mentioned a word of this since you've been here."

"I tell you Henrietta, it is true." The whistle blew, forcing her to grab Sissie and rush up the steps.

Home was no cure for the headaches. Her paranoia about being watched undoubtedly delayed recuperation. The appearance of two men at the rear of her house nearly drove her to hysterics. She knew that in times past, Milton had assigned men to keep watch of her. She was certain someone was spying and wanted a witness to substantiate her claim.

Henrietta gave her the name of a gentleman named Mulhall, suggesting he might be of help. Josephine met with the man at a street corner not far from her home. He had a brawny appearance that served him well in the running of his saloon. Josephine had no doubts as to his ability to handle neighborhood trouble. He reminded her of Cousin Thomas when he was in his prime. Mulhall and his men kept watch of the house for several days but found nothing amiss.

It had been years since she'd handled a gun, but the thought dawned on her that it might be time to renew the acquaintance. She purchased a small revolver and made a habit of carrying it in her pocket.

Josephine also decided to reach out for additional help and went to see James Brice, an Albany attorney who had once been attached to the secretary of state's office. She'd been to his office previously, begging for a solution to the difficulties with Milton Thomson.

Mulhall's failed attempt to uncover evidence of spying sent her to Brice for a second time. "I want you to come and wait with me. I know an attack is imminent. I have a club. I'll be waiting at the top of the stairs, but I need help."

"Listen to yourself," Brice commanded. "You are coming unhinged. Your accusations are irrational. I know you have Mulhall watching and that nothing has come of it."

In spite of his doubts, Brice did join Mulhall on watch. He sat in the parlor where Josephine offered her gun as protection.

"You should not sit by unarmed," she warned.

The lawyer remained until midnight. On another occasion, she sent Louis out through the roof in the middle of the night to call on her neighbor, Timothy Strong. She thought she'd heard voices, but when Mr. Strong arrived, he found the neighborhood quiet. Yet, she continued to wring her hands; her unkempt appearance was an alien vision to neighbors accustomed to her stylish flair.

Rumors of her strange behavior spread, but she could not be dissuaded in her beliefs. The Dennisons lived to the left of her Howard Street home. Edgar Dennison's employer once charged him with embezzlement. Josephine had been called to testify against him, an act that created ongoing hostility. She developed a notion that the Dennisons were part of a spying network. Who better would know her movements and the presence of witnesses? Mrs. Dennison certainly had no love for her. Shortly after Edgar Dennison's hearing, his wife had physically attacked her. She'd been holding a pitcher of sulfuric acid and instinctively sent it flying. Reports of that action had circled the neighborhood.

With nerves still frayed, she resumed her practice. The untimely death of one of her patients put her on the brink of a breakdown.

Maggie Campbell was a pretty little fool enjoying her status as mistress to a prominent politician. When she found herself pregnant, she sought out a midwife who gave her a compound of herbs. An incomplete abortion left her with unchecked bleeding. She arrived at Josephine's door begging for help, claiming her name was Fanny. Unlike most of the patients who sought her out, Fanny had money to pay her expenses. Her only request was that no one be alerted to her condition.

Dr. Burleigh's rooms were clean and her instruments sterile. Using a mild dose of chloroform, she put Fanny at ease. Then with a speculum and curette she scraped tissue from the woman's womb, padded her with gauze, and put her to bed.

"It is imperative that you rest and allow the uterus to heal. And I must warn you, it would be dangerous to resume intercourse before the healing is complete."

Since the young woman had money to cover expenses, Josephine offered to house her for a period of two weeks. One week into the stay, Fanny became agitated, insisting she needed to stretch her legs. She returned to Howard Street four hours later sporting a wily grin. Within the next two days, she developed a fever, diarrhea, and pain in her abdomen.

Josephine dosed her with castor oil and Dover's powder and put camphor cloths on her abdomen. The woman's condition continued to worsen. She sent for Dr. J.R. Boulwaire, one of Albany's most highly regarded physicians. In her note, she informed him of her patient's distress and asked that he see her immediately.

The doctor arrived at ten in the morning. Fanny was weak and suffering with pain. He found her abdomen distended and her respiration hurried. His instructions were to administer anodyne.

When the doctor returned at 6:00, Maggie Campbell was dead.

After performing a brief examination, Boulwaire inquired, "Does she have any family?"

"I don't know of any. I have the name and address of her boarding house proprietors as well as the name of a gentleman friend." She looked at Boulwaire, and her expression hardened. "An autopsy is required and will be done at my expense. It would be a relief to me if you would perform the procedure. Two additional physicians will be needed to serve as assistants—and as witnesses. I was indicted on a charge of abortion several years ago. It will likely happen again. It is difficult to defend oneself when the American Medical Association refuses to admit a female practitioner."

Boulwaire agreed. He came the next day accompanied by Dr. C.H. Porter, another well-respected physician in Albany. Mr. Brasure, the undertaker, completed the triumvirate.

Margaret Campbell's organs were sliced and dissected and her uterus removed. The ultimate cause of death was determined to be peritonitis. In the meantime, Josephine had sent messages—one to the favored politician stating that Fanny had died, the second to the proprietors of Maggie's boarding house asking them to meet with her at once.

The politician ignored his notice, an affirmation of true affection. The Misses Cleary appeared and identified Maggie by description. Josephine refused their request to see the body after the postmortem had been performed. The girl was buried and a certificate of death, signed by Dr. Boulwaire, was filed with the city register.

A dissatisfied coroner arrived on Josephine's doorstep followed by a reporter for the *Evening Times*. In spite of his fierce rapping, the door remained closed. No interviews were granted.

When a reporter from the *Sunday Press* knocked on Boulwaire's door, the doctor issued a statement. "Margaret Campbell died of natural causes. I found nothing suspicious in examining the corpse. I am familiar with Dr. Burleigh and know her to be a capable practitioner."

The press would not be satisfied. The case was published in multiple papers as a mysterious event. The public took notice, and the coroner ordered a second autopsy. Maggie was exhumed from the rural cemetery and a new set of doctors examined her remains. They pulled her apart on the bare ground without ever leaving the grave site. Evidence that the she had been pregnant made Josephine a suspect for performing an abortion. An inquest was ordered for the following day.

While witnesses testified to the evidence of a pregnancy, none could verify that the girl had been pregnant within the past three weeks. A *nolle prosequi* was entered, meaning the evidence presented had not been sufficient for indictment.

Headaches were paralyzing Josephine; the mortgage problem trailed her every movement. There were mornings when she found it impossible to leave her bed. On those occasions, young Louis took charge of the household.

In December, J. Thomas Spriggs informed her that the Howard Street house had been sold to Robert Oliver, son of the property's original owner. She immediately made contact with a lawyer from Schenectady asking that he commence action against Milton Thomson. Attorney Charles Hastings accompanied her to Utica with the intention of negotiating a settlement.

Josephine put the onus on her lawyer while she waited in the lobby of the Butterfield House. As time drew on, she scanned her surroundings appreciatively. The hotel had opened to accolades two years previously and was considered one of the finest establishments in the state. It seemed fate stamped success on every Butterfield venture.

Hastings finally returned. The Thomsons were not amenable to a settlement of any kind. They had, in fact, suggested she sue them.

"It shall be done," she stated with defiance.

With Hastings leaving the city, she contacted attorney Robert O. Jones.

"I want Milton Thomson served with papers. As mortgagee he has foreclosed on my home and cheated me out of my equity."

She then returned to Albany to await the judge's opinion. It was unlikely the ruling would come in time. A notice to vacate had been delivered. She spent her afternoon in search of storage space and worked through the evening packing cartons.

The agent called the following morning asking her to sign a lease for Charles Green.

She refused. "This paper would give possession of the house to Mr. Green. I'll sign nothing without advice from my lawyer."

She contacted Brice whose office sat not far from her home. He directed her to sign the lease, but the following day the request proved moot.

John P. Brant, the sheriff of Albany County, appeared at her door with a writ of assistance. "This is a preemptory order of eviction. I am sorry to have to present it, but I have no choice."

She gave the officer a wan smile. "I understand your position. Our things will be removed within the next few days."

The next day, Henrietta Cooper remarked at the chilling temperature as the postmaster slid an envelope across the counter. The return address was 62 Howard Street, Albany. A smile lit her face as she thought of her friend. She tucked the envelope into her bag, thinking she would savor the reading at home.

When comfortable in her fireside chair, Henrietta unfolded the letter. A frown crumpled her forehead as she read the first sentence. She read it again and gasped. *Emma and her children are being evicted!* Wasting no time, she filled a valise and took the first train to Albany. She arrived at Howard Street before the sun set.

Louis answered the ringing door bell. Josephine was descending the stairs, her arms laden with pillows and bedding.

Good God, thought Henrietta, *there are two and a half stories and a cellar to this house. However will they accomplish this on their own?*

She was surprised to find the carpets rolled and every room packed excepting the office. That one small room had been left for last. The children were hustling to assist their mother, and the work went on until midnight.

Josephine arose early the following morning, bathed, and donned the old calico dress normally worn for stable chores. But when she noticed a pail of fresh milk on the table, she realized Louis had been out ahead of her. Putting a hand to her head, it came to her that she'd forgotten to dress her hair. The discovery came as a surprise. Never in all her life had she been negligent in her grooming. Simple chores were the acts that kept one sane.

She gazed about the room and sighed. With the bulk of packing nearly complete, she needed to focus on the future. But her mind flashed backward to New York City in 1849.

Twenty-two years later, I again find myself penniless and stranded with three young children, only this time it is worse. Back then I had a farm. Now I have nothing.

Her appearance reflected the chaotic thoughts. Disheveled hair and faltering movements were a marked contrast to her known persona. She picked up a cup, placed it back on the table, and reached for a leather-bound volume of verse. Her mind began to drift again.

I've been such a fool. Robert was cruel and vindictive, driven by lust and jealousy. Milton is a diabolical monster. He has plotted against me and would see his son starve. How could I have been so blind?

Pushing a straggling hair behind her ear, she returned to the preparations for moving. Her unbuttoned shoes clattered against the stairs as she began the ascent for what seemed the hundredth time. The jangling door bell brought her to a halt.

Reversing direction, she walked to the hall and opened the door. Sheriff Brant stood before her with a half-dozen men lined up behind him.

"You have my apology, Mrs. Burleigh, but as I told you yesterday, the party holding title to this property has ordered you out. I have no choice but to enforce the eviction."

"But as I understood it, I had a few more days."

"Sorry, ma'am."

Gleaming brass doorknobs slammed against the plaster of interior walls, and seven hulking men crossed the threshold. Josephine called to the children in desperation.

In the midst of her own distress, Henrietta had the presence to grab coats and hats before everything tumbled out onto the street. Temperatures ranged in the low thirties; if nothing else, each child would have a coat on his back.

Onlookers began to circle the children as carpets and cartons were piled before them. Josephine caught hold of a cart man and hired him to move what he could to the storage location.

Mrs. Gow, a neighbor, came forward. "Mrs. Burleigh, if it would be of any help, you might store a few pieces with me."

Josephine opened her mouth to answer and quickly snapped it shut in utter dismay. A loud bellow could be heard in the alley. The horse and cow were being chased to the street. Louis raced forward to take hold of Fleet Feet while Josephine grabbed the cow by its collar. Clouds of steam billowed from the animals' nostrils. Their eyes were wide and leery. Though corralled by friends, they were fearful of an environment that had undergone such a sudden change.

Josephine was at a loss as the cow pulled against her.

Again, Henrietta displayed a quickness of thought. "I will take Fleet Feet to a livery. Mr. Cooper can pick him up tomorrow. Fear not Louis, your horse will be waiting for you at my place." She turned to her friend, "I can take the children as well. The decision rests with you."

The din and confusion made it difficult to think. Josephine took the lead strap from Louis and handed it to Henrietta. Transferring the horse was a simple decision. Proposals concerning her children were a different matter entirely. She had no idea where they would go, but for the moment it seemed imperative that she keep her family together.

"If you have an interest in selling the cow, I should like to buy her."

She turned to the man who'd spoken.

"I will pay a fair price."

She nodded. Mr. Strong's son-in-law took hold of the Guernsey's collar and pressed a bill to her hand. She scribbled a penciled receipt with no regard as to the amount of the sale. All she could see were Louis' tears, and that caused her to weep.

When they were first turned onto the street, Mrs. Gow gave the children biscuits. As the sheriff and his men moved off, she invited the family to her home for supper.

Halfway to the neighbor's house, Josephine checked her steps to look back. The expression she wore mixed sadness with incredulity. It had taken years for her to build a home. In spite of the kindness witnessed that morning, she knew the moment her back was turned, thieves would descend on the mountain in the road and the remnants of her assets would disappear.

She sat at the Gow table with her napkin in hand and her eyes lost to space.

"What will you do, Mrs. Burleigh?"

"I do not know, but I can tell you, I'm not ready to quit the world just yet. I have endured difficult times before. With the death of Maggie Campbell, people prophesied that I would lose my business and be left without recourse, yet my patient load increased.

"I pity you, Mrs. Gow. You are a widow as I am myself. People generally impose on widows. Someone I trusted has sold me out."

"I certainly have no wish to impose on you," the elderly lady murmured. "But if you would care to sell the sofa the men put in my basement. I would like very much to buy it."

Josephine's laughter turned to tears. "I haven't a single room in which to house furniture, but I would like to reflect on my situation before I make a decision."

Mrs. Gow kept the family through the night and fed them in the morning. They left in the afternoon toting a single valise.

Josephine stopped at Brice's office. The children were instructed to remain on the curb while she was in conversation.

"Brice, I am ruined. The children and I have been turned out on the street. I don't know where I shall lay my head. We have been thrown to the charity of the public and it is all at the hands of Milton Thomson."

Brice had been given the particulars several times over. Rumors could blanket Albany faster than a telegrapher could tap out the message.

"What will you do with the children?"

"I may send the boys to Saratoga. I have a friend there who is willing to take them. Brice, I want you to commence a suit to recover my house. I want you to go after Milton Thomson." As she spoke, she whipped herself into frenzy. "Damn Milton Thomson! I tell you I will get even."

"Mrs. Burleigh, stop. Think. What are you going to do?"

"I am going to Utica." With that she left the office.

The day was wearing on, but Josephine and her children were still on the street. In the past she'd leased space from Gardner Scrivens. She had been a customer at his grocery store and had seen his wife as a patient.

Perhaps the Scrivens have room for us.

Night was upon them when they exited the streetcar at a corner near the Scrivens' home. Josephine sent Louis ahead to explain their situation. He stood on the porch looking back toward his mother before cautiously lifting the door knocker.

Nancy Scrivens' shock was apparent the moment she opened the door. "Is that Louis Seymour?"

"Yes, ma'am."

"Whatever are you doing here?" She opened the door a bit wider and Louis stepped inside.

"I'm sorry, Mrs. Scrivens," he said in a hushed tone, "but we are experiencing problems. Mother is asking if we might spend the night with you."

Nancy's jaw dropped before she could recover. The child was holding a valise. She opened her mouth, but no words came out. What should she do? She'd heard of the eviction. She liked Dr. Burleigh. The family could not be left on the street.

"I am entertaining guests right now, but tell your mother to come along and I will settle you for the night.

Josephine scooted Juddie and Sissie ahead of her. It was late and the children were tired. When she reached the door she gave Nancy a mournful look. Efforts to express herself seemed to fail.

"Just follow me, ma'am, and I will light your way upstairs."

Josephine made it a point to groom herself when she awoke the following morning; then, descending the stairs, she sought her hostess.

"Mrs. Scrivens, I must thank you for your compassion."

"It is quite all right. You need to get your bearings."

"Have you ever felt that water was running through your brain? I have such pain in my head. I fear I am having an inflammation of the brain. I feel a fit of sickness coming on." She doubled over and tears streamed from her eyes. With a handkerchief pressed to her mouth, she apologized. "I am sorry, I am very sorry."

Nancy Scrivens watched as Josephine retreated upstairs. *The woman is distraught. I don't think it wise to leave her alone.* Throwing a shawl over her shoulders, she called to the children who were playing in the yard. "I have an errand to run, but will be right back. Please, stay out of trouble while I am gone."

She hustled to the grocery store in search of her husband. "Gardner, I think it best if you come home."

"But..." Gardner's eyes ran through the store.

"You have help," his wife insisted. "It isn't necessary that you be here every minute. I want you to come home."

Gardener shook his head in consternation as he removed his apron and followed orders. Whatever might happen at the store wouldn't be half so bad as the consequences of crossing an anxious wife.

When the Scrivens reached home, Nancy rushed up the stairs to check on her guest and found Josephine was crying and wringing her hands.

"Mrs. Burleigh, you must calm yourself."

"I do not know what I shall do. I have been reduced to begging. How can I care for three young children?" Folding her arms about the bed post, she continued to weep.

"Please Mrs. Burleigh, come downstairs. You should not be fretting up here by yourself."

She followed the woman to the parlor, where she spoke briefly with Mr. Scrivens. The sobbing had ceased, but her eyes held the wildness of a frightened animal. She refused all offers of food.

"I must travel to Utica. Mr. Scrivens mentioned an office might be available on Pearl Street. I would appreciate it if you could alert my patients that I will be back next week." Her statement was rational, but when she stood, she appeared disoriented.

"Mrs. Burleigh, you aren't feeling yourself today. Wait until tomorrow. The children are content. Will another day make that much difference?"

"Perhaps you are right."

Throughout the night she mulled her circumstances. *I have to place the children. The DeVeaux College for Orphans and Destitute Children at Suspension Bridge has an excellent reputation. Louis, being bright, would do quite well in such an environment. But what about Juddie and Sissie?* Closing her eyes, she squeezed the lids together and swallowed hard. *Milton promised to care for them. He has the means and must do so.*

CHAPTER THIRTEEN

Beginning on Wednesday, May 8, a parade of individuals from varying walks of life took the path to the witness stand. Doctors Frank A. Young, Alanson Jones, and Peter P. Staats were among the first to testify.

Dr. Jones gave the Court a chuckle when asked if he had a family. He responded that he did. The prosecution, not being satisfied, asked if he were married. The doctor answered no. But counsel for the people queried further, questioning the fact that he had answered yes to having a family.

"I do," Dr. Jones replied

Showing significant agitation, counsel asked for an explanation.

The doctor smiled and answered that he had a sister and a mother.

Obviously, Dr. Jones marital status had no bearing on the case, but Josephine raised a handkerchief to hide her amused reaction.

Joseph Mason took the stand identifying himself as an attorney in Hamilton. He maintained that he had brought an action on behalf of Oliver Curtiss for a mortgage assigned to him on the McCarty farm in Augusta. Mrs. McCarty's proposal for settlement had been rejected.

Warren Kelley testified to the assignment of the McCarty mortgage to Ephraim Chamberlain.

Timothy Strong related the midnight calls he'd received from his agitated neighbor.

James Brice, Nancy Scrivens, and Henrietta Cooper were all called to the stand; Mr. Scrivens was too ill to testify. There was a statement from Michael Aldridge, maître d'hôtel at the Butterfield House, as to the fact that her last meal at the hotel had been taken at breakfast the Sunday before the homicide.

Nathaniel Moak, a lawyer from Albany, was called to the stand and asked if he had been engaged in a conversation with Milton Thomson regarding provisions for the McCarty children. The prosecution objected and the question was ruled out.

William Warren of Augusta testified that he'd known Josephine Fagan as a lively, sociable, and intelligent child with a nervous and excitable mother.

Albert Newell of Marshall swore that he knew the Fagan girl to be intelligent, of good disposition and ladylike bearing.

Shaw Hawley, the lawyer from Albany, testified as to his part in drawing deeds and performing searches on the assignment of the mortgage by Virginia Seymour to Gibson Oliver in April of 1869. He stated that a gentleman had been involved and had directed him to mail the deed to Ephraim Chamberlain.

JOSEPHINE WAS THE MODEL OF DEPORTMENT as she ushered her children onto the train the Saturday before the shooting. Appearances were everything when dealing with men, and she'd taken the trouble to arrange her hair neatly under a jaunty, plumed hat. Signs of impending doom were limited to the wild flicker that sparked her eye and the tremor of her hand within the muff. In accordance with her habit of the past two years, she carried a gun in her jacket pocket.

From the depot in Utica, she led her family to the Butterfield House and signed for a room on the second floor. She supped with the children in the dining room, and then led them upstairs where they were tucked in for the night. While the children slept, she paced.

Sunday morning, she breakfasted ahead of her children, complaining to the maître d'hôtel that his men were engaging in loud conversation. Thinking her behavior rather strange, the man watched as she took a seat opposite Mrs. Hammond.

Mrs. Hammond's husband was involved in the insurance business, competing against the Thomsons. Josephine plied the woman with questions but gained nothing for her effort.

The children took themselves to the dining room a bit later that morning. Louis understood that he was bound for prep school. His mother had confided the plan before leaving Albany. Juddie and Sissie were to remain in Utica. He wasn't aware of the circumstances, but he sensed his mother had run into problems. Assuming the role of sibling in charge, he ushered his brother and sister about, allowing his mother to attend her business.

Monday morning, she dressed the younger children and sent the three of them to eat on their own. She had breakfast by herself across the street before visiting the offices of Jones and Babcock where she explained the circumstances of her eviction to Robert O. Jones. A messenger was sent to Thomson's office to inquire if he might be home. She waited until the boy reappeared. But the answer he brought was that Milton had not been seen since the previous Friday.

For the next two hours, she walked Genesee Street, inquiring at various establishments as to the whereabouts of the insurance man, Milton Thomson. When the search proved futile, she lifted her feet one after the other until they faced the Butterfield House. She walked up the steps and went to the desk where she scribbled another note to Thomson. The envelope was returned unopened.

She made a similar trek through the business district on Tuesday, uncovering the fact that Milton had a habit of riding the streetcar from his home to the office every morning.

Wednesday, just after the breakfast hour, she left her hotel, walking in a southerly direction that would take her uphill past the dwelling at 321 Genesee Street. She stopped at a corner some two hundred yards beyond the Thomson home. Frigid temperatures sent a chill up her spine as she stood in the cold and waited.

A streetcar traveling north was nearly abreast of her when Milton and another man emerged from the house.

She jumped to the curb. The conductor noticed the flutter of her handkerchief, and the streetcar halted. She climbed aboard and took a seat, adjusting her veil as she did so.

My heart is beating an unruly rhythm. Why should I be nervous at approaching this man? He sat in my home, shared my bed, fathered my child, and promised much. The least he can do is acknowledge me.

Milton walked down the aisle, directing his friend to a seat by the window. Josephine rose to her feet. Three steps and she stood beside him.

"Milton, I have brought the children you turned onto the street to starve. I cannot support them any longer."

"Go to hell and take the bastards with you," he growled.

Something happened. Suddenly it was difficult for Josephine to breathe, and then she was struck by the splatter of a warm, glutinous substance.

CHAPTER FOURTEEN

C ourt convened on Thursday morning, May 9, with further examination of the long list of witnesses. Ephraim Chamberlain was the first to be called by the defense. He denied any knowledge of the mortgage assignment. It seemed a mortgage had arrived from Albany, but he couldn't recall the particulars. He might have forwarded it to Milton Thomson.

Alderman Mulhall came next. He verified Mrs. McCarty's request for investigative services. In spite of her insistence that burglars were about, his men found nothing. He stated further that he was not an alderman during the time in question.

The audience, as a whole, seemed to hold its breath as young Louis Fagan walked toward the witness box. The boy twisted his hands as he suffered through a questioning session more lengthy and thorough than that of any of his predecessors. He testified on the history of his family life, of the homes they'd lived in, of his mother's illnesses and fear of burglars, on Thomson's visits and of having known him simply as Uncle Tom. He related events as they took place on the day of their eviction and how his mother had cried when the cow was sold. He knew she carried a gun and swore to having bought one himself. It was not a firecracker gun, he insisted, but a small pistol with a cartridge. He'd bought it in Utica prior to the announcement of the March 25 trial date. His mother took the gun and gave it to Mr. Babcock. He disputed the accusation that he'd told other boys he was going to shoot Mr. Thomson.

Josephine had been sitting in quiet composure, but she flinched at Louis' comment. There was no restitution for the theft of her children's innocence.

Police Chief Luce and LeGrand Bancroft were called to the stand to recite the facts as they knew them.

It was afternoon when defense called Dr. Charles Corey of Brooklyn to the stand. He was introduced as a practicing physician who, for a number of years, had been connected with hospitals for the insane. He cited numerous authorities, published opinions, and journals testifying that causes of insanity included intense grief, fear, prolonged anxiety, shocks, and domestic affliction. Dr. Corey described the climacteric period or change of life as a very critical period for women that left them more susceptible to disease. He also informed the jury and the audience that when hemorrhaging is excessive, women tend toward nervousness and excitability, with insanity often occurring during that period. The testimony went on for hours.

He was then cross-examined by the prosecutor. In answering their many questions, he gave the following statement:

It is true that temporary insanity appears often to persons not supposed to be insane; that is recognized by the psychological authorities in England, France, Germany and this country; it is temporary, fleeting, breaks out suddenly in automatic acts, I believe; a woman is in a building, with her child in an upper story, and a fire should take place, and she should know perfectly when she could go out, and she should throw her child out the window and then go down stairs herself, I should say under these circumstances, she lost her presence of mind, her self-control; Dr. Jarvis recognizes the doctrine of insanity from a shock.

The jury tried to remain attentive, but long questions and recitations stretching to an hour's duration were oppressing.

Judge Doolittle asked if they would like the window lowered, when what they really wanted was for the window to be thrown wide open.

Adjournment came as a relief to everyone in the courtroom.

On Friday morning, May 10, the court had no audience. The public had no interest in the theories and sub-theories of disturbances to the mind. But the morning dragged on with opinions on insanity rolling from the tongues of physicians on both sides.

Dr. Simon T. Clark of Lockport, New York, was called as a witness. The doctor was a physician and surgeon and had authored an article on transitory mania published in the *American Journal of Insanity* in January of 1872. He believed that Mrs. McCarty was suffering from this condition and that it had most likely been initiated when she was turned out of her house. His definition presumed no premeditation or intent.

The session broke for a recess at the conclusion of Dr. Clark's testimony.

When the recess came to an end, the court's assistant, Mr. Pratt, failed to appear. Messengers sent to retrieve him returned without success. After a twenty-five minute absence, the counselor returned. For those in the courtroom it had been a sweet reprieve.

Dr. C.B. Coventry then took the stand on the issue of transitory mania. He agreed with his colleagues that McCarty had the background for such insanity.

Defense was almost ready to rest their case, but they had one more witness to take the stand. Walter C. North was called. In response to questions from the defense, he answered that he was a photographer and was acquainted with Milton Thomson.

When the prosecutor objected, Mitchell insisted it was necessary to show that Milton Thomson's brother, LaMott, had called on the witness for the purpose of removing a photograph of Milton from the photographer's studio.

The evidence was not allowed as admissible.

The defense rested. Their effort to show that the plate of Thomson's photo had been stolen to keep witnesses from identifying him had failed.

The procecution then moved forward with their own slate of witnesses.

Aaron B. Pratt of Albany came first. As a lawyer representing Mrs. McCarty's former neighbor, Edgar Dennison, he made an acquaintance with the defendant when she testified in that case. According to Pratt, she had, at that time, made a claim of having been married to a man named Seymour. He noted her character as bad.

Philander Demming, a stenographer in the Court of Session in Albany, had taken notes during the Dennison trial and verified Pratt's statement.

John D. Conklin, a policeman in Albany, testified that he knew McCarty's character to be bad. But when cross-examined, he admitted he'd never heard her truthfulness or veracity questioned. In fact, he'd never heard it talked about before the trial.

Francis B. Bailey, another Albany policeman, stated that he knew her character to be bad. But again, he'd never heard her reputation for honesty spoken of until reaching Utica.

Mrs. Gow, the neighbor who had taken the McCarty family in when they were homeless, testified to the troubles that beset them. She admitted to having a disagreement with the defendant, skipping the fact that her son had stolen the McCarty's sofa. She did not think the woman insane.

Edgar H. Dennison took the stand. He had been feuding with the accused for some time and categorized her reputation as very bad.

Court adjourned, and the sheriff escorted Josephine back to her cell. She'd sat quietly as damaging testimony swirled around her. If she wasn't bad, she was crazy, and her life was on the line.

Saturday morning, May 11, brought Hattie Baker to the stand.

The servant girl testified that she had been in the service of Mrs. McCarty and had known her to be an abortionist. On cross-examination, she admitted to having been fired, but denied that she was being paid for her testimony or that she had contact with anyone in Utica.

Mary Jane Grant came next. She was asked if a man had lived with Mrs. McCarty at her house on Clinton Street, Albany. Her response that a man named Harry had resided at the house was met with another question: Had he lived there as a husband? Mrs. Grant claimed no knowledge of the relationship other than the fact that he lived with the family.

Stephen P. Franklin, a detective with the Philadelphia police force, swore the defendant's reputation at Blockley Hospital had been bad, and said he had known of her first as a student and later when she worked in the section for the insane.

John O'Donnell, bookkeeper at O'Donnell's Club House in Washington, testified that Mrs. McCarty had appeared at the club dressed in male clothing calling herself Johnny McCarty. She was in the company of a young officer who was a stranger to him. He noted that General Sickles had a room on the second floor, but he had chosen not to bother the general in regards to the woman's behavior. After she was arrested, an officer appeared at the club with a receipt to pick up her trunk. O'Donnell claimed the woman's face was one that would forever remain in his memory. He stepped from the witness stand just as a band struck up a march outside the courtroom.

The sound of a circus band was streaming through the window. As the musicians marched down the street, the small number of spectators still in the courtroom suddenly left for a livelier form of entertainment. Testimony continued.

Seth J. Mayo of Augusta answered under oath that the defendant's reputation in the town had been bad.

J. Thomas Spriggs took the stand to clarify his business with the accused as regards to the letters that had been offered as evidence.

Lyman Warren gave the opinion that Josephine's character was bad. With further questioning he acknowledged her reputation had been good up until the time she went to Europe. He admitted to having a younger brother who had gone about with her a good deal; he said he couldn't be sure whether his brother had proposed and been refused.

Then an aged and wobbling Josiah Rand took the stand. He peered at the jury through clouded eyes; it was difficult to discern the extent of his sight. "The girl was bad," he claimed. "Once caught her and a neighbor boy rolling in the hay. Sent her packing, I did. That girl was bad."

Josephine sighed. It was all so innocent and such a long time ago. Yet, she knew at the time that Josiah would make trouble. His wagging tongue spewed rumors when Camp and her mother married. The forum in which he would make his allegations against her was beyond reckoning back then.

Court adjourned.

Sunday failed to bring its promise of rest. Numb from the grueling experiences of the past two weeks, Josephine sat wrapped in the state of tight composure that she'd born throughout the trial.

Monday, May 13, brought the McCarty proceedings to its third week of court, and the jurymen complained of needing clean shirts.

For the next two days, patterns established by previous witnesses continued as Drs. Judson Andrews and John Gray testified on behalf of the prosecution. Gray's testimony was at least as long as that of Dr. Corey and was peppered with citations and names of distinguished authorities.

Dr. Alonzo Churchill stepped to the witness box on Monday afternoon. As a practicing physician, he'd maintained an office in the city of Utica for thirty-five years. He had been in the company of Dr. Gray and Dr. Bragg when they interviewed the prisoner. During this questioning period, she appeared in fair health and he had judged her as sane. As to whether she was sane at the time of the homicide, he conceded there might be some doubt. His testimony concluded the proceeding for Monday.

On Tuesday, the defense called for testimony from a new roster of Augusta neighbors. Most agreed that, up until her marriage, her character had been good; she was pleasant in nature, ladylike in bearing, and in possession of a high degree of intelligence. Many were familiar with rumors of her relationship with Thomson and the illegitimate children. The impressions of some had been altered by rumors; for others it made no difference.

In spite of objections, Albert Bentley testified on Mr. Spriggs' visit to the defendant's home community. Holding his chin between a thumb and index finger, he searched his mind for the facts. He recalled Mr. Spriggs visited his home between 1861 and 1863, inquiring as to the location of Mrs. McCarty's home. He'd given the man directions and he proceeded accordingly. The gentleman returned toward evening having been gone several hours. He'd obviously been there at the dinner hour. Bentley could not place the visit in relationship to the birth of the child. He'd known Josephine McCarty when she was a young lady; her general character was good up to the time she had illegitimate children. There'd been no conversation with

Spriggs on the nature of her condition or any mention of her connection with an insurance man. While Spriggs asked him if Mrs. McCarty was all right, Spriggs never spoke of Milton Thomson.

In response to cross-examination, Mr. Bentley stated he could not fix the year, but thought it to be around 1862.

Mazlow Cole appeared as the last witness of the morning. He testified that for fourteen years he'd resided in Marshall, near Deansboro, and prior to that in Augusta. He'd known Mrs. McCarty in her girlhood as she was a classmate of his sister. She'd left Augusta in '58, and up until then her reputation had been good.

On cross-examination he responded to questions about her being arrested for stealing in 1854. He said he couldn't remember ever hearing anything against her and wasn't aware that she had ever been arrested. If he heard she was it might have affected his impression some, but he hadn't heard enough about her in recent years to form any opinion.

He then looked boldly at his questioner and stated, "If she had been discharged, I should not have considered it against her."

Court adjourned until 3:00.

While the courtroom had been nearly empty for the morning proceedings, by afternoon it was almost filled.

For their last witness, the defense recalled Mrs. McCarty. In answer to questions posed by her attorney, she responded as follows:

Heard John O'Donnell testify; have no recollection of ever seeing him before; no officer ever paid my bill; the government paid it in order to obtain my trunk; I had receipt of my bill; have looked for the receipt at the jail; it is not there; I have papers in Albany; last saw it in Albany when I was packing my goods and papers; I never was married to any person but McCarty; I never married any man by the name of Seymour; my male attire was a dark grey; I have a photograph of it at Albany; I never had but the one suit; when I was at the jail Mr. Cole boarded me for some time; I remember the article published in the "Bee" in regard to Mr. Cole; he brought it to me.

Then came questions on the issue of insanity.

Question: "Would the fact of anger or revenge entering into the question assist your judgment in coming to a conclusion as to the sanity or insanity of the person?"

Answer: "It would increase the doubt of the insanity, although there are no evidences of insanity in the question as stated."

Mrs. McCarty then responded to cross-examination by the prosecution:

I did not hear Dr. Corey's testimony; I read the newspaper statement of his testimony; also Dr .Clark's; I read Dr. Jarvis on transitory mania; I don't agree with him; don't know how old he is; he was at one time manager of an asylum; his definition is not correct and full as a scientific definition; I have not seen a paper on this question provided by Mr. Sedgwick from Germany or anywhere else; I handed a paper to him; it was a translation from the French; I saw the paper; that translation was made at the asylum; a patient translated it; they do know something; my authority on transitory mania is Dr. Ebing; Dr. Jarvis' article was sent to the editor of the "Journal"; The French article by Ebing; was written in May 1870; later than Dr. Jarvis'; I should not consider Pritchard authority in all cases; he was considered an able writer; I could not consider him authority in all instances; Dr. Ray is a good writer on insanity; I could not agree with all his views.

Question: "Suppose that a woman went into that car without the intention of shooting, had been in the habit of carrying a revolver, did not remember the act of shooting, did not hear any noise, and didn't intend harm, would you call her insane?"

Answer: "I would call her sane."

Question: "Suppose she was an insane woman from grief, overwork, failing health, disorders of the uterus; but could write well, translate French and all that, and had gone into the car, then would there have been anything inconsistent with that?"

269

Answer: "No, sir. She might have acted under delusion. It would not have been inconsistent if she had gone about her business without attracting any attention to her insanity; such an answer might, in that case, have produced a paroxysm of insanity; I have never seen an account of Ann Broderick's case [a woman who shot her seducer] in England."

This process of questions and answers continued with Josephine displaying her intellect, eloquence, and education, the essence of which had the potential to dispel any claim of insanity.

Defense had hoped to recall Mr. Morgan, but the counselor was out of town.

On Wednesday morning, May 15, Mr. Pomeroy began a final plea to the jury.

By permission of Court, gentlemen of the jury; The last act in reference to the life or death of a fellow being is about to be intrusted to your keeping. You feel that it is solemn. That is the case, it is solemn before all others that have ever been presented to your consideration. The investigation of a question of life and death, no matter who the person may be, is of great importance; but in this case it is peculiarly solemn and impressive. We have been engaged for the last number of days earnestly, carefully and faithfully, investigating as to the death of a fellow man, and that investigation has involved the life of another human being. You have been selected carefully. We, of course, could not know what your minds were; but we could take your words for it, that you could sit fairly between the people and the accused. We could start then safely, and trust the fate of our client in your hands. You had all heard of the homicide; the people of the State had all heard of it, and discussed it. And yet you said to yourselves, "all this may be true and yet the prisoner may be irresponsible; we are not ready to jump at conclusions. We read. We think. But we are not ready to pass our judgment until we hear the whole of the case." and here we come to you to answer for the crime that is charged to this most unfortunate woman.

Some men have scruples of conscience in regard to the law under which we are called upon to act. No man but hesitates to take the life of any one under any circumstances.

I have said this is an important trial; you feel it now and will to the end of your natural existence. It will be a thing you will always think of with pleasure or regret—according to the result.

This trial is surrounded by circumstances extraordinary in character. But a little here and there has appeared of the damning influence of money in this case. It has not appeared that Milton H. Thomson and his brothers have been on the trail of the officers we have sent to subpoena witnesses. But they have.

Ordinarily the district attorney conducts a murder case alone. You have in this county an able district attorney. I say it here and elsewhere. Why such fearful odds in this case? Is it of importance except as one of the surroundings of this case? What do we find? We find in addition to the district attorney, the ablest talent of St. Lawrence brought to bear—a gentleman in whose ability and purity I have the utmost confidence. The attorney-general of the State sent here a man, I will not say his superior, for that would be disrespectful; but at least his equal. In his zeal he may be carried beyond his proper moorings, but it will be his head not his heart that takes him there.

Mr. Pomeroy went on to relate the defendant's recent circumstance to her past tragedies. "Who shall tell her thoughts as she lay rocking on shipboard thinking of her lost children—who shall tell where reason stood? In the name of Heaven, if these things will not produce insanity, tell me, tell me what will? It is not necessary that reason should be destroyed, but if distraction comes in, she is no longer herself, and not responsible."

He stated her love of children had led to the adoption of Louis; that compassion had sent her to Washington to nurse the Union's noble soldiers. She had been imprisoned by error and released on orders of General Dix. He talked of the episode in St. Louis, insisting her claim of intensified hearing was proof of an imbalanced mental state.

The counselor continued his review touching on threats made by his client. "The word revenge grates very harshly on the ears of my distinguished friend. Not murder. It means the exposure she had previously given. She meant to provide for her children more than to destroy their father......What is the revenge? I shall publish the man who has wronged me. I shall injure him in business. That is her revenge, not by shooting."

Pomeroy brought Josephine's letters to the jury's attention. Her threat, he informs them, was to bare to Thomson's wife the brutal infamy that he had exposed to her mother years ago. He read a letter written by Josephine and mailed January 1, eleven days prior to being turned out onto the street.

J. Mason, Esq. Hamilton NY

Dear Mr.:

I have been waiting your visit to Albany. I inferred from that you would soon return here on business. I have been so constantly immersed in perplexities and troubles with Thomson that I am scarcely a reasonable or responsible person.

My correspondence and business have been neglected, and I don't know that I shall ever be myself again. Will you be good enough to ascertain Mr. Curtis' decisions representing my offer for the mortgage. My attorneys here advise to open the case and pay nothing, I will wait your answer a few days.

I expect to go to Utica about the 12th, and some steps will then be taken to close up a long-pending matter. I am most gratified for your kind sympathy, and I am afraid shall tax your good services too far.

Hoping you have had a full share of the festivities of this holiday.

I am yours truly,
Josephine McCarty, 62 Howard St.

While the letter alluded to the defendants disturbing circumstances, the text implied she was seeking solutions with no hint of murderous intentions. She was in a hopeless situation, fighting a losing battle. He reiterated that Thomson's words caused her to snap. Pomeroy reminded the jury that four doctors swearing for the defense believed the accused was insane when the homicide was committed. All except Coventry were unprejudiced authorities from outside the area. Dr. Churchill stated there might be some doubt as to her sanity. How could a jury be without doubt if a learned doctor was unable to make a positive diagnosis?

The defense counselor ended his speech to the jury with these remarks:

> I leave this case with you. I leave Mrs. McCarty with you. I leave the children with you. In the name of justice save the little girl's mother. I know that justice will govern you. I ask you to render such a verdict that when you return to your homes you will not see a vision of a woman led from her cell haggard and tottering. Let the spirit of Him whose attribute is mercy govern you. Let justice have its part, but let mercy be there also. Gentlemen, I have said more than I should. I am not able to address you on this occasion properly. You have seen it. I have never been engaged in a trial in which I was so thoroughly impressed with a belief in the irresponsibility of my client. After you have heard the other counsel, I ask you to render such a verdict as will satisfy your consciences in the sight of God.

It took three hours for Pomeroy to deliver his oration. The *Herald* reported that jurors and attending counsel were affected to tears. Mrs. McCarty sobbed convulsively.

Court called a recess and Josephine was led from the room. It wasn't only her lip that quivered. Every muscle in her body had tightened, fighting the vibration of nerves. Her throat felt full, making swallowing difficult.

Her defense, silent and immobile, stood staring at her back as she disappeared through the doorway. They had done their best. They could find no stone unturned. Her fate had been handed to the men of the jury. Would the prosecution convince them that she should hang?

Before court could reconvene, the room had filled to overflowing. Judge Doolittle issued an order closing the courtroom to further entrance.

Mr. Magone faced the jury on behalf of the People. He began as Pomeroy had, paying his respect to the jury and the careful way in which they were selected. He expressed confidence that they would judge the case entrusted to them wisely, in accordance with the law.

Magone spoke rapidly as he reviewed the circumstances of Josephine's life from the prosecution's perspective. He spoke of her manner of testifying; allowing her absence of religious training, her lack of shame was deplorable. He defended Robert McCarty, insisting he had been a responsible husband. He held that her relationship with Captain Pratt was the undoing of her marriage. Had they not been intimate, why was he present at the break-up? He ranted about her return to Augusta and the indictment that exposed her as a thief. He challenged her behavior as a lobbyist, buttonholing men in the hallways of Albany. As for Louis, who could believe the story of adoption? The child was a bastard. She was caught traipsing around Washington in male attire and arrested as a Rebel spy. He discussed other men with whom she had dealt: Mulhall, who runs a concert saloon, and Brice, who willingly rode out with her, a woman of such reputation. He read a letter she had written Mr. Spriggs admitting her flagrant violation of acceptable mores:

Tell Thomson when he sends his wife away again not to send her on the same boat with myself. She said she had not thought of going until one o'clock that day, but Mister Thomson sent her on business, and he was going down the next day. I was laughing with Dodge about it, and remarked that she would not see Thomson the next day, nor the next, and it seems I was right. She said in jest that she left her children at home. I smiled, will I not enlighten her some day? She is not the woman to faint or take things very tamely. Had I have had Baby Thomson and the letters with me we should have passed a pleasant evening, discussing domestic affairs. Were you not in the enemy's camp I could tell you some funny things.

What a story teller you are!

You said I wrote you to say I was coming on. I know I never sent a letter for that purpose, but on reflection I recollected it was to send baby's photograph to your chivalrous client. I promised it once. I keep my promises. All that I have made him will be kept to the letter, and let me add another. The more law suits there are the more expenses, and he will pay it, not I. Write please by return mail. Should I not stop in Utica I will return the loan in October, unless your generous client should kindly pay you.

I do not need his money now, and he shall find me as remorseless as himself, mating more intensely than I ever loved him.

Yours truly

J.A. McCarty, 62 Howard St. Albany

Magone described Mortimer Thomson as a Christian justified in wanting his brother separated from a prostitute. When the sale of the house took place, Thomson did not want his name sullied by connection to the affair. The papers were issued in another man's name and she was carefully put out. Mr. Magone summed up the case for the people rather simply.

You are here to protect the interest of the community at large, and to stem the tide of blood which is flooding this nation. On the subject of sympathy we might mention the young widow of the murdered Hall. She, too, has a child with no father to watch over it. Who caused her misery? But you can not be asked to redress her wrongs, and you can not do her justice. You are sworn to make a true deliverance between the people and this prisoner. I have confidence in this jury. I have confidence that you will do your duty.

Mr. Mitchell then came back with his final argument, opening with the following:

> I congratulate you that this tedious trial is drawing to an end. I need not remind you of its importance. You have felt it as honest men. I will not spend time in saying a word in regard to the difficulties that have surrounded us in this case. Generally defendants are surrounded by wealthy friends who can bring everything to their aid. Upon the other side is the strong arm of the county, wealth, money and power standing against a woman, who has no money, crushed in health, and depending on charity for her counsel. I believe the true mission of a lawyer is to defend the weak against the strong, with or without money. And it was with that view that I came here to defend this prisoner, and unless I have mistaken this case, unless truth has lost its power, I can defend this woman. I ask no favor. I shall appeal to the judgment of this jury. To your judgment as sworn honest men, I appeal to show that my client is guiltless. If she is convicted, she will be convicted in contradiction to law. The gentleman can not convict my client by such a cursory running over of all the misfortunes of her life.
>
> What constitutes murder? I never supposed it had the trivial signification given by my friend; and it will not be so charged by, from that court.

Mitchell went on for some time, rebuffing charges that his client had been intimate with Captain Pratt on her voyage to England, pointing out that she slept with her children and that a nurse had been traveling with them. Protesting the slander placed upon his client by counsel for the people, he made a powerful statement:

> I shall show that she is entitled to better treatment than she has received from the government. When a woman falls, she can never get on her feet again. Men may go about destroying the daughters of the land, and no one speaks about it louder than a whisper. But poor woman! When she

falls, where is she? If my servant commits an act of indiscretion while in my house, society won't even let her stay in my house. Stand here an hour and declare against this woman, and call Thomson and his brother's conduct Christian! It will deceive no jury of Oneida County.

Mr. Mitchell continued his defense, underscoring the fact that Robert McCarty was twice the age of his bride and had presented himself falsely. After his proposal, she had insisted in waiting six months before they should marry. While she had accommodated all his wishes as a wife, he had failed miserably in providing for their family. The final insult had come with the knowledge that he was keeping a mistress. There had been no salvaging the marriage once trust was lost.

Mitchell admitted to his client's errors in judgment, but reminded the jury it was the theory of the people that men of every description were in pursuit of her—civil and military officers, doctors, politicians, and neighbors. One would have to look at the tenacity of Thomson's pursuit. And how, he wondered aloud, could she have slept with an officer at O'Donnell's for ten days without the officer being charged or some objection being made?

Court adjourned at 5:15 PM.

On Thursday, May 16, each side would make their final remarks.

The defense went first, with Mr. Mitchell citing the stress and abuse his client had endured and the resultant turmoil of her mind. He reviewed the letter that Josephine sent to Spriggs with its disparaging remarks toward Milton Thomson, explaining that it was his client's response at having been scorned. The trip to Chittenango had been made in the company of her lawyer, William Dodge. He traced her actions prior to the shooting, emphasizing the findings of Dr. Gray.

The people had painted his client to be a wicked woman. He understood the crux of their case and addressed it with the jury. "Their contention is that a wicked woman can't have her mind upset. But I shall leave it for your own good sense to answer that. We have no chance to reply. The court has the last word to the jury. We can only anticipate what they will say."

277

Court adjourned for dinner at 12:30 PM.

Mr. Sedgwick took to the floor in the afternoon speaking for the people. The courtroom was packed with spectators. He charged that the defendant left home a giddy and unrestrained girl. She accepted a marriage in haste; therefore, she had no one to blame but herself for the outcome.

He claimed not to be an advocate of Milton H. Thomson, saying: "He has put coals in his bosom and must be burned. If he has 'set the springs of law in motion' it has been without my knowledge, and I don't believe that he could corrupt the fountain of justice in Oneida County."

Sedgwick spoke eloquently and his delivery continued for nearly two hours. But the facts of the trial had been heard before and repeated many times over. When he finished the jury was given a break.

It was now up to the court to charge the jury on the scope of their duties.

Judge Doolittle's piercing eyes cased the jurors as he began a series of statements: "Gentlemen of the Jury: The grand jury, in the discharge of its duty, has presented the prisoner at the bar, Josephine A. McCarty, for trial for the crime of murder in the first degree."

He went on to review statutes of law as related to charges against the prisoner. He reviewed the facts and touched on statements made by witnesses. He pointed to the fact that statements made by the accused contradicted answers she had given in previous testimony.

"If she had deliberately and willfully sworn false in one particular, it will have a strong bearing on the question of her credibility."

After the trial commenced following dinner, the judge continued his charge.

He demonstrated the weighing of evidence. "Her examination was searching and covered the whole period of her life. You saw with what vividness of memory, quickness and keenness of perception, with what general intelligence and rationality she testified.

"Is she now laboring under such a defect of reason, arising from disease of the mind as not to know the nature and quality of her acts, or, if she does know it, as not to know whether they are unlawful and wrong? If she is not, then she is not laboring under that insanity the statute speaks of, and she is legally responsible for those acts."

The judge reviewed the finding of medical witnesses, and then charged: "You will say whether, if there was insanity, on this whole evidence, it must have been what is called either temporary mania or mania transitoria. And you will say whether such temporary insanity could have existed with the symptoms here manifested, and whether the symptoms were there which always attended mania transitoria."

The Court ended its charge to the jury with the following statement:

If you are satisfied, on a fair and candid view of the evidence, that that defense is sustained, that such was the condition of the mind of the accused at the time the pistol was fired, then your duty is to render a verdict of not guilty.

If, on the other hand, you are satisfied by the evidence in this case beyond a reasonable doubt, not beyond a possibility, that Hall was killed; that he was killed by the accused; that she fired the pistol by which he was killed with a premeditated design to kill Thomson, and in such a state of mind as to know the nature and quality of the act complained of, and that it was unlawful and morally wrong—your duty is equally plain, no matter how painful it may be to render a verdict of guilty.

But if, on a careful review of the whole case you are satisfied that the accused fired the pistol without entertaining a premeditated design to effect the death of Thomson, and was sane at the time the act was committed, then it will be your duty to render a verdict of manslaughter in the third degree—the punishment of which offense is imprisonment in the State prison for a period not exceeding four years.

I submit these issues to your final determination.

If you shall approach their final decision without passion, without prejudice, and after a patient and careful consideration of the whole case, your verdict shall reflect the honest and deliberate conclusions of your own judgments, your whole duty will be discharged.

When Judge Doolittle had finished, counsel begged the court for clarification.

Mr. Mitchell asked "If the will did not join the act, might it have been excusable homicide?"

"So charged," answered the judge.

Mitchell came back, "The killing must have been done by a person of sound mind and memory, and to have proceeded from malice."

"So charged," came the answer.

"If the proof leaves it within reasonable doubt that the prisoner was not of sound mind, she is entitled to the benefit of the doubt."

"So charged."

The list of questions went on, with the Court replying until the last inquiry had been answered.

The Court recessed, the constables were sworn, and the jury retired. After weeks of testimony, of witnesses taking the stand and being recalled, it had finally come down to the deliberation of a jury. In accordance with law, all jurors were men.

The audience seemed to swallow in unison as Deputy Cole guided Josephine back to her cell. The boys looked up at her entrance, but their mother had withdrawn to some other place.

They clung to her, knowing well the danger that loomed. But Josephine failed to acknowledge them. Her mind had moved forward to imagine the hangman. She supposed it would hurt at least for a moment. People would be gaping; some might laugh. Another swallow and she contemplated Louis and his young siblings. Would town busybodies step up to provide homes for the trio? She thought not. In a spirit of virtue, the good women of Utica would escort her children to an orphanage. Milton would maintain his presence in society, and ash would continue to fall from his high-priced cigars.

THE VERDICT

It was 6:30 in the evening when rumors circulated that the jury had agreed. Whispers hinted at a verdict of manslaughter in the third degree. A little before seven, Judge Doolittle returned to court, and jurors took their seats. Spectators were shoulder-to-shoulder in a room where no one spoke. Josephine sat in the midst of this stillness, hoping against hope that she would not faint while standing to hear the verdict.

The clerk stood. "Gentlemen of the jury, have you agreed upon your verdict?"

Mr. Spencer, the foreman, replied. "We have."

"Jurors, look upon the prisoner. How say you gentlemen? Do you find the prisoner at the bar guilty of the felony and murder where of she stands indicted, or not guilty?"

Seconds became hours. Josephine watched in what seemed delayed motion as the eyes of the jurors turned toward her.

The foreman cleared his throat before speaking. "We find the prisoner not guilty."

The clerk looked to the jury for confirmation. "Jurors, hearken unto your verdict as the court hath recorded it. You say you find the prisoner at the bar not guilty, and so say you all?

"We do," the jurors answered in unison, but the remark was drowned by thunderous applause.

Josephine's body trembled as tears stained her face. Friends appeared where previously there had been none. In great number they pressed to shake her hand. Court adjourned, but the crowd remained. Men, women, and children surrounded the acquitted defendant—members of the bar, street laborers, clerks, and in general, persons of every class. As Josephine moved toward the door, the crush of people bore her onward. A swelling crowd had collected in the street. She climbed into jailer Cole's buggy for the trip back to the jail where her children sat waiting.

Excitement spurred the community, and countless people hailed her as an exonerated woman. Their voices echoed throughout the city. "Three cheers for Mrs. McCarty!" The words were repeated three times over, and then they were heard again. Bystanders formed an entourage trailing the buggy as it took its route following the track of the Utica streetcar.

On February 3, 1872

The *Brooklyn Daily Eagle* Published the Following Commentary

A Utica paper, in the telling of the life of Josephine McCarty, who shot a man in a streetcar, traces what it calls her successive "downward steps," through marriage, infidelity, exposure, and separation, since which last event, it says, "her course has been steadily and surely downward."

Until the late tragedy, when, according to modern precedent, she began to rise, having asserted her right to commit murder, Josephine will go upward, to the level of a heroine; upward, into the affections of the aggressive women; upward to recognition as a wronged and raging representative of an injured sex; upward, as an exponent of Woodhullism*, for which Anthony and Stanton and Beecher-Hooker and their following of male curiosities cry aloud and spare not either the public or legislative bodies.

* *Victoria Woodhull, a feminist, ran for President of the United States in 1872.*

FOLLOW UP ON SELECTED CHARACTERS

THE HONORABLE CHARLES H. DOOLITTLE was born in Herkimer, New York. He attended the same school, the Oneida Conference Seminary in Cazenovia, as Josephine Fagan and Leland Stanford. He graduated from Amherst College, was admitted to the bar in 1839, and later served as president of the Oneida County Bank. Though a staunch Republican, he was elected to the Supreme Court of the Fifth Judicial District of New York in 1869, having been endorsed by both parties.

In 1874, two years after the McCarty trial, the judge boarded the Abyssina for a voyage across the Atlantic. On his second day at sea, he went overboard. It was said that he had been despondent over the unexpected death of his brother, Dr. Andrew Doolittle. Eulogies attested to the judge's legal prowess and innate sense of integrity. He left his wife, three sons, and two daughters. The Doolittle mansion was an imposing structure just three blocks north of the Milton Thomson home on Genesee Street in Utica, New York. Doolittle's daughter Isabel remained in the house until 1943 when the building was razed for the construction of a Sears and Roebuck Store.

ROSE O'NEAL GREENHOW grew up in Port Tobacco, Maryland, not far from Josephine McCarty's patrons, the Barns family. A beautiful woman of high intelligence, she married Dr. Robert Greenhow, and it was his political influence that propelled her to the top of Washington society. The couple had eight children, only four of whom lived beyond infancy. Rose was left a widow before the outbreak of the War Between the States. Her sympathies were strongly for the South and state's rights. Her Washington connections unwittingly fed her information that she promptly passed on to the Confederacy.

Arrested on charges of espionage in August of 1861, Rose was imprisoned in the Old Capitol Prison. She gained her release and was sent to Richmond, Virginia, on June 1, 1862, where she was hailed by southerners as a heroine. After a brief spell in Richmond, she sailed to England as an attaché of Confederate President Jefferson Davis. She was received in the courts of Europe sympathetic to the South. During her time in England, she penned a memoir, *My Imprisonment and the First Year of Abolitionist Rule in Washington*. On page 258, she makes reference to Josephine McCarty.

In 1864, Rose sailed for the states on the blockade runner Condor. When a Union ship forced the Condor aground at the mouth of Cape Fear River, she grew fearful of being captured. Begging the captain to put her ashore, she was lowered to the water in a life boat. Rough seas capsized the boat, and Rose was drowned along with dispatches and gold she had been transporting to the Confederates.

Rose O'Neal Greenhow was buried with full Confederate military honors in Oakdale Cemetery, Wilmington, North Carolina.

JOSEPHINE MCCARTY remained in Utica at the conclusion of her trial. While residing there, she published a periodical, the *Woman's Truth Teller*. A copy of this periodical may be viewed on microfilm in the newspaper preservation section at the Harvard College Library, Cambridge, Massachusetts. In 1873, she authored an article entitled "Blackmail" which appeared in the December issue of the *Word*, a monthly journal on reform and feminism, published by Ezra H. Hayward.

Josephine visited Augusta in August of 1889, and her arrival was covered by the *Oneida Dispatch* with a reprint in the *Waterville Times*. Unfortunately, the traditional outline of who, what, where, and when was ignored in composing the article. There is no mention of where she came from or who accompanied her. The article reads as follows:

A part of our people, who were knowing to the fact, were somewhat surprised at the appearance here, on Thursday last, of Mrs. Josephine McCarty, after an absence of seventeen years. Her trial in Utica in 1872 for murder will be remembered by most people in Central New York, as will also her wicked and unsavory career for twenty years previous. A conveyance from Oriskany Falls brought her to the ruins of her old house near Newell's Corners to see, in her advanced age of 65 years, only the bare foundations and a few rotted timbers remaining of what was in her early life a showy cluster of farm buildings and one of the pleasantest homes in the town of Augusta, a home she inherited and might have saved, but which she abandoned for a strange life elsewhere, leaving the large, old mansion unoccupied and untenantable and with all the out-buildings to drop in the ground in due time through decay. For more than thirty years her abiding places have been many but a real home probably nowhere.

Very little additional information exists on Mrs. McCarty or her children. No obituary was found.

Ironically, in 1873, one year after the McCarty trial, the Albany branch of the American Medical Association agreed to accept female members as fully accredited physicians.

CAPTAIN ISAIAH PRATT was born to a prominent family in Essex, Connecticut. His only home was that of his parents, which he purchased from his father in 1854. While traditionally the Pratts were farriers and farmers, Isaiah took to the sea. As captain of a packet ship, he became one of the finest mariners in the world. Packet ships were the first vessels to be held to a schedule regardless of weather or cargo. In 1861 Isaiah became the first captain in the United States to take and pass the America Shipmasters Association examination. Tough and independent, the captain was also kind, a characteristic remarked upon by a large contingent of Mormons who sailed with him on the Hudson in 1864.

Pratt was not only the captain of the Hudson; he was the ship's owner. He amassed a considerable fortune before passing away on April 22, 1879. Though exceedingly handsome and a man of means, the captain never married. In keeping with the charitable nature of his family, he willed his estate of nearly one hundred thousand dollars to the establishment of a school in Essex, Connecticut.

A portrait of the captain hangs on the second floor of the Pratt House museum in Essex.

GENERAL DANIEL EDGAR SICKLES came into the world with every advantage: wit, charm, wealth, and a respected ancestral heritage. Unfortunately, a recalcitrant nature hindered success and clouded his future.

The deadly shooting of his first wife's lover, Philip Barton Key, disgraced him with the public, cost him his seat as a United States congressman, and could easily have gotten him hung. He returned to prominence during the Civil War. Some hailed him as a hero; other's held that his disobedience jeopardized the Union, with casualties mounting needlessly under his command. The war injury and amputation that ended his military action endowed him with a new nickname—the One-Legged General.

He was a widower with a daughter when, in 1869, President Grant appointed him United States Minister to Spain. The Spaniards received him warmly. His alleged affair with the deposed queen, Isabella II, earned him yet another nickname—Yankee King of Spain.

In 1871, he married Carmina Creagh, the daughter of a Spanish aristocrat. Two children were born through this marriage. The general's tenure as minister ended in 1873. He moved his family to Paris, but the political action he craved was still an ocean away. In 1878, Sickles returned to New York. When his wife refused to join him, a lifelong separation ensued.

In 1888, the general became president of the New York State Board of Civil Service Commissioners, serving through 1889. He was sheriff of New York City in 1890, and he eventually regained his congressional seat as a representative of the 53rd Congress serving from 1893 to 1895.

After ninety-five years of flamboyant behavior, the general passed away May 5, 1914. The man was broke and estranged from every member of his family. His first child, Laura, predeceased him by many years. While his liaisons with women were many, it seems only one impressed him enough to make her correspondence worth keeping. The anonymously penned letter was found amongst papers he had left behind. It is printed here by authorization of the Daniel Edgar Sickles Papers, Manuscript and Archives Division, New York Public Library, Astor, Lenox, and Tilden Foundation. It reads:

> I have just come home, and have your dear note, many, many, thanks for it has made me very happy to know you still think of me. It is now six o'clock and too late to meet you…. It is best for I might sin. My wish is wanting to go home it is so dark my hand can hardly hold the pen. My husband is sitting looking straight at me. Love me still dear Edgar it is so sweet to be loved by one so dear to my sad heart. I am afraid I shall always be so. God forgive me! And bless you my so dearly loved one_____

The author of *The Balance of Justice* hoped a sample of Josephine McCarty's handwriting might validate the protagonist as the author of this letter. The text seemed a perfect fit. Alas, a copy of Josephine's marriage certificate of 1845 was nothing more than a record sheet written in the hand of a municipal clerk. It appears no source of analysis exists.

MILTON THOMSON was born in the sleepy hamlet of Paris Hill, New York, and graduated from the Clinton Liberal Institute, just a few miles removed from Josephine McCarty's childhood home of Augusta. His friendship with Ephraim Chamberlain developed while both were working in the tax collector's office in Utica, New York. He eventually moved to an insurance firm; using the knowledge he'd gained there, he opened his own business.

The company flourished and the Thomsons became appreciated donors to charitable organizations in Utica, New York. In December of 1872, Mr. Thomson bought a full page in the Sunday newspaper, using the space to proclaim innocence and decry the unfairness of the negative views weighing against him. His health never fully improved after the rigors of the McCarty trial. Yet, over the next twenty years, he traveled extensively and spent a good portion of the day at his office whenever he was in the district.

Milton remained in his mansion at 321 Genesee Street in Utica until his death on March 3, 1893, twenty-one years after the McCarty trial. No children were listed in his obituary, but there was reference to his influential connections, including ex-Governor Stanford of California. The Thomson home still stands, one of a small number of Genesee Street mansions to escape the march of progress.

WILLIAM P. WOOD was born March 11, 1820, in Alexandria, Virginia. Shrewd and fearless, he first gained recognition as a cavalryman in the Mexican War, serving under Texas Ranger General Samuel H. Walker.

His early profession was that of a model maker. His talents were appreciated by Edwin M. Stanton, and he served the attorney in various capacities. When Stanton became secretary of war, he appointed Wood superintendent of the Old Capitol Prison. Wood also served as a secret agent of the War Department reporting directly to Stanton. He was hunted by the Confederates and feared by many in Washington.

On April 14, 1865, President Lincoln created the Secret Service to halt the counterfeiting of United States currency. Colonel Wood was appointed the agency's first director. He received word of the president's assassination while working on a counterfeiting case in Cincinnati. On his return to Washington, he took an active role in the capture of Lincoln's assassins.

In January 1872, when newspapers throughout the country carried the story of Josephine McCarty's indictment for murder, her character was vilified with charges that included spying for the Confederacy. The allegation prompted Wood to speak in her defense. He was the only one to do so; his remarks were published in the *New York Sun*.

William P. Wood died March 23, 1903. In 2001, retired Secret Service agents had a monument erected at his grave site to honor his service as the agency's founding director.

ABOUT THE AUTHOR

Eileen Sullivan Hopsicker was born in Utica, New York, and spent the bulk of her life in the Mohawk Valley region. She has an avid interest in history and was serving as president of the Limestone Ridge Historical Society when she uncovered the story of Josephine McCarty.

She holds an Associate Degree in Fine Art from Mohawk Valley Community College and a Bachelor of Studio Art from Hamilton College. She retired as Director of Records and Research for Development at Utica College. She currently resides in Webster, New York.

The Balance of Justice is Eileen's first novel.